PRAISE FOR *NE'ER*

"*Ne'er Duke Well* is a delightful quicksilver romp with unforgettable characters that readers will be rooting for from start to finish."

—Deanna Raybourn, *New York Times* bestselling author of the Veronica Speedwell series

"*Ne'er Duke Well* by Alexandra Vasti is an irresistible delight from a remarkable new talent. Every page inspires a smile, laugh, or pause in reading while one hugs the book because it's just so lovely, witty, and benevolently clever. Vasti does really interesting things with genre tropes, making the historical romance fresh and exciting. I felt so enlivened after reading, I wanted to run around waving it at people, saying, 'Read this now!' Vasti has quickly earned her place on my list of favorite writers."

—India Holton, author of *The Wisteria Society of Lady Scoundrels*

"A witty page-turner with two adorable leads whose funny banter and chemistry are off the charts! I didn't want their antics to end."

—Virginia Heath, author of *All's Fair in Love and War*

"If it were socially acceptable for blurbs to be in all caps, I'd do it for *Ne'er Duke Well* and Alexandra Vasti. In fact, all caps doesn't seem strong enough to convey how much I loved this book. Vasti has quickly made her way to my list of top historical romance authors with the kind of writing that makes me scream and kick my feet in public places. Outrageously hot, tender, and brimming with wit . . . Vasti has secured herself as an auto-buy author in my book, one that I will stay up way too late reading and be glad for the lack of sleep come morning. This opposites-attract historical romance brims with the delicious restraint required of our lead characters in a society they end up defying that explodes in exceptionally steamy moments. Vasti's storytelling is this season's Incomparable, a title she'll hold for years to come with the care and craft she deftly applies to her incredible novels."

—Mazey Eddings, author of *Late Bloomer*

"Utterly delicious and undeniably clever, Alexandra Vasti's *Ne'er Duke Well* was unputdownable. I'm absolutely certain that Regency romance fans everywhere will love this warm, wonderfully witty, and oh-so-sexy novel just as much as I did. What a spectacular debut!"

—Amy Rose Bennett, author of *Up All Night with a Good Duke*

Ne'er Duke Well

ALEXANDRA VASTI

ST. MARTIN'S
GRIFFIN
NEW YORK

First published in the United States by St. Martin's Griffin, an imprint of St. Martin's Publishing Group

NE'ER DUKE WELL. Copyright © 2024 by Alexandra Vasti. All rights reserved. Printed in the United States of America. For information, address St. Martin's Publishing Group, 120 Broadway, New York, NY 10271.

www.stmartins.com

Designed by Omar Chapa

Library of Congress Cataloging-in-Publication Data

Names: Vasti, Alexandra, author.
Title: Ne'er duke well / Alexandra Vasti.
Description: First edition. | New York, NY : St. Martin's Griffin, 2024.
Identifiers: LCCN 2024000319 | ISBN 9781250910943 (trade
    paperback) | ISBN 9781250910950 (ebook)
Subjects: LCGFT: Romance fiction. | Novels.
Classification: LCC PS3622.A8584 N44 2024 | DDC 813/.6—dc23/
    eng/20240116
LC record available at https://lccn.loc.gov/2024000319

Our books may be purchased in bulk for promotional, educational, or business use. Please contact your local bookseller or the Macmillan Corporate and Premium Sales Department at 1-800-221-7945, extension 5442, or by email at MacmillanSpecialMarkets@macmillan.com.

First Edition: 2024

10 9 8 7 6 5 4 3 2 1

To librarians, to booksellers, and to every reader who's ever handed someone else a book and said, "Try this—I think you'll love it." You change lives.

And to Matt, always.

Content note: This book contains discussion of childhood illness and death of a sibling as well as references to slavery and domestic violence. There is also one use of a slur for sex workers (uttered by a villain!). I hope I have handled the challenging topics in the novel gently and with respect.

Ne'er
Duke
Well

Chapter 1

. . . You may be interested to hear that Peter Kent has finally inherited. You remember what he is like, do you not? One pities the House of Lords.

—from Lady Selina Ravenscroft to her brother, Lord William Ravenscroft, His Majesty's Army, Seventh Division, 1815

Peter suspected the project was doomed.

It had not been a good idea to begin with. Surely he could have found another way to satisfy his half sister's desire for a rapier—one that did not involve dressing her in boy's clothes and smuggling her into a fencing parlor on Bond Street.

He should have *sent* for a rapier, not gone out to fit her with it himself. He could have had someone bring a sword to his house.

He was supposed to be a duke, for Christ's sake.

Peter Kent, the ninth Duke of Stanhope—for all that he'd never set foot in England until two years ago, when he'd become heir presumptive to the dukedom and the Earl of Clermont had dragged him unceremoniously away from his home in Louisiana.

He was the duke now. Had been for three-quarters of a month. People called him Your Grace. He had more money than God.

These facts did not seem to matter to his half siblings.

"Lu," he said to his sister, slightly horrified to hear pleading in his voice. "You sure you don't want the kitten? We might buy it a little collar . . ."

He'd brought his siblings a soft, fluffy gray kitten in a basket that morning. Freddie, his ten-year-old half brother, had nearly come out of his skin at the sight of the thing, but Lu had quelled Freddie with a wordless scowl.

Freddie, at least, had wanted the kitten.

"No," said Lu flatly. "No kittens. Its tail looked like a chimney brush."

"Its tail looked soft," mumbled Freddie disconsolately.

"It has claws," offered Peter. "And teeth. Sharp little teeth."

He'd felt a right jackass in the carriage on the way to their house that morning, trying to stuff the kitten into the basket. The idea had seemed so promising. What child could resist a kitten? He'd had one brought in from his country seat in Sussex—because, in-bloody-explicably, he had a country seat in Sussex. And people who brought things at his request.

And then the damned kitten kept popping out of the basket and climbing his coat sleeve with its little needle claws and sinking its tiny teeth into his ear and *shrieking* like the hounds of hell were after it.

Pop pop went its claws as he'd pried it from his coat. Then *meeeewwwww* as he shoved it into the basket. Then *ouch Jesus blasted cockered ratsbane, let go of my goddamned thumb!*

And then Lu didn't even want the kitten. She'd turned up

her nose as if *she* were the ninth Duke of Stanhope and not his illegitimate twelve-year-old sister, the natural daughter of a dead man who thankfully would never darken her door again.

Peter hadn't even known about Freddie and Lu until he'd gotten to England. He hadn't been able to protect them from their father's neglect and cruelty. Just like he hadn't been able to protect Morgan.

But he was damned if he wouldn't protect them now.

It would help, though, if he could get the children to trust him. Or at least like him. Or even tolerate his presence without glaring suspiciously in his direction.

"I want a rapier," Lu said. "So that I might stab people with it."

You, her eyes said. *So that I might stab you.*

"I'm not sure that there's actual stabbing in fencing."

"How do you know?" Lu asked. "Do you fence? Is there fencing in America?"

"I fence."

Good God, the child didn't need a rapier to know exactly where to place the knife in his gut and twist. Yes, he was American. Yes, he was damned out of place here on this cold, foggy island, and in the fencing parlor, and in the House of Lords. And no, he hadn't been to Eton and Oxford, and no, he didn't know how to convince the Court of Chancery to give him guardianship of Freddie and Lu, and no, he didn't know how to get Lu on his side.

And no, and no, and no.

But for the rapier, he could say yes.

"I mean to demand satisfaction," Lu murmured, almost inaudible over the sounds of the street. "From the world."

God, she was a terrifying creature.

"Good," he said. "Let's buy you a rapier. But listen, Lu, don't talk, all right?"

Her brows drew together. "Whyever not?"

"Because you sound too much like a small, bad-tempered lady."

She glowered. "I am no lady."

"Well, you *sound* like one, so keep quiet."

"How would you know? Are there ladies—"

Peter frowned at her, and to his surprise, she closed her mouth mid-sentence. Frowning? Was that how he was supposed to act like a guardian? God, he hoped not, because the expression on his face made him feel like his father, and he resented it with every fiber of his being.

"In New Orleans?" he finished for her. "Yes, Lu, there are ladies in New Orleans. My mother was a lady."

"Oh," she said.

Beneath Lu's chastening hand on his shoulder, Freddie said, "Was?"

"She died," Peter said, "a long time ago."

"Our mother died too," Freddie said.

"He *knows*, Freddie," Lu said irritably. "That is why he is trying—and failing—to pry us away from Great-great-aunt Rosamund."

Ah, yes, their current guardian. The beloved Great-great-aunt Rosamund, who was not, as far as he could discern, actually related to the children, and who did not appear to recognize them whenever he returned them from one of their outings.

After their mother's death, the children had been passed like unwanted puppies from household to household, settling most recently upon a very elderly thrice-removed aunt. Rosamund nodded off mid-conversation. She rarely rose from her chair. She occasionally referred to Lu as Lucinda, but sometimes she called her Lettice and sometimes Horatio Nelson.

But despite all that, Lu acted like she *wanted* to stay with the woman—even though Peter could buy her a whole room full of fencing masters and send Freddie to Eton and give them everything he'd always wanted and never had.

"Lu," he said now, "I'm telling you, if you talk, it's not going to work. So show me how much you want the sword by keeping your mouth shut, and we'll walk out of here with one strapped to your hip."

She scowled, but she did it. They strolled quite casually into the fencing parlor.

A quarter of an hour later, they strolled back out. Lu was red-faced at the extravagant lies Peter had invented to account for her refusal to speak. Freddie buried his laughter in his hand, and Peter held the sword nearly above his own head to ensure that Lu couldn't stab anyone with it.

Which was how he found himself—bracketed by children and with a small sword held aloft out of a still-sputtering Lu's reach—when they collided with Lady Selina Ravenscroft.

Chapter 2

. . . I do remember Peter Kent. He knocked you into a mud puddle at Broadmayne, didn't he? And stole your horse. And wasn't there something about a wedding at St. George's, two sheep, and a duel?

—from Will Ravenscroft to his sister Selina, posted
from Brussels

Selina settled her poke bonnet firmly onto her head, ducked out of the back alley behind her publisher's office, and emerged into the sunshine of Bond Street.

It was extremely large, the bonnet, its brim jutting out past her face like a green silk prow. It clashed horribly with the pink pelisse she wore knotted over her yellow-striped, outrageously flounced walking gown, and if she kept her head tilted downward, her face was almost entirely obscured.

She wasn't disguised. She hadn't needed to wear the rough serge servant's dress she'd kept stuffed in the bottom of her wardrobe for well over a year, a fact that struck Selina as something of a relief.

If Lady Selina Ravenscroft, younger sister of the Duke of Rowland, were to be caught wandering about London in servant's garb, the scandal sheets would be wild with it by morning.

But in this—a shockingly out-of-fashion outfit, her hair tucked away beneath the bonnet and her face shaded by its outlandish brim—she wasn't precisely in disguise. She was simply barely recognizable, which was exactly how she preferred it.

And if she *were* to be recognized in this ridiculous ensemble, that wouldn't be enough to engender a scandal. Well, perhaps a very mild one, given that she was walking about without a chaperone or maid. But she need only cross two blocks to where the Rowland carriage waited—her delightfully bribable maid Emmie snugged inside—and then she'd be safe. No scandal today.

No scandal so far.

Of course, it was only a matter of time before someone found out the truth about Lady Selina Ravenscroft.

She angled a glance back at the office of Jean Laventille—the radical Trinidadian immigrant who was both her publisher and her only confidant. It was, decidedly, a mistake. Because with the poke bonnet's brim blocking her vision and the flounces dancing around her body, she didn't see the little boy who darted across her path until it was too late.

They collided with a *whomp*, and Selina felt the breath rush out of her. She tried to stop herself from kicking the boy in the calf and overbalanced instead.

"Hell's bells!" said the child, voice sweet, dark-fringed eyes wide as saucers.

And Selina flung her hands out in front of her, her mind busily registering a series of facts:

One, the child was, perhaps, *not* a boy.

Two, Selina's face was about to make a very abrupt acquaintance with a cobblestone.

And three, these gloves were *certainly* going to be ruined, and she really *liked* these gloves—

And then she was caught around the chest by one strong masculine arm and set, cautiously, back on her feet.

"Good God, Lu," said the owner of the arm. "You're lucky I didn't accidentally stab this woman, because even peers of the realm aren't exempt from the legal consequences of murder."

And—

Oh.

Oh *no*.

Selina knew that lightly accented voice. She knew the owner of the arm. She knew that particular brand of easy words and nonsensical charm, and she knew without looking that the expression on the man's face would be a slightly feral grin.

Peter bloody Kent.

She couldn't look up. She couldn't turn her gaze even one fraction, because then the brim would reveal her face, and he would recognize her. And she really, really didn't want him to recognize her.

She was alone, not that Peter would care. But he might wonder what she was doing out here on Bond Street by herself. He might ask. He might have seen her come out of Laventille's office, for heaven's sake. She couldn't be connected to the publisher, because then she might be connected to Belvoir's, and then she would be so thoroughly entangled in the web of deception she'd crafted that she might never find her way out.

Also, he'd practically rescued her, which was mortifying.

And, God, she was wearing this patently absurd costume.

Not that she cared what he thought of her costume. Not that she thought about Peter Kent like *that*.

Or at all. Ever.

"Beg pardon," she mumbled, sidling away, eyes downcast and fixed on his dusty boots. She couldn't look up. She thought maybe there was another child somewhere to his other side, but she dared not turn her head to check.

But then, horror of horrors . . .

He recognized her anyway.

"Selina?"

Oh *blast*.

She tipped her head back to meet his gaze. And then back, and back farther. The bonnet, which had been quite superb at disguising her appearance, was remarkably poor at allowing for normal social congress.

Finally she found his face.

Yes, it was Peter Kent—*Stanhope*, she reminded herself, he was the Duke of Stanhope now—and yes, he was grinning bemusedly down at her.

She was tall, but he was taller. His bright brown eyes were lit with warmth and the comfortable, irrepressible familiarity that had him addressing her without her proper title. His dark curls were artfully mussed—she wondered if he had his valet form them with hot tongs. His fair skin was gold-burnished from the Louisiana sun, and his lips were almost insultingly lush for a man, and—

This. This was why, in the two years since she had met him and he'd tossed her into a mud puddle, she did not think about Peter Kent.

Selina dropped into a practiced curtsy, polite but not deferential. "Your Grace. What a pleasant surprise."

Peter's grin widened. "You wouldn't say that if I'd stabbed you with Lu's rapier."

She had no idea what he was talking about, as usual. She didn't even *see* a rapier.

Peter turned and gestured to the slightly smaller of the two children at his side. "Come on, Freddie, hand it over before Lu steals it and skewers someone."

"I thought it was blunted," said the boy, sounding scandalized. "You said it was for *practice*."

"Lu could skewer someone with a spoon."

The boy—Freddie, evidently—produced what appeared to be a toy fencing foil from behind his back and handed it to Peter.

Peter's large palm practically enveloped the thing. It looked ridiculous.

He turned back to Selina. "Now that the weapons are safely stowed—"

She arched an eyebrow. Stowed, was it? He more or less held the small sword aloft.

He caught her look and ignored it utterly. "Lady Selina, allow me to present to you my siblings. Lady Selina Ravenscroft, this is Miss Lucinda Nash"—he used the foil to gesture to the taller of the two children—"and Master Frederick Nash."

Master Frederick Nash gave her a polite bow.

Miss Lucinda Nash swept her flat cap from her head, setting free a tumble of shining chocolate curls, and bowed so low she was nearly prostrate on the ground. Then she stood, regarding Selina with bright, fierce green eyes, as if daring Selina to comment on her boy's garb.

Well, Selina supposed that she had no room to criticize anyone for what they were wearing this afternoon.

"Miss Nash," she said, inclining her head in greeting. "Master Nash. It's my pleasure to make your acquaintance."

"Lu," said the girl furiously. "Not Lucinda. Lu."

"Lu," whispered Freddie, looking pained. "You're not supposed to correct the duke in public—"

"Freddie, shut *up*, they can hear you—"

Selina bit the inside of her cheek to keep from laughing. God, she would have hated to be laughed at when she was that age.

"My brother Nicholas is a duke as well," she offered instead. "I assure you, I correct him in public frequently."

Lu's eyes sparked with interest.

"No, please," said Peter. "Please do not encourage her."

"And is your brother the duke this stodgy?" asked Lu, as if Peter hadn't spoken.

Stodgy? Goodness, *stodgy* wasn't exactly the word that came to mind when she considered Peter. *Alarming,* maybe. *Confounding. Unsettling.*

Not that she thought about him, of course.

"Yes, my brother the duke is stodgy indeed." She sent an apologetic thought in the direction of Rowland House. Nicholas wasn't precisely stodgy, but when she'd been a child, he certainly had seemed rather staid. Perhaps a bit overly aristocratic.

Stodgy, in a word.

"And is your brother the duke also so *old*?"

Oh mercy, how could she not laugh?

"Why yes," Selina said. "Similarly, er, decrepit."

Peter made a choked sound.

"And is your—"

"Thank you, Lu," said Peter, slinging an arm companionably about the girl's small shoulders. "That's probably enough character assassination for one day."

"Fine," said Lu. "Pardon me for making conversation with the first interesting person we've met in London."

Somehow, this rather backhanded compliment had Selina feeling quite pleased with herself. Ridiculously gowned and half-way to scandal she might be, but at least this funny little child found her interesting.

"Surely not," Peter protested.

Selina felt herself deflate.

"I just took you to meet Angelo, didn't I?" Peter continued. "That was certainly interesting."

"You would not permit me to speak, so it's not as though I could make conversation—"

Selina couldn't stop herself. "You took your sister to a *fencing parlor?*" At least that explained the masculine attire.

Peter, Freddie, and Lu turned identical guilty gazes toward her, and Selina was powerfully struck by the resemblance among the three of them. The same brown curls, lit by hints of auburn in the sun. The bird-like bones of the children were echoed in Peter's lean, muscular frame, and in Lu's gamine face she could see Peter's same mischievous charm.

"I am going," Lu said with some dignity, "to learn how to fence."

"Though probably not at Angelo's," Peter put in.

"Certainly not," Selina said. "I was taught to fence in my own home, which is the only acceptable location for a lady of quality to learn the sport."

"You *were?*" exclaimed Lu, losing all track of her composure.

Peter's lips curled up. "Are you suggesting that Lu learn how to fence in . . . your home?"

Selina scowled. "Not at all. I meant—oh, you imbecile, you knew what I meant."

Lu grinned what Selina was starting to think of as the Kent family grin. "Oh, I like her."

"Of course you do," Peter said. "She wants you to learn how to stab people."

"Might I suggest," Selina said drily, "that you hire a fencing master to attend both of your siblings at the Stanhope residence?"

Peter frowned, and Selina felt her brows go up. She wasn't sure she'd ever seen him frown. "The children do not reside with me."

"They don't?" She couldn't help the rather appalled tone of her voice, though even as she said it, she supposed she was being absurd. Of course they didn't. What handsome single young aristocrat would house two small children in his London residence during the Season if he had any other option?

What aristocrat other than her older brother Nicholas, of course.

She and her twin, Will, had been six when their parents had died. Six years old, and half out of their wits with terror at the fear of what would become of them. They'd huddled together under the bed linens for the first time in years, wondering whether they'd be sent away to live with some ancient relative they did not know.

But instead, Nicholas had abandoned Oxford and, all of twenty years old, had come home to raise them himself.

"They don't live with me, no," Peter said, and his voice sounded uncharacteristically grim. "But not for want of trying."

For want of . . . trying?

"You don't have guardianship of your siblings, then?" she asked. And how puzzling that was. She knew Peter's parents were both deceased, like her own. Surely it would be a matter of course for the guardianship to pass to him, as hers and Will's had passed to Nicholas.

"We are *half* siblings," said Lu icily, and then understanding clicked into place.

These were *natural* children. Peter's father must have had these children with his mistress—or perhaps not even that, simply a woman with whom he'd had intercourse. Perhaps not even the *same* woman, she supposed.

Her own father had had a long-term mistress before he'd married their mother. It wasn't uncommon for aristocrats.

Male aristocrats, that is. It wasn't uncommon for *male* peers to have children with women who were not their wives.

But it *was* uncommon for the legitimate heir to recognize them—to introduce them as his siblings to an acquaintance on the street.

Goodness, Peter Kent did have a way of surprising her.

"I see," she said. "And where do you reside now, Miss Lu?"

Lu jerked up her chin. "With Great-great-aunt Rosamund. We *love* Great-great-aunt Rosamund."

Freddie emitted a little squeak—Selina thought maybe Lu had kicked him—and then he was nodding along agreeably. "Oh yes, we love her. We love her, um . . . her, um . . . her . . ." He gazed at Selina and then inspiration seemed to strike. "Her bonnets!"

Peter gave a strangled cough.

Lu rolled her eyes. "Thank you, Freddie."

"She sounds like a paragon," Selina said.

"Oh yes," said Peter, "certainly. What did she say this morning when I arrived to collect you? I don't think I quite understood her."

Freddie produced an imitation of a quiet snore.

"We love Great-great-aunt Rosamund," repeated Lu. "And her home is where we shall stay."

"Unless I can pry you out by means of legal action," said Peter, and there was that frown again. Selina found she didn't like to see him frown. Which was probably the most bizarre thought she'd had all day, and that included all the eye-popping combinations of colors she'd imagined plucking out of her wardrobe.

"Don't you know," Peter was saying to his sister, "I could fill the drawing room of the Stanhope residence with fencing masters, if you so desired it, Lu."

"I do not." Her small chin was still lifted, her dark brows arched in challenge.

"I have to admit," Selina said, "it is a particular pleasure to have a fencing master attend you at your leisure."

Lu turned a scowl in Selina's direction.

"Listen to Lady Selina, won't you?" Peter said, his face softening. "You like her. She's interesting. She's easily the cleverest woman of my acquaintance."

A little frisson of delight curled up like a cat inside Selina's chest, and she tried to get hold of herself. Good God, there was something about these offhand Kent compliments that could charm the hat off one's head. Even this monumental green silk bonnet.

"In fact," he said, and he turned to Selina as if about to speak. He paused for a moment, and then said, "Yes—I think that—" His warm brown eyes rested on her face consideringly.

"You think that . . . ?" she prompted after a moment. Her cheeks were starting to feel a bit warm, and she really did not want to blush, for goodness' sake. Selina did not blush. She *refused* to blush.

"I'd like to speak to you and your brother about this exact situation. Can I call on you at Rowland House?"

She wasn't entirely sure what situation he was talking about— curse the man, he always made her feel as though she'd lost the plot—but . . .

She knew herself. She knew her fatal flaw.

She was curious. She always wanted to know more.

"Yes," Selina said. "I am living at Rowland House with the duke and duchess."

"Excellent," Peter said. "I'll call on you there."

And then he clapped a hand to the back of Lu's head and said, "Try a curtsy this time, Lu."

Lu's mouth pinched, and she held out imaginary skirts and swept Selina a rather magnificent curtsy that almost reached the depths of her previous bow.

"You know," said Selina, "I quite like you as well."

Chapter 3

. . . Have you any new interest in politics after spending the last eighteen months with His Majesty's Army, Will? You might be interested to know that the new Duke of Stanhope (Peter Kent, I'm sure you remember him) delivered as his maiden speech perhaps the most devastating opprobrium against slavery ever heard in the House of Lords. I am well pleased by his ascension to the peerage.

—from His Grace Nicholas Ravenscroft, Duke of Rowland, to his brother, Lord William Ravenscroft, His Majesty's Army, Seventh Division

"Tell me again," said Mohan Tagore, "why we are walking to Rowland House."

Peter made himself slow down to keep pace with his barrister's shorter strides. Then he realized he'd been whistling a Carnival song he hadn't thought of in years and he made himself stop that too.

"It's a fine day," he said. "Use your legs, Tagore. I have it on good authority that an unused muscle atrophies. I worry for you."

"Are you saying that if I were to gag you for a month or so, your *tongue* would atrophy? Because if so—"

"God forbid," Peter said. "I assure you, while you might not regret the loss of that particular organ, there are a number of ladies of my acquaintance who might disagree."

Tagore choked briefly on air. "I am going to pretend I did not hear that and ask you again why we are walking to Rowland House."

Peter took a moment to meditate on the question. He'd considered taking the Stanhope carriage to Tagore's office, picking up Tagore, and then having them conveyed together to Rowland's door. But it seemed too absurd—to ride barely a dozen blocks to Tagore's office, then back again as far to Rowland House—when they could walk. The sky was painfully blue, a color that made him think of Louisiana with the mixture of love and nostalgia and loss that he'd felt ever since he'd arrived in England with the Earl of Clermont two years prior.

He wanted to look at the sky. He wanted to talk to Tagore before they got into Rowland House and everything became all caution and pleading-without-seeming-to-plead.

"Or perhaps," Tagore said, apparently tired of waiting for Peter to answer, "you might tell me why we are meeting at Rowland House at all."

"I want to talk to Rowland about the next six weeks. I want to see if he has any ideas as to how we might make the lord chancellor more amenable to our petition."

In six weeks, Peter's petition for guardianship of Freddie and Lu would come before Lord Eldon, the chancellor of the High

Court. And unless something changed quite drastically in that span of time, Peter was going to lose.

"Eldon is a problem," Tagore agreed. "But I meant, rather— why Rowland House? You are a member of Rowland's club, are you not?"

Peter was. He was fairly certain Rowland had exerted no small amount of pressure to encourage the manager of Brooks's to extend a sponsorship to him, because he'd been offered membership nearly a year before his ducal elevation. Rowland was brilliant at those sorts of things—easing the way, making the track smooth. Peter had never had the talent for it. Nor the inclination, even, until he'd moved to England.

"I wanted you to talk to Rowland as well," he said easily. "You'll be at the Court of Chancery with me, and Rowland will not. I'm hopeful he'll have some suggestions."

Tagore drummed his fingers against his thigh. "It's a challenge. Lord Eldon moves in entirely different political circles than Rowland, for all that Rowland is a duke. Rowland's a Whig, a reformer, and Eldon is the most entrenched of the Tories."

"I know it. I'm hopeful that we might be able to think of another approach. Not direct political pressure, but . . . something."

"Rowland isn't in the habit of bribery. Nor Eldon, for that matter."

"No bribes," Peter said. Not that he would be opposed to bribery, if it would get him Freddie and Lu, but he'd already talked the matter over with Tagore and decided it wasn't practicable. But he was damned if he was going to let his brother and sister go without a fight.

He had lost a sibling, back in New Orleans, when they had both been children.

He would not let it happen again, not for all the dukedom or for all the world. There had to be something they could do. There had to be another way.

And he wanted to talk to Selina Ravenscroft.

That, as much as he couldn't say it aloud to his barrister, was the reason they were going to Rowland House. At Brooks's, Selina wouldn't be there. At a ball, he couldn't lay his cards on the table in front of her and watch her clever, busy mind puzzle away at the problem.

In the two years since he'd met her, he'd seen her at work a number of times. She distracted maidenly aunts to help facilitate unchaperoned marriage proposals. She rearranged conversational groups, murmuring in response to his curious glance, "Lady Stratton can't abide the Earl of Puddington. I'd hate to see fisticuffs ruin my aunt's party."

He'd seen her identify a fragile dowager missing a glove from across a crowded room and produce a new glove as if from nowhere.

Once, at the Breightmets', he'd seen her thrust her friend Lydia Hope-Wallace into a potted palm. He'd watched with interest as Lydia had cast up her accounts, hidden from all passersby, and then stood by in frank amazement as Selina somehow managed to remove Lydia from the ball without a single other person seeming to notice their departure.

Just last December, she'd organized the elopement of Clermont—who had become one of Peter's closest companions—and her own dear friend Faiza Khan. Clermont and Faiza had given every impression of despising each other. Peter had been quite certain no one but he knew that Clermont carried Faiza's earring in his pocket like a blasted talisman.

But Selina must have known. She had certainly known *some-*

thing, because one day Clermont and Faiza had been shouting at one another over dinner and the next they were well on their way to Scotland, in a post-chaise personally hired by Selina.

She was so damned efficient. She seemed like she could be in two places at once. She could light up the room like the most popular woman of the *beau monde,* but he'd also seen her fade into the background when she chose to. Though how she managed that, he had no idea, what with her acres of honey-blond hair and that wide, expressive mouth.

And her eyes, light amber, like a cat's eyes, or a wolf's. He'd thought about those eyes from time to time these last two years.

Not as often, though, as he'd thought about how infernally clever she was, and how much he liked that about her. She fixed things, like her brother—but not in his same way. Rowland was a politician, all careful talk and social grace and terrifying ethical code. Selina wasn't afraid to sneak about, to hide in a potted plant or steal a glove if she had to.

And when he'd seen the way Lu had warmed to her, and the way Selina had known instinctively how to win Lu's confidence, it had occurred to him suddenly that if anyone might have a fresh thought about how he could gain custody of his siblings, it would be Selina Ravenscroft.

He was still thinking about her when they arrived at Rowland House.

The butler ushered them inside and set out to determine if His Grace was receiving callers.

"And Lady Selina," Peter added. "I'd like to see His Grace and Lady Selina."

He felt rather than saw Tagore's sharp dark-eyed gaze.

Like a penknife, that look.

"Social call, is it?" said Tagore blandly.

"No," Peter said. "No. Have you met Lady Selina?"

"I have not had the pleasure. Rowland's sister?"

"That's right. When you meet her, you'll see why I want her here as well."

Tagore snorted. "I'm sure I will."

Peter ignored him, and the butler returned to deliver them into a drawing room decorated in blues and creams. Nicholas Ravenscroft, the Duke of Rowland, stood to greet them as they entered. He was tall and dark-haired, perhaps half a dozen years older than Peter's own nine-and-twenty. His wife, Daphne, was there as well, a welcoming smile on her face and her riotous mahogany curls springing in all directions.

And in the corner of the room, rising to her feet from a leather armchair, was Selina.

Today she wore demure white, and there was no trace of the immense green thing she'd had on her head when he'd met her on Bond Street. He couldn't quite say whether he missed it—he'd rather admired the way she had worn it, all defiance, as if it were a crown and not a hat the size of a barque. Her gloves were neatly buttoned at her wrists, and she gave him the politest of curtsies as he greeted her. Her eyes were downcast, and for just a moment he doubted this whole damned thing.

Then she looked up, and that fierce tawny gaze caught his, and he knew down to his bones that he'd been right to think of her.

And he had the strangest thought then: that he'd been right *every* time he'd thought of her. That every time she had crossed his mind—her keen wit and her capable manner and even, if he were being honest with himself, the plump curve of her mouth and the tender spot at the nape of her neck—every time, it had been right. That she belonged exactly there, inside his head.

Which was ridiculous, even for him.

He shook off the peculiar notion and seated himself as the duchess poured tea for all of them. He noticed when Daphne stripped off her gloves that there were ink stains on her fingers, and he recalled that she was intimately involved in the steward-ship of several of their country estates. He wondered if asking *all* of the Ravenscrofts for advice about how to manage his affairs would be a bit beyond the pale.

They made polite small talk for a few minutes, and then Selina helpfully directed the conversation where Peter wanted it to go.

"And did you see your brother and sister safely home to Aunt Rosamund then?" she asked, her fingers nudging her teacup to the exact center of its saucer.

"I did, yes," Peter said, and then turned to the rest of the group to explain. "Lady Selina had the rather adulterated pleasure of meeting my brother and sister last week in town while I took them shopping."

One corner of Selina's mouth quirked up, but she didn't say anything about the fencing, which was probably good, since he wanted Rowland to think of him as a responsible guardian and not an impulsive degenerate who would permit his sister to behave like a hoyden.

Which he was. And she did.

"How did they enjoy London?" asked Daphne. "Remind me again how old they are. I think they're quite a bit older than our boys, are they not?"

"My sister Lucinda is twelve," Peter said. "My brother Freder-ick is ten." He took this opening to outline in circumspect detail their background—attempting to be mindful of *faux pas* such as "talking about your father's sexual escapades in the company of ladies" and "insulting benevolent elderly women."

"We've been laying the groundwork these last two years, preparing legal arguments and encouraging a relationship between Stanhope and the children," Tagore said. "But we didn't want to put forth the application for guardianship until His Grace inherited. Once that happened, I petitioned the lord chancellor immediately. Our case is set to go before him six weeks hence."

Rowland toyed with his cravat. "Eldon is the sticking point. If you'd gotten the new vice chancellor, Plumer, I wouldn't be so concerned. But Eldon . . ." He trailed off.

Selina's brows were drawn together. "Nicholas, I don't understand. Why wouldn't Stanhope automatically be granted the guardianship, as you were?"

There was a moment of awkward silence, and Selina's lips pursed. "I mean—that is to say—I know what natural children are. I understand why the guardianship wouldn't be assumed." Peter noted with fascination the flush that slowly worked its way up the fair skin of her neck. In the last two years, he'd rarely seen her blush. Even the first time they'd met—when he'd stumbled upon her in the woods, still damp from bathing in a stream at her country estate—she had not blushed, merely delivered a scorching glare.

He had to admit, he liked that sweet strawberry flush on her skin. Rather alarmingly.

He *had* seen her grind her teeth on numerous occasions, and she was doing that now too. "I simply meant that I don't understand why this is a problem. Stanhope is a duke. He wants his siblings. What could possibly be the difficulty?"

"The problems," Peter said, "are twofold. First, my father never formally acknowledged the children. In fact, I don't believe he recognized them at all. We know from the Stanhope account books that their mother went to my grandfather for financial support, not to my father. Between Tagore and my Sussex steward, we've produced any number of records that show that the previous duke supported them for years, but they aren't mentioned in his will or my father's. For all legal purposes, I might as well be a stranger who's come to snatch them from the clutches of the court's noble servant, Great-great-aunt Rosamund."

Selina took that in with a stubborn set to her jaw. "Nonetheless. We are all here well acquainted with the power of a dukedom. Whyever would Eldon stand in your way?"

"Eldon was born the son of a coal-fitter," Nicholas said. "He's rather less impressed by the peerage than you might expect, for all that he's now Baron Eldon and the voice of the king in the High Court."

"But what objection could he possibly have to Stanhope's taking the children?"

"Me," Peter said, wincing at the bluntness even as he said it. "His objection is me."

"I see," said Selina, though her expression said plainly that she did not.

"I have not endeared myself to Eldon this year," Peter continued. "Or any year, in point of fact. He has a particular sense of English pride that resents the sudden elevation of an American upstart to the highest levels of the government."

"But your father was English," protested Selina.

"Yes," Peter said, "and my mother was French. To many, the latter is more consequential."

"And, as I may have mentioned," Nicholas added, "Eldon is a Tory. The worst of them. He hates reformers with a passion. Thinks England was at its best in 1688."

"It would have been better," Peter said, "if I had not made that speech in the Lords just after I took my seat."

Tagore muffled a snort, and Daphne coughed a laugh into her teacup.

"What speech?" Selina asked. "What happened?"

"It was," Nicholas said delicately, "certainly rousing."

Peter spun his teacup in its saucer and then watched in some horror as tea arced up the sides of the cup and sloshed onto the porcelain beneath. "I argued for total abolition of slavery across all British colonies. In a few, er, choice words."

"'The greatest practical evil ever inflicted upon members of the human race,' I believe it was," said Nicholas. "'The severest and most extensive calamity in the history of the world and an irremediable stain on our national character.'"

"Er," Peter said. "Yes."

And though he'd always known that Rowland was perhaps his strongest ally in the Lords on the question of abolition, the fact that Rowland seemed to have memorized the words he'd used to condemn slavery was . . .

Well, Peter felt speechless for perhaps the first time in his life.

"I begin to see the problem," Selina said. "You are requesting a favor from a man who is not disposed to like you, whom you have sparred with politically, and who has no legal requirement to give you what you want."

"All that," Tagore said, "and then there was the cognac."

"Oh for God's sake," Peter said. "I couldn't possibly have known about the cognac."

Nicholas arched one dark eyebrow. "I am unaware of this particular concern."

Tagore's eyes were gleaming like he'd just been handed a brand-new inkpot, or whatever the hell barristers liked. "Before His Grace inherited the title, it came to his attention that his grandfather was a particular connoisseur of cognac, and so before the former Stanhope passed on, the *current* Stanhope—"

"Kent," Peter interrupted. "I beg you. Call me Kent. This story makes no sense when everyone involved has the same title."

Tagore waved his fingers in dismissal. "Fine. *Kent* here decided he wanted his grandfather to have the very best in cognac before his death."

"Before *his* death," Peter clarified. "I am not dead in this story."

He was pretty sure Daphne laughed again. Selina shot him a chastening glare.

"Not yet," mumbled Tagore. "In any case, Kent talked to Stanhope's steward and found out where the man used to purchase the highest-quality bottles—smuggled, of course, because they are produced in France. Begging your pardon, Lady Selina, Your Grace."

"I am aware of smuggling," said Selina.

"Indeed. Er. Of course. In any event, that particular cognac was no longer for sale. So Kent hired a band of highwaymen—"

"Blatant defamation," said Peter. "They were perfectly respectable members of their own particular kind of trade—"

"A band of highwaymen," Tagore said, rolling right over his objection, "to steal the cognac from the smugglers. And they did. All eighteen barrels of it."

Nicholas appeared on the point of speaking, then stuffed an iced biscuit into his mouth instead.

"I really don't know what they were thinking," Peter said. "Eighteen barrels! I meant for them to take a bottle."

"But the real problem," continued Tagore, "is that the smugglers had been hired personally by Lord Eldon. He is, as it turns out, obsessed with cognac himself. And those eighteen barrels were the last production of an ancient distillery that was destroyed by Napoleon's armies."

"They were very expensive," said Peter morosely. "Thousands of pounds."

"And Kent stole them all. And then, because he did not want to store eighteen barrels of illegally obtained cognac in his house, he had them decanted and passed the extra bottles out to every public house and tavern in the county of Sussex."

"So now," Peter said, taking up the story, "Eldon is buying up every single bottle, one public house at a time. But the word has gotten out about the cognac, and the tavernkeepers are all charging him twenty times what they're worth." Twenty *thousand* pounds. Surely Eldon could not want to spend twenty thousand pounds on French brandy.

"Good heavens," said Daphne. "I'm not sure you could have made a more calculated project of indisposing Eldon if you'd tried."

"Believe me," said Peter. "I did not try."

"Did your grandfather like the cognac?" Selina asked.

Peter felt his chest twist. God, what a question. Had he ever met a woman so clever and also so damned sweet?

"Yes," he said. "He liked it very much."

Nicholas looked like he couldn't decide whether to laugh or tear off his cravat in disgust. "Stanhope, you have not exactly made this easy on yourself."

"I know," Peter said. "I know." He couldn't stop himself from rising, though he knew it wasn't quite the thing. But he had to move. He had to do *something*. Damn him, he would not accept that his own recklessness had lost him the chance of getting custody of his brother and sister. He *couldn't* accept it. He meant to care for them, to protect them, and he would manage it, no matter what it took. Even if it meant becoming an altogether different kind of man.

He walked to the window and pressed a finger to the glass, then rubbed the smudge clear with the sleeve of his coat.

Back in New Orleans, he hadn't been able to protect his brother, Morgan, and Morgan had died. But Peter was grown now. He was a goddamned peer of the realm. He would not let his father hurt these children—not through neglect or cruelty. Not even from the grave.

"Your Grace," said Tagore, "have you any influence in Eldon's circle?"

"Not as much as I'd like," Nicholas said. "I will certainly exert what pressure I can. But Eldon isn't in the Lords now—though I have it on good authority that he would be open to such a thing when he leaves the Court of Chancery. I hate to say this, Stanhope, but I'm not sure how much I can help."

When she spoke, Selina's voice sounded almost abstracted. "What else do you know about Eldon?"

Peter turned away from the window to look at her. Her eyes were half narrowed, and her lips compressed as she looked into the middle distance.

Nicholas fiddled absently with his cuffs. "He's a Tory. He supported Pitt for prime minister. He has been painfully resistant to any calls to reform the courts, despite the backlog of cases and the shocking bureaucratic inefficiency of the system."

"Not about politics," said Selina. "What do you know of *him*? Eldon. What's his name?"

"Lord Eldon? John, I think," Nicholas said. "John Scott."

"He's from Newcastle," put in Tagore. "You can hear his northern accent when he speaks."

"What does he care about?" Selina asked.

"England," said Nicholas. "And our sterling national character."

Peter winced.

"Cognac, apparently," said Daphne.

"Perhaps Stanhope could deliver him cognac?" suggested Selina. "Or—perhaps not. Mayhap we should avoid reminders of your past misdeeds."

"They say he was a rotter at school," Nicholas said consideringly. "A devil for pranks and truancy."

"Is that right?" said Tagore, looking suddenly intrigued.

"And of course," said Nicholas, "there was the matter of his wife."

Four gazes fixed on Rowland with interest.

"Eldon kidnapped her. Quite famously."

Selina's brows climbed nearly to her hairline. "He *kidnapped* her?"

"Well," Nicholas temporized, "perhaps *kidnapped* is not the word. He was a law student at Oxford, at home on school break, when he fell violently in love with the daughter of a neighbor. Both sides objected to the match—his parents wanted him to focus on his studies, and her family thought the son of a coal-fitter beneath them. They wouldn't back down, and so Eldon removed her from her family home by way of a window in the dead of night, carried her off to Scotland, and married her on the morrow."

"Now, that," Selina said, "is something."

"Do you think to appeal to Lady Eldon?" asked Daphne. "Does she live in London with the chancellor, Nicholas?"

"I believe so. I understand them to be quite a devoted couple."

Daphne tapped an ink-stained finger on her chin. "Shall we have them over for dinner?" she asked. "Is that too transparent?"

"Not at all," said Nicholas. "I'm happy to arrange it, Stanhope, if you like."

"Yes," said Peter. "Anything you think might help."

"I like this idea," said Selina. "I'd like very much to speak to Lady Eldon. But I wonder . . ." She trailed off, her fingers absently nudging the cup on her saucer again. "I wonder . . ." Her eyes came up again and fixed on Peter's. He felt her gaze almost like a tug, pulling at him from across the room, and he took a half step toward her before he could stop himself.

"Call here again," she said. "Tomorrow. I want to talk to Lydia Hope-Wallace first. And then I want to talk to you."

She had something in mind. Peter was certain of it—not just from what she'd said, but by her eyes, distant with concentration, and the decided set of her jaw. She had an idea, and he knew her well enough to think it would be a good one.

He felt a sudden rush of warmth that he recognized as relief, because . . . Because for the first time since he'd learned that Lu and Freddie's mother had died, Peter thought that the children might just be all right.

Although now that he thought about it, there was something about the stubborn angle of her head that reminded him a bit alarmingly of Lu.

"You don't think I should *kidnap* the children, do you?" he asked. "I mean, I would do it. But I'm not sure I'd survive the experience, now that Lu has a sword."

"Um," said Selina. "No. I do not think you should kidnap the children. I would . . . No. Certainly not."

This was something of a relief, though in truth he'd already started spinning out ideas for how he might lure them out a window in the middle of the night. Tiny kittens armed with tinier spears, perhaps. Éclairs in the shape of épées.

Tagore seemed to be shaking his head. "I am going to pretend that I did not hear that, Stanhope."

"Nothing to hear," Peter said, and he strolled back toward his teacup from where he'd been standing at the window. "Cookie?"

"Perhaps one for the road," Tagore said, and shortly thereafter they took their leave of the Ravenscrofts. Peter caught himself whistling again and tried to tamp down the sudden emotion that had blossomed inside him at Rowland House: relief and cautious hope and bright amber eyes.

Chapter 4

. . . I had a letter from Selina just last week that mentioned Stanhope as well. I am almost afraid to inquire: Whose new project is he? Selina's or yours?

—*from Will Ravenscroft to his brother, Nicholas,*
posted from Brussels

The morning after the Duke of Stanhope's fascinating interview at Rowland House, Selina sat again in the drawing room.

This time she was in her stocking feet, her legs curled up beneath her on the cream-colored divan, chewing on her lower lip and waiting for her best friend, Lydia Hope-Wallace, to arrive.

She'd dropped by the Hope-Wallace residence—just half a block away from Rowland House—the previous day, but Lydia had been out with her mother, doubtless being tormented at a modiste or a milliner. And why Mrs. Hope-Wallace could not leave Lydia well enough alone, Selina would never understand. They were richer than Croesus. Like Selina herself, Lydia certainly did not *have* to marry, and torturing her by thrusting her into the public eye at every single engagement to which they were invited had not, thus far, produced results that Lydia or her mother were happy with.

With her four older brothers and even with the Ravenscrofts, Lydia was a gem. She was far and away the smartest woman Selina had ever met, with an encyclopedic knowledge of parliamentary politics and a head for gossip that rivaled any dowager.

But at balls and dinners—anywhere she was expected to make conversation among large groups of people—Lydia was too terror-stricken to speak.

The Marriage Mart had not been pleasant for Lydia. The 1815 Season was her fourth—she, like Selina, was three-and-twenty—and her mother, rather than resigning herself to Lydia's lack of popularity, seemed bent on redoubling her efforts. Lydia had more gowns and hats than a member of the royal family. "As if a peacock feather on my head," she'd said briskly to Selina in an undervoice at a recent dinner, "might distract a gentleman from my inability to unlock my jaw in his presence."

Selina had left a card for Lydia at the Hope-Wallace residence, and Lydia had dashed off a note in response that said she would call this morning. So Selina was back in the drawing room, demolishing a scone and tapping a quill pen against a sheet of foolscap while she waited for her friend to arrive.

When their butler finally announced Lydia, Selina had crumbled the scone into pieces and made two dozen tiny black dots on the paper.

"All right," said Lydia without preamble. "I'm here for all the chatter and idle talk you have for me. What's the scandal of the day?"

Selina winced. "No scandal. In fact, I would like to discuss the opposite of scandal."

Lydia raised her brows consideringly and settled her lush figure into the divan beside Selina. Today her orange-red hair was caught in a low knot beneath a pert straw bonnet that Selina quite liked. For all Mrs. Hope-Wallace was a meddlesome devil, she had excellent taste in hats.

"What in the world is the opposite of scandal?" Lydia asked. "Or must I guess?"

"Marriage," said Selina. "Marriage is the opposite of scandal."

Lydia took this in but then shook her head. "Marriage might be the solution to a scandal, I'll grant you that. But I can think of a good half a dozen marriages that caused more scandal than they eliminated. And by the by, whose marriage are we talking about here?"

She gave Selina a long look through coppery lashes, and Selina felt herself start to blush. *Again.* Twice in two days. It was offensive.

"Not mine," she said quickly. "Definitely not mine. Lyddie, believe me, if I ever consider accepting a proposal, you'll be the first to know."

"I was wondering if I was about to be," Lydia said.

"No," said Selina. "No, certainly not."

Since 1812, when they'd both made their bows, Lydia and Selina had each turned down several offers. The majority had been in their first Season. Lydia had been disgusted. "Beaumont," she'd said, rolling her eyes. "I have danced with the man a single time. I have spoken a grand total of four words to him. Good evening. And then later: Good evening."

That first Season, every single male member of the *ton* with substantial debt and a total lack of interest in the personality of his future wife had proposed to Lydia. She'd rejected them all.

If Lydia could just bring herself to *speak* to men, Selina felt certain she'd have made an excellent match in a heartbeat. But Lydia didn't—or couldn't—and after the first two years, the proposals had slowed to a trickle.

Selina had had offers too, from fortune-hunters and men who wanted a closer connection to the dukedom and even occasionally a nice gentleman who seemed legitimately interested in her company.

But 1812 had been something of an education. It had started with ribbons.

Purple, if Selina remembered correctly. Lydia had informed her that aubergine would be *à la mode* in late 1812, which was why she had been holding purple ribbons when they'd discovered that Selina's suitor, the Marquess of Queensbury, was in the millinery shop not to pay his attentions to her, but to set an assignation with his mistress.

Good heavens, Selina had been such a fool then. *Whyever could he have come into the shop?* she'd asked. *He didn't even make a purchase.*

As though a marquess might come in to purchase a hat for his mother or buttons for his own coat.

She'd heard the term *mistress*, of course, but only at a distance. Whispered beneath discreetly cupped hands. Not as the name for real women whom real men of her acquaintance engaged for the purpose of carnal conversation.

But she'd learned quickly. First an illusion-puncturing explanation from Lydia—*Your older brother has kept you sheltered from the real world, Selina*—and then a book. *The* book. The book that Lydia had brought over to Rowland House and told Selina to keep out of sight if she had any sense.

The Courtesan's Revenge: The Memoirs of Harriette Wilson, Written by Herself.

Selina recalled the cheap cloth binding, the way the rough

navy starched cotton had felt under her hands, so different from the smooth leather of the books in the library at Broadmayne, their country estate.

She remembered curling up beneath her counterpane, squinting in the moonlight at the words on the page.

I shall not say, the book began, *why and how I became, at the age of fifteen, the mistress of the Earl of Craven.*

Selina had learned quite a bit from Harriette Wilson's book. She'd learned a great deal more in the three years since 1812, and all of it came back to Belvoir's and its expansive catalog of emerald-green books.

She had also learned—between her brother's marriages and her growing understanding of the lifestyles of male peers of the realm—that the regular kind of aristocratic marriage was not good enough for her. She had no need to marry for security or social position.

She was endlessly grateful for that privilege, because she had discovered, in her heart of hearts, that she wanted *more*. She wanted something better than a political and economic match based on an appropriate lineage and a desire for heirs.

She wanted love. She wanted someone who wouldn't be afraid of her connection to Belvoir's. She wanted someone to look at her and see more than just the sister of a duke or the recipient of a substantial dowry. More than difficult and prickly and too opinionated and too *much*.

So far, no such candidate had presented himself. It was extremely lowering.

"All right," said Lydia. "My curiosity is piqued. If we're not here to discuss *your* incipient marriage, whose are we planning?"

"What do you know," Selina said carefully, "about the Duke of Stanhope?"

Lydia's brows arched. "Stanhope? Why, practically everything, I think."

Selina permitted herself a snort, because it was Lydia. "Of course you do."

Lydia gave a small ironic smile. "Did you expect anything else?"

"Not in the slightest."

"His father was a third son," Lydia said, "who was sent to the colonies to marry the daughter of an absurdly wealthy French hotelier. The Stanhope coffers were not at their best at the time, but as I understand it, the marriage—and the work of the rather savvy eighth duke—shored up the Stanhope fortune well enough. Given his father, his uncles, and his two male cousins, there was no reason to think that he would ever inherit, so Mr. Peter Kent was raised in blissful American splendor in New Orleans. But thanks to Napoleon, among other misfortunes, the younger Kent men did not outlive the old duke, and so, two years ago, Peter Kent became the heir presumptive to an ancient dukedom."

"Precisely," said Selina. "The American Duke."

Lydia inclined her head. "The Earl of Clermont retrieved Kent from Louisiana when he became the heir—to meet his elderly grandfather and the rest of the *ton*—and he's lived a figure of some, er, notoriety ever since."

"You know that he's spoken against slavery in the Lords?"

"Of course I do," Lydia said. "He's a radical abolitionist. I'm surprised that *you* do."

"He was here yesterday," Selina said by way of explanation. "He wanted Nicholas's help in his efforts to secure guardianship of his half siblings."

"Intriguing. I take it they are natural children?"

Selina nodded. Goodness, she adored Lydia, who knew everything and was shocked by nothing. "As I understand it, they're concerned that the Court of Chancery is unlikely to grant Stanhope's petition for guardianship."

Lydia took this in, and Selina knew she was mentally reviewing her knowledge of Lord John Scott, first Baron Eldon and the lord high chancellor.

"Nicholas says he's not sure what he can do to help."

Lydia huffed a laugh. "Of course he's not. Your brother is too terrifyingly honorable to curry favor with Tories he doesn't care for."

Selina nodded. That was certainly Nicholas.

"To be sure, the lord chancellor despises Stanhope, because he's American and a radical," Lydia continued. "And there's some precedent for denying guardianship to an elder brother because of inheritance concerns, not that I suspect Stanhope's father's by-blows have money or property. But it would be justification for Lord Eldon to deny Stanhope if he chooses to do so. A real tangle, Selina."

"I was thinking," Selina said, "about Lord Eldon. About his famous love match and about his reasons for disliking Stanhope. And I was wondering—well. If Stanhope were to marry—quite suddenly, and to a woman of the most upstanding reputation and perfect English background—"

Lydia's blue eyes were narrowed in thought as she gazed at Selina. One finger tapped the sprigged muslin of her skirt. "You think if Stanhope marries respectably, the lord chancellor will find him less objectionable?"

"I think if Stanhope marries respectably, he will *be* less objectionable. And I also think that if he marries out of impassioned ardor, perhaps Lord Eldon will find him more sympathetic. And I do wonder if Stanhope and his new bride might be able to get

Lord Eldon's wife on their side as well, if their story is charming enough."

Lydia's lips curved up. "Selina. You have the mind of a politician after all. I'm impressed."

Selina gave a little shake of her head. "Don't say it. Don't even *think* it, or Nicholas's single Whig friends will suddenly start calling in droves."

Lydia laughed. "God save you from that fate. All right, so you mean to see Stanhope married?"

"I had intended to suggest that course of action to him, yes," Selina said. "I thought you might help me draw up a list of suitable ladies for him to court." She gestured to the dotted foolscap in front of her. "I'm prepared with pen and ink."

"Of course you are," said Lydia. "I've never seen you other than prepared. Have you any candidates in mind for the future Duchess of Stanhope?"

Selina chewed her lower lip. "It must be someone with an impeccable reputation."

"That puts the Halifax twins right out then," said Lydia.

Selina winced. The Halifax twins had made their bows the previous year and had spent the entire 1814 Season popping up on scandal sheets across London, smoking cheroots in libraries and emerging from closed carriages with gentlemen at dawn. Selina loved Margo and Matilda, but—

"Absolutely no Halifaxes," she agreed.

"An impeccable reputation," said Lydia, "and if not a daughter of a peer, then at least someone who is English to the bone. Eldon will like that."

"And someone sensible," Selina said. "Someone with enough backbone that Stanhope won't run right over her."

Lydia considered this. "Stanhope is rather . . ."

"Forceful?" said Selina.

"I was going to say impulsive," Lydia said. "Reckless. A bit outrageous."

Selina thought about Lu and her rapier. About his offer to kidnap his siblings. About those ridiculous curls that simply *could not* be natural, and . . .

"Yes," she said. "He is rather all that."

"He doesn't need a fortune, so that makes this a bit simpler. What do you think about Lady Georgiana Cleeve?"

Selina blinked. "Georgiana Cleeve? No. No. My goodness, Lyddie, no."

Lydia looked taken aback. "Why on earth not? She's the daughter of an earl, for all the Earl of Alverthorpe is rather unbearable. She's been widely regarded as the Diamond of this Season. She is a bit young, I suppose, but she's a perfect innocent."

Selina pictured Georgiana Cleeve's lamb-like blue eyes. The immaculate moonbeam ringlets of her hair. The clustered knot of lordlings that surrounded her at every ball.

"Lydia," she said, "Georgiana Cleeve has the brains of an eel. *After* it has been boiled and jellied."

Lydia pressed her lips together, smothering her amusement. "Surely that's a bit uncharitable."

"I once heard Tresidder ask her if she liked Coleridge. Georgiana told him she didn't know that particular ridge, but that she believed walking in nature to be hazardous for young women of good breeding."

Lydia's eyes widened. "I am so sorry I missed that conversation."

"Even Tresidder looked alarmed, poor man."

"All right," said Lydia. "Let's add a modicum of intelligence to the list of characteristics. What about Beatrice Villeneuve?"

"Lydia," Selina protested. "She is awful. You cannot mean to suggest her."

Lydia cocked her head. "Goodness, Selina, you didn't say 'pleasant' was a required characteristic as well."

"I wouldn't wish a lifetime with Beatrice Villeneuve on my worst enemy." And Stanhope was far from that. She liked him. She had always liked him, even though he was terribly unsettling. "Plus there are children involved. Beatrice Villeneuve would eat Stanhope's little brother for breakfast."

"All right," Lydia said. "I give up. Clearly you've someone in mind already."

"Um," said Selina. "Well. I did have one woman."

"Who is this paragon of virtue?"

"Er. You, Lyddie."

Lydia's mouth fell open, then snapped closed with a click of her teeth. "I?"

"It's perfectly logical," Selina said quickly. "Your family is one of the most well respected in England. There's never been a hint of scandal attached to your name—"

"Only because no one has yet seen me vomit at a ball—"

Selina ignored this. "You are beautiful and clever, and you'd never let Stanhope make a fool of himself."

"Selina," Lydia groaned. "Not you too. My mother has been tormenting me for years. Even you cannot suddenly make me into a different person."

"That's the beauty of it," said Selina. "You need not charm him if he's already looking for a bride. It's a wonderful idea, and he'd be lucky to have you. And"—her voice turned wheedling—"if you were to marry Stanhope, your mother would never bother you again."

"How do you think we would get on in our marriage then,"

Lydia asked, "if I am unable to speak? Seems like it might make day-to-day life rather awkward."

"This is promising!" Selina said brightly. "Already thinking about your married life."

Lydia spluttered. "I—what? I meant precisely the opposite!"

"Consider it," Selina said. "Just consider it. Let me put you on the list."

"I cannot be a politician's wife. How could I host a dinner party? It wouldn't work, Selina."

"It would. You'd be the duchess. You could do whatever you liked. And truly, Lyddie—I think you would be happy in a house of your own."

"I hate this," Lydia said. "I hate you."

"You do not," said Selina. "You adore me."

Lydia rolled her eyes. "What about Iris Duggleby? If we're considering awkward wallflowers for the position."

"Stop that," said Selina. "She is not. *You* are not."

"There's no sense in ignoring reality," Lydia said. "What do you think about replacing me on your list with Iris?"

Iris Duggleby. Selina twirled her quill pen between her fingers. She hadn't considered Iris, but in truth she rather liked Iris for the role. Like Lydia, Iris hadn't precisely been a hit on the Marriage Mart. She was a well-known bluestocking with an abiding passion for antiquities, and she made no apparent effort to pretend interest in the social whirl.

Iris did not suffer fools. Selina recalled the expressionless stare Iris had directed toward a baron's son that first Season when he'd asked airily if she thought he should follow the Prince of Wales's example and polish his boots with champagne.

"I cannot imagine having an opinion on this matter," Iris had replied.

Selina had nearly choked on the desire to laugh.

But Iris's disinclination toward false politeness had offended some preening blockheads, and her mother's insistence on jamming Iris's generous figure into a torture device of a corset had not helped matters either. The combination of it all had led one of the crueler lordlings to nickname her Miss Puggleby in her first Season. Even her father's viscountcy hadn't been quite enough to overcome *that* for most of the *ton*'s eligible young idiots.

But Iris had survived. In fact, Selina would not have thought she knew about the nickname, so little did she seem to attend to society's taunts. But then she'd bought herself a charming little pug and started to walk the thing up and down the Serpentine, a half smile on her face.

Beneath that distracted scholar's exterior, Iris was all steel. Selina thought Iris might make an excellent ninth Duchess of Stanhope.

"I'll add her," Selina said. "But I'm not taking you off." And in between ink splotches, she jotted down Lydia's name, and then Iris's.

"How about Lady Westcott?" asked Lydia.

"Goodness, Lydia, she's *old*."

"She can't be more than thirty."

"She's a widow!"

Lydia's flame-colored brows drew together. "So? Remarriage is perfectly legal."

"She has a *lover*," Selina hissed.

"Is that right?" Lydia sat back, impressed. "How do you know that? Even I did not know that. She must be quite discreet."

Belvoir's. Selina knew because Lady Westcott was a member of Belvoir's, and so was her lover. And Belvoir's did seem to strike its more reckless members as quite the ideal location for a tryst, as much as the staff tried to discourage it.

But Lydia didn't know about Selina's connection to Belvoir's, and so Selina said, "I do hear things occasionally, you know. From other friends."

Lydia pursed her lips and looked skeptical, but said, "Fine, strike Lady Westcott. Too scandalous, it seems. Hannah Harvey?"

"Too sweet by half. Stanhope will trample her."

"Oh for goodness' sake. Lady Victoria Eyles-Styles?"

"You must be joking," Selina said. "Stanhope isn't a horse. He'll never attract her attention."

"You are rejecting Lady Victoria because she is too fond of horses?"

"I'm rejecting Lady Victoria because unless Stanhope rolls about in hay and dresses in nothing but leather, she won't even notice him."

Lydia blinked and said nothing.

"Like a saddle," Selina said quickly. "I meant leather like a . . . like a saddle. And bridle. Like what a horse wears." It just seemed to be getting worse and worse the more she spoke. Good God, Belvoir's had completely ruined her.

"Indeed," said Lydia drily. "How about Elizabeth Yardsley? Oh, or Elizabeth Swinburn? Or even Lady Elizabeth Maye?"

"No. And no, and *definitely* no. I reject all of the Elizabeths."

"Selina, I think you have rejected every eligible woman of the *ton*."

"Not all of them," Selina protested. "I put Iris on the list."

"You know," said Lydia thoughtfully. "There is someone we haven't considered who fits all of your requirements. Clever and sensible, sterling reputation, and unparalleled English lineage."

Selina took up her pen. "I knew you would crack this for us. Who is it?"

"You."

Selina dropped the pen. "Absolutely not."

"Why not?" said Lydia. "You want me to be on the list, do you not? Obviously you can't think Stanhope such a terrible prospect as a husband."

"It's not that," said Selina. She picked up the quill again and nervously flattened the feathered end.

Lydia had no idea that in 1812, Selina had convinced her brother Will to buy Belvoir's. And that since January 1813, Selina had been almost single-handedly running the most popular circulating library in London.

Lydia didn't know. Selina's dear friend Faiza did not know, and neither did her brother Nicholas.

No one but Will knew. Because behind the pristine surface of Belvoir's Library on Regent Street, where patrons could have their books bound or order volumes for their home libraries, Belvoir's provided salacious literature to any literate woman in London.

No more, she'd thought to herself as she'd built the Venus catalog. Never again would she be the sheltered fool she'd been that first Season, flabbergasted by the discovery of mistresses and bastard children.

There was such power in knowledge. She knew that now. And she meant to make that knowledge as broadly available as she could.

Selina had two rules for Belvoir's:

1. Anyone could purchase a membership for one guinea per year.
2. Only women were permitted to check out books from the Venus catalog.

There was a third rule, but it was for Selina alone: No one could ever, ever see Selina enter or leave the bookshop, and she could never have a Belvoir's book on her person.

And somehow, quite miraculously, it had worked. Selina had been running Belvoir's without a hint of scandal for well over two years now. The young women of the *ton* were vastly more educated in matters of the sexes than Selina had been, thanks to the combination of radical philosophy, erotic memoirs, and titillating novels that made up the Venus catalog.

She was proud of what she'd accomplished with Belvoir's. Word of mouth had brought hundreds of women to the Venus catalog; Selina had seen more and more debutantes and housemaids and even venerable matrons clustered together around green-bound Belvoir's books each passing month. When Lydia's maid had reported a sudden and complete departure of female staff from the Marquess of Queensbury's household, Selina had felt a heady combination of satisfaction and relief.

But nothing could last forever. As the knowledge of the Venus catalog spread through the *beau monde*, people who opposed female education were sure to discover it. Just last week, Jean Laventille had reported to Selina that he had fielded two separate inquiries into the ownership of the Belvoir's property.

When Selina's connection to Belvoir's got out—and it would get out, Selina had no doubt of it—the scandal would be cataclysmic. If Selina were ever to select a husband, he would need to be someone who could weather the scandal with equanimity.

Peter—who required a wife entirely above reproach—was not that man.

No. She could not put him at risk with her secret. She felt too much for him: his half-concealed vulnerability, his earnest desire to take care of his siblings. She wanted to help him. And exposing him to the scandal of the decade would decidedly *not* be helpful.

"Well," she said to Lydia, trying not to seem like she was hedging, "for one thing, I plan to deliver this list to Stanhope personally. I can't exactly present myself as one of the three most eligible women in London."

"Fair point," said Lydia. "I can tell him myself."

Selina almost wanted to agree, just to see if Lydia could manage to utter such a thing in a strange man's presence, but . . .

No. She could not let Lydia entertain the possibility.

"Also, I . . . I simply do not think of him that way. As a . . . potential spouse."

"Oh, please," said Lydia. "Try it. You'll manage. He's not exactly difficult to look at."

Hang the man, he most certainly was not. His eyes had been so bright and intense on hers the day before, and then there were those irritating curls that made her want to lift her fingers to his brow and . . .

Blast, she was losing this argument with Lydia.

What could she say? Her affections lay elsewhere? Lyddie would know that wasn't true. Perhaps she could tell Lydia that she preferred the company of women to men—but somehow she felt she'd deceived her best friends enough these past years.

"I can't," she said. "Lyddie, I can't explain it. I just . . . can't marry him."

Lydia sighed. "All right, fine. I trust you to know your own mind."

Well. Selina had all the moral rectitude of a ham sandwich.

"Here it is then," she said, looking with some misery back down at the sheet of foolscap. "My grand plan to save Stanhope's siblings. You and Iris Duggleby."

"And you might as well add Georgiana Cleeve," Lydia said. "Some men like women with feathers between their ears."

Yes, Selina knew that by now too.

"To be sure," she said, and she penned Georgiana's name at the bottom of the list. Way at the bottom. Far, far down at the bottom of the page. "Three candidates. One future duchess."

"Wonderful," said Lydia blandly. "Let the games begin."

Chapter 5

. . . I know what you're going to say. I'm taking this too far.
Managing too much. Actually, I take it back. You would
never say such a thing, and I adore you all the more for it.

—*from Lady Selina Ravenscroft to her friend Lady*
Faiza Greenlaw, Countess of Clermont, currently visiting
her family in Awadh, accompanied by her husband

There was no duke this time, Peter thought as the butler escorted him into the blue-and-cream drawing room of Rowland House.

Or—no, damn it. There *was* a duke. *He* was a duke.

Surely at some point that fact would become simply part of the way he conceived of himself and not a freakish anomaly he was forced to remind himself of multiple times a day.

In any case, there was no Duke of Rowland and no Duchess of Rowland either in the drawing room. Just one Lady Selina Ravenscroft. And one Peter Kent.

It made him strangely nervous, which was also a freakish

anomaly. It wasn't as though he avoided the private company of women. In fact there had been times in his life when he'd quite sought it out, though his father's habit of dipping his wick in anything in skirts and fathering children on multiple continents had made Peter too damned cautious to ever be a buck of the first head.

Indeed, he had spent plenty of time in Selina's presence in the past. Had danced with her, had dined with the Ravenscrofts and watched her face shimmer with amusement at her twin's soft-voiced jokes. On one memorable occasion he had offered to carry her portmanteau—perhaps *offer* was not the right word; he'd practically *wrestled* with the cursed stubborn woman—and accidentally knocked them both onto their asses in a slick patch of mud.

But for some reason, sitting across from Selina while she neatly poured tea unnerved him.

It might have been the way she'd stripped off her gloves, all efficiency. No wasted movements, just quick tugs on each finger before she peeled off the fine leather gloves and stacked them in her lap.

There was nothing seductive about the way that she moved, about the quick gestures of her fingers, and yet somehow a little part of his brain was optimistically imagining that same ruthless competence directed toward the removal of other garments.

Hers. His.

And God, wouldn't it be a pleasure to slow her down. To see if he could turn those sharp amber eyes unfocused, watch her dark lashes flutter down to her cheeks.

And, right. He'd gone wildly off track here, and evidently he'd been right to be nervous, because five minutes alone in a room with Selina Ravenscroft and he'd mentally gotten them both naked and engaged in some mutual heavy petting.

"The truth is," Selina said, and he blinked at her, because even though he'd been undressing her in his head—well, to be fair, she'd been undressing *herself* in his head—he'd also been listening. And "the truth is" was apropos of exactly nothing she'd been saying a moment ago.

"The truth is," she said again, "I'd like to know if you are open to marrying."

"Er," he said.

To . . . marrying?

Did she mean marriage in general? Or marriage to *her*? Was she offering him the most frank proposal he could possibly imagine, or was his mind so enraptured by the fantasy of what her capable fingers could do that he'd totally lost the plot?

And how in the world did he delicately try to find out?

"Yes," he said decisively. "I am open to marrying."

There, that did it. He'd either accepted her proposal or agreed to some kind of scheme she had in mind, and either way, he'd have his answer in about a minute.

Her eyes lit up. "Oh good," she said in a relieved sort of way. "I'm so pleased. I think it's an excellent idea."

Amazingly, he still had no idea if she thought they were now betrothed.

"Me . . . too?" Hmm, he sounded awfully tentative. If they *were* betrothed, surely he should sound more eager. "I also think it's an excellent idea."

She was nodding away cheerfully, and a dark-blond curl slipped free from her coiffure and coiled along the pale skin of her neck. "For the children, of course," she said.

He had no idea what she was talking about, but he nodded manfully and tried not to think about what all that hair would look like loose and cascading over his chest. "Certainly the children do need . . . a mother?"

She looked rather startled at that. "Why, yes, I suppose so. But I meant for the purposes of securing their guardianship, of course."

"Oh," he said, but as he thought about it, it did make a kind of sense. "I suppose I'm rather less objectionable if I'm married."

"Yes!" she said eagerly. "That's exactly what I said to Lydia."

She'd said he was *less* objectionable? As though his current state of objectionability needed to be remedied?

Perhaps they weren't betrothed.

The bizarre twinge of disappointment in his chest did not bear thinking about.

"What's more," she was saying, "I think Lord Eldon must secretly be a romantic, what with the story of how he eloped with Lady Eldon. I think if you marry by special license in the next handful of weeks, he might find your appeal more compelling. And I'm hopeful that we might get Lady Eldon on your side as well."

All right, they *definitely* weren't betrothed. It was a scheme, then. A scheme in which he identified some unknown woman willing to become the Duchess of Stanhope and then tied himself to her for life for the purpose of getting what he wanted from the Court of Chancery.

The whole thing felt a trifle cold-blooded.

"You think I should find a woman to marry in the next six weeks so that I might be more popular with a capricious old baron who dislikes me because I have had the temerity to be born in Louisiana and to say outright that slavery is an abomination?"

"Um," said Selina, and she looked somewhat agonized. "That's . . . it . . . It sounds much worse when you put it like that."

"How would you put it?"

She lifted her chin a bit, and he liked the way she didn't back down. "I would say that you should devote a considerable part of the next six weeks to the project of matrimony. If you discover a woman with whom you think you might make a suitable match, then you should make it. And if that action leads Lord Eldon to approve your petition for guardianship of Freddie and Lu, then you've achieved your goals and gotten a wife in the bargain."

Freddie and Lu. Yes. Damn it, that's what this was about. He wanted to be better for his brother and sister. More cautious and prudent and bleeding parental.

But Selina was still talking. "And of course there's nothing wrong with being born in Louisiana, and there's nothing wrong with speaking the truth about slavery. I think you should continue to speak against slavery. You must. I believe in doing what's right even if it isn't in one's own best interests." She pressed her lips together. "And your wife should understand that."

The woman was as persuasive a talker as her brother.

"All right," he said. "I see the wisdom of this plan. And in truth I *am* open to matrimony. And I am willing to do whatever it takes to secure Freddie and Lu's future. Anything."

Her wide mouth curled up at the ends. "Perhaps it won't be as bad as all that."

The prospect of hurling himself into the sea of marriageable daughters of the *ton*, along with their ambitious mothers and condescending fathers, didn't exactly strike him as pleasant. For the last two years, he'd discovered precisely what kind of prospect he was: highly desirable as the heir to a wealthy dukedom, yet indubitably suspect because of his French mother, and an accent that marked him as not-quite-English-enough. Watching the members of the *beau monde* try to work out the contradiction had been gratifyingly amusing, so long as he maintained his detachment.

Less amusing, he supposed, if he had to take it all seriously.

He had never been one of those men who regarded marriage as the parson's noose. Marriage seemed perfectly fine as a social institution. Better than fine, if one actually liked the woman to whom one attached oneself. He'd always meant to marry eventually. The timetable was simply accelerating. At a rapid pace.

Hopefully he could find a woman he liked in the next six weeks, because Freddie and Lu needed him to do whatever the situation damn well required.

His mind helpfully suggested one woman whom he liked quite a lot, and who happened to be sitting within arm's reach. He gave his mind a very firm squelching.

"I'd like to help you," Selina said, and to his surprise, she reached out and cupped a hand over his own. Her long, tapered fingers touched the back of his hand lightly, and then withdrew.

He wanted to flex his fingers, but he made himself be still.

"I've made up a short list," she said, "of women I'd like to introduce you to. Women I think you should get to know better. Each, I think, would make a superb duchess."

Good God, "superb duchess" wasn't exactly the primary characteristic he'd imagined using to select a future wife. Not that he'd imagined many characteristics beyond *likes my jokes* and *grabbable rump*.

"Er," he said. "All right. I appreciate your assistance."

"Excellent," she said, and then she plucked a folded sheet of paper from the table beside her and handed it to him.

He unfolded it.

Matrimonial Candidates, it read. *Miss Iris Duggleby. Miss Lydia Hope-Wallace. Lady Georgiana Cleeve.*

Peter wasn't entirely certain how he had progressed from thinking they were maybe, possibly, potentially affianced to accepting a list of women she'd hand-selected for him to woo and win.

"Surely," he said, "you did not need to write down a list of three names. I am confident I can recall all three without a textual aid."

"Don't be ridiculous," she said crisply.

He couldn't stop himself from grinning at her. "I've been told from time to time that it's my defining feature."

She tucked the wayward curl behind her ear. "If you don't need the list, then you may simply"—she waved a hand—"toss it away. Do you know any of these women?"

He glanced back down at the paper in his hand.

"Ha!" she said. "You *do* need the list."

Well, point to her for that one.

"I certainly remember your friend Miss Hope-Wallace," he said.

He looked up in time to catch the expression of glee on her face, which she hastily smoothed away into something more restrained. "Do you?" she said. "That's wonderful. Lydia is incomparable. I'd be so delighted for you to marry her."

Perhaps it was all the imaginary nudity or the brief whisper of time in which he'd thought she was asking for his hand, but somehow Peter felt mildly insulted by the sheer enthusiasm of her desire to see him married to someone else.

"I shall, er, certainly consider it," he said.

He hadn't actually ever spoken to Lydia Hope-Wallace beyond a cursory good evening—in fact, he didn't think he'd heard her speak at all, ever—but he wasn't opposed to getting to know her. He figured she probably had a good reason for vomiting in a potted palm.

Though what, he wondered, would be a *bad* reason for vomiting in a plant? A pointed dislike of indoor foliage?

"Lady Georgiana you are likely to have met this Season," Selina said, returning to the list. "She's just been brought out this year. The daughter of Alistair Cleeve, Earl of Alverthorpe—and for all the man is widely disliked, his daughter is popular indeed."

The name didn't call anyone in particular to mind, though there were plenty of fresh-faced debutantes to go around. "I have to say, the idea of a bride closer in age to Lucinda than to myself is somewhat unsettling."

She gave him a forced-looking smile. "I suggest you hold off on making a judgment until you meet Lady Georgiana."

Hmm. Perhaps Selina meant to imply that Lady Georgiana was an older-than-average eligible daughter.

"Nor do I know Miss Duggleby," he said.

Selina winced. "You have probably seen her about. At balls. She's not precisely the most popular girl of our set." Her brows—dark, like her lashes, in startling contrast with her blond hair—drew together as she looked at him. "But Iris is exceptional, even if most men of the *ton* are too foolish to realize it."

Peter felt chastened for some reason. "I look forward to meeting her as well."

Selina picked up the gloves in her lap and put them decisively back on. "Marvelous."

He supposed the donning of her garments meant their tête-à-tête was finished. He wasn't sure if the meeting had gone about as well as he'd expected—Selina did, after all, have a fresh thought on how he might secure his siblings—or if it had veered quite off course.

Certainly he was feeling rather less optimistic than when she had been taking her clothes *off*.

Mother of God, he needed to get hold of himself. Removing her gloves to pour tea could not, under any reasonable definition, be termed taking her clothes off.

"Would you like to walk with me in the Park on Sunday?" Selina asked as they both rose.

"To . . . plan out my marital campaign?" he inquired cautiously.

And there went that look of delight again. "Precisely. Yes. *Campaign* is just the word for it, don't you think?"

"I do now."

"Hyde Park will be packed. It's the ideal place for some early reconnaissance."

He'd told Lu and Freddie that he'd take them for an outing on Sunday afternoon, so why not the Park? He supposed it couldn't hurt to mix business with pleasure.

Although upon further consideration, he wasn't sure either his siblings or his incipient entrance onto the Marriage Mart really deserved the label of *pleasure*.

Business with business, maybe? Family with business? Alarming familial responsibility of overwhelming magnitude with additional alarming responsibility slightly offset by the possibility of regular tupping?

"How about a picnic?" he said. "I'll have someone pack us something."

"Even better," said Selina.

She rose, and he was quite certain now that he was dismissed.

Chapter 6

. . . The truth of it is—I love the children. I don't know how else to say it. I love Stanhope's brother and sister. I want the three of them to be a family. Why does love have such a way of leading one into trouble? (And don't think I don't mean you!)

—from Selina to Faiza, again

He lured Freddie with the picnic basket and Lu with the promise of more Selina Ravenscroft.

"Are there cream cakes?" Freddie asked, trying unsuccessfully to peek into the basket.

"I have no idea," Peter said. "But there's a cake house in the Park if you're unsatisfied by my cook's offering."

"I still don't understand why I couldn't bring my rapier," Lu said sulkily.

"Because it doesn't go with your dress."

She scowled up at him. "Then I should have worn breeches."

"When we get to Rowland House, we'll ask Lady Selina how she dressed when her fencing master attended her."

Lu sat back, accepting the suggestion with unexpected equanimity.

They all jumped down when the carriage reached Rowland House—Lu disdaining the hand he offered her, of course—and crowded up under the white portico at the front of the residence.

Freddie was blinking at the honey-colored brick and gridded Palladian windows with no little amazement. "This is someone's house?" he said. "Not a church?"

Lu rolled her eyes. "It's just a house, Freddie."

"Can we go inside? I want to see what it looks like inside."

"I suspect we can," Peter told him.

Rowland's liveried butler was at the door then, and his sober expression cracked into a hint of a smile when he saw the children with Peter.

"Your Grace," he said. "And how may I introduce your companions?"

Peter gave his siblings' names as they entered the house, but before the butler could retreat to find Selina, she was coming around the corner, dressed in blue and flanked by members of her family.

"Oh," she said as she glanced down at the children, and then she looked back up at him, tawny eyes bright with amusement. "I see we've both brought company. We're going to need another carriage."

Had he not mentioned that he was bringing his siblings? Perhaps he hadn't.

Peter presented Lu and Freddie to Selina's terrifying dragon of an aunt, Lady Judith, and her longtime companion, Thomasin

Dandridge. Thomasin was a small, round woman with a cloud of sandy ringlets that bobbed about her face like cheerful springs.

"My darlings," she said, bending to take in the children more closely. "What a delightful surprise you are! I would be so pleased if you would accompany me in the carriage. Will you do me the honor?" And she held out her arms for the children to escort her like a plump little queen.

Freddie and Lu exchanged puzzled looks but agreed.

"Are you Lady Selina's mama?" asked Freddie as Thomasin allowed them to pull her out of doors.

"I'm not her mama," said Thomasin, smiling down at them. "Lady Selina's mama died when Selina was only six. But I love her just as well as any mama ever loved a daughter."

As they followed Thomasin and his siblings, Peter watched Selina's face soften with pleasure. "No child was ever more pet-ted," she said on a laugh.

"That superlative," said Lady Judith drily, "might apply to you or Will equally."

Selina's expression grew momentarily shuttered, and Peter thought about Will Ravenscroft, her twin. Peter knew they had been close, had seen them share a quip or an embrace half a dozen times his first few months in England. But then Will's wife and son had died in childbirth, and Will had bought a commission and sailed to the Continent to lose himself in war and violence.

"You must miss him," he said to Selina, and her eyes flickered up to his in surprise.

"I do," she said. Her voice was a little rough. "Every day."

"Do you hear from him often?"

One corner of her mouth lifted. "As often as the post can deliver. Sometimes we get four or five or ten letters at a time, all the regiment's mail coming to us at once. But come," she said, and she reached out to take his arm. "We should follow our families."

"I'm not sure Miss Dandridge is prepared for my sister."

"Don't let Thomasin fool you," said Selina. "She's tougher than she looks."

"Is she ready with a rapier, then? Because the promise of swordplay is really the only way I got Lu into the carriage this morning."

Lady Judith made a sound of amusement as they caught up to Thomasin and the children. "You might be surprised to know that Miss Dandridge was the one who supported Lady Selina's desire to train in fencing with her brother. For my part, I was entirely against it."

"It's true," said Selina. "Thomasin convinced Nicholas to let me learn to fence with Will. And Thomasin taught me to play all sorts of card games ladies aren't expected to know."

"I drew the line at pugilism," said Thomasin cheerfully.

"What's pugilism?" asked Freddie.

"Boxing," Selina said. "I really wanted to learn to box. Still do, in point of fact."

Lu looked as though she might collapse to the cobblestones in shock.

"I had another carriage brought 'round," said Thomasin. "Are we waiting for Lydia, or is she meeting us at the Park?"

"She'll meet us there," said Selina. "She and Nora went ahead this morning." She peered at Peter as he helped Lady Judith up into the Stanhope carriage. "I hope you don't mind. I've taken the liberty of preparing some topics of interest you might converse upon with Lydia and the others."

Apparently all the Ravenscrofts knew about his impending . . . What to call it? Duchess hunt? Courtship in triplicate?

"I look forward to hearing your suggestions."

And so, in the carriage, she plied him with recommendations. Lydia Hope-Wallace, it seemed, had a considerable interest in political machinations. "I've no idea what she's talking about half the time," Selina said. "But if you talk to her about the work that interests you in the Lords, she'll know precisely what you're referring to and will have suggestions about how you might achieve your goals."

He had to admit, Lydia Hope-Wallace did sound like a very useful duchess.

"She seems a bit diffident," he said, hoping that wasn't a wildly inappropriate thing to say.

"Oh," said Selina, and her mobile mouth turned down. "Well. Yes. Well, no, actually, not at all. Not once she gets to know you. You simply need to make her feel comfortable with you."

"Er," said Peter. "All right." He wondered if Selina had any suggestions for *that*, but none seemed forthcoming.

"Miss Duggleby," Selina said, "is also quite clever. She is fascinated by antiquities."

"By antiquities?" he repeated.

"Yes. Etruscan art. Roman coins, classical sculpture." Her gaze sharpened on him. "You don't approve of Elgin's acquisition of the Parthenon marbles, do you? If so, better keep it to yourself."

"I . . . er. No. I can't say that I do."

Good Lord, he needed a study guide for the interests of his matrimonial prospects. Why on earth had Selina not prepared a textual aid for all of this?

"And Lady Georgiana? What topics do you suggest I discuss with her ladyship?"

Selina nibbled her lower lip consideringly. Peter tried not to think about it.

"Perhaps the weather?"

The *weather*? Well, at least he wouldn't need a crib sheet for that.

"In truth," said Selina, "you might want to just talk to Lady Georgiana."

"Pardon?"

"Just . . . talk. Avoid, um, asking her things."

For some reason, this advice struck him as the most alarming of all. He chanced a glance over at the silver-haired Lady Judith, who was looking distinctly amused. Peter didn't think that boded well.

Once the carriages stopped, they reunited with Thomasin and his siblings. Freddie was tucked under Thomasin's arm, dreamy and a bit sticky-faced.

"Sweetmeats," murmured Selina. "Thomasin is always prepared with sweetmeats."

Even Lu looked rather taken with the woman. She flitted in between Selina and Thomasin, asking questions about card games and fencing.

"Have you ever seen a boxing match?" she asked Selina.

Selina looked around surreptitiously, and then leaned down to whisper something in Lu's ear. Lu's face lit up, and she dashed off to catch up to Thomasin again, who was now walking beside Lady Judith. Lady Judith's hand rested at the small of Thomasin's back.

"If I could persuade Lu to like me half as well as she likes you," Peter told Selina as they followed a handful of footmen to the banks of the Serpentine, "I'd have the children living with me by next week."

Selina's lips quirked. "Give her time. She's twelve, yes?"

Peter assented.

"It's a difficult age. I never was more angry at my brothers than I was at twelve."

"What did they do?"

She smiled at him, and she was tall enough that she barely had to tilt her head back to meet his eyes. The afternoon sun made her a study in monochrome shades of gold: gilded ivory skin, the rich honey of her hair, her amber eyes clear and luminous like . . . whiskey, perhaps? Rum. Something bright and intoxicating.

"They were men," she said. "They did whatever they pleased, while I had no control over anything in my life, I thought. Will had gone to Eton, while I was stuck at home with my governess. My fencing master wouldn't come back after Will left. I was too big for my pony, but Nicholas thought me too small for the bay gelding I really wanted." She gave a little self-conscious laugh. "Petty things, I know. But I wanted to be in charge of my own life, and instead it seemed as though I had charge of nothing at all."

"Do you still feel that way?" He liked listening to her. He liked how carefully she thought things through.

"Sometimes," she said. "But, no, not really. I've taken my life in my own hands these last years."

"Sounds dangerous," he said, and he meant it as a jest, but her eyes sharpened a bit as she looked at him.

"Perhaps," she said. "Perhaps it is."

They'd reached the picnic area that the footmen had arranged, and Freddie and Thomasin were unloading wrapped foods and corked wine bottles and lemonades. They set out crystal and silver and small porcelain plates—dukes and their relations, it seemed, did not eat cold chicken with their hands.

Actually, as he surveyed the children, it seemed perhaps that they did. Lu's busy fingers were separating chicken from bone, and Freddie held a joint of the cold meat to his mouth.

"Er," he said. "Lu. Freddie."

They glanced up at him, and he wasn't exactly sure what to say. *Best not to act like barbarians in front of these important people?* Good Christ, surely they were old enough that he didn't need to teach them table manners, weren't they? He had no blasted idea what he was doing.

Thomasin cleared her throat and gave a rather studious nod toward the silver and linens beside them. "Just in case you find that you need them, my darlings."

Freddie went red to his ears, and he grabbed up a fork so quickly that he dropped it again. It clattered off his plate of chicken and came to rest on Lady Judith's neatly spread indigo sarcenet skirt.

"Oh," he said. "So sorry. Let me just—"

He grabbed for the fork, but it had somehow become entangled in the embroidered fabric, and when he picked it up, Lady Judith's skirt lifted with it. They were all treated to a flash of white petticoat.

Freddie dropped the fork as if burned. "Oh monkey," he said miserably. "That's gone wrong."

"Thank you, Master Nash," said Lady Judith blandly. "I was hoping for an additional utensil. Allow me to secure you one of your own."

But Lu was already there, handing a fork to Freddie and glaring up at Lady Judith like an angry terrier. "Don't tease him," she said. "Leave him alone."

"Lu," Peter started to say, but now she too had flushed deeply, and she fixed her gaze furiously on her own lap. Her small bare fingers were in fists at her sides.

Selina laid a hand on his arm, and her expression was gentle when he turned his head.

Give her time, Selina had said.

But how much time did they have?

He had to get this right.

They ate their picnic, Lu and Freddie in disconsolate silence. Even Peter felt not quite up to the task of polite conversation, and when Thomasin asked the children if they fancied a walk with her to the cake house, he hated that their escape felt like relief.

"I'm sorry," he said when they were out of earshot. "About Freddie and Lu."

He hated this. He hated apologizing as though there were something wrong with them, when really there had been something wrong with their goddamned father who had abandoned them. With Peter, who didn't know how to raise them now.

But to his surprise, Lady Judith was regarding him with a hint of a smile. "I like a spirited child," she said. "I trust you won't let anyone break her."

Peter didn't trust that about himself at all. These Ravenscrofts—with their sturdy confidence, their obvious affection for one another—were outside his realm of experience. When he thought about family, he thought about fear and grief—his father who had gone and his brother who had died. He had no frame of reference for what it could be like to bring up a child like Lu and protect her from the harsh realities of their world.

But he wanted to. He wanted better for her than to wake up each morning gripped by the unpredictability of her future. He wanted to be steady and certain. And he did not know if he could do it.

•   •   •

Selina watched Peter watching his siblings as they scampered off with Thomasin. His face was almost impassive, but she could see the tension in the set of his shoulders. The faint flush at his cheekbones.

When Lu had taken Aunt Judith to task, Selina had felt a rush of tenderness so powerful that she'd wanted to cry.

It was her family that she saw when she looked at them, she realized. She saw her brother Nicholas in Peter—so determined to do what was right. She saw her twin's sweetness in Freddie, and in Lu, brimming with stubborn pride, she saw herself.

She'd felt that same protective ferocity toward her own little brother. Will, seven minutes younger, and now impossibly far out of her reach.

He'd fractured apart when Katherine and the baby had died, and Selina hadn't been able to fix it. He'd purchased a commission six months later and sailed, hard-eyed, away from her. Away from all of them. She wrote him every single day, and perhaps it was madness—perhaps he hated getting dozens of letters from her at a time—but he'd never complained.

He also hadn't come home.

And perhaps this was more madness, seeing them in Freddie and Lu, but she didn't care. They could be a family, Peter and his siblings, and she would help Peter make it so.

Chapter 7

. . . .

—from Selina's private journal, page titled

PROPOSED TOPICS OF CONVERSATION

FOR STANHOPE AND GEORGIANA

Peter understood now what Selina had meant about talking to Lady Georgiana Cleeve.

They'd made a little party as they wandered the riverbank: Lady Georgiana with her hand on Peter's arm, Selina and Lydia just behind them. Lady Georgiana's mother, the Countess of Alverthorpe, made up the rear, flanked by a truly startling number of maids and footmen. The Earl of Alverthorpe had, fortunately, not deigned to join them—in fact, he had scarcely acknowledged Peter at all, a fact that Peter found he didn't much mind.

His impression of this whole project had risen slightly when he and Selina's path had intersected with that of the Cleeves and Lydia Hope-Wallace. Lady Georgiana—though precisely as young as he'd feared—was almost unnervingly lovely, and she smiled at him brightly enough to rival the sun reflecting off the Serpentine as he'd approached. Lydia, for her part, had looked a bit green, but she too was a beauty, all red hair and neat curves beneath her trim walking dress.

Then they'd all started trying to make conversation.

"And are you enjoying your first Season out, Lady Georgiana?" Peter asked. Damn, he had already asked that. Would she notice? Maybe she wouldn't notice.

"Oh yes," she said, and she gave him that same brilliant smile. Her teeth were perfect, he noted distantly. Literally perfect. She could have been an artist's model for teeth. She could turn a tidy sum if she were to sell them.

No one else said anything. Peter tried to think of a remark less terrifying than *Have you considered selling your teeth?*

Selina piped up—with a kind of clenched-jaw cheer—from behind them. "His Grace too is fairly new to the Season, Lady Georgiana. He's only just arrived in London these last two years."

"Has he?" said Lady Georgiana, turning wide cornflower-blue eyes to Selina. "But wherever did he come from?"

Selina closed her eyes briefly. Peter thought she might be praying.

"From New Orleans," Peter said to Lady Georgiana.

She turned her head slowly to regard him. "I've never heard of that. Is it in Sussex?"

"Er," he said. "No. It's a city in Louisiana. In America."

"How fascinating," she said, blinking rapidly. Her eyelashes were long enough to create a small breeze.

"Most recently I have come from Cuba, which is an island in the Caribbean." His voice sounded tinged with desperation.

"An island." Georgiana gave a knowing nod. "England is an island too. Or, wait, is it? Or is that Great Britain? I always forget." A small line appeared between her exceptional eyebrows. "I am all thumbs when it comes to geology."

He attempted to parse the last several sentences.

"Great Britain," said Lydia hoarsely, "is the island."

Peter turned to her and attempted to smile. *Make her comfortable*, Selina had said. What would make her more comfortable? "Have you done much traveling, Miss Hope-Wallace?"

"No," she whispered, staring down at her boots.

"Have *you* traveled?" asked Lady Georgiana. Peter turned back to her and realized that she was addressing him.

"I seem to have spent most of the last decade going from one island to another," he said.

She appeared stunned by this. "There are *more* islands? How many?"

"I don't mean to imply that I have visited all the islands in the world," Peter said hastily. Was she jesting? Surely she had to be jesting.

"*All* the islands in the *world*?"

"I—" He honestly didn't know how to respond. "No. I have not been to all the islands in the world. I have been to several islands in the Caribbean. Cuba, Jamaica, Barbados. I spent some time in Haiti after the revolution to learn about self-government."

"How many islands *are* there in the world?" murmured Lady Georgiana dreamily. "There must be at least . . ." She paused, looked around, and then said triumphantly, "Seven!"

Peter looked desperately to Selina. If she was laughing, then surely he too could laugh.

She wasn't laughing. She looked as though she were experiencing physical pain.

"Haiti," she said, voice brittle. "That is the former French colony Saint-Domingue, is it not?"

"That's right. The revolution was led by former slaves, and the freed men now run the government there."

"Isn't that interesting, Lyddie?" Selina said, giving her friend a little nudge.

"Yes," muttered Lydia. "Haiti . . ." She trailed off.

Peter waited to see if Lydia was going to continue.

She didn't.

"Lady Selina tells me you are familiar with my political work on abolition," Peter said to Lydia—though to call his handful of weeks in the Lords "political work" seemed a bit of stretch. But he meant to do real work, damn him. He had stumbled into this position of immense power and privilege, and he meant to use it, if he could. He intended to learn, to try to help tear down the world of plantations and brutality he'd grown up in and build a new one.

"Yes," said Lydia, and now she looked absolutely wretched, her face growing even paler, her lips almost white.

"Are you quite all right?"

Lydia stopped walking and clamped her jaw together, and Peter had no idea if he was meant to continue to walk with Lady Georgiana or stop to keep pace with Lydia. He attempted to do both and thrust the arm with Lady Georgiana forward while twisting his body to continue to look at Lydia. His hat fell off.

Sweet Jesus, he was a disaster. This was a disaster.

"Have you lost something?" asked Lady Georgiana, peering up at him in concern and drawing to a halt. "You seem different."

"Oh dear God," mumbled Selina, and she leapt forward to grab his hat.

Lydia Hope-Wallace turned on her heel and took off away from their group at a pace that might have been termed a sprint.

Peter looked longingly after her.

He could run. He could disentangle Lady Georgiana's fingers

from his forearm and run back to Freddie and Lu. He could scoop one up under each arm and carry them to the Stanhope town-house and lock them in the nursery and never let them leave.

He could be the Kidnapper Duke. The Abducting Aristocrat.

He turned his gaze back to Selina and Georgiana. Selina stuffed his hat into his hands. Lady Georgiana blinked down at it.

"That's it!" she said in amazement.

"That's . . . what?" He was almost afraid to ask.

"A hat," she said, and there went the teeth again. White and even and surely too numerous for one aristocrat's daughter. "That's a hat."

He could not introduce this woman to his sister. Lucinda would gnaw on her bones.

Peter turned to Selina and mouthed, *Help.*

The expression of tooth-grinding misery on her face shifted suddenly as she looked at him. One corner of her mouth twitched up, and she blinked desperately, and, thank God, now she too was about to laugh.

"Lady Georgiana," she said on a smothered gasp, "are you fond of hats?"

"Oh, exceptionally." Georgiana grinned blissfully at them both. "I have fourteen hats."

Peter felt the muscles of his abdomen clench as he tried to contain himself. Oh, to hell with it. "Do you know," he said, grinning back at her, "so do I."

"Truly?" Her blue eyes widened in amazement. "For your head?"

Damn it, the girl could not be serious. This had to be some kind of elaborate ruse. "Several for my head. Others for my . . ." He trailed off.

Selina gave a sort of strangled sound.

"For my valet," he said, giving her a chastening look.

"You are dreadful," she hissed.

"I am being polite."

"I would love a valet," said Georgiana dreamily. And then, "Mother! Might I have a valet?"

Lady Alverthorpe, who had been meandering at some distance behind them, came abreast of their trio. "Georgie, darling, certainly not."

Georgiana's face fell.

"A valet would know nothing of gowns," said the countess. She was as blond as her daughter, and nearly as slim, though her blue eyes were a bit watery and her nose wriggled disconcertingly like a rabbit's when she spoke. "And hair! Heavens, a valet wouldn't know how to dress your hair."

"But surely a valet dresses His Grace's hair," protested Georgiana. She smiled winningly up at him. "Your valet curls your hair so prettily."

Selina appeared to choke.

"Georgie, sweet," said Lady Alverthorpe. "Men do not like to be reminded of their efforts at beautifying themselves. Not since the French Revolution."

Good Christ, there were two of them. "Do you have any brothers? Perhaps you might try out one of their valets."

"My brothers' hair is much less pretty than yours, Your Grace," said Georgiana. "And my father is quite bald, so his valet would be no help at all."

Peter could practically hear the response in his head—*Lady Georgiana, it would be my pleasure to offer you the services of my valet*—or perhaps *I can't countenance the idea that your hair could be any more lovely*—and yet he found he could not bring them to his lips.

He looked again at Selina. The berry-colored curve of her

mouth was set in a crooked smile, and her eyes on him were encouraging. He was meant to be courting this girl, and Selina's expression said, *Go on, then. Say something charming.*

And, damn him, it shouldn't have rankled, but it did.

"My valet, I'm afraid, would be a disappointment." He resettled his hat on his head, trying not to be too obvious about the desire to smother his own coiffure. "I hate to admit it in polite company, but I've yet to let Humphrey take hot tongs to my head. My hair grows this way." He'd never even had a valet until he'd inherited. It was bad enough to let the man dress him, as if he were a child.

Selina's brows drew together in an expression of unguarded skepticism. "You cannot mean it."

He felt himself smiling helplessly at her. "God's truth."

"Insulting," she mumbled. "Truly insulting."

"It runs in the family. You've seen Lu's hair. You can't imagine she lets Aunt Rosamund at her with curling implements."

Selina tilted her head in acknowledgment. "I suspect Aunt Rosamund doesn't wish to find herself at the wrong end of extremely hot metal."

"You haven't met Aunt Rosamund. *I* suspect she wouldn't know curling tongs from a salad fork."

Selina pursed her lips. "To be fair, she could probably use curling tongs on a salad."

"Point to you," he said, and her eyes sparkled at him so brightly in the afternoon light that he almost lost his breath.

Lady Alverthorpe cleared her throat, and Peter started. He knew enough about English society to know that he was being outrageously rude to talk in company about people they didn't know. He tried for a moment to explain his siblings and Greatgreat-aunt Rosamund.

Georgiana blinked up at him. "They all sound very nice."

Well, *nice* wasn't really the word for Aunt Rosamund—or Lu, for that matter—but he appreciated her effort. "They're very important to me."

Her perfect teeth peeked out as she bit her lower lip. "Who did you say they are again?"

Selina groaned quietly from beside him, and he didn't have to turn toward her to know she was clenching her jaw again.

"Georgie, my girl, you must listen better," chided her mother. "Surely you heard His Grace say that they were his valets?"

It was only because Peter was still marveling at Lady Georgiana's teeth that he saw it. Her gold lashes fluttered down to her cheeks, and her nose twitched, and the corner of her mouth . . . shivered. Once, and then again.

And if he didn't know any better, Peter would have sworn that Lady Georgiana was a very, very talented actress who was trying very, very hard not to laugh.

Her eyes blinked open again, and the impression was gone. She was all curls and limpid blue eyes, and her voice was spun-sugar sweet when she said, "Valets! Of course. The ones who curl His Grace's hair." She nodded smartly. "I can see it must require several men."

He narrowed his eyes at her, and her eyelashes started working again like feathered fans. "Your Grace," she said, "I'm afraid we must take your leave. The afternoon grows a bit warm for my mother."

The countess was already nodding and scooping up her daughter's arm.

"Oh," said Selina. "So soon? Perhaps we shall see you at the Strattons' ball this week?"

Lady Alverthorpe kept right on nodding. "To be sure, my dear. To be sure."

"Might I call on you?" Peter heard himself ask. "Lady Georgiana?"

Three faces turned toward him, with varying expressions of surprise. Selina looked rather startled, but not at all displeased. Of course she did. Peter ignored the little flush of irritation, because, damn it, this was what they'd agreed on. This was the damned plan.

"To be sure, Your Grace," Lady Georgiana said politely. "That would be an honor. Perhaps you might bring your valets."

"I will try to do so. Armed with salad tongs." He stared at her, practically daring her to laugh.

She didn't. "I love salad," she said breathily. "It is my first passion."

And then they made their farewells.

He escorted Selina back along the Serpentine toward their families.

"That went . . . well," he offered. Well enough, except for the part where he hoped that Lady Georgiana's entire personality was an intricate facade and then the other part where Lydia Hope-Wallace had sprinted away like Pheidippides at Marathon.

"Do you fancy her?" Selina asked. "Lady Georgiana? Is that the sort of woman you favor?"

He echoed Georgiana's words from earlier. "She seems nice."

In truth, he wasn't sure he'd ever had a type of woman that he favored. Women came in all sorts of shapes and sizes, and he liked soft bits he could hold on to as much as he liked long elegant lines. Blondes or brunettes. French accents or English ones.

He supposed he liked clever women. With ruthlessly efficient fingers. Eyes that danced and flashed by turns, eyes that soothed him and challenged him at once.

None of which described Lady Georgiana Cleeve, but *did* very accurately describe—

Damn it.

Chapter 8

. . . Stanhope, find below the details for the paper at Cambridge on ceramics of the Etruscan period. For the love of God, I do not want to know why.

—*from Mr. Mohan Tagore, barrister, to His Grace Peter Kent, the Duke of Stanhope*

"You needn't talk." Selina resettled a pin into Lydia's hair in the Strattons' retiring room. "There's no need. Remember that *he* must charm *you*."

Lydia groaned and put her face into her hands.

"You must simply endeavor not to run away." Selina tugged a lock of red hair loose and swirled it at the base of Lydia's neck.

"Oh, certainly. I shan't move a muscle, and then I'll vomit on Stanhope's boot."

Selina winced.

"In any case," Lydia continued, "do you think this even necessary? Did you not tell me he meant to call on Georgiana?"

Selina chewed on her lower lip. "He did say so."

Lydia arched a brow. "I told you. Men like that sort of thing."

"Lyddie, it just got worse after you left. I cannot countenance it."

"Go have a look at Georgiana in the ballroom, and see if you can countenance it."

She'd seen Georgiana, surrounded as always by suitors, swathed in virginal white and blinking around like she couldn't imagine what all the fuss was about. Selina understood the appeal—Belvoir's and four years on the Marriage Mart had taught her enough to know that men preferred Marianne Dashwood to Elizabeth Bennet, as unaccountable as it seemed.

But she'd seen Peter struggling against laughter at Georgiana's non sequiturs. Curse him, the man had had the temerity to turn those liquid chocolate eyes on her and plead for help. Half-amused, he'd looked, and half-agonized. And she'd thought, *Yes, I will help you. Anything.*

For the children, of course. Because she cared about the children. Because she wanted them to be a family.

Only when Peter had looked at her as though she were his partner in some great adventure, she'd felt something bright blossom in her chest. She'd felt like his friend. She'd felt like she mattered. For once in her life she didn't feel like too much—she felt exactly *right*, there in the warm embrace of his eyes.

And then, for some reason, he'd changed his mind. He'd smiled at Georgiana. He'd offered to call on her. And he didn't need Selina after all.

Selina smoothed the seam of her gloves between her fingers and tried to shake off the maudlin thoughts.

"Come along," she said, and she linked her arm through Lydia's. "If he's going to marry someone, he couldn't possibly find a better partner than you."

In the ballroom, they found Georgiana and Peter just finishing a set. Selina could hear Peter rattling on—something about his sister, Selina thought, and her fencing—while Georgiana looked at him with an expression of puzzlement.

She led Lydia over to intercept them as they left the dance floor. "Good evening, Your Grace. Lady Georgiana."

Peter stopped talking. His eyes caught on hers and held there. Her fingers itched to sweep the dark curls off his forehead, and she wondered if he'd been lying when he said his valet didn't form those bloody ringlets with hot tongs.

He must have been lying. Her own hair took Emmie an hour to arrange.

He seemed to come to himself with a start, and he bent to kiss her hand and then Lydia's. Lydia was rather pale but not yet that familiarly ominous pale green. Selina squeezed her upper arm encouragingly.

"Your Grace," Lydia muttered. "Have you heard that Brougham is running this year in Winchelsea?"

Selina hadn't the faintest idea who Brougham was, or why his campaign would be relevant to Peter, but Peter's eyes sparked with interest.

"I had, yes. I've been meaning to meet with him—I have a great deal to learn about abolition work in this country."

"You should," said Lydia. She was staring grimly down at her slippers, but she was still talking. Selina wanted to clap her on the back in delight but restrained herself. "He was instrumental in passing the Slave Trade Felony Act. If you want to work on legislation, he can help you do it."

Peter grinned at Lydia, and Selina felt a hot sensation in her chest and her fingers.

"You should dance," she said abruptly. "The next set."

Peter's gaze shot to hers. "Lady Selina. It would be my pleasure to escort you onto the dance floor."

"Oh," she said, and now the burning feeling rushed up to her cheeks. "No. I—I meant with Lydia." Devil take it, had she implied that she wanted to dance with him? Surely she had not. "You must ask Lydia."

He took her stuttered protest with equanimity. "To be sure. Miss Hope-Wallace, would you care to join me for the next set?"

Lydia managed to nod, and when the music shifted into a quadrille, Peter and Lydia made their way into the crush of men and women in the center of the ballroom.

Lady Georgiana was scooped up promptly by a small knot of suitors. Tresidder—poor foolish man—seemed to come out the winner, and he led Georgiana into the fray. Samuel Bowbridge, among the rejected, nervously angled his gaze toward Selina. She gave him a withering look.

"Beg pardon," he mumbled. "Good evening, Lady Selina."

And then she was mercifully alone to watch Peter dance with Lydia and to think.

They would have made a brilliant couple if Lydia didn't look miserable. She was an excellent dancer—not that she had the chance to demonstrate it often—but her face was set, and she kept refusing to look Peter in the eye. He was talking easily to her, though, and he didn't seem offended by her silence.

He was good at this—dancing, talking. Selina had not thought he would be quite so good at it.

She had, of course, some sense of his appeal. She had sat across from him at Rowland House more than once and had forced herself not to look too hard as he smiled and spoke easily of New Orleans. Once, when she and Faiza had encountered Peter and Clermont at the opera, she'd had to bite her cheek to keep from laughing aloud as Peter caught her elbow and drew her behind a screen while Faiza and Clermont argued.

"If I throw my glove at Clermont," he'd whispered, grinning down at her, "will it distract them, do you think? Because right now they're drowning out the soprano."

She'd noticed the way he had of focusing on her, his eyes bright, his expression suddenly serious—as though he was listening intently to what she had to say. As though it mattered.

She'd simply never seen him deploy the expression on someone else.

It didn't rankle. It didn't. She was *glad* he was so bloody charming.

Funny how *glad* felt like a sting in her chest.

She set her jaw and turned to look for Iris Duggleby. She still meant to present Peter with options for his future wife, after all. Even if he didn't seem to need her help nearly as much as she'd thought.

She found Iris in a chair on the side of the ballroom, an abandoned champagne glass at her side and her dark head bent over a book. Iris's mother, Lady Duggleby, was Italian, and Iris had inherited her thick, glossy black hair. Selina felt quite confident that the twists and ringlets into which Iris's hair had been tortured—along with the flounced pink satin gown Iris wore—were also the products of Lady Duggleby's influence.

She took the chair beside her friend. "Iris. I've missed you."

"Hmm?" Iris appeared engrossed in her reading, and Selina felt her lips tug into a smile. After an extended pause, Iris looked up, and her expression came into focus. "Oh, Selina! Have you read this?"

Selina looked down at the book in Iris's lap and promptly froze, mouth half open.

It was a Belvoir's book.

She had expected a treatise on archaeological practices or perhaps something in a language she did not recognize. She had absolutely *not* expected—

"Is that," she choked out, "a, er—"

Iris nodded cheerfully at the book. "A phallus. With a bow on it. Yes."

Selina looked around the ballroom, then tried to pretend she had not done so. *Do not look guilty*, she told herself. *Don't you dare.*

She reached over and flipped the book in Iris's lap closed. "Fascinating," she said on a wheeze.

"Isn't it? My lady's maid left this in my bedroom. I thought it was some kind of hint, but perhaps she just forgot it. I really did not know what a French letter was until this evening. Nor that one must tie it on with a ribbon like that."

"Indeed," Selina managed.

She recalled that book quite clearly. It was a guide to various forms of contraception, and she had been so pleased with it that she'd made Jean Laventille send it into a second printing. That was precisely the kind of text she wanted for the Venus catalog—a clear, lucid, scientific discussion of how to prevent pregnancy, with diagrams and even suggestions for where to purchase the various products therein.

She had not supposed she would encounter it in a ballroom, in the lap of Iris Duggleby.

But then again, this was exactly what she wanted Belvoir's to be: an attainable resource for women who would not otherwise have access to knowledge that could change their lives for the better.

The flush on her cheeks was not all guilt, she supposed. Some of it was pride.

Iris was drumming her fingers on the cover of the book and looking abstracted. "Do you know," she said, "this makes me wonder if we've misinterpreted some of the findings from Clarke's excavation last year. Something in these illustrations struck me as familiar . . ." She made to reopen the book, and Selina clapped her hand atop Iris's in alarm.

"Perhaps," she said weakly, "you might examine the illustrations at home?"

Iris looked down at their hands on the book. "Ah. Perhaps you are right."

Cautiously, Selina withdrew her fingers. When Iris did not immediately move to turn the cover, Selina gave an inward sigh of relief. "Listen, Iris," she said, "I wanted to speak to you about something. About *someone*, I should say. Have you met the Duke of Stanhope?"

Iris tapped the green-bound book meditatively before responding. "The American duke? Of course I have. My mother seems to think he might be persuaded to accept me, given that he missed the Puggleby debacle of 1812."

"Oh," Selina said. That was good, she supposed, that Iris had already considered marriage to Peter.

Really, it seemed as though *everyone* would consider marriage to Peter. Which was what she wanted. Of course.

"Why?" Iris asked. "Has he an interest in Clarke's excavation?"

"Um," said Selina. She rather hoped he did. She had told him to prepare for this, had she not? "I cannot say. But I do know that he is looking to marry. Soon. I'd like to bring him over to speak to you, if you're amenable."

Iris nearly upset the book. "Good Lord, Selina. My mother has delusions of grandeur; I've always known that. But *you*?"

"Stop that." Selina ground her teeth. Why were her friends so bloody resistant to the idea that they were desirable candidates for marriage?

But of course, she knew why. Because society had told them they were undesirable for years now. And as much as Selina wanted to transform their narrow-minded world, she had not figured out yet how to change *that*.

"Let me bring him over," she said. "You'll like him, Iris. He's a good man."

"Hmm." Iris gave Selina a considering glance. "That's a better recommendation than I've heard you give most men of the *ton*."

"Most of the men of the *ton* are fools."

Iris's mouth tipped up in a crooked smile. "Don't I know it."

•   •   •

Exhaustion had sweat pricking his brow as Peter whirled Lydia Hope-Wallace to a stop at the close of their set and watched her make her way toward her mother.

Thirty minutes. Had he really just spoken nonstop for thirty minutes? It was like a parliamentary speech, only he hadn't prepared remarks.

Well, that wasn't quite fair. At some point, he'd resorted to quoting his own maiden speech on abolition. And then a second speech he'd been writing these past weeks. Also William Wilberforce, William Pitt, and possibly several other Williams.

Lydia had slowly relaxed, though, as he'd babbled, and she'd even darted her blue eyes up to meet his once or twice. But then they were forced to change partners, and when she'd returned, the whole process had begun again. Terrified Lydia. Nonsensical Peter. Extended rambling followed by gradual thawing of Lydia's fright.

Perhaps they might suit. Perhaps if he had weeks alone with Lydia at the Stanhope residence, she would find her voice, find herself willing to share what was happening behind the pale facade of her face.

It was clearly a measure of his personal distraction that when he thought about weeks alone with his hypothetical new bride, he imagined spending their days talking politics. There was no good reason that Lydia Hope-Wallace, with her ginger hair and generous figure, shouldn't inspire him to all sorts of erotic daydreams.

No good reason. One very bad reason.

The very bad reason herself was making her way toward him through the crush, and he felt himself smiling at her. She walked with long, impatient strides, her legs eating up the distance in a way that seemed to declare the ballroom and all its inhabitants in the way of her plans.

He wondered what it would be like to have all that singular focus to himself. On himself. Just for a day. A night. One long cold English night, with nothing but starlight and Selina's bare skin to keep him warm.

Good Christ. He blinked at her as she approached, trying to remember the expression on her face when he'd mistakenly thought she wanted to dance with him.

She hadn't. The very idea filled her with horror. She was trying her damnedest to marry him to someone else.

"Your Grace," she said, her greeting barely acknowledging his bow at her approach. "I'd like for you to meet another one of my dearest friends. Do you remember when we spoke of Miss Duggleby?"

Of course he damned well did.

"I'd be delighted. I've studied up on Etruscan art."

Selina gave him a narrow-eyed glare, evidently trying to determine whether or not he meant it. He smiled innocently at her, and she pursed her lips in a way that had blood rushing away from his brain and decidedly southward. A pout. Who knew Selina Ravenscroft could pout?

"Come along, then." She linked her arm through his and gave him a solid tug. Her hair was undecorated this evening, pulled back into some kind of twist that had waves of gold spilling down her back. He was close enough to smell her, and he couldn't put his finger on her scent. Something spiced. Cloves, perhaps, or rum.

He followed her lead, and she took him to one of the corners of the ballroom, where a dark-haired woman of about Selina's own age sat alone, her head bent over a green-bound volume in her lap.

As they approached, Selina cleared her throat.

The woman did not move. She did not even seem to hear them.

Selina coughed again, rather more loudly. Peter bit hard on the inside of his cheek.

Selina muttered something incomprehensible under her breath, reached down, and plucked the book out of Iris's hands. She snapped it closed and stuffed it into her own reticule before Peter could see what it was that Iris had been reading.

"Miss Iris Duggleby," Selina said loudly, "may I present His Grace, the Duke of Stanhope?"

Iris blinked up at them, her eyes a dreamy gray-green. "Oh. Already? That was quick."

Selina made a slightly strangled sound, and despite Miss Duggleby's less-than-enthusiastic reception of his arrival, he found that he wanted to laugh. He turned to look at Selina, who was staring daggers at Iris. Evidently he wasn't the only one who could earn that whiskey-colored glare.

He wanted it back. That fierceness. He wanted *her*, curse him for a fool. He wanted her so much he could barely stand the heat from her body at his side, the way her fingers held his arm through his jacket sleeve. He wanted to drag her fingers up to the back of his neck and pull her long body against his and watch the shape her lips would make just before he took her mouth.

He clenched his teeth against the hard pulse of arousal and forced himself to turn back to Iris Duggleby, who didn't appear to want him either, but who at least didn't send him out of his head with addled lust.

"Miss Duggleby," he said, "it's a pleasure to make your acquaintance. Would you like to dance?"

Iris directed a single longing glance at Selina's reticule. Selina tucked it under her arm and glowered so powerfully that even Iris seemed to feel the heat of it.

"To be sure," Iris said, and took his hand.

She wasn't nearly as accomplished a dancer as Lydia Hope-Wallace, but when she made to turn the wrong direction, she didn't appear overly perturbed. He thought she was still staring off in the direction of her book.

He *had*, in point of fact, attended a lecture about Etruscan ceramics. He'd even attempted to listen, though his knowledge of antiquities could fit in a teacup with room to spare for an entire serving of oolong. Never let it be said that Peter Kent wasn't willing to do whatever it took for his damned ungrateful siblings.

But the introduction of the topic was enough for Iris's attention to finally land upon him. She had, as it turned out, also attended the lecture. She worked out his total lack of familiarity with the topic in the time it took them to exchange partners and then return to one another—that was to say, about four minutes—but he managed to ask her a reasonable question or two. She *was* clever, as Selina had said. He could discern her expertise in the subject matter, and he liked the way she spoke about the lecture—judicious and fair, even as she dismissed several of the lecturer's conclusions with a toss of her dark head.

He was in the middle of composing a third question on the subject when she interrupted him.

"Why are you doing this?"

"Beg pardon?" He wanted to pretend he didn't understand what she meant, but he had a sinking feeling that he did.

"Dancing with me. Talking about my interests as though they could possibly matter to you. Do you need money? Because I assure you, while I may be the daughter of a viscount, my dowry is passable at best." She didn't sound angry, precisely, but rather coolly factual. Maybe a little resigned, those eyes calm on his own.

Christ. What could he say? It crossed his mind for a heartbeat to try to charm. Something about her cleverness, and the way her eyes caught his gaze—it wouldn't be a lie, not really—and yet he found he couldn't do it.

So instead, he told her about Freddie and Lu. About Lord Eldon and the Court of Chancery and Selina's scheme to make him less objectionable.

When he finished, Iris gave him a considering look. "I see. And you've selected me because you think I am desperate enough to accept you anyway?"

Peter choked. "No," he protested. "Of course not. You—are—"

Iris tipped back her head, and to his extreme relief, laughed.

"Don't look so alarmed," she said, her lips still curled as she looked at him. "I won't balk at being thought desperate so long as you promise not to object to the same."

He thought about Freddie and Lu. About Morgan and their goddamned father. "Not at all."

She nodded. "I don't particularly want to marry you, Your Grace. But I can't say I don't respect your motives. And the way you told me the truth. I have a strong aversion to men who tell me lies."

"A reasonable objection."

The orchestra was winding down, he could hear, and dancers were starting to fall away to the sides of the room.

"I have no illusions about my ability to attract a husband on my own merits," said Iris. Peter started to object, but she cut him off with a lifted hand. "As a scholar of antiquities, my confidence in my own abilities is unparalleled. As a debutante—" She gave a little half shrug, and her voice stayed so stubbornly bright he wondered if she'd practiced it. "I have other talents."

"Of that, Miss Duggleby, I have no doubt."

"I have no special desire to marry at all. But if I were to marry, I would like it to be to someone who sees me as more than simply a means to an end."

They'd stopped dancing, and Peter released his grip on her small fingers. "Thank you for the dance, in any case."

She stopped him with a measured look. "However. You are more than welcome to continue to pay me your attentions. If anything, it can't hurt my reputation. And if, in the next week or two, you can persuade me that I am *more* than an avenue to achieving your desires, then I will consider your proposal."

Peter wasn't sure if he was impressed or terrified. "I'll call on you, then."

Iris gave him a little nod. "You may."

He bid her farewell. And then he looked around, trying to catch a hint of dark-blond hair. Because after that conversation, what he really wanted to do was recount the whole thing to Selina. He wanted to know what she would say.

Chapter 9

. . . Of course, Lady Jersey, my brother the duke and his wife are eager to continue their patronage of Almack's. But you must know that my brother takes a personal interest in His Grace, the Duke of Stanhope. I forbear to suggest that my brother will not attend if Stanhope's voucher is withdrawn—and yet . . .

—from Lady Selina Ravenscroft to Lady Jersey,
patroness of Almack's

"Don't tell me there's another one."

Aunt Judith raised one silver brow and then deposited the newspaper onto the breakfast table. It slumped in front of Selina's plate of buttered brioche.

Selina dropped her forehead to the table with a groan. "I simply cannot look at it."

Daphne reached out from several seats away to pluck at the paper. "I can."

"I'll admit to some interest myself," Nicholas said. "What's Stanhope done this time?"

Selina raised her head from the table to peer at Daphne while she perused the paper.

"It's quite a good likeness," Aunt Judith said drily. "No doubt whom the engraving is meant to represent."

"Hmm," said Daphne. "Well, it's not as bad as the time he climbed the exterior wall at the Cleeves' townhouse—"

"Please do not remind me," Selina moaned.

"And certainly less exciting than when he rescued Lydia from a runaway horse—"

"Oh for heaven's sake, you know as well as I do that Lydia was *riding away*—"

"But it's pretty bad."

Selina pinched the bridge of her nose. "Just get it over with."

"It seems he took Iris Duggleby to an art exhibition yesterday— all appropriately chaperoned, no need to worry, Selina—and he started a fistfight."

Selina dropped her head back into her arms. "I don't understand."

Daphne's voice was muffled when it reached Selina's ears. "Honestly, I don't think this gossip columnist was even there. Really, *why* Lord Ambrose would take issue with Stanhope's aspersions on the portraitist is not entirely clear to me."

"I believe"—that was her brother's cautious interjection— "that Lord Ambrose and the portraitist are quite close."

"Is that right?" This was Aunt Judith, who never turned up her nose at *ton* gossip.

"Well, one can hardly blame Stanhope for not being aware of that," said Daphne.

"I can blame him." Selina lifted her head and glanced around the table at her arrayed family members. "I can absolutely blame him."

It had been two weeks since the Strattons' ball, and Stanhope had applied himself to the project of courting Georgiana Cleeve, Lydia Hope-Wallace, and Iris Duggleby with purpose. With *disastrous* purpose.

He'd taken Georgiana Cleeve for a ride in his curricle, which—according to Lydia's extremely capable maid, Nora, who had a cousin in the Cleeve household—had gone reasonably well. Then, when he'd returned Georgiana to the Cleeve residence, she had left her hat in the conveyance.

It had, Selina supposed, probably been some kind of flirtatious offering on Georgiana's part. An invitation to Stanhope to come back to call on her another time. But Stanhope had taken the accessory as some kind of a challenge, and had decided to return the thing to Georgiana directly.

By climbing the clematis on the side of the house while carrying the hat between his teeth, according to the print that was now being sold at several Bond Street news stalls.

The scandal was just beginning to break when he'd dropped by Rowland House to describe his progress to Selina. He'd seemed flabbergasted that she knew about the hat. And the climbing.

"I didn't want her reputation to be damaged if her damned *clothing* were to be seen in my curricle," he'd protested. "I know what it's like to be the subject of all that icy English disdain. I thought I could get it back to her before anyone saw me. I went up through the blasted back garden!"

"Peter," she'd found herself saying, the shock of his Christian name on her lips like a little warm spark, "you cannot have thought that no one would notice your climbing their house like Romeo at the Capulets' garden wall."

"Wasn't that a balcony?"

"You—what?"

An errant curl fell over one dark eyebrow. "Doesn't Romeo climb a balcony?"

"I— That's not at all the point, but no, it is a garden wall."

"I really think it is a balcony."

She wanted to smack him, but she restrained herself for fear she'd end up brushing his stupid hair back into place. "Peter! You probably have a First Folio in the Stanhope residence. Check when you get home. Don't climb anything else."

He hadn't. He'd been all decorum for at least a day. He'd gone to Almack's—Selina had had to apply to Lady Jersey directly to ensure that his voucher to the exclusive social club wasn't revoked after the climbing incident—and danced quite nicely with everyone.

He'd walked with Iris in the park. He'd called on Lydia at the Hope-Wallaces' house, and Selina had dashed down the street to confer with Lydia as soon as she'd seen the Stanhope carriage trundle away.

It had, according to Lydia, been fine.

"Fine?" Selina had demanded. "That's all you have to say?"

Lydia had shrugged. "It was fine. He talked. I listened. Everyone left satisfied."

Everyone, that was, except Selina, who found herself decidedly unsatisfied by the whole affair. Of all the ways she'd ever thought to describe Peter Kent, the ninth Duke of Stanhope, *fine* certainly would not have made the list.

In fact, the list of words she might use to describe Peter Kent had taken something of a turn.

It had started with the dream. She had been reviewing several texts for inclusion in the Venus catalog and had fallen asleep after reading one particularly salacious memoir.

That was all. She had simply been reading. And reading had translated to dreaming. It had nothing to do with the man himself.

But whenever she thought about Peter Kent—and she seemed to be thinking of him quite a lot—she could not help but recall it.

It had been hot in the dream, so *hot*. That was what came back to her the most strongly. He'd been smiling, that sharp pleased grin, as he'd slipped her frock from her shoulders. Sweat had beaded between her breasts, and he'd pressed his mouth to her skin and licked her there.

His hand had burned as he'd slid the fabric down her torso. She could not have said where they were. Somewhere dark and fragrant, the air heavy. His mouth on her skin made her feel boneless, her body drifting, need rising in a long, slow crest.

Her dress was gone. She could see the long, muscled expanse of his body. His mouth was between her legs, her fingers tangled in his hair. She had no thoughts but desire, her body a conflagration that began and ended with Peter's touch.

When she'd woken, she'd been damp with perspiration, her body sensitive and achy, and now every time she tried to organize Peter's courtship, her mind tumbled her back into that strange, hot dark.

Infuriating, she might have described him. *Impossible.*
Not for her.

Not for her to dream about. Not for her to think on as she flipped the pages of a Belvoir's book, and most especially not when desire tangled in her belly, and images—of his dark curls between her thighs, of his mouth, of the bare skin of his throat—rose in her mind.

She swallowed and tried to turn her mind back to his marital endeavors. That was what she needed to think on. His marriage. To someone else.

He hadn't even made half a week of sedate courting. There had been the incident with Lydia's horse in Rotten Row, and then another memorable outing with his brother and sister that had involved Lucinda, ices, and a large wolfhound she'd enticed into Gunter's Tea Shop. Selina and Lydia had been able to hear the shrieking from down the block at the millinery.

Stanhope was, in truth, a walking scandal. He'd made no inroads thus far in appearing to be swept away by romance and—if her conversations with Lydia were any indication—rather little progress in securing a wife besides.

"He needs help," Selina said now, drumming her bare fingers on the table beside her plate.

"Mm." Her brother somehow made this wordless grunt sound deadpan. "And you know just what kind of help to offer him?"

Selina pushed back from the table. "First, I need to find him."

"And second you need to tell him where he's gone wrong?"

She had a lifetime of ignoring the teasing of brothers, so rather than respond, she tugged her gloves on wordlessly.

"I rather think," said Aunt Judith, a half smile on her lips, "that Selina is prepared to tell him how to get it right."

•   •   •

Peter still didn't know if Georgiana Cleeve was faking it.

It had happened once more, when he'd said that eggs were the roundest animal. The downcast eyes, the shiver at the corner of her mouth as though she was ruthlessly biting her cheek. He'd been nearly certain she was trying not to laugh.

But only once! In two weeks of his attempts to out-ludicrous her. When he told her that he'd hired a valet for each of the fine grays that pulled his curricle, she'd merely blinked rapidly at him and said, "I'd have thought the cattle needed two each, at least."

Several times now he'd considered demanding whether or not she meant one-quarter of the things she said—and if not, why in the world she said them. But there was something peculiar and fragile in that bizarre brand of defiance, something that reminded him strangely of Lu. So he took her for walks, and said whatever absurd thought came into his head, and decided that there was no way he could marry this woman, but he'd do what he could to see that she didn't get hurt.

"I say," Georgiana said, pulling to a stop from where they were walking on the banks of the Serpentine. "Is that a dog?" She lifted a hand to shade her eyes, though Peter couldn't possibly imagine why, given that she was also wearing a substantial bonnet.

He peered out in the direction of her gaze. "In the water? Maybe a duck."

"I rather think it's a dog. On sort of a log?"

He couldn't help but laugh, but when he glanced down at her, Georgiana's blue eyes were a little impatient.

"Look there," she said. "Isn't that a dog?" She pointed a long, doeskin-clad finger out at the Serpentine.

He looked, and looked again, and by God, Georgiana Cleeve had incredibly sharp eyes to go with her perfect teeth. He could just pick out the little white clump of fur she was pointing to, a wet, miserable-looking thing afloat on a tangle of branches. It didn't seem to be in imminent peril. It did, however, look decidedly pathetic.

"Whatever it is, it's certainly not a duck."

"I really think it's a dog," she said, her tone edging toward insistent. "I think it's stuck."

"All right," he said. "Can you hold my hat?"

She looked up at him, her blue eyes so startled that he was almost certain it wasn't feigned. "I . . . yes?"

He gave her his hat and started to tug at his boots. Cursed English fashions—he wasn't sure he could get the damned things off unless he sat down. He needed an armchair. Perhaps a valet, lowering as that was.

He looked again at the little dog, or kitten, or possibly loosed piece of knitting. Hopped on one foot as he yanked at his heel and wished pathetically for a flat rock.

And then a familiar cool female voice met his ears, and he stopped hopping.

"Do not tell me you are going for a swim in the Serpentine in front of half the *ton*?"

Peter realized he was still standing on one foot like an overdressed flamingo, and so he put his foot down. Tried to squelch his sheer delight at the sound of her voice as he turned.

Selina stood on the bank behind them. Her face was a little flushed, her breath coming quickly. He meant not to look at the way her breasts rose and fell, pressed taut against the lace-edged neckline of her thin blue walking dress. Meant not to, and then did anyway.

He blinked at her. "Did you run here?"

She scowled at him, and he liked it far more than he had any rational reason to. "That is entirely beside the point."

"Surely," he protested, "if you can sprint through Hyde Park, then I can take a casual afternoon swim."

She stalked closer. He took a step back.

"I," she hissed in an undervoice, "*I* am not the one who cannot keep himself out of the scandal sheets for two days running. *I* am not the one who is attempting to improve his reputation in English society."

She was so damned lovely with those hectic spots of color on her cheeks, her eyes as ferocious as her tone, and for once in his life Peter managed to control his unruly mouth and not tell her so.

"There's a dog," he said instead, "in the Serpentine. There's a little dog on a branch, and I'm just going to retrieve it. No one will see."

Selina threw out a hand at their surroundings. "Peter! I understand your concern. I'm sure it will float free, or someone else will secure it. But it cannot be *you*! Everyone in the Park will see. There are a hundred people within eyeshot right now, and another thousand who will hear about it in the papers tomorrow."

"Surely the circulation is higher than—"

"Peter!"

He liked the way she could shout in a whisper. He liked his name on her lips, and he liked her lips, and he needed to throw himself into the river before his physical reaction to her proximity became any more obvious.

"I'll be quick," he said, backing another step away. "No one will notice. Maybe you can make a distraction across the Park. Sing a ballad. Do you know 'Rosemary Lane'?"

She launched herself at him and caught his arm, the warmth of her fingers palpable through her gloves and his coat sleeve. "Peter, for heaven's sake. You are not taking this seriously! Do you not *want* the guardianship? Is that what this is about? You want Lord Eldon to dismiss your suit?"

He tugged his arm back, and she came with it, pulling their bodies within inches.

He couldn't have made himself step away from her for all the world. Instead, he reached up and closed his hand around her shoulder. Her lips parted, and she took a quick, gasping breath. Her gaze fell to his mouth. His groin tightened in response, and so did his fingers on her arm.

"I'm taking this seriously," he said. "You have no idea how seriously I am taking this or what I would do for my brother and sister."

She licked her lips. He felt the inches between them like a physical thing.

"Then why"—her voice was soft and he fought the desire to lean into her words, into *her*—"then why do you do this? Do you not think before you act—about what others will do? What they will say?"

Reckless. He could hear his father's voice in his mind as clearly as if the man were not six years dead. *Selfish. Thoughtless.*

Damn his father, and damn *him*, for hearing the words so many times and never backing down. It had become almost a badge of honor—to be precisely what his father accused him of being.

He was reckless. He took the things he wanted, and he wanted his brother and sister. He would take Freddie and Lu because he damned well *knew* he could protect them better than a stranger the courts had given them to. And if when he thought about them, he also thought about Morgan, and Louisiana, and the way Morgan had looked before he got sick, swimming like a silver-limned dolphin in the bayou—well. Peter already knew he was a selfish bastard. He'd known that for a long time.

A thousand words boiled in him as he stared at Selina. He

did want the children. He *did* mean to get the lord chancellor on his side.

He wanted too much.

"There's a dog," he said finally. "I'm not going to leave the dog in the water."

He watched her throat bob as she swallowed, and he realized he was still gripping her shoulder. He pulled back his hand, let it fall to his side.

"All right," she said, and then she started to pluck at the fingers of her gloves. "All right. You walk with Georgiana. *I'll* get the dog."

Christ! Georgiana. He'd forgotten her completely. He looked back to where she'd been standing and saw that she'd wandered closer to the bank with her maid. Her gaze was still on the river—presumably on the scrap of wet fluff gently meandering down the Serpentine.

He turned back to Selina, who had pulled off her gloves and crouched, at work on her half boots.

"For God's sake, Selina, you don't mean to—"

She raised challenging eyes to his. "What? Go into the water?"

"In a word, yes."

He could see her jaw tighten. "I mean to stop you from hurling yourself into scandal once again."

"By hurling yourself into a river instead?"

She had one boot off. "Yes, if that's what it takes! I don't have anyone I need to impress. I don't have"—her voice shook—"anyone who needs me. Freddie and Lu don't need you to rescue a wet puppy, they need you to act like the ninth Duke of Stanhope."

"Well, I need *you* not to drown in the Serpentine," he heard himself bite out. He could barely recognize his tone, barely recognize the anger swirling inside him. He knew she was right. He knew, in the stretched-thin part of himself that was so damned tired of trying to be what he was supposed to be, that her counsel was sound.

But this goddamned society—this goddamned *country*—cared more for the state of his hat and his boots than a living animal.

He didn't know where to aim the frustration and resentment that twisted in his gut. At England? At himself?

Not at her. He forced it back.

"You say you're willing to do anything for Freddie and Lu?" she asked. She was in her stocking feet now, and she seemed smaller, her head tilted farther back to meet his eyes. "Then do this. Take Georgiana's arm. Walk away. I'll get the dog."

He gave her a short nod, not trusting himself to open his mouth.

God only knew what he would say. *I want you* or *Don't drown* or *I can't be who you want me to be.*

He watched her go to the bank, watched her quick precise fingers spreading tall grasses, tugging apart some kind of reed.

He made himself walk over to Georgiana.

"Is Lady Selina going after the dog?" she said without pre-amble.

"Yes," he said. "She wants us to walk away. So we don't draw a crowd, presumably." So he didn't get caught up in any more gossip.

"Not bloody likely," murmured Georgiana.

Peter felt his brows lift as he stared down at her.

"I'm not moving," she said, "until I see that she's gotten the dog. I'd be out there myself if I thought I could manage it."

Where was the blinking? Those brilliant smiles and acres of white teeth? She seemed a different person entirely with the pretense of absurdity dropped. Crisp, business-like, perhaps a little stubborn.

"I . . . see." His voice came out faint.

"And Your Grace?" She looked up at him. Gave him two rapid flutters of her thick gold eyelashes.

"Yes?"

"I think it best if you cease your attentions toward me after today."

Surprise caught him with her words, but somehow it made sense. Without that brittle shell of hers, she was a different woman. And now that he'd seen that woman, she wanted distance. From him? Or from the truth of who she was?

He watched Selina, her head dark with damp as she waded into the water toward the dog, which had drifted close enough now for Peter to make out slightly bulging eyes in a head too large for its small body.

"Lady Georgiana," he said finally. "Do you need some kind of help?"

He felt the sudden press of her fingers squeezing his. "No," she said. "I just need to make sure this dog is all right."

So they watched. In a minute or two Selina had gotten close enough to tug at the little raft of branches upon which the dog was perched. She angled her body back toward the bank and towed the dog behind her with ruthless efficiency.

Peter made himself look around as she made for dry land. There were people in all directions—she'd been entirely right about that. She'd probably been seen swimming through the water, but with nothing except her head visible, she likely hadn't been recognized.

"Lady Georgiana," he said, eyes tracking back to Selina as

she approached the water's edge. "Do you know where they rent the rowboats?"

"I do."

"How quickly do you think you could get there?" He chanced a glance away from Selina's progress to find Georgiana's face, bright but somehow steadier than he'd ever seen her.

One corner of her mouth kicked up. No visible teeth. "Ten minutes, if I walk fast. Shall I hire a boat for you?"

"Tell them to bill it to Stanhope—" He hesitated. Devil take it, how did he get Selina out of this and still manage to avoid having his name in the scandal sheets? Absurd, how much he didn't want to let her down.

"I'll pay," said Georgiana. "If you promise to bring me the dog. I want him."

"I'll bring you the dog with a giant velvet bow on its minuscule neck if you can get someone to row a boat to this exact spot in less than a quarter hour."

"Done," she said. "And Your Grace?"

He'd turned back to Selina, but he dragged his gaze away to look at Georgiana again.

"Thank you. Now go make sure she stays hidden in the bulrushes."

• • •

Selina had done quite a bit of mental swearing since she'd started swimming—and thanks to Belvoir's, her mental vocabulary was extensive.

She'd cursed Peter Kent thoroughly, and with several words she wasn't entirely sure how to pronounce.

She'd cursed the dog, whose fur was so plastered to its small white body that it barely looked canine, all huge eyes and mouse tail.

She'd saved the largest vocabulary of vulgarities for herself. Why had she insisted on tracking Peter down in Hyde Park? Why did she let him goad her into recklessness that she normally reserved for Belvoir's and nothing else in her life? Why was she always so certain she knew what was best for everyone else?

Why, why, *why* had she kept her stockings on? She had liked these stockings.

Now she was going to be in the scandal sheets *and* she was going to have to throw away her favorite stockings.

Bloody. Larking. Bollocks.

She pulled the dog on its makeshift raft into a small copse of reeds and pushed her sopping hair out of her eyes. "I hope you're grateful. I'm bloody certain you could swim if you gave it a try."

"Selina!"

Peter's voice was a drawling, lightly accented whisper, and she jumped so high she nearly fell on her backside and had to grab a fistful of bulrushes to remain upright.

"Keep your head down," Peter's voice went on. "Stay in these grasses. You're practically invisible from the footpath. I checked."

"What on earth—Peter, where *are* you? What are you doing?"

His dark head popped out from within the rushes. "Going for a row," he hissed. "Stay here until I can come around with the boat. Ten minutes." And then he vanished.

She wasn't sure whether to curse more or sit down and cry. Surely he wouldn't throw himself into scandal anyway, would he? After she'd swum straight into the current of public humiliation for him, and ruined her favorite stockings besides?

She picked up the dog, which whined and nuzzled its face into the sodden fabric of her bodice. "Poor thing," she whispered. "You're rather chilly."

In answer, it licked the wet, ruined lace and sighed pathetically, relaxing into her body. It made a small damp weight against her chest.

"I've got you," she said. "You're all right."

She had no way to tell the time, but before long she could see a rowboat making its way toward her, Peter alone at the oars, his head bare and his dark curls burnished red in the sun. She stayed crouched in the rushes, and he maneuvered the craft up into the copse in moments.

"Come on," he whispered. "Can you get in? Stay low, if you can."

She waded into the water and handed him the dog. It gave a little moan of dismay, but Peter soothed it with gentle hands before placing it on the wooden seat beside him.

Selina eyed the boat warily, trying to think how she could get in without tipping them both. She hiked up her dripping skirts, grateful she'd worn her lightest muslin, and tossed one leg over the side of the boat.

Wordlessly, Peter reached out a hand, and she locked her arm with his at the elbow. In one quick pull she was over the side and in the boat, water splashing and pooling into the bottom.

"Sorry about this," Peter said, "but I think you'll have to lie down if you don't want to be seen once I row away."

She glanced up at him, but he was staring seriously down at the craft as though wondering how she might fit.

"Oh bloody fine," she mumbled, and wedged herself in between the two wooden benches, curling her body into a tight C and tucking her head onto her arm. She had an excellent view of

Peter's right calf, tightly encased in his leather Prussians. Water slopped into her ear as he started to row away.

"Wait," she said abruptly, and he paused mid-stroke, lifting the oars out of the water. She could see the muscles of his shoulder bunch beneath the close-fitting fabric of his coat. It rose in her mind—her dream, the planes and angles of his body, his bare skin all pressed to hers in the humid dark—and she bit her lip for focus. "My gloves. My boots. They're still on the bank."

"Georgiana got them," he said. "And this boat, and my carriage too, which she's hopefully sent down to the dam to meet us."

Selina squeezed her eyes shut and then opened them again. "Lady Georgiana Cleeve? Arranged this?"

One side of his mouth lifted in a crooked version of his usual grin. "Sometimes I suspect there's more to her than meets the eye. Or ear, as it were."

Selina puffed a breath between her lips and turned her gaze from his shoulders and his infuriating curls to the water puddled in the bottom of the boat, sluicing back and forth as he started to row once more.

Lady Georgiana had fixed things. She had saved Selina from unwanted attention from half the *ton*. Peter thought there was more to her.

That was delightful. This was all delightful. Better than she could have hoped for.

Absolutely bloody stupendous.

Water splashed up into her nose and she coughed and snorted out the most indelicate, un-lady-like, un-Georgianan series of noises that she had ever heard in her life.

"Christ, Selina, are you well?" Peter was peering down at her, and she forced herself to meet his gaze from her spot curled up at his feet.

Like a dog. *She* was the half-drowned dog in this scenario.

"Stupendous," she mumbled. "Just great."

"I don't think anyone saw you," he offered. "And you . . . aren't very recognizable right now anyway."

Something occurred to her, and she struggled up onto one elbow. "Peter?"

"Hmm?"

"Why didn't you get a boat and row out to the dog?"

The powerful rhythm of his arms at the oars stuttered for a moment, then restarted as smoothly as before. "Sorry?"

"If you knew the boats were close by. Why didn't you just *row* to the dog?"

"Honestly? I didn't even think of it."

She slumped back down onto her arm in the puddle, water saturating her hair. "Neither did I."

The silence between them was broken only by the splashing of Peter's oars. And then, very quietly, by the laugh that bubbled up in Selina's throat and slipped out from between her lips.

She couldn't help herself. She couldn't squelch the sudden hilarity. He was ridiculous. *She* was ridiculous, and maybe running Belvoir's should have been enough outrageous behavior for one lifetime, but she found suddenly that she couldn't be angry. She'd swum in the Serpentine. She'd rescued a dog, and she'd prevented Peter from ruining his reputation further, and, drat her foolish adventure-loving heart, she'd had fun.

She curled herself even more tightly around his legs and laughed so hard tears came to her eyes. She wiped them away with damp wrinkled fingertips, and when she glanced up at Peter, he was staring down at her, absolutely boggled.

"I'm sorry," she wheezed. "I'm not really weeping. I just—can't stop—"

And then he pulled the oars into the boat, leaned over his lap and fairly roared with laughter.

His brown eyes crinkled at the corners—she could see that even through the wash of moisture in her eyes. He caught her cold wet fingers between his hands as he bent at the waist, laughing so hard he couldn't catch his breath, the sound of his unfettered amusement ringing alongside her muffled giggles.

His hands held hers.

He warmed her. Her fingers. Elsewhere. A hot rush that began in her belly and curled up into her chest. Need stirred in her. Need and the memories of her dream.

Amusement shifted in her to something else, something dark and sweet. She tried to catch her breath, tried to pull herself free from the tangle of his eyes and hands.

"Peter?" It came out a rasp.

He tried to stop laughing before he responded, but little choked sounds kept bursting free. "Yes?"

"Have you thought about how I'm going to get from the boat to your carriage without being seen?"

He dropped her hands to wrestle with the oars and came up holding something long and covered in green silk.

A parasol, she realized. Lady Georgiana's parasol.

He grinned at her, and this time it was the real thing, that shiny impossible Kent grin. "You're going to stand in between me and this very large decorative object. I told Georgiana to instruct my driver to pull up as close to the dam as he can. And if we walk very fast, no one is going to suspect a thing."

Chapter 10

. . . Tell me again why it is that no one listens to my superb instructions.

—*from Selina to her brother Will, again*

At the Townshends' dinner party, Selina suffered through eight courses with Lydia seated four chairs down and across the table from her. Veal consommé. Glazed ham. Quail. Asparagus in butter. Summer peas. *Des tendrons de veau aux carottes.*

Selina thought she might scream. She was just close enough for her to watch Lydia converse—haltingly, but at least vomit-free—with Peter beside her. Close enough to watch the play of Peter's elegant fingers on his wineglass.

Too far for her to hear what the two of them were saying. And much too far for her to clutch Lydia's hand and demand to know whether she thought Peter was on the verge of proposing.

He'd inexplicably stopped calling on Georgiana, but he'd kept up his attentions toward Lydia and Iris Duggleby this last week. He hadn't done a single thing that had even whispered of scandal.

Selina chewed on her lower lip and made tiny designs in her lemon ice with her spoon. A cross. An X. A little V that looked like a heart.

They had five days left until the dinner party at Rowland House with Lord and Lady Eldon that Daphne and Nicholas had managed to arrange. She'd hoped he'd be able to announce an engagement there, and she and Thomasin had conspired to leave an empty place for his future bride. In fact, part of her had rather hoped Peter might have already married by special license by the time the dinner party came around.

But so far, Peter hadn't proposed to anyone.

There were three weeks remaining until the Stanhope guardianship case came before the Court of Chancery, and devil take him, if he wanted to present a picture-perfect future family to the Eldons, the man needed to *get moving*.

And if, when she thought about Peter on one knee before Lydia or Iris, she felt a spiked tangle of feelings rise in her, she forced it back down and refused to let herself think about why that might be.

She could not think about wanting him, about the flip of need in her lower belly when she watched him slide a finger along the edge of his plate.

The dreams were bad enough as it was.

Isaac Villeneuve to her side said something about the weather, and she gave him a wordless glare. He stopped talking.

When the last course was taken away by a bevy of footmen, Selina nearly overturned her chair in her haste to make her way over to Lydia. From several places down, Aunt Judith arched an eyebrow.

Selina refused to be chastened and arrowed straight for her friend.

"Well?" she said when she reached Lydia's side.

Lydia blinked up at her, several white feathers twining through her red curls. "Well?" she repeated.

"Stanhope, for goodness' sake. I saw you speaking at dinner."

"Ah," Lydia said. "Yes. We talked about Brougham's campaign in—"

"Lydia!" Selina's voice was a whisper-shriek.

Lydia's feathers bobbed in surprise. "Er . . . yes?"

"What of *marriage*? Did you speak of your—" She found herself hesitating on the words, and forced herself to spit them out. "Of your future life together?"

Lydia's brows drew together in surprise as she looked up at Selina. And then, quite deliberately, she rolled her eyes.

"Lyddie," Selina hissed, "what does that mean?"

"I know you dislike your plans going awry, but it's not going to happen."

"I really think—"

Lydia fixed her with a clear blue stare. "Selina. The man has no intention of marrying me. I am absolutely certain of it."

Selina felt a curious sensation unfolding in her chest. A twist, and then a shudder, like her heart was beating too hard for her body.

Frustration. Surely it must be frustration at Peter's lack of progress.

It certainly wasn't relief. It couldn't possibly be.

She scrubbed her gloved fingers together restlessly. "I've got to talk to Iris."

"Do you think he's making more progress on that front?"

"He'd bloody well better be."

•   •   •

Peter had done his due diligence. He'd conversed with Lydia Hope-Wallace. He'd danced with Iris Duggleby.

He'd kept his eyes and his hands and every other part of his body off Selina Ravenscroft, even though he could nearly smell her unnameable spiced scent, almost hear the hum of her voice from across the room.

He felt like he had a blasted tuning fork that vibrated at the sound of her. Except it was his cock.

He needed fresh air and maybe some awful frigid English rain, but failing that, he was going to get something alcoholic to drink.

He was halfway down the hall between the ballroom and Townshend's office where half a dozen men had gathered for brandy and smoking when a silk-gloved arm stretched out from behind a partially closed door, caught his wrist, and yanked.

He stumbled into what appeared to be a library and fell into a pair of rum-colored eyes.

"Peter," she whispered. "Finally! I've been in here an age."

She shut the library door behind him.

And then she turned the key.

"Selina? What—"

"I've been talking to Lydia."

Her eyes were bright, her hair dotted with pearls and spilling in heavy waves down her back. Her dress was bronze, darker than her skin, lighter than her eyes, and he wanted to run his fingertips across it all: satin and skin and antique gold hair.

Peter coughed and backed judiciously away from her. "Should we . . . open the door?"

She scowled at him. "I have been talking to Lydia," she said again. "I asked her if she thought you might be on the cusp of proposing. And do you know what she did?"

"I really think perhaps we should open the—"

"She rolled her eyes," Selina continued, as if he hadn't spoken. "And then I asked Iris Duggleby the same question. And do you know what *she* did?"

Peter had a feeling he could guess.

"She rolled her eyes too!"

"Selina," he said, and felt behind himself awkwardly for the key to the door. Nothing. Just carved wood and a door handle. He tugged off his glove with his teeth and then reached for the door again.

She took a step toward him. "Peter, I know you said that you mean to pursue marriage in earnest. But somewhere between your intentions and what actually happens, you're going wrong."

"I'm sorry to tell you this"—had she not left the key in the lock? Christ, the woman had probably secreted it in her reticule using some kind of sleight-of-hand—"but you've just described most of my life."

She sank her teeth into her lower lip. "I want to help you."

Peter bit back a sigh. "Listen, you are exceptional at arranging things, I'll give you that. But I don't think it's going to work out."

"I think you simply need to practice."

"Selina." He blew out his breath. "Why do you want this so much? Why is it so important to you to see me married?"

She looked agonized, and he regretted the words as soon as he said them. "I—it's not that I want to see you married. I want—I want to help you, Peter. I want you to have your family. I think this will help you get the children!"

"All right," he said. "Fine. How do I practice?"

"You are too—" She hesitated, as if searching for the word, and his pride winced in horrified anticipation. Her lips made that little pout again. "Charming."

His pride rebounded. "And that's . . . how I'm going wrong? With women?"

"Indeed. I'm sure you are very successful with"—her lips compressed—"women. But you are not trying to marry *women*, Peter. You are trying to marry *one* woman."

"I . . . see?"

He did not see.

She waved a hand through the air. "You deploy your charm indiscriminately. You smile that Kent smile at all sorts of women in the exact same way."

That Kent smile? He felt as though he'd gotten locked not in a library but in some kind of alternative country where he didn't speak the language.

"If you want Lydia or Iris or Georgiana to take you seriously as a marital prospect," Selina continued, "you must show her that she means something to you. Something special. Something unique."

Christ. He raked a hand through his hair, and Selina's eyes followed the movement of his arm. "They *are* unique. They're all very unique."

She scowled. "That is precisely the problem. You cannot say things like that and expect them to believe that you are sincerely interested in marrying them."

"And you have ideas about what I should say?" Did she mean to provide a script for his proposal, then?

Good God, this whole situation had spiraled out of his control. It had seemed simple. Find a woman he liked. Marry her. Get the children.

Was it his impulse for self-destruction that had made it all such a snarl? Why else would some part of his brain be shouting that there was one woman who was special. One woman he could imagine in his life, in his bed, and here she was, carefully instructing him on how to marry someone else.

"I have a few ideas," she said. "Choose one of the women, Peter. Tell her that you value her. Tell her that you respect her as a person, and not just for her dowry or her family name or her pretty face."

"Fine," he said. "I understand. I'll try."

He started to turn to the door, but her voice stopped him. "Wait."

He looked back. She bit her lower lip, just for a moment, and then she said, "I told you. I think you should practice. On me."

"Selina," he tried to say, but she was already protesting, her hand held out to him in appeal.

"Just practice," she said. "Tell me what you would say."

He could feel the steady rhythm of his heart against his ribs as he looked at her, with her wolf's eyes, that wide mouth he wanted to taste more than he'd wanted anything in his life.

And he took the things he wanted. He was selfish that way. Reckless.

It was a terrible idea. This was a terrible idea.

He took a step toward her. She held her ground, and damn him, he liked that about her.

"I respect you," he said, his voice low. She swayed toward him, and he took another step. "I value you. I've never met anyone like you."

She licked her lips, and he brought his hand to the side of her long, slender neck, his thumb just brushing the skin behind her ear.

Alarms were sounding in his head, shrieking, *Stop talking* and *Back away* and *She's not for you, you ass.*

He ignored it all, and savored the impossible softness of her skin.

"I think about you. All the time. Even when I shouldn't think of you, I do." Blood was roaring in his ears now, pounding through his body, but he made himself be easy, let his thumb explore her racing pulse.

Her lips trembled apart, but she didn't speak, so he kept going. He couldn't have made himself stop.

"I am so glad I know you," he said. "You are so clever. So damned sweet. I can't stop wondering what it is that you smell of. I dream about how you would taste. And Christ, Selina, I want to taste every part of you."

Her lips came back together, pressed into a pout, and he realized it was the start of a little plosive *P*. She was going to say his name. She was going to tell him to stop being such a damned fool.

And so instead of letting her finish, he caught that pout with his own mouth and kissed her.

She stood frozen for a moment beneath his mouth. It felt wrong, somehow. This was *Selina*, fire and life and abundance, and he did not think she was afraid.

So he touched her, softly, behind her ear, then slid his thumb questioningly along the line of her jaw. *Please*, he thought dazedly.

And she seemed to hear him. Her mouth came open on a gasp, and then she was pressed against him, her slim body coming warm and full into his, and he nearly groaned in relief and shifted his fingers into her hair.

She tasted—oh Christ, her mouth was heaven, was sweetness and tart lemon ice. He would never taste lemon again without being here in this moment, drowning in this woman.

She nipped at his lower lip, and he shuddered and sucked and tried to pull her harder into his body. She wanted—he could feel her desire in the unsteady whisper of her breath, in the press of her breasts against his chest. She reached up and found the nape of his neck above his cravat, and her cool silk glove felt like paradise against his heated skin.

He broke away from her mouth and shifted downward. God, he had dreamed of this—this exact place where her neck met her shoulder, the sounds she would make when he kissed her this way.

But he should have known she would be more than he could have imagined. She rocked against him and made a soft, impatient sound that made him want to yank her skirts up to her waist.

But slow, he told himself. *Slowly now.*

"You taste so good," he murmured into her skin. "You are so sweet. So lovely."

He closed his teeth around her earlobe, and she made another one of those sounds, a sound so low and heated he thought he might go blind with wanting.

"Peter," she whispered. "Don't stop."

He wanted to please her. He had to please her. He dropped his hands to her buttocks and made to tug her body up, just a bit, to feel her against his chest and his cock.

And oh *God*, beneath all those layers of silks and skirts, Selina Ravenscroft had the sweetest, roundest, most magnificent ass he'd ever encountered.

He turned an oath into a wordless growl and dragged her against him, suddenly desperate to feel, to hold, to possess . . .

And it was that—that rough desperation—that brought him back to himself.

He could hurt her like that. He could not be careless with her.

He wanted more than this—more than frenzy and flesh. He wanted so much more with her.

He let her go and lifted his head. She blinked open her eyes and looked up at him, her face flushed, her lips parted. It took every scrap of his limited self-control not to bend his head back, not to spin her around and push her up against the door and find her skin with his hands.

"Marry me," he said.

Her lips parted further. She stared at him, and the flush in her cheeks faded, degree by agonizing degree.

"I—" she said. "Are you—practicing? Still?"

Oh Jesus Christ, this woman. "I was never practicing. It's you, Selina. I want *you*."

Some part of him was shouting that he needed *words*. He was good with words. He could tell her that she was extraordinary. He could tell her that when she walked into a room, all the candlelight gathered itself upon her face.

He could tell her she was lemon ice and spiced rum and the dawn.

But somehow he knew already that it would not matter. He knew from the milky pallor of her cheeks and the frozen look about her mouth that fancy words would make no difference. He knew what she was going to say.

"I'm sorry," she whispered. "I can't—Peter, I *can't* marry you."

He had not expected anything different, not really.

If she wanted to marry him, she wouldn't have presented him with a list of other women for him to court. She was the sister of a duke; he knew for a fact she'd turned down at least half a dozen proposals from men altogether more suitable for her than Peter. Steady English peers who weren't reckless and selfish. Who didn't need fixing.

And yet he felt cold, a bitter English cold, and sick with disappointment.

He eased back from her. "Of course," he said. "I understand."

"Peter," she said again, and her hands clung together in front of her. "I'm sorry—it's not—it's not—"

He backed away from her a little farther, moving toward the door. He was no saint; he did not want to hear her pity. "It's all right. Thank you for the advice. I shall—try to put it into practice."

She stared at him. "Oh. You're welcome. I—"

She was blinking rapidly now, no more words making their way from her mouth, and so he turned to the door and yanked at it.

It did not open. It was still locked. For God's sake, what a time for Selina to be so utterly competent and for him to be such a consummate fool.

He spun back toward her, clenching his jaw so no more idiocy poured out.

She was already fishing for the key in a hidden pocket of her skirt. "I'm sorry. I have it. The key, I mean. I have—here it is. I'm sorry."

She shoved the key into the lock and turned. Started to open the door and then stopped herself and shut it again.

"You should . . . exit first," she said. "For your reputation. You should exit first, and I'll follow in a few minutes."

He stared down at her. "For *my* reputation? Selina, you do understand that if we were discovered in here, yours is the reputation that would suffer? It's not right, but it's simply a fact."

She laughed unsteadily. "I'm not nearly so worried about my reputation as I am about yours."

God, his heart squeezed at that. He could not think of anyone he had ever known who cared the way she did. "You shouldn't be."

"I cannot help myself!" Her voice cracked a little. "I care for the children. Your brother and sister need you, Peter, and I—I don't have anyone who needs me."

He lifted his still-ungloved hand halfway to her face. *I need you*, he wanted to say.

But he would not continue down that road. He dropped his hand.

"Put your glove back on," she said, "before you go."

He did. He gave her a ghost of a smile and then closed the door between them.

Chapter 11

. . . We'll need at least a hundred copies of the new translation of Catullus. And two dozen more of Fanny Hill, *I suppose. For a sixty-six-year-old book, it does seem to fly off the shelves.*

—from Lady Selina Ravenscroft to
Jean Laventille, publisher

The following afternoon, Selina sat at her escritoire and stared blankly down at the paper in front of her.

She knew what it said. She had intended to write a letter to Laventille—he'd passed along word of another inquiry into Belvoir's ownership, this time via a "potential investor"—but she had altogether failed to pen the note.

Instead she had tapped several dozen clustered dots on the top of the page and then written in her quick, neat hand: *What the bloody hell were you thinking?*

He'd been pretending.

That's what she'd told herself there in the Townshends' library, Peter before her, his eyes intent upon her own. He was pretending, he was practicing, he was making it all up because she'd lost her mind and told him to act like he wanted her.

The worst part was, she'd wanted to believe him. She'd wanted to think he meant it, meant every word as he searched her face. She could almost let herself imagine it was true—until he'd called her sweet.

No one, in her entire life, had ever called her sweet. He must have been imagining someone else.

Except then he'd said her name. And then he'd kissed her.

It was not the first time she had kissed another person. But it was the first time she had done so and felt—all of that. Everything in her liquid, her mind cloudy with need.

Marry me, he'd said to her. And he had not been pretending then.

Something dangerous had lit the air between them. In that moment, Selina could name the feeling that had twisted in her chest these last weeks as she'd watched him dance and laugh with Lydia and Iris and Georgiana.

Wanting. She wanted him for herself with a possessiveness she had never before known. She had looked up at him and tasted it on her lips—her *yes* and the kiss that would follow, his hands in her hair, his mouth on her own.

And then reality had cut through the haze of desire.

She had meant to help him, for heaven's sake. She'd meant to fix things, to make it so his family could be together.

He needed a perfectly English, perfectly scandal-free wife so that he could convince the courts to give him Freddie and Lu. And Selina was always, on any given day, a hairbreadth from social ruin. She couldn't do this to him. She couldn't have him.

Oh, but she *wanted*.

She wanted his hands on her skin and his body pressing into hers. She wanted the sweet warmth of his brown eyes, his intense focus as he listened to her speak. She wanted him. She wanted everything.

It was some wild, impulsive, uncontrollable part of her that had made her decide to buy Belvoir's and start the Venus catalog. She had been so angry with the deceptions and hypocrisies of the *beau monde*, the different rules for men and women designed to keep her sex ignorant. Men seemed to do as they pleased—to press their advantages in finances and politics and sexual relations— and Selina had no longer been able to tolerate it. She had taken the privilege that was hers as wealthy duke's sister, gathered it up in her hands, and thrust herself into reckless action to try to make a difference for naive young women like she herself had once been.

And somehow that same irrepressible fire seemed to come out when she was around Peter. Swimming in the Serpentine, dragging him into the library and locking the door. Telling him to pretend that he wanted her.

He'd frustrated and unsettled her—but in a way that challenged her carefully controlled life. He respected her, more than any man she'd known except perhaps her twin. He asked her questions and really listened to her answers, his gaze so steady and absorbed upon her that she felt like the center of his world.

He made her laugh. He made her burn.

She gritted her teeth, smothering the memory, and turned her attention to the books on her escritoire.

She could not think about Peter like that. She could not let herself feel all that wanting.

The Belvoir's books were bound in emerald-colored cloth— Selina liked how recognizable it made the books, and cloth was far cheaper than the calfskin used for bindings in her brother's library here at Rowland House. But these samples weren't bound at all, merely sewn together, their edges still uncut. The books she chose would be covered in the Belvoir's style and added to the catalog.

Sometimes she made rapid selections at her publisher's office, but she had the Venus catalog options sent to her directly, ever since the memorable afternoon in which she'd flipped open an illustrated text in front of Jean Laventille that had turned out to contain cartoons comparing women's breasts to various pieces of fruit.

Ridiculous. Her readers knew perfectly well what their own breasts looked like. A pamphlet on *male* sexual organs—now, that was something she might have considered.

There seemed some viable fruit candidates. Bananas, certainly. Cucumber—was that a fruit? Perhaps an aubergine.

She sliced neatly through the pages with a penknife and wondered if she were completely cracked.

The first text was another Covent Garden memoir. She chewed on her lower lip and flipped the pages. She appreciated the frank humor of the memoirs of ladies of the night, but in truth the Venus catalog already held quite a few. She liked having them, though—it made a useful contrast with the romantic novels that fairly flew off the shelves. No declarations of love here. In fact, this one featured a wildly unflattering comparison of the phalluses of the pleasure worker's most frequent customers.

Perhaps she'd add this one to the list.

She sliced through the second set of pages and then glanced at the title. *The Use of Flogging in* . . . She blinked and stuffed the pages back into her escritoire. Absolutely not. She was after a gentle introduction to sexual matters for sheltered women of the *ton*. Definitely no flogging.

Where did Laventille *find* these books? She'd had to send him a tersely worded note the third time he'd sent her *Lady Bumtickler's Revels*.

The last set was a translation of erotic Greek poetry. These, too, were popular, and she turned the pages slowly, her eyes catching on the words. *Whence is this*, she read. *What strange tumultuous throbs of bliss? What raptures seize my fainting frame?*

She licked her lips and set the pages down, but it was too late. The next line of the poem whispered in her mind.

And all my body glows with flame.

Yes, that was how it had felt. As though her body were glowing. Sparking to life and then catching fire.

She'd burned from the inside out when Peter had touched her, when he'd kissed her.

And she'd wanted more. What she'd read about and seen in illustrations—his mouth on her breasts. His hands beneath her skirts.

She wanted it now, as she thought about the sweet pressure of Peter's lips, his long fingers digging into her hip, the hoarse sound of pleasure he'd made.

She realized that the heel of her palm was pressed hard into her thigh. Somehow her legs had loosened, splaying open wider as she sat at her desk. Her hand drifted closer to the apex of her thighs as if called by the ache there.

It was all tangled in her mind now—her dream of Peter's body, his hands clamped hard on her flesh, his teeth grazing the skin of her neck.

Peter's mouth. Her fingers in his hair. His—

A knock sounded at her door, and Selina let out a strangled cry and leapt to her feet.

"Selina, darling? Are you quite all right?"

It was Thomasin. Sweet, gentle Thomasin.

Selina looked frantically about the room as if for evidence of her erotic crimes. She shoved the book of poetry into the drawer of her escritoire, avoided her flushed and guilty reflection, and hurled herself into her bed.

She buried her face in a decorative pillow and tried to cool her flaming skin. "I'm perfectly well," she mumbled into the brocade. "Come in, please."

She managed to look up as Thomasin entered, her round face creased in a smile. Thomasin made her way to the bed and sat down, unfolding a handkerchief and spreading it out on the counterpane to reveal a handful of dried fruit.

Apricots. She knew Selina had loved apricots since she was a child.

"Just wanted to check on you, dear one. You were quiet at breakfast."

Selina plucked one of the golden fruits from the handkerchief and stuffed it into her mouth to avoid having to respond. She chewed methodically and sought to calm her nerves.

Her brother Nicholas had raised her and Will himself—but Aunt Judith and Thomasin had been there since she and Will were six. They'd arrived the day of their parents' funeral and never left. Thomasin knew Selina better than anyone. It was extremely difficult to hide anything from her.

When she finished chewing, she said, "I'm feeling out of sorts, that's all." Good Lord, what a way to describe *gripped by uncontrollable erotic fantasies*. "Nothing serious. I'll feel better in a few days. I'm sure."

Thomasin's gray curls bobbed as she tilted her head. "What's going on with Stanhope?"

It was fortunate she'd finished the apricot, or she would have choked. "N-nothing," she stuttered. "I . . . I don't think of him that way." *Oh, Selina, you lying liar.*

Thomasin appeared to be smothering a grin. "Indeed. I'd only meant, how goes his marital campaign? But—good to know."

Oh Lord, she had a turnip for a brain. "Right," she said. "It's . . ."

What did she say? *Not too well, I think, considering he spent last evening kissing the single most ineligible debutante in England.*

"I'd hoped he would have made more progress by now," she said carefully. There, that was relatively neutral. Not too incriminating. She hoped.

"My darling." Thomasin tucked a wayward strand of Selina's hair behind her ear, and Selina wanted to curl into her soft, rose-scented touch like a little girl. "You don't need to take care of everyone, you know."

She looked down at the pillow in her lap, tracing the brocade whorls. "I know."

"Do you?" Thomasin's voice was gentle, but Selina still felt the faintest bit stung.

"I do know. I know my own limitations." She knew she was too overbearing, that she came on too strong and intimidated people. She knew there was so much in the world that she couldn't fix.

"I am not quite sure I believe that you know your limitations, my dear. But nor do I think you know your own strengths."

Selina drew back in surprise. Her own strengths? No one had ever accused her of not knowing her virtues—if anything, it was much the opposite. She always thought she knew what was best. She always believed she could take on anything and anyone. It was what had made her take up fencing and card games as a girl. It was what had driven her to chase Peter down in Hyde Park and throw herself into the Serpentine.

It was what had made her start the Venus catalog. Society had cast the women of her generation adrift—they were meant to be playthings, meant to be innocent and empty-headed and leave practical knowledge to the men who controlled their lives.

To hell with that. Selina had read books. She had learned. And she had taken it upon herself to change the way the women of the *ton* saw their own place in the world.

"I'm not sure what you mean," she said to Thomasin, one corner of her mouth rising wryly. "I'm quite confident in my knowledge of both."

Thomasin gazed at her, blue eyes soft. "We both know you can command a room, of course. You can organize a dinner party for twenty without a blink, and you've probably secured marriage proposals for half of the debutantes of the last four years."

Selina tilted her head in acknowledgment. True, true, and—well, half might be an overstatement. She'd had a hand in probably a third.

"Those are strengths, to be sure. But your greatest strength is your heart."

Selina bit her bottom lip and then let it go and pressed her lips together. "I care about my family."

"You *care*, Selina. About us, yes. About Lydia. But also about Iris Duggleby and Ivy Price and the Halifax twins. About Stanhope and those precious children. You care so much that I worry, sometimes, for you. You cannot solve every problem, Selina, no matter how hard you try." Her face was gentle. "Stanhope may not get the children. He may not marry before his petition comes before the courts, and he almost certainly won't be engaged by the dinner party we're hosting for the Eldons next week. And if it doesn't go as you planned, I don't want you to be hurt."

"I know," Selina said. "Believe me, I know."

If Thomasin knew about Belvoir's, she'd realize that Selina lived every day with the knowledge that she couldn't predict what the future held. If Thomasin knew, she'd realize that Selina's fierce wrangling for control over the rest of her life was bound up in the way that she couldn't control when and how the Belvoir's scandal would eventually break.

Not for the first time, Selina considered telling Thomasin about Belvoir's. Thomasin wouldn't be angry—she was never angry.

But she might be hurt. She might blink back tears of shock and disappointment, and if that happened, Selina didn't think she could bear it.

She was *proud* of what she'd done with Belvoir's, the difference she'd made for the women of her generation. And she couldn't stand it if her family knew the truth and didn't feel the same way.

"Tell me," said Thomasin quietly. "Does your Stanhope project have anything to do with Will?"

Selina drew a quick breath. "No. No. What would it have to do with Will?"

"After we lost Katherine and the baby. I know how desperately you wanted to fix things for Will."

"I did." Her voice rasped a little, even now, when she thought of her brother's wife and the baby who had died. "I still do. I want him to come home and I want to wrap him in cotton wool and never let him be hurt again."

"But you know you cannot."

She swallowed against the burning in her throat. "I know I cannot. He'll come home when he's ready." It was hard to think of him so far away, to read letters written weeks or months before, not knowing if on any given day he was safe and whole.

She didn't know if her twin would ever be whole again.

"I wondered if you saw Will in Stanhope's younger brother. If you thought by rescuing those children, you might be rescuing Will, somehow. It would be perfectly understandable."

Selina shook her head. "I want to help Stanhope and the children because they deserve to be together. It's not because of Will. I know—" Her blasted voice broke, and she coughed shortly, angry with herself. "—I know I can't fix Will. Nothing can repair what he's lost."

"He'll come home," Thomasin said. "In time. He'll smile again, Selina. I promise."

Her vision was blurred, and she reached up to press the heels of her hands to her eyes. They came away wet. Senseless tears.

"I hate it," she said finally. "I hate that I can't make things right."

Thomasin reached across the abandoned apricots to pull Selina into an embrace. "I know, my darling. I know."

"I love him so much," she said, and let herself be held. Just for a moment. "I wish that was enough to bring him home."

"It is. It will." Thomasin passed a hand gently over her hair, and for once it felt good to let someone else be in charge. To let someone else do the caring. "Love and patience and bravery are always enough. And you have those in abundance."

"Patience?" Selina laughed into the soft roundness of Thomasin's shoulder. "I wouldn't say I have that by the thimbleful, let alone in abundance."

"Isn't this where we started? With your strengths?" Thomasin waited until Selina pulled back and met her gaze, and then smiled up at her. "You have a whole well of patience, my darling. You simply haven't needed to use it until now."

Chapter 12

Cauliflower velouté with hazelnuts. Eight quails, garnished
with watercress. ~~*Beef braised in brandy and mustard.*~~
Charlotte of apples and apricots.

—from the menu of Her Grace Daphne Ravenscroft, Duchess
of Rowland, hastily annotated by Selina: "No cognac!"

Peter took the carriage to Rowland House for the dinner party
with Lord and Lady Eldon.

He'd have preferred to walk. Hell, he'd have preferred to ride,
gallop a horse down Rotten Row and back half a dozen times
before dropping it off in the mews at Rowland House. Perhaps
he'd be worn out enough to stop his mind from spinning through
frustration and guilt and simmering regret before he had to face
the Eldons.

And Selina. He had to face Selina.

What had he been *thinking*?

Christ, he knew the answer to that. The answer was the same
as it always was—he hadn't been thinking. He'd been wanting, so

desperately that his mind had gone quiet and all he'd been able to see was Selina, her mouth trembling as he pulled back from the impossible heaven of her body.

He wanted her, nothing but her. And he hadn't been thinking of the children and how he needed to marry for them. He'd been thinking of the harsh gasp of her breath and the raw-silk sound of her voice. *Peter. Don't stop.* He'd been thinking about how god-damned much he liked her, and how tired he was of hearing her try to pair him with someone else, and how much he wanted to lift her skirts and taste even more of her.

Even *that*, surely, would have been less idiotic than asking her to marry him.

He didn't know if he wanted to find her and apologize or hide out in his office with one of the last remaining bottles of cognac and lick his wounds.

But instead, he was on his way to Rowland House, because she'd been right when she said that the children needed him. He was dressed in the most ducal thing he owned—according to Humphrey, his valet, who had far more experience with English dukes than Peter did—and he'd taken the carriage just as he was supposed to. He would be perfectly polite. As English as he could manage. If he could've stripped away his accent for this one night, he would have, as much as it burned him to admit it.

For the children, he would do more than that.

Lord and Lady Eldon were already at Rowland House when Peter arrived. He was ushered into a sitting room that he hadn't previously encountered—this one held a pianoforte, fine mahogany furniture upholstered in ivory, and a handful of liveried footmen.

He couldn't keep his eyes from flickering across the room. Lady Eldon was deep in conversation with Lady Judith Ravenscroft and

Thomasin Dandridge, Lord Eldon with Rowland. On the settee, the Duchess of Rowland had her head bent over the cover of a book—and beside her, equally engrossed, was Selina.

He tried not to look at her face, at her mouth. Tried not to see if her expression changed when their butler announced his name.

Judith Ravenscroft was the first to welcome him personally. She barely inclined her silver head, and a footman was already at his side to offer him refreshment.

"Good evening, Your Grace," she said. "Welcome back to Rowland House."

"Thank you. I'm only sorry I couldn't bring Freddie and Lu this time. Freddie hasn't stopped talking about this house since we left. Something about Palladian windows?"

Her face, normally severe, softened slightly. "A future architect, perhaps. Bring them back another time."

He wanted to. After his disastrous proposal in the Townshends' library, it didn't seem terribly likely. But he merely nodded and let Lady Judith shepherd him toward John Scott, Baron Eldon and the lord high chancellor.

Also the arbiter of Freddie and Lu's future.

The chancellor himself stood in a corner, chatting with the Duke of Rowland. Nicholas was tall—an inch or two taller than Peter and probably a full four or five above Eldon. Eldon was a solidly built man in his mid-sixties, his worn face bracketed by heavy white brows. He was scowling.

"I tell you, Rowland, you've got this by the wrong end," he was saying grimly as Lady Judith and Peter approached.

"Your objections, Lord Chancellor, while noted, will have to wait," said Nicholas easily, turning his stance to bring Judith and Peter into the conversation.

Eldon made a gruff sound of disgust and turned a sharp blue gaze onto them.

Lady Judith presented Eldon to Peter. He still wasn't used to it—having people presented to him ever since his ducal elevation, rather than the other way around. It seemed absurd to pretend that Eldon needed to beg for Peter's gracious acceptance of the introduction, when they both knew perfectly well that Peter was the petitioner here.

He tried a relaxed smile on Eldon.

Eldon's thick white brows drew down. "Stanhope. Don't think just because we haven't met socially that I don't know who you are."

Peter considered his options for response. *Why whatever can you mean, Lord Chancellor? Is it simply that I stole thousands of pounds of your illegally obtained cognac? Or do you also recognize me from every gossip rag currently printed in this city?*

He settled for, "Nonetheless, it's a pleasure to finally make your acquaintance."

"Hmph. For a duke, you're not very good at lying."

Nicholas choked slightly into his glass of wine. Lady Judith looked like she wanted to laugh but absolutely did not dare.

Before long, footmen signaled them into the dining room for dinner. Peter escorted Lady Judith to her seat, and as he led her in, she said in an undertone, "For goodness' sake, Stanhope, don't let Eldon make you sweat. You belong here just as much as he does. Act the part."

He wasn't sure if he felt cheered or rather chastened by her advice. Possibly both.

He found his own seat, in between Lady Eldon on his left and—hell—Selina on his right. Lord Eldon sat across the table from all of them, and he peeled off his gloves like a man preparing for a fencing match, rather than an elegant dinner.

"Your Grace," said Lady Eldon from his side, and Peter turned to her. She was several inches shorter than Lord Eldon, and her once-dark hair was now liberally streaked with gray. She had a deeply engraved dimple on each cheek, and her eyes sparkled like champagne.

"Lady Eldon."

"I'm so pleased we've been seated near each other," she said confidentially. "I'd like to hear everything you have to tell me about New Orleans. I keep telling John"—she angled a mischievous glance toward her husband—"that he needs to take me on a pleasure cruise before I die. And *he* keeps telling *me*—"

"That I'm busy trying to keep the bottom from falling out of our legal system?" Eldon broke in. "And that you're nowhere near your deathbed, Bess?"

Lady Eldon heaved a sigh. "Do you see what I live with? My children are grown. I mean to enjoy the years I have left to me. Now—tell me all about New Orleans. And make it good so John feels tempted."

Based on the expression on the chancellor's face, Peter thought that Lady Eldon might be wildly overestimating Peter's powers of persuasion.

Still, he did his best. He told her about New Orleans—the colorful houses and wrought-iron balconies, the shimmering Carnival masquerades and the drowsy heat of the Vieux Carré. He described his mother's home, the hot lushness of the bayou, and the dozens of children who played there all year round.

Peter tried not to look at Selina while he was talking, but he couldn't stop his gaze from drifting toward her. She wasn't looking back at him, but her head was tilted in his direction, her expressive face soft with pleasure.

He dragged his eyes away.

"How lovely that sounds," said Lady Eldon. "You must have had many playmates as a child. Had you any siblings?"

Beneath the table, Selina's foot gave his a little nudge. He wanted to catch her eye and grin—*Don't worry, I won't miss that wide-open opportunity*—but he didn't.

"My mother's family employed a great number of locals, so yes, there were many children," he told Lady Eldon. "And of course, I grew up with a brother. Morgan. He died in childhood."

From his side, he heard Selina draw in a short, sharp breath.

"I'm so sorry to hear that," said Lady Eldon. He could see the soft smile lines around her eyes as she spoke. "I, too, lost a brother in my youth. I still miss him, even fifty years on."

There was a strange sort of comfort in that. That even when the image of Morgan's small square hands and hazel eyes grew blurred with time, Peter would never forget how much he'd loved his brother.

"I learned in recent years that I have two more half siblings," Peter said. "It's been quite an experience to come to England and get to know them."

Lady Eldon's eyes lit. "You had two siblings you didn't know about? What an extraordinary surprise. Are they of an age with you?"

Peter hoped like hell that the lord chancellor was listening. He took a cautious sip of his wine, and then he told Lady Eldon all about Freddie and Lu. He told her about Lu's protectiveness and Freddie's gentle reserve. He told her about the kitten. He told her about the guardianship petition.

At one point during his story, Nicholas Ravenscroft tried to say something to Lord Eldon. Judging by Nicholas's abruptly cut-off speech and the offended look he shot Selina, Peter had a feeling that her foot had also encountered her brother's. Evidently with rather more force than what she'd directed toward Peter.

Lady Eldon asked all sorts of eager questions about Freddie and Lu—enough questions that he began to wonder if she had been let in on this whole scheme by Lady Judith and Thomasin.

If so, he blessed the machinations of intelligent women.

He'd just started on a description of how he meant to buy the children a puppy and send Freddie to Eton when Eldon broke in. His eyebrows looked skeptical. "Tell me, Stanhope—how do you mean to raise these children in between all the responsibilities of your new position? Or do you plan to dodge the Lords and rid yourself of your estates like the rest of the young bucks of your generation?"

Peter was grateful his mouth didn't require much input from his brain in forming a response, because in truth, he had no idea how he meant to raise his siblings. Not one. "Not at all. There's no inherent conflict between attending to my brother and sister and taking my place in the Lords."

Eldon scoffed. "Easy words from a man who's never had children of his own. We've raised four between us, Bessie and me, and there's no sense in thinking you can do it alone." He cast a fond look at Lady Eldon, which promptly dropped off his face when he turned back to Peter.

"Surely you know I raised my siblings as well," Nicholas cut in smoothly. "Ten years younger than Stanhope to boot—and we survived, didn't we, Selina?"

Selina smiled warmly at Nicholas, Eldon, and the general company, and nodded. She opened her mouth to speak, but Eldon again harrumphed, and she closed her mouth, wincing.

"I think we all know you had plenty of help, Rowland," Eldon said, tilting his head toward Lady Judith and Thomasin. "What does Stanhope have? A pack of hired nursemaids? Or simply a fully paid tuition bill so he can get the children out of his house?"

A clamor of voices broke out at his words.

Peter stuttered a rejection—he hadn't meant that at all when he'd mentioned Eton, surely they must realize—

Lady Eldon said gently, "Now, John, Stanhope seems to me—"

Selina's irate voice barely bordered on polite. "Surely if His Grace meant to do nothing more than send the children off to be cared for elsewhere, he would simply leave them where they are."

And Lady Judith, when the tumult died down, said sternly, "Come now, Eldon. Stanhope has all of us. Ravenscrofts do not abandon their friends."

Footmen entered the room then, one for each guest, and presented tiny crystal glasses filled with raspberry ice. On each a sugar-paste flower blossomed, fragile and delicately painted in pinks and violets.

Peter ate the dessert course mechanically, barely tasting the sweetness, hardly wondering which company had imported the sugar.

Frustration and resentment swirled in him—at Eldon, yes. But also at himself. If he'd just gone along with Selina's plan, he might have an affianced bride here tonight to answer Eldon's queries. And for once, it seemed like it would have been a damned good idea. How *did* he think he was going to do this all by himself?

He appreciated Lady Judith's support, down in some bone-deep part of himself that had always wanted to be part of a family like the Ravenscrofts. But he scarcely knew what she meant. The children were his. His family, his responsibility. And somehow he was already failing at that responsibility as he sat here, unable to tell Eldon what the man wanted to hear.

He should have listened to Selina. He should have picked a duchess from her carefully selected list. But he couldn't. How could he, when everything he wanted was right here, beside him, and he never wanted to let her go?

The subject turned from his family to politics, and Peter let it flow past him, unheeding. When the dessert course was cleared, they made their way out of the dining room. Rowland invited Peter and Eldon for port—not cognac, which was something of a relief—in his study, and the ladies made their way back into the sitting room. Peter heard the soft sound of the pianoforte and wondered who played.

Rowland and Eldon spoke of their mutual acquaintances in Parliament, and Peter dutifully agreed with whatever they were saying. He mentioned the imminent date of the guardianship petition on the Court of Chancery schedule, and he didn't say anything about the colonies or stains on any national character. He might not be able to marry as Selina had wanted him to do, but he was on his best bloody English prig behavior.

When they finally left the office and the port to make their way back to the ladies, Peter excused himself.

He told them he needed to piss—not quite in so many words—but in truth he needed to breathe. He needed just a moment to remember how to inhale and exhale, enough times so that he could pretend the world wouldn't end if he cocked this all up and didn't get the children.

He made his way past the retiring room, past the library and the sitting room to another door, partially shut, its gold handle gleaming dully in the candlelight of the hallway. He had no idea what sort of chamber it was or what was inside, but he needed a minute. He needed a quiet room.

He pushed open the door the rest of the way and let himself in. It was dark—his eyes adjusted slowly to the dim space, lit only by the glowing embers of a banked fire and the starlight out the window.

He half turned back to the door and started to close it, until his movement was arrested by a whispered feminine shriek.

"Wait! Don't!"

He whirled, his shoulder clipping the side of the door and sending it careening into the jamb. "Selina?"

Her face was a pale circle in the dark room, and she leapt toward him. "Did it close?"

He blinked idiotically at her, at the door shut tightly behind him. "Yes?"

She said something that sounded vaguely like a curse, but he honestly didn't quite recognize her words.

"I beg your pardon?"

She groaned, repeated the inexplicable oath, and put her head in her hands. "Peter. This door is broken. We're locked in here."

Chapter 13

. . . Here may they learn to shun the dreadful quicksands of pain and mortification, and land safe on the terra firma *of delight and love . . .*

—*from* HARRIS'S GUIDE TO COVENT
GARDEN LADIES

"We're . . . what?" He couldn't have heard her correctly.

"We're locked in here. That's why I told you to wait. When you close the door to this room, it can only be reopened from the outside. Sometimes it requires a crowbar to sort of prise the—"

Somehow it seemed he had. "Why the devil were you in here in the first place?"

"I?" She stared up at him, amber eyes dark in the half light. "I live here! Why are *you* in here?"

He stalked over to a looming dark shape that he was fairly confident was a settee. Maybe a chaise. Something he could sit on, at least. He dropped himself down. "I needed a minute away from that bleeding circus. And that's saying something, because I'm typically fond of a circus."

Selina made her way back from the door and perched on another low shape across from him. They were closer to the window now, and the starlight silvered her hair. "Well, you'll have a minute. Or ten, or maybe thirty before someone thinks to come look for us in here." She sighed. "I could pound on the door, I suppose. Seems a bit dramatic."

"Maybe," he offered, "I can climb out the—"

Her head snapped up and her fierce gaze caught him. "Peter, I swear to you, if you say that you will climb out the window, I will never speak to you again."

He stopped talking and considered her expression. He wasn't quite sure if she meant it. "I just meant that I could—"

She fixed him with a terrifying glare. "Do not say climb. That window opens to the street, and truly, if there is an engraving of you in the papers climbing out the window of the Duke of Rowland's house, I will buy Lucinda a dozen rapiers and let her loose on the streets of London."

He felt his lips twitch. God, he liked her much too much.

"Listen," he found himself saying. "I wanted to apologize. I should've—I've been wanting to apologize."

She stiffened. "I'd really rather that you did not."

For God's sake. Now he was an ass if he didn't apologize and an ass if he *did*, because she'd asked him not to.

"All right. I won't apologize. But I need to tell you that I can't follow your advice. I know you're not wrong. This evening made it even clearer to me than it already was. But I can't do it, Selina. And I know you don't want me to say it, but I *am* sorry about that."

Her dark brows drew together. "You're sorry that you can't follow my advice?"

He gave a little shrug and didn't speak.

"About marriage, you mean? You're sorry that you can't propose to someone else?"

Her voice had shifted slightly. It had been guarded before, tense like the set of her shoulders. And suddenly it was vibrating with . . . something.

He looked back up and found her intoxicating eyes.

"That's right," he said.

"Why?"

"Because you told me to." His mouth was talking away, talking, talking, and his senses had fixed on the one bright point in the dark room that was Selina. "You told me it was a good idea, and you're right. Eldon would've loved it. I'd be halfway to the guardianship by now. You're clever, and right, and I'm sorry I can't stick to the plan."

"I didn't mean why are you sorry," she said when he wound down. "I meant—why can't you marry someone else?"

Christ. He rose to his feet and took a step toward her. Another. When he spoke, his voice was thick and deep, almost hoarse. "You know why."

Her lips had parted. They looked like the heart of a fig, soft and ripe and impossibly sweet. He wanted to taste her. He couldn't keep breathing and not taste her again.

He reached out and took her shoulders almost roughly, tugging her up to her feet. She stood tall and slim and lovely before him, her skin not ivory now but something else in the silvery light, something shimmering and unreal.

She looked down between them at her own hands, her fingers twisted together in a gesture he'd seen her make before. And then, quickly, as though she couldn't give herself too much time to think, she uncurled her fingers and peeled off her white satin gloves.

He watched the fabric slide over her skin and felt his mouth go dry.

When her fingers were bare, she reached up and put her hands on his shoulders. Then, cautiously, slid one hand across the tight wool of his coat and brought it to the line of his jaw.

"Again," she said. "Once wasn't enough."

Everything in the world went still. *Again. Yes. Again.*

He gave a muffled groan and dragged her hard to his body, angling his head down and claiming her mouth.

She tasted like raspberry syrup, and thank God his gloves were still tucked in his jacket because he needed the feel of her bare skin on his hands like he needed the lungs in his chest. More.

He ran his fingers up her bare arms, touched her shoulder, the line of her collarbone. He gave in to the temptation to slide his tongue along the seam of her lips, and when her mouth parted under his, he couldn't control the way his hand tightened on the back of her neck.

When she took his lower lip between her teeth, he groaned again.

Mother of God, she was so deliciously herself, even in this. Fearless and bold and electric with life. He ran a hand down her back, traced the line of her spine, and moved his mouth to her neck, licking, tasting her delicate skin.

She tipped back her head, wordless, and arched her body into his.

Her breasts met his chest. His hand curled around the generous weight of her bum and his cock leapt against her belly. God. He'd spent the last five days trying to forget the feel of her. He had tried to tell himself he'd imagined the perfect backside on this impossible woman.

He hadn't imagined. And he hadn't forgotten.

Two hands. He needed two hands to fully appreciate it. He slipped his other hand out of her hair and brought it to the curve of her buttocks, lifting her against him as he did.

His hips jerked at the contact, and she moaned breathlessly, rolling her pelvis against his. Her fingers locked around his neck.

God. It wasn't enough. It still wasn't enough. He lifted his head, trying to find a wall he could press her against, but his eyes caught on her breasts, straining against the tight fabric of her bodice, and he gave up and bent his head to the line where satin met skin.

He licked. She whimpered, her hips dragging against his own, and he did it again.

Somehow, despite her skirts, she had one of her legs wrapped around him. Had he done it? Had she? He didn't care. He pulled a hand under her leg, lifting it higher and cursing her skirts, cursing anything that separated his skin from hers, his aching cock from her heat. He had to feel her. He had to taste her.

There was a loud scrape of wood against wood. His mind registered the sound and couldn't make sense of it—his world was all Selina and heat and starlight.

In his arms, Selina stiffened and tried to leap away, but he, like an idiot, tightened his grip. She stumbled back and her skirts caught around his legs, and he was so damned dazed, his brain still trying to work out where they were and what in hell was happening, that when she started to fall, he fell with her.

He turned as they fell, pulling her on top of him, taking their combined weight on his hip and elbow.

Which was why, when Lady Eldon peered into the room, her

bottom lip caught between her teeth and her gaze slightly puzzled, he was on the floor, Selina half on top of him, her buttocks still carefully cupped in both his hands.

Peter froze. Atop him, Selina seemed to do likewise. Her fingers still clutched the lapels of his coat, and as he watched, her gaze flicked between his face and Lady Eldon's.

Selina looked almost panicked, and he fought the mad impulse to cradle her against his chest.

Lady Eldon was still standing stock-still, as stunned as the rest of them, when a voice intruded.

"Bessie? Have you gotten turned 'round? That's not Rowland's library."

Eldon. That stern, hearty voice was certainly Eldon.

Lady Eldon turned and tried to block the doorframe with her diminutive frame. "Oh! No, my dear. Nothing—nothing—"

And then Eldon was in the room too, and Lady Judith, and Nicholas Ravenscroft, and Selina was trying frantically to scramble off his lap, but her hair was mussed and one of her slippers had fallen off, and he was pretty sure he'd heard something tear when they'd fallen.

He registered it all in the time it took him to stand and steady Selina on her feet.

Eldon's glower. Lady Judith's unreadable calm. Nicholas—Selina's *brother*, damn it all, what had they *done*—appeared absolutely incensed.

But when he looked back at Selina's face, it had gone calm and smooth, almost impassive. There was no trace of panic in her voice when she spoke.

"Lady Eldon," she said, placing her hand on Peter's forearm. "Let me be the first to present to you my future husband, the Duke of Stanhope."

Chapter 14

. . . If then women are not a swarm of ephemeron triflers, why should they be kept in ignorance under the specious name of innocence?

—*from Selina's private copy of* A VINDICATION OF THE RIGHTS OF WOMAN, *annotated in her hand:*

"Why indeed!"

Selina was not entirely certain if she had lost her mind.

Here was Lady Eldon, her eyes dancing, congratulating them on their betrothal. Their *betrothal. Their* betrothal.

Here was Nicholas, furious but ever-polite, taking Peter's hand in what looked to be a vise grip and murmuring, "We will discuss this tonight, Selina."

Aunt Judith and Thomasin and Daphne and Lord Eldon, saying all sorts of things she couldn't quite make out.

And Peter. The only thing she was certain of was Peter's warm solid form beside her, his hand unmoving from the small of her back.

The dinner party broke up rather quickly. Lord and Lady Eldon took their leave, Lady Eldon dimpling at all of them and taking her husband's arm in hers as they made their way to their carriage.

Then it was just Peter and an array of her family members, whose expressions ranged from amazed delight—Thomasin, naturally—to cool censure—Aunt Judith—to barely banked fury.

That last was Nicholas.

"Stanhope," he said icily. "Let me speak to you in my study."

Somehow this cracked Selina's dazed stupor. "I should think not," she managed to say. "Do you truly believe I would allow two men to discuss my future as though I have no say in it?"

"Selina." Nicholas caught her in his stern hazel gaze, and he yanked at his cravat in frustration. "I am not sure how much say you have, at this point."

She tossed back her hair. "I have every bit as much say as the two of you, and—no, blast it—"

"Selina," said Aunt Judith censoriously.

"*Damn* it, I have *more* of a say in what happens to me than my brother!"

"Selina!"

"Enough," said Daphne, and her crisp tone was enough to silence the rest of them. "Enough. Did the two of you truly come to an agreement?"

Selina's heart thudded against her ribs, and she turned toward Peter.

He had looked terrified, there in the darkened music room, with her body crushed to his and Lady Eldon standing stunned in the doorway.

He had been afraid. He must have thought that this was the end of his guardianship petition. To be caught by Lord Eldon in the process of compromising the Duke of Rowland's sister—in Rowland's own house! It would have been one scandal too far, one final disaster.

And she could not let that happen to him.

So she had said the only thing that came to her mind.

What was the solution to a scandal?

Marriage, Lydia had told her. Marriage is the solution to a scandal.

And now, here in the drawing room, with her family clustered around her, she did not know if she had done right. She looked up into Peter's eyes.

He looked at her the way he always did. Warm, and sure, and so intent upon her that the rest of the world could have faded away, and she thought he might not notice.

"Do you still want to marry?" she whispered.

"Yes," he said. "Regardless of all the rest of this. And there's nothing I wouldn't do to keep you safe."

It was like a fantasy and a nightmare come to life. She wanted him. She wanted him, and she was afraid she would hurt him, and she had to go forward with this betrothal, because Eldon had seen them together and Eldon controlled the children's guardianship.

And she wanted to go forward with it. Almost as much as she wanted not to ruin his life.

"Yes," she said dazedly to Peter. And then, more firmly, to Daphne, "Yes. We came to an agreement. We're betrothed. We can be married right away, by special license." She turned back to Peter. "That is, if that's all right with you."

"Yes," he said, and his fingers pressed harder into her back, so steady and safe that she wanted to cry. "Yes. The sooner the better."

"I would still like to speak to you, Stanhope," her brother said. "Very much. I have a great deal that I would like to say."

"Of course," said Peter. But he made no move to pull away from Selina.

"Alone!" Nicholas's voice was practically a roar.

Everyone jumped into motion. Thomasin started to usher Selina away, and Peter angled his body in the direction of Nicholas's office. Before she could think the better of it, Selina tugged out of Thomasin's grasp and grabbed Peter's arm. She pulled his head down toward hers and whispered in his ear, softly enough that she was certain no one else heard. "I have to speak with you. I'll come to your residence. Tonight."

•   •   •

It was good, she supposed, that she had two years of secretly running Belvoir's to her name, because Selina knew perfectly well how to sneak out of Rowland House and make her way to the Stanhope residence without getting caught.

Her maid, Emmie, had quirked a brow when she'd come to help Selina prepare for bed and found her instead dressed for an evening of stealth. She still had the heavy charcoal serge gown that covered her from chin to toe, and though it was warm, she'd tugged on a dark and slightly threadbare cloak that she usually kept hidden at the bottom of her wardrobe.

"An extra week's pay," she said to Emmie, her voice determinedly cheerful. "And a pithivier for you and Olive to split when I can make my way to Comfrey's tomorrow."

Emmie plunked herself into a brocade chair that matched Selina's coverlet and slipped off her sturdy slippers. "This one's on me."

Selina blinked. Emmie was a very, very good maid—practical, sensible, and absolutely delighted to receive a bit of extra money to pretend she was unaware of Selina's nighttime absences when necessary. "Whatever do you mean?"

Emmie smirked. "Don't think we haven't all heard the news, m'lady. I thought you and the duke might need the evening to"—she coughed—"finish your conversation." Her blue eyes were perfectly guileless. "Take your time."

Selina groaned but didn't deny it. Although the conversation she meant to have with Stanhope was probably far less carnal than the conversation Emmie was imagining.

Certainly less carnal. Entirely carn-free, and consisting mostly of an attempt to explain her wildly scrambled life.

"But actually," said Emmie, as Selina made her way toward the door, "I'll take you up on the pithivier." Her lips curled. "You know how much my little sister likes those pastries from Comfrey's."

Selina snorted. She had her suspicions about how much pastry was consumed by four-year-old Olive.

And then it was down the back stairs into the mews, and a few coins for her favorite groom to procure her a hired hack, and then she was in the carriage on her way to Peter's house.

It was less than a mile away, so she didn't have much time for fretting.

The Stanhope residence was a peculiar-looking building—tall and narrow, its white-plastered front gleaming even in the near-darkness of the cloudy night. She had the hired carriage drop her off at the end of the block, and she made her way quickly to the servants' back entrance.

The door came open at her knock, and a tall and very slender manservant peered out at her. "Yes?"

She tossed back her hood. "I am Lady Selina Ravenscroft."

The young man—he couldn't have been more than twenty, though his hair was visibly thinning—stared at her with a kind of bemused horror. "Yes?"

"Er," she said. "Yes." That hadn't been quite the reception she was anticipating. "I believe His Grace is expecting me."

The man's eyebrows sailed toward his hairline. "I don't think so."

Oh for goodness' sake. She had told Peter she was coming, had she not? Had he expected her to use the front door, where she could be seen by all and sundry?

Though, she thought, with a tinge of hysteria, it wasn't as though she could be *more* ruined. Perhaps he had.

"Never mind," she said. "I assure you, he's expecting me. Can you take me to wherever he spends his evenings?"

"His . . . bedchamber?"

The boggled look on the young man's face was slightly gratifying. At least it didn't seem likely that her future husband often received nighttime visitors in his bedchamber.

Her future husband.

Dear Lord.

"What's your name?" she asked.

"Humphrey, my . . . lady?"

"Humphrey," she said. "All right. As untoward as this seems, I am probably going to be living here soon. I have a very nice maid named Emmie with a lifetime supply of French pastry, and if you help me locate His Grace right now, I will make sure that she shares with you."

Selina Ravenscroft, pastry fairy, did the trick. Humphrey opened the door the rest of the way and led her through a series of narrow and puzzlingly dark rooms.

Where was the rest of the staff? Were they all abed?

But she shook off the thought, because Humphrey led her up two flights of stairs and then—she winced—started shouting, "Your Grace! You have a caller! Your Grace?"

Peter materialized in the hallway.

He was still dressed as he'd been at their house for dinner, but his cravat was untied and dangling around his neck. His dark curls were wild, as though he'd scrubbed his hands through them a time or ten.

He looked baffled and a little vulnerable, and the way his cravat framed his bare throat made her want to put her mouth just there and lick him.

Oh God, she was going to hell, wasn't she? She was here to explain why marrying her would ruin his life and tell him he ought to reconsider.

She was *not* here to lick him.

"Selina," he said, coming close enough to grab her hands in his. She felt a shock of warmth in her body as his bare fingers met hers. "Why—how did you get up—" He paused and turned to his manservant. "Thank you, Humphrey. That's all for tonight."

Humphrey looked extremely relieved to be dismissed. He fairly sprinted back down the hallway as Peter ushered Selina into a firelit chamber. It was dim, but the whole house had been rather dark, and her eyes were adjusted well enough to make out a sparsely furnished room. A desk, a few stacks of books upon it, and several more stacks on the floor. Two chairs pulled together in front of the fire.

"Peter," she said, and then promptly ran out of courage. "Maybe we should . . . sit. We should sit."

"Yes," he said. "All right."

Her backside had barely met the chair when Peter started talking again. "I'm sorry," he burst out. "God, Selina, I'm so— I'm so sorry. I know you didn't want this. I just couldn't"—he hesitated for the briefest of moments and then forged on—"I couldn't think of anything else to do except to go along with it."

He reached out and took her hands in his again. "Tell me what I can do to make it right."

It was so altogether unexpected that Selina stared. "You're . . . sorry?"

"I'm sorry," he said again. "I didn't mean for any of this to happen, I swear it. I know you didn't want to marry me."

"Peter." His hands were warm and steady as they held hers. His fingers were long, his skin callused but not rough. She stared at his hands for a moment longer and then willed herself to look up and meet his gaze.

His eyes were dark in the flame-lit room and intent on her face.

Courage, she told herself. *You are the woman who runs the most popular circulating library in England. Act like it.*

"Peter," she said again. "It's not that I don't want to marry you. I turned you down because—because—"

She could not say it. She was afraid to say it.

"It wasn't because I don't want you," she whispered. "I do."

His eyes flared with heat, with hope, so she rushed on.

"But there is something you must know before we marry. Something about me that will likely make you reconsider this union. You needn't feel obliged to wed me after you hear this, Peter. You didn't know."

"Selina, for God's sake, you must know that I don't feel obliged—"

She gathered her nerve and cut him off. "Let me tell you something that very few people know."

He went quiet, but his hands stayed on hers.

"Do you know the circulating library Belvoir's?"

He nodded, his expression baffled.

"My brother Will owns it. And I"—God, it was so hard, so

hard to make herself say the words—"I run it. Two and a half years ago, before Katherine died, I asked Will to buy it for me, and he did. I meet with my publisher, Jean Laventille, monthly, in secret. I have two men of business who carry out the daily operations. I oversee the library maintenance, the price of our subscription, our membership rolls, all ordering and binding, and—of course—the catalog selection. I have made Will a great deal of money, and we keep most of it in a bank account that neither of us touches. I am a female aristocrat, the sister of a duke, and yet I engage in trade."

Peter, God help him, appeared absolutely delighted.

"Good Lord," he said. "I knew you were infernally clever, but I had no idea—*no* idea—Selina, I see Belvoir's books *everywhere*. Those green covers—my God, *you* came up with that?" He grinned at her. "I don't think I could be more impressed."

Despite herself, her foolish heart leapt in astonished pleasure. Leapt, and then plummeted right off a cliff instead of landing, because he'd barely heard the half of it.

"There's more," she said. "Quite a bit more. It gets worse."

"All right," he said, still smiling. "Tell me."

"You may not have realized it, but you have probably seen Belvoir's books more often with women than men. That is because of something called the Venus catalog, which is accessible only to women. I had Will buy Belvoir's for one very specific purpose."

She paused, long enough for Peter to prompt, "And that purpose was . . . ?"

"Sexual relations."

Well, that had certainly taken him by surprise.

She kept talking. "A number of years ago, I learned that my father had kept a long-term mistress. I scarcely knew what a mistress was. In the year I made my bow, I discovered that Vernon Whaley, the Marquess of Queensbury, whom I considered a most excellent catch, was known for having relations with his servants and then putting them out on the street.

"I didn't understand it. I couldn't. I was entirely sheltered from the realities of life in the *beau monde*. And I wasn't alone."

Her voice was trembling now. "At the end of that year, my dear friend Ivy came to see me at Rowland House. She was terrified, weeping her heart out. She was pregnant, you see. And she did not understand how it had occurred. That was how little she knew about intercourse, Peter. She did not understand what physical mechanism had gotten her with child. She did not know how to prevent it. And she had no idea what to do when the bastard of a man who impregnated her refused to stand by her."

She knew the expression on her face had to be a little frightening—a half-wild smile, a smile of rage and ferocity. "Her parents threw her out, but she's tough, my Ivy. We set her up in a little house near our estate in Gloucestershire, and she lives there with her son. And now Belvoir's pays for it all. But I swore that year that whatever it took, I wouldn't let another naive woman suffer that way—not if I could help it.

"So I had Will buy Belvoir's, and I developed a selection of books that can only be checked out by women. Memoirs by courtesans. Erotic poetry. Gothic novels. Each month, I read perhaps a dozen such books and choose the most useful for the Venus catalog."

She tried to relax her fingers on his, because her knuckles were nearly white. "It's very popular. Most of the women of the *ton* are members. And absolutely no one knows that it's mine."

There was a long moment of quiet, and she stared at their linked fingers, trying to think of how she could make him understand what had been going on in her mind that year. The fury that had animated her and her single-minded determination to fix what was wrong, no matter the cost.

"Selina," he said gently.

She looked up. The expression of delight on his face was gone, replaced by a softer expression.

Pride, she thought it was.

"That's spectacular," he said. "*You* are spectacular. You are a bright, brilliant light on this benighted country."

"Oh," she said. And then, "Oh no." He meant it, she realized. He was proud of what she'd accomplished. But he didn't grasp the potential consequences. Perhaps, having been raised outside the insular world they inhabited now, he couldn't.

"Peter, you have to understand. Eventually someone is going to figure it out. It's not at all difficult to uncover the fact that Will owns Belvoir's, and he's been out of the country for over two years now. As our circulation has grown, so too has curiosity about the library. One hard look at the catalog, and what I've done will be in the papers."

"And, Selina, what you've done is extraordinary."

Oh God, she wanted to shake him. "Peter, I cannot tell you how much it means to me to hear you say that. But you must think of your own position. You need a wife who makes you *less* scandalous, not more. This would destroy your guardianship petition if the truth were to come out before the hearing. And if it comes out after, your political career would be in shambles. Your reputation will be destroyed. And, Peter—I could go to prison for this. John Cleland did, after he wrote *Fanny Hill*." She winced. "Do you *know* how many copies we have of *Fanny Hill*?"

"Selina," he said. "You will be a duchess. I don't even think they *can* throw you in jail. And if they did, I would tear the thing down brick by brick if necessary to get you out."

Her eyes burned. "What about the children? If I raise them—

and then my reputation is destroyed—Lu could never be brought out in society—"

He laughed. "You've met Lu. Do you think she *wants* to be brought out in society?"

"You're not thinking this through," she said, and one wayward tear slipped free and ran down her cheek. Another. "I don't want to ruin your life, Peter."

"Selina," he said, and then he tugged on her hands, pulled a little harder until she half tumbled out of her chair and into his lap. "Sweet. My reputation is already in shambles. If you are discovered—"

"When," she corrected into his coat.

"Fine, *when* you are discovered, we'll simply be a matched set. England's most scandalous duke and duchess. We'll thumb our noses at the *ton* and get invited to everything anyway. And if we discover that we can't stand it, we'll move back to Louisiana."

"But your—your political goals—"

"Can be accomplished just as well in America. Perhaps better, in some ways. Come to think of it, sweet, *shall* we move to New Orleans? In my experience, there's a real dearth of erotic books for ladies there."

It was so Peter—so ridiculous and easy and so bloody perfect—that she buried her face in his chest and wept.

Part of her wanted to choke back the tears that stung her eyes and clogged her throat. The same part of her that wanted to say, *I'm sorry—I don't know what's come over me—I never cry.*

But she knew precisely why she was crying. It had been two and a half years now with no one to talk to about Belvoir's—no one who knew except Jean Laventille and Will, who was gone. She hadn't told Nicholas or Thomasin or Lydia, all the people she trusted most in the world to love her no matter what errors in judgment she'd made.

Now she'd told Peter, forcing back any part of her that had hoped he might see Belvoir's the same way she saw it: as something with value. Something that was worth the cost.

But he *had*. He'd taken in her words and looked at her with that single-minded focus and seen . . .

Something worth it.

She let herself cry for at least sixty long seconds before she pulled back from his now-damp chest and wiped at her eyes.

"Well," he said, "I had a feeling this night would end with weeping."

She choked out a laugh. "Did you?"

"Oh yes. Just wasn't sure which of us it would be."

"Peter."

"Yes?"

She lifted a hand and stroked back one of his dark curls. Just because she could. "Are you absolutely certain?"

He lifted a hand to cover hers, cradling it against his cheek. "Yes." He turned his face into her hand and kissed her palm. Just once. "I'm absolutely certain." Twice. "Are you? Because if you don't want to do this, we can find another way out."

His gaze was on her—that encompassing gaze, that saw all of her and shut out the rest of the world.

She looked down at her lap, the soft press of his hand on hers suddenly all she could think about.

She wanted him. She wanted him so much she wasn't sure if she was thinking clearly. Would she ruin him, if she said yes? If she gave in to his easy assurance, would that make her unforgivably selfish?

But—Eldon had seen them together. There was no simple way out.

"I am certain," she said, her voice barely audible.

She wasn't. She wasn't certain at all. She felt terrified that by accepting, she would lead Peter headlong into disaster.

He pressed another kiss to her palm and she squeezed her eyes closed, fighting the urge to weep again.

If she did this—if she took what she wanted—she could not let her secret get out. She would not permit the guardianship hearing to be anything but a success. This was what she did—she organized, she planned, she managed circumstances. She would use every trick at her disposal to ensure the children's position as Peter's wards, and in the end, she would make him *happy*. She would not let him down, she vowed, not on her life.

When the burning sensation in her eyes receded, she lifted her gaze to Peter's again. He had a half smile on his lips and a strange hint of vulnerability there too, lurking in the curve of his mouth.

He brought his hand to her chin and then stroked his thumb across the curve of her lower lip.

Her mouth trembled open. "Peter," she said. "I—"

He kissed her. It was a slow, searching sort of kiss. His mouth was gentle. His big hand still stretched warmly over hers, and his fingers moved, whisper-soft, to trace the lines between hers.

She heard herself gasp against his mouth.

He pulled back. "Yes?"

She stared at him. "Yes?"

"You were starting to say . . . ?"

"I don't remember."

A grin curled across his lips, more smug than she'd ever seen. "Good."

And then he kissed her again.

Talking, it seemed, was at an end. Selina took a moment to consider and decided she approved entirely.

His mouth on hers was almost cautious, and when her tongue tentatively touched his, he gave a soft groan of pleasure. The sound of his desire undid her completely, and she stroked his hair, his jaw, his neck, trying to chase more of his response.

When she slipped her hand beneath the line of his jacket and traced the hard muscles of his abdomen through his thin linen shirt, he made an inarticulate sound. His hands fastened on her rib cage, his thumbs stroking the undersides of her breasts.

Without her conscious volition, her head fell back, her back arching. Sweet heavens, if his touch felt that splendid through her gown, just imagine if she was . . .

Peter seemed to be having much the same thought. His fingers moved to the side hooks in her gown, unfastening one after another until her gown sagged open at the seam. Beneath her gown, she wore only a chemise—she didn't bother with stays with this dress, as she couldn't lace them herself.

One of Peter's hands eased the heavy serge fabric off her shoulder, and it fell to her waist. The other hand had already claimed her breast, shaping and kneading the small globe through the thin cotton of her chemise. His fingertips traced her areola, then slipped softly across one tight, aching nipple.

"Ah," she gasped. Her hands were still on his abdomen, and she felt her nails tighten on him. "Peter, I—oh *God*."

He kissed her, hard and deep and urgent, his tongue thrusting into her mouth with a need that echoed in her breasts, her belly, her fingertips. She whimpered and shifted in his lap, trying to pull closer to him.

Somehow he'd disentangled her other arm from her gown,

and now both of his hands were filled with her breasts, both of her nipples taut under the gentle, relentless torment of his fingers.

Her skin felt tight and hot. She needed him to touch her. She needed—God, something, she needed something or she would go mad. She pressed her thighs together and writhed on his lap.

He groaned again. "You—that's—God, I have to—"

His pelvis rocked, and she recognized suddenly the hard line of his arousal pressing into the soft flesh of her hip. Oh. *Oh.*

One of his hands abandoned her breast, and she whimpered in disappointment. No, he couldn't stop, he'd barely touched her, only stroked and teased and tormented.

Then she felt his hand beneath her skirt, warm through her thin silk stockings, and then his mouth came down to her breasts.

Where his fingers had grazed, his mouth was firmer, hotter, more urgent. He laved her nipple through the fabric, then spread the wet cotton tight with his fingers. "So lovely," he said roughly. "So beautiful, sweetheart." Then his mouth came back, hot and wet, and he sucked hard at her nipple, making her gasp and then moan.

She felt—she hardly knew what she felt.

Wild. Drunk. Barely in control of her body as she gripped the back of his head, holding him tight. She didn't know what to do, but she knew what her body wanted. Pressure. Friction. More.

She rolled her hips, searching for the hard pressure of his arousal. Then she felt his hand move past her knee, past the garter that held her stocking, and on to the bare flesh of her upper thigh.

His fingers. Skin. Yes.

"Selina," he scraped out. "Can I touch you?"

"Yes," she gasped. "Please."

He growled appreciatively, his hips jerking against her, his hand sliding farther toward the part of her that was slippery and aching. She felt her leg fall open, inviting his touch at her core.

His fingers were featherlight at first, and she took a little sobbing breath. He stroked her gently, so gently, tracing her folds, circling the bundle of nerves at the apex. Her body felt like a bow-string about to snap as he circled, retreated, circled again.

"Peter," she said desperately. "Peter, I need—"

"Hush," he murmured into her ear. His tongue traced its curves. His fingers teased her sex. "I've got you, sweet. Easy."

She writhed, pressing herself into his hand. "I don't want *easy*, Peter. I want *harder*."

He huffed a laugh that turned into a moan. "God," he said, and slipped a finger inside her. "You make me—you are—Christ, you're so wet. I want to be inside you."

His finger teased her, stretched her, and then he added another finger, curling deep inside her, his palm firm against her mound.

She gasped at the intensity of the pleasure and rolled her hips frantically against his hand.

"Yes," he said. "God, Selina, you're lovely. Perfect. Don't stop. I have to—"

Then his mouth found her nipple again and suckled, fast and firm, and she felt her body coil tighter and tighter, pleasure chasing the throbbing tension as she rode Peter's hand.

When she climaxed, an earthquake of pleasure rolled through her, shock after shock of sweet, impossible, life-altering bliss.

And while she shook apart, he whispered little words of praise and tenderness, and when her body stopped shaking, she felt the trembling go on for a long time somewhere deep in her chest.

She came back to herself in fragments. She felt Peter's lips at her temple, his breath rushing through her hair. She felt his arm locked around her waist, keeping her in his lap.

She felt the rock-hard insistence of his erection pressed into her hip, defying all vegetal comparison.

Her heartbeat was slowing now, but she could still feel Peter's, thudding sharp and strong against her back. His muscles were tight, even as his murmured approbations were soft and easy.

Oh dear Lord. She had . . . And he hadn't . . .

What was she supposed to *do*? How was she meant to approach it? She had seen references to licking. Stroking. Larking, whatever that meant. But how did she *do* it?

And now that he knew about Belvoir's, would he expect her to be good at it?

Belvoir's. Thank God, she had Belvoir's, and at least seven key volumes from the Venus catalog secreted in her bedroom, plus another several dozen in her office at the library.

She needed books. She needed detailed descriptions, and full-page illustrations, and possibly a series of diagrams, if such a thing existed.

She leapt to her feet, nearly stumbling as her bodice slithered down to her hips and then caught there, too tight to slip past her bottom half.

Which, she wondered wildly, would be more humiliating: Her dress falling to the floor? Or the blasted thing ripping as she tried to peel it from where it currently clung to her hips?

She yanked her bodice back up, heedless of potential tearing, and started fastening its hooks.

"Well," she said. "That was . . ." Oh for God's sake, how did she finish that sentence? *Nice* sounded like an insult to his abilities, but anything more fervent might remind him of the fact that he hadn't . . . he hadn't . . .

She didn't even know the word that ladies used for it. *Was* there a word that ladies used for it?

She gave up on her sentence. Peter was staring at her as though she'd grown a second head somewhere between his lap and the middle of the darkened room she had backed into. She struggled into her cloak, which had puddled on the floor at some point earlier in their conversation. "I should go," she said. "Back to Rowland House."

He squeezed his eyes shut and then opened them again. "Right," he said. "Right. I'll have Humphrey ready a carriage for us."

She let out a little squeak of protest. "Peter! I can't be seen getting out of your carriage in the middle of the night!"

He bounded to his feet and approached her, took the tapes of her cloak in his hands and tied it for her. Then he pulled the hood up over her head, hiding her hair and shadowing her face, and grinned at her. "You won't be."

Chapter 15

Not the pink. Definitely not the pink. The scarlet, I think. The one that looks like blood. (Before you ask—yes, this is for the duke's twelve-year-old sister. And no, he will not mind.)

—from Lady Selina Ravenscroft to Mrs. Maria Pierpoint, modiste, in response to fabric samples sent to Rowland house for her perusal in preparation for her wedding

Two days later, Selina stood on a small platform in a back room at her favorite dressmaker's shop, wearing nothing but her undergarments and a feather on her head.

"No," said Lydia decisively. She reached up to pluck at the feather, but between the platform and Selina's six inches of height on her, her fingers caught nothing but air. "Not that one. Bend down. I should've had my mother come with us. You know she's brilliant with millinery."

"I agree," said Daphne. "Not that one. She looks like a peacock."

Selina's sister-in-law sat on an upholstered armchair in the corner, smiling so smugly that Selina was put in mind of a house cat with a feather dangling from its mouth.

Everyone, in fact, looked a trifle smug. Thomasin appeared delighted as she sorted through lace night rails and embroidered chemises more lurid than anything even Selina's jaded eye had before encountered. Aunt Judith wore a distracted half smile as she busied herself with the dress that had just been removed from Selina's person by the dressmaker. Even Mrs. Pierpoint, the modiste, had looked rather pleased with herself. From the hasty conversation Selina had overheard at her first fitting the day before, she understood that her wedding dress was to be made in one-tenth the time such a dress would typically require and cost thirty times as much.

Lydia, for her part, was grinning while she examined the options they'd acquired at the milliner for atop Selina's head. A feather. A little cap made of fur. A bandeau of pale-blue forget-me-nots.

For Selina to wear at her *wedding*. Good Lord.

Selina was not quite sure how any of this had transpired, and if she focused very hard on all the details—on what slippers would adorn her feet and what they would serve for the wedding breakfast and who would collect the children—she could almost distract herself from the anxiety that swamped her at the thought of the potential consequences of this union.

"How about this?" Lydia held up a cake-like confection made of white satin roses and lace. "I think it's a bonnet. I know you favor these enormous hats. Bend down."

"Absolutely not."

Lydia's eyes crinkled with amusement. "You mean you *don't* favor enormous hats? You could've fooled me. My goodness, Selina, so many secrets—first a covert *tendre* for my former suitor and now an unrevealed preference for small headpieces—"

Daphne coughed a smothered laugh into her glove.

"I don't—"

Oh God, what could she say? She certainly could not deny having harbored all sorts of illicit feelings for Peter Kent while shoving him in the direction of her closest friend. Not now, when she'd been caught with her shoe off and her arse in his hands in her brother's music room.

Not now, when they were about to be *married*.

"I'm—" she tried again. "I'm so—"

Lydia laughed then, a real laugh, and dropped the cake hat on the ground to pull Selina down into an embrace. "I'm teasing! Don't fret."

"You don't—mind?"

"Of course not, you ninny. I never wanted him. He talks *far* too much. My, you are absolutely crimson about the face!" Lydia pulled back and turned gleefully toward Selina's relatives. "Crimson! Have you ever seen it?"

"Vermilion," offered Daphne cheerfully. "She is the color of beetroot."

"She is the color of *guilt*." This last was Aunt Judith, but Selina could hear the thread of amusement that laced her voice.

Thomasin set down her pile of shocking nightwear and tugged Selina down from the platform, lacing one arm about Selina's waist. "My darling, ignore these three for a moment. What I want to know is—are you happy?"

Selina opened her mouth to reply, but no words emerged.

Was she happy? She had scarcely allowed herself to be. She thought perhaps she was: happy and afraid of that happiness. Afraid of how easily she could lose it all.

Thomasin looked up at her, blue-eyed and dimpled. "You need not go through with it, darling girl, unless you want to. Unless this marriage—this *man*—is the one you want. We will be beside you either way."

Selina's eyes burned, tears threatening to spill over. "Thank you," she managed, her voice catching in her throat. "This is what I want, Thomasin. It truly is."

"Then all will be well," Thomasin said. "I promise."

From beside them, Lydia put in, "Don't act as though you are surprised, Thomasin. I know you saw through her as long ago as I did. The sheer *passion* Selina displayed for Stanhope's bridal prospects was not particularly subtle."

Selina blinked.

Before she could reply, Daphne added in her soft voice, "Surely I cannot have been the only one to notice the way she ogled Stanhope's hands over dinner."

"I—"

Oh, she *had*. It was true. The man had beautiful hands, curse him.

"Personally," offered Aunt Judith, "I rather thought she wanted Stanhope for his buttocks."

Selina's mouth fell open.

Hers was not the only one.

Daphne and Lydia were still recovering themselves when Thomasin plucked a headpiece from the pile and presented it to Selina. "This one, darling. This is the right one, I think."

Selina looked down dizzily at the coronet of pearls and little stars made from delicate brass wire. "Yes," she said. "Yes."

• • •

They were on their way out—Thomasin having bundled *eleven* separate items of nightwear into their purchase of Selina's wedding dress—when they encountered the dowager Marchioness of Queensbury and the Countess of Alverthorpe.

The two women appeared to be on the point of entering the modiste's shop, and so Selina stepped back to let them in.

She tried to hold in a wince at the sight of Lady Alverthorpe, Georgiana's mother. The last time she had spoken to the countess was in the Park, when she had been busily organizing the courtship of the woman's daughter to the man Selina now meant to pledge *herself* to in roughly eighteen hours.

Of course Lady Alverthorpe knew about the impending marriage. Everyone knew.

But Lady Queensbury and Lady Alverthorpe didn't enter after all. They looked into the shop, their gazes sliding over Selina and her family as if they did not see them, and then stepped delicately back into the sunshine of Portman Square without a word.

Selina stared after them, agog.

"Did they—" Her voice cracked, and she started again, furious with herself. "Did they not acknowledge us? Are we to be cut simply because Stanhope has decided to marry in haste?"

She had not anticipated this at all. Surely the precipitate wedding would be seen as *romantic*, would it not? At least to Lord and Lady Eldon?

She did not care, really, for the opinions of a couple of matrons. Only—she did not want anyone to think less of Peter.

But Daphne pinched her lips together, her face paling. "It's not about you and Stanhope, I promise. No doubt Lady Alverthorpe is listening to that miserable husband of hers. It's—" She cut herself off mid-sentence and shook her head. "It's something to do with Nicholas. An idle political rumor. Ignore it and it shall dissipate on its own in time."

"A rumor? About what?"

But Daphne only shook her head and did not answer, directing the conversation rather forcefully to what she had planned for the wedding breakfast at Rowland House on the morrow.

Once they made their way into Portman Square, however, Selina dropped back behind her family and caught Lydia's arm. "Do you know what Daphne meant? A political rumor—about my brother?"

Nicholas was often the subject of debate, what with his progressive politics within the reactionary Lords, but he had never before been the subject of enough scandal that his own family was given the cut indirect in public.

Lydia grimaced. "It's stupidity."

"What? Tell me, Lyddie. I want to know."

Lydia lifted one shoulder in a shrug. "Lord Alverthorpe has never been fond of your brother, not since Nicholas defended the mill workers' riots in Nottingham two years ago. Alverthorpe thought they all ought to be shot."

"Of course he did." Selina refrained from rolling her eyes.

"Alverthorpe is just one of a group of peers who've taken up against your brother in the Lords, only this time it's grown rather personal. It's foolish, Selina—I scarcely believed my ears the first time I heard the latest rumors. Nonsense, all of it."

Selina felt a sudden anxious tilt of the pavement beneath her feet. "Rumors?"

"Indeed. It's recently been put about that your brother secretly owns Belvoir's Library and is using it to distribute seditious political pamphlets."

"*Nicholas?*"

"Absurd, I know."

Selina pressed her fingers hard against her mouth. "Oh," she said. "Oh no."

In all of the times she'd imagined her secret coming to light, she'd never once thought the blame would fall upon Nicholas. If someone discovered that Will owned Belvoir's, then surely suspicion would fall to *her*. She was his twin. She was a woman, had free time in abundance to organize a salacious circulating library for ladies.

But—she was a *woman*. Of course they would not think her capable of such a thing.

Lydia set her fingers atop Selina's arm. "I have no idea what has instigated this bizarre new infamy, but truly, Selina, don't let it worry you. Like all nonsense, it will flare up brightly and then die down just as fast."

Selina tried to compose her face, even as her stomach clenched. *Nicholas.* She had never predicted this turn of events, not once in the last two years.

Will had known all along, had plotted it out with her. He had been part and parcel of the arrangement, as willing and consenting as she to take the damage to his reputation if necessary. But Nicholas—who *loved* his work, who *believed* in his work—who had already made a difference for the lives of British citizens—

He had no part in her scheme. She could not let him suffer for her choices.

But no more could she let Peter and his siblings suffer. She could not reveal herself as the responsible party. Not yet, at least. Not until the guardianship hearing was over.

"Of course it will," she made herself say.

Lydia blinked up at her, a line forming between her brows. "Perhaps I shouldn't have told you. This won't spoil your day tomorrow, will it? Because I mean to compliment you for several straight hours and call you Duchess enough times that your cheeks catch fire."

"I shan't let it spoil anything," Selina said. Her voice sounded strange and far away, and she hoped Lydia would not notice. "As you said, it's only a rumor, and an absurd one at that."

Even as she said it, she felt the cold terror in her belly. It had been almost thawed by Peter's reception of her revelation about Belvoir's, the errands and minutiae she had been swept into with her family these last two days.

But it had not gone away.

Perhaps this rumor would die down. Perhaps nothing would come of it; perhaps no suspicion would be turned in her direction before the hearing. But someday she would have to face the situation head-on. If the rumors about Nicholas turned more poisonous, she would be forced to reveal herself to clear his name.

And in doing so, she would hurt Peter. She thought of the warmth in his eyes as he'd looked down at her in his study, the pride on his face as she'd told him of Belvoir's, and she felt sick with it. Someday he would realize what a terrible position she had put him in. Someday, she thought, he would regret it.

Not yet, she said in her heart, a silent gritted-teeth prayer. *Not yet.*

Chapter 16

. . . I cannot believe I have married without you at my side. Tell me you forgive me.

—from Her Grace Selina Kent, Duchess of Stanhope, to her brother Will

It turned out that together they were something of a force of nature.

Not in the bedchamber. Peter wasn't thinking about the bedchamber. He certainly hadn't been spending at least nine-tenths of his waking hours imagining Selina naked in his bed. Recalling the sounds she'd made when she'd climaxed. Dreaming about the thick need in her voice as she'd asked for *again*, and *please*, and *harder*.

He'd taken matters into his own hand more than once, and yet he was pretty sure he'd had a cockstand for roughly seventy-two hours now. He'd never before thought that his cock might be worthy of a medical case study, but here he was.

So yes, damn it, inside the bedroom they might very well be a force of nature, but outside of it as well. When their two wills were set on the same goal, they seemed capable of making quite a lot of things happen. Which was why, three nights after they'd been caught in flagrante delicto by the Eldons, they were standing at the front door to the Stanhope residence, dressed in some outrageously expensive finery.

And married.

He'd managed the special license. Had secured what Lady Judith informed him was the second-nicest chapel in London and therefore acceptable for a ducal wedding.

Securing St. Margaret's had involved a shocking amount of bribery in the form of a promised installation of a commemorative stained-glass window and a consolation gift of a Continental honeymoon tour for the displaced bride and groom, but Lady Judith didn't ask for details.

Selina had arranged the guest list, and the wedding breakfast, and appropriate attire for not only the two of them, but for Freddie and Lu as well. Lu's resistance to wearing a formal frock had been forestalled by its color—a rather alarming carmine—and an introduction to Selina's former fencing master.

They'd both forgotten to buy rings, and had only realized their oversight when they arrived at the chapel within minutes of each other. Selina had vanished into an alcove at the church's entrance and reappeared a few moments later sans hairpiece and bearing two circlets twisted out of the brass wire that had formerly held a little crown of pearls atop her golden hair.

"Good enough," she said, and Peter felt something shift in his chest.

She was so clever—always fixing things—and he . . .

He had failed at enough things that at some point it had become safer not to try. Better, it somehow seemed, to deliberately flout convention than to try to please some impossible standard, stretching ever farther out of his reach.

Yet somehow now he found himself wanting to try. He wanted to give her better than good enough. He wanted to be more to her than a problem to be solved.

He shook himself and took the little brass circle, vowing to buy her something better—for God's sake, he'd bought two perfect strangers a wedding tour. And then, almost before he knew what had happened, they were married.

They'd breakfasted at Rowland House, and then they'd taken Freddie and Lu back to Great-great-aunt Rosamund's house in Bloomsbury. The children had been disturbingly civilized all morning. Peter felt a trifle concerned for their health.

And now here they were. Back at his house.

Which was now *their* house.

Which meant that his bed was now *their* bed. Which meant—

"Peter," said Selina. "Do you think we should . . . go inside?"

He looked dazedly at her and tried to pretend he hadn't been thinking about licking the curve of her inner thigh.

"Yes," he said. "Listen, Selina, perhaps I should warn you about the house."

Her brows drew together. "I've been in the house."

"Ye-es. It was dark, though."

She looked mildly alarmed. "Go on."

"Well, when I inherited, you know that the duke was in his late nineties."

"Yes, of course."

"And that he'd been living at the estate in Sussex for quite a while."

"So I understand."

"He hadn't been in London for some time."

"Peter, if you do not get on with this story and tell me what is on the other side of this door, I shall push it open and find out for myself."

He winced. "He hadn't been to London in many years. Many, many years. Decades. And he'd rented out the house for quite a while, until the last year or two before his death. So when he died and I took possession, it was a bit, er . . . empty."

She blinked. "Yes, I'd have assumed as much."

"Not of inhabitants. I mean, it was completely empty. I believe the last several families that rented it simply took the furniture with them when they left. The art too, and the curtains. The wall coverings, in some cases."

"I . . . see."

"I've been meaning to furnish it," he said, a little weakly. "But once I hired Humphrey and Fleming—that's the cook—things seemed to crack along all right. I did fix the plaster that was falling down. And of course there's . . . a place to eat. Er, and sleep."

She turned suspicious amber eyes from his face and opened the door with one slender-fingered hand.

"I sent my lady's maid ahead this morning, along with several footmen and most of my garments," she said. "I wonder where she's put them."

They didn't have long to wonder. A small woman in cinnamon-colored muslin stepped around the corner. She seemed to have been waiting to pounce.

"My lady," she said, ignoring Peter altogether. "That is, Your Grace. I am not sure we were . . . you were . . . entirely prepared. I'm not quite certain we've brought enough . . . er, anything."

Peter winced and looked around the house, recalling how it had appeared to him the first time he'd entered after inheriting.

The front hall featured two soaring columns. A rose-print paper covered the walls, but it was faded, with large dark rectangles suggesting the shape of the art that had once hung there. To one side lay the sitting room, looking traitorously free of places to sit. On the other side, an archway framed the dining room, its black-and-white marble tiles seeming to stretch on and on. The impression was rather exaggerated by the fact that Peter and Humphrey had been dining together at a square oaken dining table surrounded by exactly two chairs.

In truth, it looked quite substantially better than it had when he'd moved in. He'd spent some time removing strips of peeling fabric from the walls of the sitting room. And the mice—he and Humphrey had removed all the nests of mice.

He was pretty sure. Mostly all of them.

He had meant to furnish the house before the children came, but to do so before the guardianship hearing had seemed like hubris. It felt impossible to believe they would ever really be a family.

Selina was taking in her surroundings with astounding equanimity. "Peter?"

"Yes?"

"Do we . . . have any staff?"

"We have a full complement of grooms in the mews. There's a cook. And Humphrey."

Her maid let out a loud snort.

Selina arched a brow. "Yes, Emmie?"

"Humphrey," the woman said with a disdainful sniff. "Thinks he runs the house, does he? We'll see how he feels when you've brought in a butler. And a housekeeper. And perhaps a valet."

"Humphrey *is* my valet," protested Peter.

Emmie snorted again.

"He's very handy with an iron," Peter told Selina.

"He told me there is no bedchamber prepared for Her Grace." Emmie sounded appalled. "And no wardrobes for her clothing and no clothes-brush for me to use and no iron and no—"

If she continued to list things that the house didn't possess, Peter feared they might be there all afternoon and well into the evening. "I'm sure that tomorrow we can set up—"

"We'll share," said Selina crisply.

He couldn't have heard her correctly. Surely she would want her own bedchamber. Hell, he was not entirely certain she had wanted to marry in the first place—she had said no, after all, until the Eldons had discovered them together at Rowland House.

Emmie appeared to have the same reaction. "You'll . . . share?"

"Indeed. We will share a bedchamber. Tonight. Every night."

God above, his eyes nearly rolled back in his head at her words. The images they evoked contrasted with the business-like tone of her voice in a way that he found quite painfully arousing.

He was fairly certain that if a drop of water had landed on his skin at that exact moment, it would have sizzled.

"You may select a room near to our bedchamber to be my dressing room," Selina was saying. "Can you begin a list of the furnishings we'll need to acquire tomorrow?"

"Of course."

She turned to Peter then. "Perhaps we should speak to your cook about tea?"

Right. He had to think about something other than dragging her upstairs and sharing their bedchamber that very second. "Tea," he repeated. "Right."

•   •   •

The fires of lust could be extinguished quite quickly, it turned out, with the unexpected application of tears.

They'd dined, and then Selina and her maid had retired to the bedchamber to set about unpacking Selina's garments and making ready for a shopping expedition on the morrow. Peter had offered to help and had been shooed away, so he'd been reduced to wandering the house like a randy ghost, whistling and alternately thinking about furnishings and Selina.

Well, that was a flat-out lie. He'd thought of furnishings at least once, though. He was fairly certain.

He paced his study and then wandered back down to the first floor, where the stairwell obscured the entrance to one of the only rooms in the house left mostly untouched by former tenants. It was a portrait gallery—the wall coverings were a bloodthirsty shade of red, and generations of Stanhope dukes and duchesses and children loomed menacingly out of the shadowed portrait alcoves. He could see why the previous inhabitants had ignored the room. He preferred not to think of it himself, and the grim faces were his immediate relations.

This time when he approached the tucked-away room at the base of the stairs, his ears caught the sound of muffled sobs.

He was in the room before he could think the better of it. He had half a beat to hope—rather uncharitably—that it was Selina's maid crying her heart out and not his wife.

But, blinking against the dark red shadows of the room, he made out Selina's tall form. She was tucked half in one of the alcoves, her head buried in her arms. And she was weeping.

He felt a queer sharp stab in the vicinity of his heart. Twice—twice in three days he'd reduced this fearless, remarkable woman to tears.

He came up behind her, trying to make some sound as he walked so she wouldn't startle.

"Selina?"

She stood and turned, furiously swiping at her face. "Oh! Peter. I'm sorry. I didn't think you'd come in here."

She'd been hiding, then, down here in this dim, uncomfortable room. From him.

He swallowed against that bright sharp thing in his chest. "I heard you. I'm sorry, I—oh, the hell with it."

He reached out and yanked her into his arms. She stood stiffly for a moment and then, by degrees, she relaxed against his body. He tucked her head beneath his chin.

What had he to offer her? He was a duke—but she was the sister of a blasted duke, and marrying him gave her scarcely more social standing than she'd had before.

He had money, but so did she—from her family, from Belvoir's.

He had a big empty house, and a brother and sister he didn't know how to get or how to keep. He had himself, such as he was—selfish and reckless and heedless of all the things he was expected to care about in the *beau monde*.

He thought of her family at their wedding breakfast, their mutual love and respect never more obvious. It was nothing like what he had known back in New Orleans, with his mother and the crumbling old house, with Morgan's painful gasping breath in his ears.

He felt suddenly certain that she had realized what a dreadful bargain she had made with him. He was as emptied-out as the house—nothing more than a crisis that needed to be managed. He had nothing to offer her, and she had realized it, and she was drowning in regret.

"I'm sorry," he said. His voice was rough in his throat. "I know it's not what you wanted, Selina. But it won't be so bad. You'll see."

He scarcely believed himself. A lifetime of fixing her husband's disasters—that must be what coming into this townhouse had taught her to look forward to. Unless she had decided she'd had enough already. Perhaps she wanted to go back to Rowland House.

She pulled her head back to look at him, tilting her chin up to meet his eyes. She stayed in the circle of his arms, soft and yielding. "What on earth can you mean?"

"This house." He shrugged against her body. "Marriage. To me."

She stared up at him. "You thought you'd found me in here weeping over the lack of furnishings?"

"Yes?"

She tried to flail a hand around at the room, but he was still holding her, so she mostly smacked him in the side. "Peter. It's just a house. Just things."

He winced. "It's more than just things. It's what they represent." Perhaps if he made it plain for her, she would go now, before he started to hope for more. A future. A family, together, like the Ravenscrofts. "I know it must seem like you've done nothing but clean up after my errors, Selina, but I mean to put things right. With the house. With Freddie and Lu." *With you,* he thought, but managed not to say.

She turned her head and tucked her face back into his chest, and he inhaled the almost-spicy scent of her body. "I was crying because of the portraits."

He looked around the room. "Should I take them down? They *are* alarming."

"No." She laughed a little damply into his shirt. "No. I was looking at your family, and the truth is"—her voice wobbled, but she didn't weep again—"I miss Will. I never dreamed I would marry without him there, without Faiza and her husband. I was so angry when Will eloped and married Katherine without me. And now I've done the same to him, and I feel I've betrayed him. I feel like my life shouldn't keep going on when his seemed to stop two years ago. And I just wish he were *here*."

Her voice had grown louder and higher with her final words, and she fisted her fingers in the back of Peter's shirt, her face still hidden against his chest.

God, he was an idiot and a selfish bastard besides. He hadn't thought at all about how much she must be missing her twin today.

Perhaps he did have something to offer her, though. He had these two arms, he supposed, and so he wrapped them tighter around her. He had this one body, to give her comfort and pleasure. He pressed a kiss to her honey-colored hair.

"Sweetheart. His life didn't stop. And neither should yours."

"I know," she said. "I do know. And I know that eventually he'll come home. I just miss him today."

If he could have, he would have switched places with her brother at that moment. To make her smile. He kissed her hair again, which was loose about her shoulders. It was so thick he could've spent hours tangling his fingers in all the gleaming strands.

She pulled back suddenly, looking up, and her nose nearly bumped his chin. "Peter?"

"Yes?"

"I'm glad to be here. I *want* to be here."

God, she was so beautiful it hurt. He wanted to touch her, and he was afraid to touch her at the same time. Touching her made him start to imagine a different kind of a marriage, not a patched-up affair in an empty house designed to save them both from scandal.

But he couldn't help himself. He rubbed his thumb across the sweep of her lower lip. "Good."

Her fingers suddenly unknotted from the fabric of his shirt and swept up his back. Without a coat, he could feel the soft warm brush of her hand. Her fingers stroked the back of his neck, and, without meaning to, he pressed his thumb harder against her lip.

He made himself pull his hand back from where he wanted— intently, desperately—to push into the wet heat of her mouth. Instead he nudged her hair back from her face.

"Are *you* glad I'm here?" Her voice was tentative.

God. "Yes," he said, his voice rasping again. "I'm very glad you're here, Selina."

"Good," she said, echoing him. Her tawny eyes, darker in the shadowed room, came to rest on his. Her fingers found the nape of his neck and brushed once, and then again. Softly. Her body was pressed against his, and he could feel the heat of her skin through the layers of fabric that separated them.

"Tell me again," she said. Almost a whisper, her face inches from his. And then, "Show me."

Gladly.

He brought his mouth to the curve of her ear. "I've dreamed of having you here. Anywhere."

She gasped and tilted her head to the side, exposing her neck. He kissed his way from her ear down the long tender line of her throat. He felt her pulse beating, quick and light, at her collarbone, so he kissed her there too. So like her, that pulse—bursting with strength and life. "I could spend an hour right here," he said into her skin. "Tasting just this part of you." He slid his fingers along her collarbone, and she breathed out a moan. "Touching you. You're so soft, did you know that?"

He closed his teeth gently along the delicate ridge. She arched her back, her breasts pressing into his chest.

His mind blurred at the sensation. Warmth and soft sweetness. He wanted—Christ, he wanted to bury himself inside her right there in the alcove. He wanted her arms locked around his neck and her heels digging into him as he drove deep into her body.

Instead he soothed the small bite with his lips, then traced the hollow of her throat with his tongue. He let his fingers play at the line of her bodice, not quite slipping beneath. "You are so lovely. So responsive. I think of nothing except having you."

Her breath came quickly, and her pulse throbbed harder under his mouth. "Peter," she whispered. "Show me. Show me everything."

Chapter 17

. . . Such ardent desires, such ungovernable longings . . .

—*from Selina's private copy of*
FANNY HILL, *underlined*

Her skin was on fire. His fingers trailed flames as they swept, back and forth and back again, along the line of cloth-of-gold that made up the bodice of her wedding dress. Selina breathed in Peter's warm, clean scent and felt the swells of her breasts push up, seeking the pressure of his fingers.

His breathing was ragged. She could tell, could hear the shudder-stop in his chest, and yet he didn't hurry.

He touched, traced, then bent his head and tasted.

She was shaking, she realized, as she gazed down at the dark head bent over her body, at her fingers threaded into his curls. Each whisper of his breath seemed to pass over her nipples, drawing them tight. Each small bright bite of his teeth sent a pulse between her legs.

And he had barely touched her! She was still fully dressed.

Bloody hell, she had read every volume she could get her hands on from Belvoir's these last days. She was ready. She was prepared to consummate their union.

Both of his hands framed her rib cage, then pressed up, cupping her breasts, pushing them upward. His thumbs found her nipples, his touch softened by layers of fabric and not nearly enough.

"P-Peter," she stuttered, shocked by the sound of her voice, breathy and pleading. "Peter, I need you."

"God." He didn't look up, but first one hand, then both abandoned her aching nipples to spring free the fastenings of her gown. "The things you say. I'm already half out of my mind."

And then her dress sagged down her body, and his long, tapered fingers slipped beneath the filmy white of her chemise to find her skin. *There* was the rough callused touch of his fingertips on her breasts—this skin that had felt no touch but her own. And *there* was his mouth, coming down to suckle her hard and fast, and *there* was the insistent demand of his erection, her hips swiveling against his, her mind emptying of anything but need and want.

She clutched at the back of his head, the thick softness of hair cropped close at the nape of his neck. "Peter—" It was a moan, almost a cry.

His voice was dark. "I have you. I have what you need."

Her head tipped back, resting against the wall of the alcove. She sought the line of his shirt, traced the shifting muscles at his shoulders, and tried to tug at the soft lawn. She wanted to feel his naked skin, wanted to press her bared breasts against his chest. She wanted to *see* him, the golden skin she'd glimpsed at the neck of his shirt and imagined tasting.

But instead he dropped to his knees before her.

She blinked down at him. His face was fierce, as if in turmoil, as he worked his hands under her skirts, circling her ankle.

"To hell with it," he said. "To hell with the bedroom." And then he looked up and met her gaze, his eyes dazed and wild, his mouth curving into a grin. "Lean back. I've got you."

Bemused, a little dizzied, Selina leaned against the wall. His warm hand around her ankle pulled her foot from the ground and she gasped, off balance. His other hand steadied her hip even as he lifted her foot higher, stroked her calf, then set her knee around his shoulder.

His face—his mouth was—

"Don't worry," he said. "I won't let you fall."

His busy hands pressed back the yards of fabric around her hips, satin crumpling in a rush. She felt the sharp nip of his teeth again at the edge of her stocking, a pleasure-pain that traveled up, up her thighs like a wick caught fire. He settled one hand onto her buttock, kneading, and groaned softly. "Lovely, luscious. Sweet Selina."

A sudden panic bolted through her. She had thought to do this under the covers. She had seen the engravings in her Belvoir's books—the heavy breasts that balanced the swell of hips, the sinuous dip of a woman's waist. She didn't look like an engraving. Her breasts were small, her hips wide, her thighs inelegantly dimpled. She hadn't meant for him to be close enough to *see*.

"Peter," she whispered. "Perhaps we should—"

And then her thoughts scattered like dandelion seeds, because he pressed his lips directly to the curls that guarded her sex.

He murmured inarticulately, and the vibration traveled right through her, humming deep into her body, settling in her lips, her nipples, her belly. With her leg around his shoulder, she was open to him, shaking and vulnerable and needy. She felt the wet heat of his mouth, firm lashes of his tongue against her.

She gasped out his name. The strokes were slow, deliberate, as unhurried as he'd been when he'd tasted the skin at her collarbone. He licked into her and she whimpered at the gentle intrusion, moaned when his fingers chased where his tongue had been. Her hips rolled, unbidden, as his fingers filled her. His mouth roved, quick licks and sucks, and she heard a needy sob that she knew to be her own. He was so slow, so easy, and yet still she felt the pressure of her climax mounting, quick and violent within her.

She felt her thighs start to tremble and tightened her knee over his shoulder. So close, she was—

He paused, pulled his head back, and blew a cool stream of air against the bundle of nerves at the apex of her sex. Her rising orgasm retreated, and she gasped for air.

Peter made a little hum of approval between her legs. His free hand stroked along the cleft between her buttocks and then his fingers curled around the soft flesh of her thigh. "Lovely," he murmured, and licked her again, harder this time, quicker, his fingers moving inside her. Again, again—the pressure built, the sweet hot pulse riding the backs of her thighs, tightening in her belly.

Again he stopped.

Her head pushed back hard into the unforgiving plaster. "Peter," she choked out. "What are you doing?"

He lifted his head. His eyes were dark, heavy-lidded. "Pleasing my wife, I hope."

"You—you're doing it wrong!"

His lips curved and curved until he laughed. "God," he said. "God, I'm mad for you." His gaze swept down her body, fixed again at her sex bared to him. "Hold fast. And then we'll see who's wrong."

Once more he lowered his head. Once more his fingers moved, curling deep inside her. Once more he suckled her clitoris, softly at first and then harder. She was filled by his fingers, a thick delicious fullness, and she had never felt this, not when she'd explored her own body, not even when she'd touched herself and thought of him.

This time when her climax arced up, higher and higher, he didn't stop. He kept on, merciless and unrelenting, as her hips bucked, her heel digging into his back, her eyes going blind as pleasure burst through her, wave after wave of senseless, incomprehensible bliss.

Finally, slowly, he pulled his head away. Gently he resettled her foot on the ground. She'd lost her slipper, she thought dazedly, as her foot came into contact with the marble floor, cool through her stocking. Somehow even that felt erotic—the chill of the stone contrasting with the heat of Peter's body as he eased himself up and surrounded her.

He was talking to her, and the sounds slowly resolved into words she understood. *Lovely* and *beautiful* and *good*.

Her mind was clearing. "All right," she whispered, sliding her hands around his waist. "You weren't wrong."

His eyes were still dark, even though his expression was easy, undemanding. "I'll take your forfeit, then," he said, and took only her mouth.

He was gentle. So gentle, his lips so soft, and she—she tasted *herself* on his lips. She'd read of that, the taste of a woman's wetness, of a man's seed. She hadn't expected the dark pleasure it would set off in her. She licked at his lips, wanting more, and his mouth came open, his fingers fisting in her hair.

She felt, rather than heard, him groan. She swallowed the soft exhalation of his breath and felt herself suddenly freed by it.

He was mad for her. That's what he had said. She caught up his shirt, drawing it from his breeches and thanking his entirely irregular valet for letting him wander the house in nothing but his shirtsleeves and silk wedding breeches. His skin was shockingly hot under her palms, and she slid her hands wonderingly up the lean, muscular planes of his back, the wings of his shoulder blades, then down, inside the band of his breeches and around the tense curve of his buttock.

His hands tightened in her hair, and she felt him draw her head back. "Selina," he said slowly. "Let me take you to our bedroom."

Almost she said yes. She could picture it—Peter bracing himself above her as she lay on her back in his bed.

But here was the recklessness. She had it inside her, she had always had it, and he made her feel *right* just as she was.

"No," she said instead. "Here." Then she brought one palm forward to cup his shaft.

His eyes went black, his face almost pained. "Selina—"

She brought her other hand around, slowly, as he had, letting her nails glide along his skin. He shuddered, the muscles of his belly tightening, and she felt a matching pull at her center.

She wanted her fingers around him. She had seen the pictures, could imagine how his cock would rise between her hands as she stroked him up and down.

But—blast! No book had mentioned how to unfasten his breeches. She fought with his falls.

"Stupid," she muttered. "Odious garment." She tugged harder, her fingers brushing clumsily against his shaft. Buttons, fabric, and then somehow another set of hidden buttons beneath.

He buried his head in the curve of her neck and laughed.

"Don't you dare—"

"Selina," he mumbled, his face pressed against her skin. "I am thanking Providence for this delay, so that I might not spend in my smalls."

"Oh." That, she understood, was considered a shameful thing. And yet the idea of him so completely undone . . .

His breeches were loosened. Her fingers were inside his smallclothes. His shaft was hard as the marble beneath her feet, but hot, curving against her palm. She curled both hands around his length, and he gave a muffled cry into her shoulder.

Curiously, she traced the broad head with her thumb, gathering the moisture that beaded at the tip, spreading it in a circle.

"Now," he said hoarsely, "we should go upstairs."

"No."

"The . . . door is open."

"Then it is a good thing you have no staff."

He took her face in his hands then, looked hard into her eyes. "You want this—here?"

"I want you here."

He muffled a curse with a kiss, vehement and sudden, before breaking away. "Slow," he said, as if to himself, as he looked down at her small, high breasts, at his cock caught in her hands. "I will take you so slowly." He pressed her back into the wall, lifting her leg around his waist. "I will make you ready for me. Wet and desperate and greedy for my cock."

She wasn't shocked by the frank speech—she had read those words and more, much more, much coarser. But she *was* shocked by how his words thrilled her. Her nipples tightened beneath his gaze; heat and moisture slicked her sex. His palm cupped her mound.

"Do you like that?" His breath was hot in her ear. "When I tell you what I'm going to do to you?"

"Yes," she gasped. Her fingers tightened on his shaft, as if to draw him closer, and he hissed.

Not in pain. She was certain of that. She stroked him again, a little clumsy, a little rough.

He answered her in kind, the heel of his hand firm against her clitoris as he worked two fingers inside her. She rocked against him helplessly, seeking more and somehow more.

"Yes," he said. "That's right. Take what you need."

She didn't know how she could be so close to climax again, yet she could feel it building already. She tossed her head, almost frantic. It *hurt*, didn't he understand—she *needed*—

And then, suddenly, she felt the pressure of his cock at her entrance, firm and insistent, and she whimpered with relief. He was talking again—*wet* and *sweet* and *good*—but she was well beyond hearing. She tightened her leg around his waist, trying to urge him on, push him faster and deeper into her body.

More words—*fuck yes please*—and then he was easing into her, pressing her harder against the wall, canting her hips up as he worked in and out, stretching her body to receive him.

She had read about virginity, about the maidenhead, but she felt no such barrier as he moved patiently inside her. Only a hint of burning as she strained to take him, a pressure-pain so deep inside her she thought she might break apart.

She was clinging to his shoulders, and she felt his muscles work as he slid a hand between their bodies and found the sensitive nerves just above where he entered her. His fingers were deft and sure, stroking in time to the beat of her pulse. His other hand braced against the wall beside her head, holding them both steady as he withdrew. Slowly. Then entered her again. Less slow. Less steady this time.

Undone. They were both coming undone.

It was—she had never expected this. The throb of her heartbeat, the thrust of his cock inside her body, the rhythmic working of his fingers that sent her shuddering and gasping into a bright nowhere.

His hand withdrew after her climax broke, then fastened on her hips, lifting her onto her toes as he thrust into her again, faster now. His breath sawed out unevenly, and still he held her, pinned against the wall and tilted up for his access, his pleasure.

Only one word now, her name, again and again, wild and uncertain, until finally he withdrew, shuddering, and spilled his seed against her thigh.

He dropped his head again into the curve of her neck, his fingers loosening their hold on her buttocks. A bead of sweat slipped down between her breasts. A cool whisper against her heated skin.

Peter lifted his head and then blinked. "Oh hell."

She angled her head to see what he was looking at, but couldn't quite make sense of it. "What is it?"

"Seems I've put my hand through Great-uncle Francis."

"*What?*"

She wriggled away, twisting to see—

His hand, which she'd thought had been braced on the wall beside her head, had gone straight through a tightly wrapped oil portrait. A man's dour face drooped pathetically next to Peter's thumb.

"Oh, *Peter!* That was a *Lawrence*—it should have been in the Academy!"

He grinned down at her, curls spilling over his brow. Something uncoiled, loose and warm in her belly.

"Somehow," he said, "I don't regret it."

Chapter 18

Dearest Duchess!
I knew you had a tendre *for Peter Kent. I knew it! Ha!*
(Clermont says I am waking my cousins with my cackling. In
truth he is only surly because he was wrong.)

—*from Lady Faiza Greenlaw, Countess of Clermont,*
to Her Grace Selina Kent, Duchess of Stanhope

The bed must have been assembled in the ducal bedchamber. It was the only piece of furniture that had remained when Peter had moved into the Stanhope townhouse, likely explained by the fact that it was too large to fit out the door. It was a great heavy wooden thing that reminded Peter of an immense ship, its prow extending nearly to the opposite wall.

And in that huge boat of a bed, lapped by little mounded-up waves of bedclothes, lay Selina. His wife.

The linens—he'd had Humphrey iron them the day before— were crisp and white. They lay softly over her calves and ankles, twisted under her hips, then flared out around the long curve of her ribs and shoulder. She slept. She slept and he stood on the other side of the room, marveling at her.

He'd kissed that bare, luminous skin. Had licked across the curves of her thighs, cradled her delectable bum as he'd entered her. Once in the portrait gallery. Again in the bed. He'd tasted his way across her body and he thought there were perhaps one or two places he'd missed. He had the whole morning to remedy that.

He'd risen to go downstairs and fetch coffee for himself—tea for Selina, because he'd only ever seen her drink tea. He should go. He should go, or at least turn away, stop staring at her like a lovesick fool and put his damned trousers on.

Hang the coffee. He dropped the trousers he'd been holding and stepped back to the bed.

He sat beside her, and his weight caused the mattress to dip. She stirred, blinked open her eyes, and found him with a sleepy half smile. "Peter."

He found some knot of tension uncoiled in his chest at the sight of her face. Her smile, her eyes.

He thought perhaps she was happy to see him. He *wanted* her to be happy to see him. Almost as much as it terrified him.

If she was happy, there was something to lose. If she thought him more than a selfish idiot, he was bound to disappoint her in the end.

He leaned down wordlessly and kissed the tip of her long elegant nose. *This*, he thought. This he knew.

He kissed the corner of her mouth. He traced one finger down the side of her neck, and she shivered beneath his touch. "Good morning," he said to the freckle at the top of her shoulder.

She made a little squeak. "Peter. I must clean my teeth."

"Surely not. You're naked."

She laughed and squirmed, and he meant to let her go, but

when he looked at her face, she was staring at him. Her eyes were bright as morning.

"You have this way of looking," she said softly, "as though you cannot see enough of me."

"I cannot." He lifted the rumpled sheet, smoothed it over her bare shoulders, then slid his hands down slowly, caressing the sides of her breasts, her rib cage, the curve of her waist through the thin linen. A flush bloomed on her cheeks again. "I can't touch enough of you either. I'd thought to spend the morning on it. Touching you. Tasting you. But mere morning won't suffice."

She lifted her chin, exposing the column of her throat, so he placed his lips beneath the line of her jaw. A kiss. A small bite.

"What is it that you smell of? I can't tell you how long I've been wanting to know. Years, I think."

She laughed shakily, one hand coming up to cup the back of his head. "My soap. Oil of bergamot."

He paused in his attention to her collarbone. "You smell of tea?"

"I am sorry to say that bergamot is a very sour orange."

He ran his tongue along the valley beneath the delicate rise of bone. "Impossible. You smell of spice and sweetness. Perhaps it's your skin itself." He couldn't help himself. Her nipple was inches from his mouth and he found it through the sheet with his lips.

Selina gasped and arched her back, pressing into his mouth.

She wanted, too, it seemed. Christ, he was so goddamned ready for her. But slow. He must go slowly.

He pulled back and framed one breast in the curve between his thumb and forefinger. "You have," he said conversationally, "stupendous bubbies."

She twisted her fingers into his hair. "Don't tease."

"I assure you I am not. I've spent a great deal of time thinking on them."

She blinked at him, dark brows drawing together. "I have seen engravings, Peter. They are too small for larking."

Now it was his turn for bemusement. "For . . . what?"

"For larking!" At his expression, she paused. "Is that . . . not a common activity?"

"I couldn't say. I don't know what that is."

"To put a man's member between one's breasts and—" She gazed up at him, her cheeks growing pink. "Never mind."

He could not speak. All the blood had drained from his head.

She was still talking. "Blast it all. Belvoir's. So hard to know what is usual and what is not." She shot him a look of concern. "But . . . flogging. That's surely not usual. Is it?"

"*Flogging?*" Evidently he *could* speak, though his voice seemed to have attained an unusual register.

Selina ground her teeth. "No, obviously not. Damn you, Jean Laventille, and your peculiar interests!"

He tried manfully not to laugh. "Are you interested in flogging, wife?"

"Of *course* not!" Her flush deepened. "I suppose I don't know."

"Oh my God." He gathered her into his arms and fell back onto the bed. "I beg you. Tell me every last thing you've seen in image or text that's intrigued you."

"I . . . I am not sure . . . there's time."

He groaned. "You cannot imagine what you do to me."

One long-fingered hand found its way in between their bodies and stroked up his thigh, stopping just short of his cock. "I have some idea."

"Mmph," he muttered, and kissed her, quick and hard and deep, trying to recall why he needed to slow down.

"Peter," she said, when he came up for air. "Last night. In our bedsport"—she hesitated—"is that quite the right word?"

"It is the *best* word. But I urge you to try out all the words you know, just for comparison."

"Absurd man." But her rum-colored eyes were soft. "In our bedsport, why did you withdraw? Is that your preference?"

He paused, startled. "I—don't know. I doubt it. But we had never discussed children, Selina. I didn't want to assume. Do you want to discuss it now?"

"I . . . oh." She looked surprised but not displeased. "I suppose I just presumed—you are the duke. You must want an heir?"

"Not especially." He had been a duke for more than a month now, but he had never expected the title. Never *wanted* the title and felt no particular attachment to the dukedom. "Do you want to have children, then?"

Her dark eyelashes were working rapidly up and down. "I'm not sure. I . . . don't know."

"Well, then," he said, pausing to kiss her before continuing. "We'll wait. Until we both are sure."

And then he pressed her back against the mattress and kissed her again.

•   •   •

Several hours later, Selina hummed as she fastened her earbobs. Humming! It was outrageous, really. She had only Peter to blame—Peter, and his tendency to whistle at inappropriate moments. Peter, and his infectious joy.

She kept on humming as she buttoned her gloves and slipped out of her dressing room. Peter was already in his study, working on his next parliamentary speech. She had plans to drop by Laventille's office later in the afternoon—ostensibly to discuss purchases for the Stanhope residence's plundered library, but in fact to talk about the print run she needed of Walter Scott's upcoming novel and to discuss the recent rumors connecting Nicholas to Belvoir's.

At the bottom of the stairs, she stopped in delight. "Lydia!"

Humphrey was ushering Lydia Hope-Wallace into the sitting room, and Selina mentally added a stop at the registry office to her afternoon schedule. Staff—they desperately needed staff. Humphrey and Lydia both paused at the sound of her voice.

"Perhaps the dining room," she said to Humphrey. It was, at the moment, the only room on the lower level with chairs. She tried not to laugh at Lydia's expression of bemusement as they seated themselves nearly knee-to-knee at the square dining table.

"I'm so pleased to see you!" she said instead. "You should have sent a note—I was just on the cusp of leaving, and then I would have missed you entirely."

"Selina." Lydia's voice was low and grave, and Selina's eyes snapped to her face. "I wouldn't have come the morning after your wedding if it were not urgent."

"What's wrong? Is it your mother? Has she made further demands of you? Oh, Lyddie—"

"It's not me," Lydia said. "I'm not here about myself."

Selina blinked. "Oh. I'm glad. What's wrong, then?"

Lydia looked down at her lap. She shifted the large netted reticule that she'd been carrying, then lifted the flap. She withdrew from its depths a book bound in bright emerald green.

Selina felt her heart thump hard against her chest. She tried to fix her face into an expression of casual interest. "A book?"

"Yes," Lydia said. "A Belvoir's book, as you know perfectly well."

"Have there been new rumors about Nicholas?" The tension

that had simmered inside her these last two days knotted tight beneath her breastbone. "Is that why you're here?"

"No. At least, not that I've heard of. But you, Selina—you are a member of Belvoir's, are you not?"

"You know I am not. I've a membership with the Royal Colonnade." She did. The Royal Colonnade Library was her primary competitor.

"Indeed. But we've talked about the Venus catalog, have we not?"

"Yes, of course. Most intriguing."

Lydia's blue eyes held her gaze. "And you have never considered becoming a member yourself? That strikes me as . . . not at all like you, Selina."

Selina felt hot and cold at once. "I never felt the need."

Lydia tossed the green-bound book down onto the smooth surface of the table between them. "Hang it, Selina, I know it is you!"

She could not even try to deny it. Not to Lydia, who was the smartest woman of her acquaintance, who knew everything.

It had always only been a matter of time.

"How?" It came out a whisper.

"For heaven's sake, Selina, I used my head. It was not so very hard to figure out, not after I saw how upset you were at the dressmaker's shop two days ago. I asked myself why Belvoir's would have been connected to the Duke of Rowland in the first place— goodness knows that his political projects are not the same as the ones promoted by the Venus catalog." The blue of Lydia's eyes was dark with agitation. "He owns it, doesn't he? The Belvoir's property."

"No," Selina said hoarsely. "Will does."

Lydia's lips compressed. "Of course. Of *course*. He has been out of the country for years now, so they must have attributed the running of the library to Nicholas instead. But as soon as I thought about it for more than a moment, I knew it could not be Nicholas. You, Selina. *You* run Belvoir's. *You* started the Venus catalog."

"I did." She gritted her teeth, then forced herself to continue. "I do. After Ivy Price and the revelation of her pregnancy. After I learned about the lords and their mistresses and their wives. I was so tired of feeling like I had no control over my life. So I . . . I took control. Will bought Belvoir's for me. I ran it."

Lydia's eyes had gone bright and wet, and for a moment Selina thought she was furious. And then she realized Lydia was *hurt*, and the knot of anguish inside her tightened further.

"Why didn't you tell me?" Lydia asked. "Didn't you trust me? Did you really think I would not keep your secret?"

"I didn't want you to be disappointed in me. I didn't want you to hate me."

"Did you truly think I *would?*"

"No. I—I don't know. I was afraid, Lyd! I couldn't tell anyone but Will."

"And your *husband?*"

"He knows," Selina said miserably. "I told him before we wed."

"There's that, at least."

Her brain didn't seem to be working properly. She could see the grain of the oak table before her, a twisting pattern of dark and light. She pressed her hand against it, her fingertips flattening against the table's wooden lines.

Lydia had figured it out. How long did she have until more people did? Until everyone in the *ton* knew?

She needed more time. Just a bit more time—just until the

guardianship hearing was over. And then everything could fall apart.

"Selina." Lydia's voice was gentler now, and Selina looked up to find that Lydia's eyes were no longer wet with tears. "I understand. Why you did it."

It was almost too much to hope for. Selina wanted to ask her to say it again, but only swallowed hard against the desire to ask for comfort. She did not deserve it.

"I remember how upset you were when Ivy . . ." Lydia trailed off. "When Ivy." Her eyes sharpened. "Do *you* pay for her house? In Gloucestershire—near your family's country estate. I cannot believe I did not see it before."

"Yes. Well, Will does, officially. I simply arranged it."

"You . . . simply arranged it." Lydia laughed, amused and slightly harsh. "You arranged to finance a single pregnant woman's living—presumably for the rest of her life. As you arranged the running of a circulating library and the re-education of the female half of the *ton*."

"Yes."

"Good Lord, Selina. How did you even have time?"

"Honestly? I dislike French, watercolors, and needlework. Once I mastered dancing, there seemed to be plenty of hours to fill."

Lydia's eyebrows rose. And then she started to laugh.

Selina stared at her in horror.

"Oh God"—Lydia pressed her palms to her eyes, half bent over her lap—"I am so sorry. I know this isn't funny. But only you would turn up your nose at embroidery and resolve to overturn society in its stead."

"There's nothing wrong with embroidery," Selina protested inanely. "I am simply very poor at it."

Lydia plucked up her now-empty reticule and threw it at her. "For heaven's sake, Selina. What are you going to do?"

"I have to find out who is spreading the rumors," she said. "Whether it's Alverthorpe or another peer or someone else entirely. I have to stop them."

"But the children," Lydia protested. "Stanhope's brother and sister. It will not look well for Stanhope, Selina, if this comes out."

It would be a nightmare—her worst fears coming true.

Peter had come to her in the first place because he wanted her help in securing the guardianship. That was what she had to offer him. That was what she was good at. That was the only thing that had allowed her to permit herself to marry him—her certainty that she would be able to maintain her deception long enough for the lord chancellor to rule in Peter's favor.

"I will pay them," she said, half-frantic. "I will find out who it is and pay them for their silence. The hearing is less than two weeks away—I will make it worth their while to keep it to themselves."

Lydia sighed. "You have an answer for everything."

"I don't," Selina said miserably. "I wish I did."

She considered for a moment going to Rowland House to unburden herself to her brother—but no. No. She needed to come to him with a plan in place—with the situation well in hand. She could not fling her problems in his direction any more than she had already.

Lydia tucked a coppery curl behind her ear. "You know I am beside you, yes? Whatever you need."

"I know. That means—a great deal to me." She pushed against the notched wood of the table, needing the way it grounded her. "More than I deserve."

But when Lydia left the dining room, Selina did not stand.

She did not leap to her feet and plunge into reckless action. She stared at her bare fingers against the wood and heard her unsteady breath echo in the silent room.

If she did not succeed—

She almost could not make herself think of it. If she was not able to find out who was behind the rumors—if she could not persuade them to keep silent—if somehow the truth of her involvement came out *before* the hearing—

And yet she had to think of it. She needed to make a plan.

How would Peter feel if her secret came out now, when the guardianship hearing was so close at hand? He would be crushed—he would blame her—

But no. She did not think he would blame her. And that was worse, somehow. That she would be the means of ruining his happiness, and that he would try to forgive her for it.

It would be unbearable, to disappoint him that way.

She thought about Ivy Price, and the house Will had bought for Ivy and her son in Gloucestershire.

They could do it again. If the scandal broke before the guardianship hearing, she could leave Peter and the children, buy a house as far away as she could manage—in Cornwall, perhaps, or Wales. They could have the marriage annulled. Peter could denounce her publicly and perhaps manage to avoid the worst of the damage.

Things could never be the same between them. No more openhearted declarations, no more easy Kent grins. Even if he did not intend to resent her after the scandal broke, he would not be able to help it.

It would be better to make a clean break. He might not like it—he might not agree at first. But the children were more important. The children were the most important thing, and he would have to accept her plan, because his guardianship meant more to him than anything else in the world.

Her fingers were blurry, and she stared hard down at her hands until her sight cleared. And when it had—when her breath in her ears sounded normal—she got to her feet.

She needed to write to Will. She needed to look at her accounts and her membership rolls and perhaps write to her man of business about Cornish cottages for ruined ladies. She meant to try everything she possibly could to prevent the truth from getting out before the guardianship hearing. But if she failed and the scandal broke anyway, she needed to be prepared.

And if the thought of leaving Peter—of leaving him alone in this big empty house—splintered something inside her, she would do it anyway if she had to. There was no other choice.

Chapter 19

. . . I was drove to it by a passion too impetuous for me to resist, and I did what I did because I could not help it.

—*from* FANNY HILL

She had to tell Peter.

Not everything. She did not want to tell him that she meant to leave, if she had to. She did not even want to speak the words.

But she had to tell him about the rumors, and her plan to find out who was behind them. She needed to tell him that their respectability—such as it was—was threatened. And she did not want to.

That was the bare, humiliating truth. She didn't want to tell him. It had been difficult to tell him about Belvoir's before they married—hard to share what had been hers and Will's alone for so long.

But now they were married, and it was a thousand times worse. *Married.* Every rash, impetuous thing she'd done in her life was now part of Peter's future, not just her own. Her good intentions seemed a poor comfort for the reality of her secrets crashing headlong into his life.

She spent the afternoon buying furniture for the lower floors. It felt a hollow sort of satisfaction—to try to turn this peculiar house into a home for them. She was excellent with planning, with direction, and yet an utter disaster at making choices to protect the people she cared about.

The house would be full of staff in a few days, the bedchambers stocked with beds and linens. She had imagined which rooms might suit the children.

And now, because of her secrets, perhaps the children would never reside there at all.

It was painful: to make lists of furnishings and imagine a future that she did not know if she could bring into being.

She tried all day to bury herself in trifles, and when Peter came into their bedchamber that evening, she thought about running away. She wished powerfully that she hadn't kissed him at Rowland House—that she'd convinced him to marry someone else instead of her.

And even as she thought it, something greedy and possessive in her rejected the very idea. He was *hers*.

She felt the same reckless part of herself flare to life as it always did around him. She was never satisfied with half measures, was she?

She could not just assist Ivy Price. She had to upend the entire state of female education among the literate London public.

She could not simply help Peter marry. No. She had kissed him and pressed herself to him, and when he'd given her his body, she had wanted more and more and never enough.

"Peter," she said. "I have to tell you something." She touched her thumb to the brass circlet twisted around the fourth finger of her left hand.

He settled himself on their bed, crossing his feet at the ankles. "How concerned should I be? On a scale of, 'We've run out of eggs in the larder' to 'Lucinda has acquired a small army and means to invade France'?"

"Oh God," she said, "closer to the latter."

He sat up, alarmed, and she hated herself for the fear in his expression.

"Someone has found out about Belvoir's," she told him. "Not that it's mine—not yet. They think it belongs to Nicholas, and they're spreading the story through the *ton*. I need to find out who is responsible and make them stop. I—I may need to reveal that I am the one behind Belvoir's, not Nicholas. But if I must do so, I promise I will wait until after the hearing. I swear it."

"Oh." He sat back against the enormous carved bed. "I thought it was going to be worse."

"Worse?" she exclaimed. "Worse than the fact that it may soon be public knowledge that your *wife* works in an *office* and procures books about *sexual relations*?"

"God above, Selina, it sounds much worse when you use the word *procure*."

She ground her teeth.

He laughed. "Will you be very angry if I tell you that the look on your face is extremely arousing?"

"Yes!"

"All right," he said. "I won't say it. Should I go downstairs and have Humphrey ready us a carriage? After I put my boots back on?"

Good Lord, the man so often made her feel as though she were sprinting to catch up.

"Where on earth do you mean for us to go?"

He blinked at her. "I thought you'd want to go to Belvoir's. Review your records. Write to your publisher. See if you can ascertain who's responsible for the rumors."

Well. She *had* meant to do all that.

"You . . . want to come with me?"

He grinned and swung his feet off the side of the bed. "Of course. I promise I won't distract you. I'd like to see where you work."

"You aren't upset?"

"Selina," he said, his voice gentling. "Nothing's happened yet. Perhaps nothing will happen at all. We'll face the consequences when they come."

It felt almost radical—his equanimity in the face of potential disaster.

It was also infuriating. It was as if she were the only one who grasped the potential consequences of her secrets.

Suddenly she wanted him to see Belvoir's. Perhaps when he saw the Venus catalog spread out in rows of emerald bindings, he would understand the magnitude of the catastrophe that threatened.

Perhaps then he would realize what a mistake it had been to marry her. Perhaps then she would look into his face and see regret. And if someday she had to leave him—well, perhaps he would understand why.

·   ·   ·

After close to three hours in the office, Peter did not seem to be grasping anything besides the books on her shelves.

Selina had made copious notes on every member of the Venus catalog who might have the social cachet to spread rumors about a rich and powerful duke. She had penned notes to Jean

Laventille and to her banker, firmly requesting more information about anyone who had made inquiries lately into her business. She verified that she had more than enough capital to finance a small Cornish cottage. She thought about writing a letter of reference for Emmie, and her fingers shook so much that she could not quite manage it.

She had considered carefully who among her rolls might be a political enemy of her brother and resolved to find out more via Lydia's gossip network about which of her members were avowed Tories.

Peter, meanwhile, prowled.

He didn't talk at all, but he kept pulling books from the shelves. The green bindings—which so effectively disguised the Venus catalog books, allowing them to be carted about by even the most innocent of debutantes—made it impossible for her to tell what he was reading.

Was it *Waverley*? A treatise on abolition that he wanted to take note of?

Was it the book of erotic Greek poetry that she had most recently acquired? Her personal copy of the Covent Garden memoir wherein she had—horror of horrors—spent a full hour making notes in the margins?

God forbid that he was reading *Lady Bumtickler's Revels*. Although—she had not had that one bound in Belvoir's green, so it could not be *Lady Bumtickler's Revels*.

Which was a relief.

Scratch, scratch, went Selina's pen.

Flip, flip, went the pages in Peter's hands. He replaced the book on the shelf and took down three more.

She couldn't stand it any longer. "Find anything of note?"

"Mm," he said abstractedly. "I'm researching larking."

Selina tossed down her pen. "You are *not*." Did the man not realize they were in the middle of a crisis?

"Fine, then I'm not. By the by, did *you* make these notes? You have beautiful handwriting."

She leapt to her feet and strode across the room, snatching the book from his hands. "No! Of course not." She blinked down at the text. Yes, that was most certainly in her hand: *Can this be physically possible???*

She was going to die of mortification, right here in her own office. "Peter," she said, pretending her face wasn't red-hot, "this is a place of business. Sit down."

He let her shove him into a chair, then caught her arm and pulled her down into his lap. He wore only his shirtsleeves and a jacket, and his throat, bare of cravat, lay tempting inches from her mouth. "Tell me you're almost finished. Tell me I can take you home."

"I—I—" She *was* almost finished. In addition to the research she'd done directed toward finding the rumormonger, she'd also completed a great deal of the incidental labor that kept Belvoir's running. She had reviewed the previous week's circulation numbers, written out orders for new purchases, penned a note to her secretary to review a handful of texts that had not been returned. *Fanny Hill*, mostly—she simply could not keep the library stocked with enough copies of *Fanny Hill*.

But something deviled her, and she wriggled out of Peter's grasp, leaving the book he'd been perusing beside him. "Not yet."

"All right," he said equably, letting her go. "Have I mentioned that I'm developing something of a fetish for the sound of your pen at work? Thankfully just yours, or I might get thrown out of my club."

She felt twin spikes of desire and exasperation. "Peter! Are you taking this seriously?"

His lips twisted, a wry expression that seemed somehow far from his usual grin. "I am. Truly, I am." He glanced down at the book and then met her eyes, his face gone sober. "Take as long as you need, Selina. Never let me rush you at your work."

She sat down at her desk. Suddenly, unaccountably, tears stung her eyes, and she turned her gaze down, not wanting him to see.

She couldn't understand him. She was worried—so bloody worried that Belvoir's would ruin his life, that her reckless choices—well intentioned as they were—would come between Peter and everything he wanted.

But he didn't seem to feel the same. She wanted to believe him—that he understood the risks. That he saw in Belvoir's something that was worth the cost.

That he saw that in her.

She didn't know what to believe. She felt tangled in her emotions. Why had he sat here, cooling his heels in her office for hours?

Was he waiting for her to make a plan? Had he some blind confidence that she could sort out the mess she'd made of their lives?

She hoped he trusted her. She wanted to be worthy of his trust, and she was not sure she was up to the task.

It seemed to her, here in her office, surrounded by the library of her heart and the evidence of her commitment to Belvoir's, that she wanted too much.

She wanted, she realized now, to keep Belvoir's. She did not want to give up her involvement with the Venus catalog, not even when her secret came out. She *loved* Belvoir's. In some strange contrary part of her soul, she was proud of what she had done, and the thought of abandoning it all—of leaving London in a hushed flight of shame—almost made her angry. She had made a difference for women, and she did not want to give that up.

And even as she thought it, she felt guilty and greedy and stubborn. She wanted Belvoir's, and she wanted her husband too. She wanted a thousand nights like this: books and conversation, quiet work and Peter. Timeless days and nights of learning him, learning how he teased and played and laughed. Learning who they could be together.

Perhaps it was foolishness, or blind stubborn recklessness, that made her flip closed the account book on her desk and look up at him.

Perhaps it was a mistake to allow herself to grow closer to him. To crave him this way. But he was here at her side, patient and confident, and she wanted him too much to let herself dwell on how everything might fall apart.

She let the world go out of focus as she looked at him, his dark head bent over a book.

"Chapter eleven," she said.

He lifted his head. "Sorry?"

"Chapter eleven. In the book with my marginalia. I made quite a lot of notes in chapter eleven."

He plucked the book up from where it lay beside his chair and turned the pages. Not quickly—no, that wasn't his way, he never rushed. But easily, as though he had all night.

Selina listened to his breathing as she meticulously drafted a note to her man of business. Moments passed, and then—yes, there it was. A little hitch in the steady rhythm.

Her quill traced out the words, the scratching audible in the silent room.

"Selina," Peter said finally. "If you imagined I could look at your notes and remain unaffected, well . . ." He trailed off, his eyes still fixed on the page. "I am sorry to disappoint."

She laughed, and it came out throaty, seductive. She'd never known her laugh could sound that way. "I imagined something else entirely, if you must know."

He looked at her, and there it was, the expression that was as precious to her as breathing. Fierce and covetous, as though he wanted to possess her. Hungry, as if he might swallow her whole.

Reckless, she thought to herself. *You are getting in too deep, Selina.*

But she could not bring herself to stop. She licked her lips, and he followed the movement of her tongue.

"Come here," he said. "I want to touch you."

She felt her lips curl at the ends, almost involuntarily. "No."

"No?"

"This is a place of business," she said, and though the words were prim, her voice was not. "I must refuse."

He gazed at her appraisingly from the other side of the small room. "Is that right?"

She rose from her seat behind the desk and stepped in front of it. She kept her eyes locked with his and slowly unfastened the buttons at the side of her bodice. "I am the superintendent of this business. I could not engage in relations at my place of work."

Her bodice gaped down, and she slipped the capped sleeves from her shoulders. Slowly, slowly, she let her fingers play over the front of her stays, tracing the underside of her breasts. Peter's eyes were hot and dark, following the circles she drew, up and around the soft curves.

"Of course," she said, "I could not let you touch me here." She reached behind herself to unfasten her stays, and her breasts thrust forward, nearly spilling over the top of the garment. Peter didn't move from the chair, but she sensed him growing more intent, his focus narrowing down to a point.

It was all she wanted in that moment. For the rest of the world to fall away.

"That does not mean," she said, slipping free the buttons at the front of her chemise, "that I could not touch myself. That I have not sat here." She nodded down at the book that lay forgotten by Peter's side. "Reading that book. Thinking of your hands instead of mine."

In truth she had never done any such thing at Belvoir's, had rolled her eyes at the customers who felt the library a suitable location for a tryst. But here, now, with Peter's hungry gaze upon her, she wanted to do so very much indeed.

She cupped her breasts through the fabric of her chemise, lifting them as though offering them to Peter. Then she let the sides of the garment part, the pink-tipped globes standing out against the white cotton.

"Selina," he said hoarsely. "I have to touch you."

A dark thrill rose in her. Unhurried, was he? Always so easy, so slow and teasing. Two could play at that game.

"No," she said. "But you may touch yourself."

• • •

Peter's mouth was dry as he watched her from the chair by the hearth. His *wife*. Merciful God.

He knew she had been worried before they came to the office, and he'd felt the impact of her pale, tense face somewhere inside him. He knew she feared that they would lose the guardianship, and he hated that he could not do more to reassure her.

But somehow in the office, she'd lost that drawn look. A half smile had played around her lips. And he'd seized that hint of happiness with both hands and held on tight.

She had so much inside her—the businesswoman, the radical, the practical stubborn woman he'd always respected. And this too: bravery and independence and sensuality, burning in her like an ember.

Her long, efficient fingers coasted along her skin, made gold by the candlelight. She thumbed her nipples, rolling the hard peaks beneath her fingers, then pinched them. Her face was flushed.

"Lift your skirts," he said. His voice was hoarse.

Her chin rose, a faint challenging smile on her lips. "Unfasten your falls."

Christ in heaven, the woman was going to kill him. Blood beat painfully through his body, racing toward his cock. He made quick work of the buttons at the front of his trousers, where his erection strained fervently against the fabric.

"Take yourself in hand," Selina said, and helplessly he palmed his shaft.

"Now," he said. "Lift your skirts now."

She caught her lower lip in her teeth as she looked at him and then let it pop free. His skin felt fevered, his cock twitching beneath his hand.

Then she leaned back against the desk and took the fabric of her dress in her fists. It was a dark, dark blue, almost black, and as she inched the frock and petticoats upward, the pale-white lace of her stockings made a startling erotic contrast. With the fabric just above her knees, she paused.

"Higher."

"So demanding." Instead of raising her skirt, she slipped one hand beneath. He could see the muscles of her shoulder flex, the fabric shifting as her hand moved.

He swore, his fingers tightening involuntarily as he stroked his length.

"Is there something you want?" Her eyes were lit with amusement, but her voice was uneven.

What *didn't* he want—he wanted to bury his face between her thighs, he wanted to thrust hard inside her body, he wanted to fuck her until she forgot her own name—

He wanted to please her. He wanted to make her happy.

"I want to watch you come. I want to see your fingers inside your sweet, wet cunny. Then I want to taste them."

She withdrew her hand from underneath her gown. Her first two fingers shone with moisture. She arched her brows. "Like this?"

And then she took her fingers into her mouth.

Christ—*Christ*. The room was too hot, going dark around the edges as though all the candlelight poured itself onto Selina. The light lavished her with gold and shadow, flickering upon the dampness of her lips, the dark hidden cove beneath her gown, the white-lace arch of her calf.

"I am holding on," he said precisely, "by a thread. Lift your goddamned skirts."

She eased back farther onto the surface of the desk, so she was sitting, her feet not quite touching the ground. She bunched the fabric of her gown and petticoat in her fingers, sliding it up and up and up. He saw the tiny bows of her garters at the top of her stockings, wine red against her pale thighs.

He let himself imagine that *his* hands were sliding that dress up her thighs. He let himself imagine shredding the frail lace, licking the small strawberry mark at the top of her thigh.

He let himself pretend, just for a moment, that it was *her* hand wrapped around his cock, and he pumped hard into his fist, moisture welling at the tip, as Selina finally pulled the dress up to her hips and let her legs fall open.

Her fingers came to the dark-honey curls. She circled, delicately, advancing and then retreating, touching her folds, the crease of her pelvis, the hood at the apex of her sex.

"Both hands," he ordered.

Her eyes were growing glassy, drunk with desire, but instead of listening, she nodded at him. "You first."

He was bloody delighted to oblige—perhaps this would make her stop teasing and *come*, damn her. He cupped his sac in one hand, his other fisted around his desperate erection.

With one hand, she parted her folds, sliding two fingers inside. Her other hand moved to her swollen bud, a brisk, circling rhythm.

Part of his mind was memorizing this, the way she touched herself, the pace that pleased her most—he could have guessed, his Selina, quick and hard, the way she came—and the rest of him was going quietly mad, as he watched her climax and could not touch her.

Her head tipped back. Her eyes closed. She whimpered, almost a sob.

Peter groaned aloud, his fingers so tight on his cock it verged on pain.

Her thighs trembled when she came. He knew that already. But now he could see it all, her glistening sex, the brilliant rose of her flushed cheeks, the darkened tips of her breasts. She came, hard and gasping, her mouth open, her midnight skirts flared around her body.

He was upon her before she'd stopped trembling, before she'd even opened her eyes.

"Home," he said. He could barely hear his voice over the pounding in his blood. "I'm taking you home."

Her eyes fluttered open. "Home?"

"I'm trying not to fuck you on this desk." He yanked up her bodice. "We are going home. And then you're going to touch yourself again. While you ride me."

Chapter 20

. . . Yes, I told him. He took the news of Belvoir's with ~~enthusiasm eagerness~~ equanimity. Oh, hang this letter!

—from Selina to Will, crumpled and discarded with
a blush

"I want you to know," Peter murmured into his wife's ear, "that you may take me to your office anytime."

Selina's expressive face crashed right through pink and made a strong foray into scarlet. It was impressive—he wouldn't have known it from her voice, which was rather crisp. "I am used to working alone, but I think I can make an exception from time to time."

"Oh, can you?" He eased the bedsheets down, exploring the long lines of her body in the heady light of day.

He should have let her sleep longer. They'd been late at Belvoir's, and when they'd arrived home—well. It had been a long time before they'd made it up the stairs.

He hadn't meant to wake her, not really. He'd only meant to brush her thick curls back from her face.

And then kiss her ear. And then ease his impatient body against the generous curve of her bum with an appreciative whimper.

So. Perhaps it had not been so surprising that she'd woken. God, she was soft beneath him, mouth and breasts and warm, heavenly, welcoming thighs—he could not get enough of their creamy inviting curves . . .

He was moving down toward them deliberately when the knock came on the door.

"Your Grace!"

It was Humphrey's anxious tenor.

"Go away." He continued his leisurely progress southward. Selina clapped a hand over her mouth, stifling a horrified laugh.

"Oh—Your Grace . . ." Humphrey knocked again. "I am *so* sorry. My—my deepest apologies . . ."

Peter devoted a long moment to the strawberry mark at the top of Selina's thigh, near the crease at her pelvis. "Stop apologizing," he said deliberately when he came up for air, raising his voice to make sure his message carried. "And go. Away."

"I—I would, Your Grace. It is only that—well, at the door, Your Grace. The children are here, and—they're alone. I couldn't leave them on the street."

His vision swam before him. "The children?"

"Yes, Your Grace. Your brother and sister."

• • •

Selina sat up so quickly she nearly bashed Peter's nose with her knee. He was still frozen on the bed, staring at her in stupefaction.

"Humphrey," she said. "Can you send up Emmie? With a gown? Immediately, if you please." Her gaze shot back to Peter, naked and aroused. "Er, perhaps in a few minutes."

"Yes, of course, Your Grace. Shall I come in now and help His Grace ready himself?"

"No!" She and Peter spoke in unison.

"To be sure," said Humphrey, in tones of indignation.

Peter was suddenly in motion, leaping from the bed, laying about for smallclothes. Or—no, the man had forgone smallclothes and was tugging on his trousers. Truly, what was even the point of the Venus catalog if she'd had no idea a man could wander about bare-bottomed beneath his breeches with no one any the wiser?

"Humphrey," he said. "I'll be down momentarily. Whatever you do, do not let them leave."

By the time Emmie entered the room, Selina was wrapped in a dressing gown and Peter was dressed in trousers and shirtsleeves—no waistcoat, no jacket, no cravat. His curls were tousled, and he dragged his fingers through them as Emmie bustled in, laying out a mint-green morning gown, an embroidered chemise, and light stays.

Peter splashed water from an ewer onto his face and started for the door. At the threshold, he paused and turned back, and Selina stopped disrobing long enough to wave at him.

"Go," she said. "I'll be right behind you."

He stood there a moment longer, looking so intently at her that she glanced down to see if her dressing gown had slid off her shoulders and puddled on the floor. It hadn't. She looked back at Peter, whose encompassing gaze took her in for another heartbeat. Then he turned and was gone.

She and Emmie made rapid work of her toilette, Selina talking all the while, explaining Lucinda and Freddie to her pragmatic lady's maid. In minutes, she too was downstairs.

Where had Humphrey put them? There was a sitting room, to be sure. A large, chairless sitting room with a cold hearth. The dining room featured a sad deficit of chairs as well, and no breakfast for two growing children. Surely not the portrait gallery? She prayed Humphrey had not put them in the portrait gallery.

She found them still standing just inside the front door, Peter on one side of the entry, Freddie and Lu facing him. They had one trunk between them. Freddie carried a satchel in his hands. And—her heart twisted in her chest—they wore the same finery that she'd picked out for the wedding breakfast.

They had come, with their things, dressed in their very best clothes.

"What's happened?" she asked.

Lu turned to her, regal and cool as a queen, her chin high. "Great-great-aunt Rosamund is dead."

The words were small shocks in the air, rattling everything that had come before.

"Oh no," Selina said reflexively. "I'm so sorry to hear that."

"We came here," said Freddie. His voice sounded smaller than Selina remembered, as if the house's cold marble floors muffled it. "We didn't know where else to go."

"We've brought our cat," Lu said. "We will remain with the cat or not at all."

"You brought the cat?" Peter said, sounding stupefied. "The gray kitten I gave you?"

"It is *our cat*." Lu's voice was fierce, her green eyes bright. "We aren't going to leave him behind."

"Of course not," Selina told the girl, trying to make her voice soothing. "Of course you must not leave him. Of course he may stay."

"We've named him Peter," said Freddie proudly, flipping open the satchel.

Selina choked on air.

Peter's eyebrows ascended heavenward. "You named *the cat* Peter?"

Freddie nodded. A pair of gray ears emerged from the top of the bag. And then with a hiss, Peter-the-Cat shot out of the satchel like a rocket, leapt onto Peter-the-Duke's shoulder, rebounded to the ground, streaked around the corner, and vanished into the portrait gallery.

Chapter 21

Dear Duchess—how is Peter? (I mean, of course, the cat.)

—from Will to Selina

Selina had taken all of them shopping.

She'd managed it seamlessly. Almost before he knew it, Peter was fully attired and handing Lu up into the Stanhope carriage, while Selina followed behind with Freddie beside her and a carnet under her arm.

"Lucky for you," she had said to the children, "that we were on our way to purchase furniture just this very moment. Now you can choose the finishings for your own bedrooms, rather than having your stodgy duke of a brother select them for you."

He'd had no idea she meant for them to go shopping that day. *Had* she? Or was she simply inventing the errand to fold the children into their morning's activities?

Freddie and Lu were where they were supposed to be, she told them without words. They had bedrooms. They had a brother who wanted them. They belonged.

He swallowed back the tightness in his chest and tried to answer Lu when she asked if her bedroom could include a collection of ropes. She had, she informed him, taken up learning marine knot-tying.

Of course she had. Visions of himself tied hand and foot, at the point of Lu's practice foil, flitted alarmingly through his head.

Across the carriage, Selina sat beside Freddie, their heads bent over her carnet. She seemed to be showing him a list of furnishings she and her lady's maid had drawn up.

"For the sitting room," she said, "I had thought to have the walls re-covered in dark green."

Freddie nodded eagerly. "You'll need draperies."

"Chairs. Sofas."

"Ottomans." Freddie was warming to the theme. "Books. Candelabra. A pianoforte!"

Next to him, Lu sniffed disgustedly.

Selina looked up. "And for your bedroom, Lu? Is there a particular color you have in mind?"

Lu scowled. "I cannot imagine why I would care."

"Lu!" said Freddie, his voice a whispered reproach.

Lu's eyes were bright, her tone brittle. "My apologies. I cannot imagine why I would care, *Your Grace*."

Christ. He wanted to ask Selina to be patient with them. He wanted to shake his sister, and he wanted to hug her and tell her it was safe. No one would make her leave ever again.

But of course, that wasn't precisely true. If he did not get the guardianship, Lu and Freddie would have to leave. Any promises he made would be lies.

He had tried not to show his worry to Selina last night in her office. Yet he could not help but think on what would happen if he did not succeed in Chancery. They would lose Freddie and Lu, and he—

He would have failed them all. It would be one more way that he had not lived up to Selina's expectations, one more black mark against him. A disaster even she could not solve. And as he sat in the carriage with his wife and his siblings, he realized how desperately he wanted to be something more than a disappointment. For all of them.

"Selina," said his wife. She sounded unflustered, even gentle. "Please call me Selina."

Lu sniffed again but didn't reply.

When they reached Bond Street, Selina made for the registry office and gestured for him to take the children on ahead. "First, staff. I'm going to arrange for interviews this week." She eyed him. "You need quite a lot of staff. And a tutor for the children."

He made himself smile. "And a fencing master?"

Her eyes softened. "I will try my best. Can you take them down to R. S. Barrett's? The Ravenscrofts have patronized Barrett for many years. Perhaps we can purchase his whole showroom. I'll follow on shortly."

Barrett's turned out to be not one shop but a whole building, a rabbit's warren of room after room, each stuffed nearly to the eaves with furniture, rugs, fabrics, and artworks. Lacking Selina's list, Peter decided to let Freddie and Lu wander at will.

For Freddie, that meant speechless amazement as he took in his surroundings.

"Inform the shopkeeper if you see anything you like," Peter told him. "Tell them to send the bill to the residence."

Freddie nodded, wide-eyed and eager.

Lu, meanwhile, surveyed the furnishings before her coolly.

"You may as well choose something," Peter said. "For your

bedchamber. Hell, you can make up a bedchamber for the cat, if you like." He refused to refer to the feline by its apparent moniker.

Lu, he was certain, was behind that one.

Even she could not fail to be overcome by the offerings at hand. When Selina arrived a quarter of an hour later, Lu was engrossed in a stack of maritime maps.

"Piracy," he said to Selina with a nod at his sister.

Selina blinked at him. "I beg your pardon?"

"Lu. She's plotting out routes around the Atlantic as we speak. First fencing, then the knots, now the maps—piracy is the only explanation for it."

Selina tipped her head, considering. "Perhaps you ought to encourage privateering instead."

He wanted to laugh, but instead he nodded seriously. "A government contract, you mean?"

"Indeed. A pirate with papers. The Royal Navy can only be improved by Lucinda's collusion with its efforts."

"I'll take it up in the Lords."

Selina laughed, a warm sparkling sound in the musty dimness of Barrett's. His heart did a strange slow roll as he looked at her, flushed and happy.

She was *happy*, here in this dusty shop, buying furniture for his awful empty house.

It felt as fragile as the calm surface of a pond. As easily shattered. If they did not get the children, would she look at him this way again?

"Come," she said, tugging him into the next room, away from Freddie and Lu. "I want to show you something."

But once they crossed the threshold, she maneuvered him around a series of dark mahogany sideboards and enameled end tables into a shadowed corner.

He tried for a grin. "You wanted to show me dusty plaster?"

She rolled her eyes. "No. We've enough of that at home."

Home. There went his stupid heart, thudding against his chest to the rhythm of the word. Solid and steadfast and terrifying. *Home. Home. Home.*

"I wanted to talk about the children," she continued, as if his vital organs weren't splayed open in front of him for her to trample upon. "Peter, this is brilliant. They've come to you of their own accord. Surely Eldon will take that into account at the hearing."

"Yes," he said, trying to focus on her words. "Yes. I hope you're right."

"I am certain I'm right. We've less than two weeks until the hearing, but that's plenty of time to discreetly ensure Eldon knows the children are living with us. We might invite the Eldons over for dinner—or, no, perhaps that's too obvious. We can endeavor to run into Lady Eldon in the park. Make mention of the children's new residence with us. Or"—her eyes lit up—"even better, I can ask Lady Eldon for a recommendation for a tutor and governess." She bit her lower lip as she thought. "I can call upon her tomorrow."

She was so damned *certain*, his wife, and the confidence in her tall golden form drew him like a magnet.

"We cannot let them go," he said, surprised to hear the rasp in his voice.

Selina blinked up at him. "The children, you mean? But they're here now. Where would they go? And *why*?"

"Lu, she . . ." He hesitated. "She doesn't trust me. My father . . . our father. He wasn't a trustworthy sort. He left no provisions for them." Shocking, how it still blazed up, the fury and resentment toward Silas Kent. "Freddie wants to believe, I think. That we can all be together. But Lu is poised to bolt."

One corner of Selina's mouth quirked up. "Then we shall have to make everything too tempting for her to depart. And, given enough time, she'll realize there's nowhere she'd rather be."

It was painful, how much he wanted it all. Wanted the world she imagined so easily, where the children came home to rooms of their own, to dinner and kittens and adults who kept them safe. Wanted *her*—so much he was afraid to touch her for fear he might hurt her by grasping too tightly.

"Peter?" Her wolf's eyes had caught on him, clear and penetrating. "Are you quite all right?"

He wasn't. He wasn't all right. He felt too much, too hard, and it terrified him.

•   •   •

Two days later, Selina ladled coddled eggs onto plates for Freddie and Lu.

"And a kipper?" said Freddie. His hazel eyes were wide and guileless, his cheeks flushed.

Selina pretended not to notice the gray kitten twining about his ankles and added a kipper to his plate.

She crossed to the dining table—a great polished thing from Barrett's that would serve excellently for hosting Peter's political allies—and laid the plates before the children. Rolls and butter and fruit decorated a sideboard, and a newly hired footman had poured them both cups of frothed chocolate.

"Tomorrow," Selina said, "your tutors will attend you. And your governess arrives, Lu."

Lu snorted.

"Do not forget our bargain. *You* refrain from scaring off the governess for three weeks, and *I* shall take you to a private boxing exhibition."

Lu didn't respond but dug into the eggs with relish. Evidently the food at Great-great-aunt Rosamund's had been less salubrious than one might have hoped.

Peter came into the dining room then, and at the grim look upon his face, Selina rose to her feet. "What's happened?"

He looked at her, then at the children, who'd paused mid-bite in alarm. One corner of his mouth turned up, a ghost of his grin. "All's well. The guardianship hearing has been postponed. Backlog in Chancery, it seems."

"Postponed?" Freddie's voice was thin, and he had not touched his eggs. "Does that mean we have to leave?"

"No," said Selina hurriedly. "No, of course not, Freddie."

"You never need to leave," Peter told him.

Lu said nothing, picking up her fork and mechanically eating again, her gaze fixed in the middle distance.

Selina felt a cold weight in her belly. She wanted to believe Peter's promise to Freddie, but the delay felt ominous.

She wanted this to be over. She wanted the children secure and immutably *theirs*. Never before had Belvoir's felt so much like Damocles's sword, dangling above her and liable to fall at any moment.

Despite her efforts, she had not yet found out who had started the rumors about Nicholas. She'd dropped her pride and written a half-frantic note to Lydia asking if she could put her domestic spies to work to find out more.

She felt sick, though, as she stared at the children, at Peter's almost-frown. How could she do this? How could she welcome them home without knowing whether they would truly be able to stay?

Her reputation simply could not be destroyed until after the hearing. She would not permit it. She set her jaw, forcing the fear out of her expression.

"Don't forget to save some room for sweetmeats," she said. "Especially now that Miss Dandridge has learned your favorites."

They had an outing planned for after breakfast with Aunt Judith and Thomasin again. Aunt Judith had suggested they meet in Hyde Park; Selina suspected some subterfuge involving Lady Eldon but was uncertain of the details.

Even Lu was eager to see Thomasin. Selina felt her lips curve as she watched Lu scrape the plate of eggs clean and then bound up the stairs, Freddie and the kitten trailing her.

Peter laid his hand along her back, and she tilted her head into the solidity of his chest.

"It'll be well," he said. "You'll see."

She almost believed him.

In the park, Aunt Judith and Thomasin arrived not with Lady Eldon, but with grooms, footmen, and two ponies, a black and a shaggy bay.

Selina laughed aloud when she saw them. Peter's aspect suggested alarm.

"You," Selina said to her aunt, "are a menace as a grandmother. Ponies! Merciful heavens, Aunt Judith, I had to marshal an extended essay—in French!—when I wanted a dog at Broadmayne. And Freddie and Lu get ponies four days after they join the family?"

Aunt Judith gave Selina an arch look beneath her silver brows. "These children are considerably less spoiled."

Thomasin patted Selina's shoulder. "If you are still feeling bitter, my darling, allow me to remind you that you made Will write most of your essay for you anyway."

Selina felt herself blush as the interested gazes of her spouse, aunt, and two tousle-headed children swung her way. "I most certainly did not."

She had. Her French was execrable.

"Hmph," said Aunt Judith. "That explains why you forbore to read it aloud."

Peter made a muffled sound of laughter, which Selina pointedly ignored. She ushered the children toward the ponies. Lu leapt forward enthusiastically, demanding to know the black pony's name and asking whether she might try to mount it. She stroked its velvety nose, crooning over the white star beneath its forelock.

Freddie hung back.

"Have you ridden before?" Thomasin asked him, her sandy ringlets bobbing beneath a white lace cap.

He nodded, his face flushed. "I am—not sure I was fond of it."

Thomasin's lips quirked. "Let me tell you a secret. Do you remember Selina's brother, the duke? Tall, black hair, rather grave?"

Freddie nodded.

"He was terrified of horses as a boy. Not that you are terrified, of course."

Selina cocked her head, listening. She had never heard this story before.

"I am a little terrified," admitted Freddie.

Thomasin laughed softly. "And how very courageous of you to admit it. Well, Nicholas was quite, quite frightened, and his papa—who loved him very much, but was very stern himself—was determined to teach him not to be afraid."

Selina remembered their father, but only fuzzily—his dark hair, the signet ring he'd worn, the smile line carved on the left side of his mouth. The way he'd let her ride on his shoulders.

"His papa hired a riding instructor, and then a handful of grooms, and no one could convince young Nicholas to mount the horse. But Nicholas was frustrated too—he hated being afraid and wanted to please his papa. So one night, he snuck down to the kitchen and stole a bag of apples, then carried them out to the stable. One by one he fed every single horse there, befriending each in turn. And every night after that, he brought his pony an apple. He fed it while he stroked its nose, then while he brushed its coat and saddled it, and finally when he mounted for the first time. And soon enough he rode his pony, proud as any duke ever was—and do you know? The bedeviled pony had grown so accustomed to the apples that he would not permit a rider other than Nicholas ever again!"

Selina grinned at Thomasin. "I remember that pony! So fat, it was, and the poor thing followed Nicholas around like a dog every time he came home from school."

Thomasin's eyes danced. "Precisely." She fished in a hidden pocket of her pink ruffled gown. "And do you know what I've brought for you, Freddie?"

"An apple?" he said hopefully, and Thomasin laughed.

"Indeed."

Freddie took the proffered apple and approached the shaggy brown pony. It eyed him rather mournfully as the apple bobbed up and down in Freddie's nervous grasp.

Peter came forward and murmured something in Freddie's ear. Selina was reminded with a little whisper of amusement of the first time she had met Peter. He'd thought her horse abandoned in the woods at Broadmayne, their country estate, and the gelding—a great beast of an animal that she adored—had dumped him flat on his arse when he'd tried to mount.

She wondered if he was telling that story to Freddie.

He showed Freddie how to hold the apple out to the horse, his long fingers cupped beneath Freddie's smaller hand. They made a pair, two heads of dark curls bent together, Peter's hat clutched under his other arm. The sun glinted red on their hair.

Freddie finished feeding the apple to the pony. Aunt Judith and Lu had abandoned their little party—Selina suspected Aunt Judith was giving Lu a lesson in horsemanship she wouldn't soon forget. Thomasin spoke in an undervoice to the groom who held the bridle of Freddie's pony.

Peter fell back beside Selina, and she smiled to look at him. His curls fell over his brow, and she reached up to brush them back. She could almost pretend that their marriage did not threaten his future. Here in the sunshine, she could almost believe that he would not come to regret it.

"Did you ride often in New Orleans?"

He turned from where he'd been staring after Lu in the distance and looked distractedly down at her. "Often enough."

"Is something wrong?"

"No," he said, but his voice was strained. "No."

"Is it the hearing? The postponement?" Her stomach clenched. Part of her wanted to cry—she'd *known* he would understand the consequences of Belvoir's eventually. She'd *known* it.

What had she thought? That she was worth the cost?

"We must think of it as an opportunity, Peter," she said and cursed herself for the words.

She had secured a cottage in Cornwall to go to, if the worst happened. She had the note from her man of business tucked into her desk at Belvoir's. She ought to be preparing Peter for her potential departure, not trying to reassure him that all would be well.

It would be better for him if she left. She couldn't make herself say the words.

"An extra week means more time to show the Eldons how perfectly content the children are with us," she said instead. "The tutors, the ponies—all of it will help."

He clasped her hand in his own, the soft leather of her glove thin enough that she could feel his warmth. "It's not the hearing."

He didn't go on. Did he think she did not notice his abruptness? It was not like him—he was always so easy with his words, his charm. She wanted to demand to know what was wrong, but she fought back the urge. She was too much, too insistent. She knew that about herself.

He tucked her hand into the crook of his arm and he didn't look at her when he said, "Freddie asks if he might call Thomasin Grandmother."

She blinked at the non sequitur, but her chest loosened a trifle. "Oh—but of course! Well, no, in fact. Aunt Judith is Grandmother. Thomasin is Grandmama." She smiled at the retreating back of her aunt, tall and straight beside Lu on the pony. "Aunt Judith wanted to be Grandmother Ravenscroft for my nephews—heaven knows why—but they can't manage all of those syllables. *Grandmother* alone is asking quite a lot of wee Teddy." She glanced again at Peter, who was still looking away. "You must tell him to call her Grandmama. Thomasin will be ecstatic."

One corner of his mouth turned up, but it wasn't right. No flash of white teeth, no warm brown eyes capturing hers. Selina cast about for what could be bothering him. "Lu," she said awkwardly, "may call them whatever she likes. I—we—Will and I always called her Thomasin, though she was in so many ways our mother. She's—so good at that. Thomasin. Making a family."

Now he met her eyes. "I'm so glad that the children have you all." His forearm tensed beneath her hand. "I am so damned glad they have you, and Miss Dandridge, and Lady Judith. Your family."

Your family.

She recalled, suddenly and forcefully, the way that Peter had stolen eighteen barrels of French brandy for his grandfather. A man he had never met before coming to England two years past.

"Did you know your grandparents on your mother's side?" she asked. "In Louisiana?"

"They'd died. Long before I was born. When she was a girl."

His tone was not encouraging, but Selina was not easily put off. "What was she like, your mother?"

His dark lashes came down over his eyes for a moment, then lifted. "Brave. Fragile." His voice was steady. "I was raised, mostly, by the mother of my half brother."

"Morgan?" Selina remembered the brother he had mentioned to Lady Eldon at the dinner party, the little boy who had died.

"Yes. My mother struggled with our life in New Orleans, but Morgan's mother"—his lips curved, a fond smile—"she was so good. Sturdy and steadfast and patient with me. It won't surprise you to hear I needed a lot of patience, as a boy. I haven't changed in that regard."

She didn't like the way he said it. "All children require patience. Did you not hear the story of how I made Will write my persuasive essay about *les chiens*?" That more or less exhausted her recollection of the words in the essay.

He huffed a little laugh. "I would have liked to have seen you then."

"You wouldn't. I would have made you fence with me. Or tried to punch you in the nose."

He looked at her then, truly looked, all the force of his gaze trained upon her face. She felt heat rise in her cheeks at the intensity of his regard. "I have always wanted to look at you."

She swallowed. "You . . . may."

She gave herself a little mental shake. Honestly, nearly one hundred salacious volumes in the Venus catalog at Belvoir's and she couldn't come up with anything better than *you may*?

"I'm glad," Peter said, "that Freddie and Lu have your family. I'm glad they will grow up with your family to be patient with them. I—" He broke off.

"You love them," she said.

"Of course."

It was so sweet and sharp in her chest the way he said it, immediate, as if there could be no doubt.

"I do too," she said. "I love them." Her gaze was caught on his. The tilt of his lips, the way the sun glanced off his cheekbones. Her heart kicked up, and she was suddenly terrified because she wanted—she wanted to say—

"And Aunt Judith," she said instead. "And Thomasin—and Nicholas and Daphne, and Will—when he gets home. He will love them." She was babbling. She did not typically babble, but her blood was loud in her ears, because she loved Peter, she *loved* him, and she had almost told him so.

She could not tell him that. Fear gripped her, and not just fear that he might not return her feelings. She was as afraid—perhaps *more* afraid—that he did.

If she spoke the words aloud, it would be real—to him, to her. It would be so much harder to leave him, if she had to.

She could not say it now. Not before the hearing. Not before her secrets were revealed and she judged just how disastrous her effect had been upon his life.

There was a sudden commotion up ahead of them, where

Freddie had been leading his horse by the halter, and Selina broke away from Peter almost desperately, needing distance from the warm pull of his body.

"Lu's probably taken off for the docks," said Peter wryly.

But as they drew closer, Selina saw that it was not Lu and Aunt Judith at all, but rather Thomasin, seated on the ground, her pink skirts crumpled around her.

She darted forward, Peter just behind her. "What's happened?"

In Thomasin's lap, half-curled, lay Freddie.

"Selina," Thomasin said, and the tone of her voice sent ice crawling down the back of Selina's neck. So calm. So perfectly even. "Freddie has taken ill. I've sent a footman around for the carriage."

Selina dropped to her knees beside the older woman. "Taken ill? Why—he seemed—"

She thought of Freddie—his cheeks flushed pink, his hand trembling as he held the apple. His face still burned with hectic color as he lay in Thomasin's lap, his eyes barely open.

"I'm all right," he said, his voice thready.

Selina brushed a hand over his hair, and she felt his fever—so *hot*—straight through her gloves.

"What do we do?" she asked Thomasin. Her own voice was somehow unaffected as well, though she felt dizzy with sudden fright.

"Take him home," said Thomasin. "Put him to bed. Cool cloths for his forehead. I always liked to use lavender essence when you and Will were small."

The crisp, calm instructions steadied her, and she rose, turning to Peter. "Shall we go to the—"

Her words died in her throat.

Peter's face was stricken. His brown eyes were unfocused, almost dazed, and his skin had taken on a strange, unhealthy pallor. He looked *through* her, through Freddie, into some distant place she could not follow.

"Are you well?" she demanded. "Peter?"

"He was warm." He sounded puzzled. "I thought he felt warm. When I helped him feed the apple to the pony. I thought . . . his coat. I thought he might need new clothes."

Selina licked her lips, her mouth dry, her throat tight. "All right. Can you go 'round and wait for the carriage? I'll get Lu."

"Lu," he breathed. He looked at Selina, abruptly intent. "Don't frighten her. I don't—want her to be frightened. Tell her . . . tell her everything will be well."

"Everything *will* be well." She said it as much for herself as for him. "In a day or two. Children take ill often." Nicholas and Daphne's boys certainly did—earaches and coughs and small head colds.

"Yes," said Peter bleakly. "They do."

Chapter 22

Lyd—can you find Gabe and send him here? Right away, if you can. I don't like to write it but—I'm frightened.

—from Selina to Lydia, sent with a footman to the Hope-Wallace residence

Freddie was still sick the next day.

They'd brought the children home, and Peter had stood, dazed and helpless, as Selina tucked Freddie into the bed they'd acquired from Barrett's. She'd produced a folded linen and a crystal cup full of water and violets.

"When we were children, it was lavender," she'd told Lu with sturdy cheer. "But I always thought lavender a most unpleasantly potent scent."

She'd dipped the linen and then laid it against Freddie's brow. She'd had tea sent to the sickroom, and then—when Freddie began to toss and turn uneasily—she'd ushered Lu out the door.

When she came back, she'd thrown open the windows and

told Peter that Lu was to be sent to Rowland House, for fear of contagion.

But really, Peter thought, she didn't want Lu to see her brother like this. Little, in the big rosewood bed. Sweaty and miserable as he twisted in the white bedsheets. Peter thought perhaps she didn't want Lu to feel as helpless as he felt, sitting pointlessly beside the bed and watching his brother cough and cough and cough.

It had been a long night in the sickroom. Selina had tried to persuade him to come to bed—"Emmie will watch him, or Humphrey"—but he couldn't make himself leave. He didn't trust his own legs.

And when the sun cracked the horizon, nothing had changed. When the shadows lengthened with the afternoon, Freddie had taken two sips of beef tea, Selina had gone through an ewer of cool water and half a dozen linens, and the room, despite the open window, smelled sour with sickness. Peter remembered that smell.

"All right," said Selina. "I don't like this. I'd like to call a physician, if you don't mind." She laid a hand on Peter's shoulder. "Do you mind?"

He should have done that. He should have managed it himself—the linens, the water, the physician. He should have realized Freddie was ill and kept him home. He had known he would fail them, in some critical moment, when it mattered the most. He had known he would not be enough.

"Yes," he said. "Call the physician."

The man who came into the room several hours later was roughly of an age with Peter, and Peter—when he forced his gaze away from his brother's thin, restless form—thought he looked vaguely familiar.

"Gabe," said Selina, leaping to her feet from the chair on the opposite side of Freddie's bed from Peter. "Thank goodness you're here." She caught the man's arm in hers, bringing him to the bed beside Peter, who'd managed with an effort to bring himself to his feet.

"Peter," she said, "this is Lydia's brother, Gabriel Hope-Wallace. He's a year out of the Royal College of Physicians. Gabe, this is my husband Peter, the Duke of Stanhope."

The doctor was tall and fair, though the new growth of beard on his jawline was as red as Lydia's hair. He bobbed a quick nod at Peter, his gaze already trained on Freddie. "How long has he been ill?"

"Since yesterday," Selina said. "He fainted yesterday afternoon in the Park. He's been feverish, and last night he started to cough."

"Conscious?" the doctor said.

Peter felt his jaw tighten painfully. Once again, Selina responded. "Yesterday, he was. Today he's been lucid at—at times." Her voice broke a little.

"All right. Anything else?"

Selina shook her head wordlessly, and Hope-Wallace strode forward to examine Freddie. He felt along his body, rolled him to his side like a doll. He pressed his ear to Freddie's back for a few long moments then stood, casting about with an expression of frustration.

"Have you a heavy sheet of paper?" he asked.

Selina darted for the door. "I'll get one. I'll be right back."

Peter looked at the doctor, panic chasing circles in his chest. "Paper?"

"Mm," said Hope-Wallace. He'd returned to the boy, lifting Freddie's hand to examine his fingernails, cupping Freddie's jaw to look into his mouth. "Helps me listen to the lungs when auscultation by ear is insufficient."

Selina returned with an engraved sheet, and Hope-Wallace rolled it into a long, thin tube. He placed it against Freddie's back and put his ear to it.

Mad, Peter thought. It seemed mad—the doctor, the fragile roll of paper. He bore no instruments, no lancets for bleeding or small glass jars of laudanum and oils.

Eventually the doctor stood, satisfied by what evidence had emerged from the paper tube. "Pneumonia," Hope-Wallace said. "His lungs are inflamed."

"Consumption?" Peter forced the word from where it had lodged, painful as glass, in his chest the moment he'd heard Freddie's cough. His voice was raw.

Hope-Wallace turned to him, sharp blue eyes softening. "No. Not consumption at all. His symptoms are entirely different."

Relief slid through Peter, making his joints weak.

"Consumption," said Hope-Wallace, in the tones of one giving a lecture, "has symptoms for weeks—even months or years—before the crisis. His fingernails would be pitted and, at this stage, quite blue." He gestured to Freddie's hand. "See for yourself. A bit pale, perhaps, but those are healthy digits."

Peter blinked at Freddie's fingers, his vision hazed.

"All right," Selina said hesitantly. "What can we do?"

There was a long silence, long enough for Peter's vision to clear, for him to watch the tightening of Hope-Wallace's whiskered jaw. "Nothing, I expect."

"You can't mean that." Peter scarcely recognized his own voice.

The doctor turned to him, his expression kind. "He will likely recover. But bleeding, leeches, starving—I have hundreds of observational studies from my colleagues in England and India showing that they do not help in cases of catarrh and pneumonies.

I have—" He broke off. "Keep him cool. Yarrow tea for the fever. I mislike willow bark for children. Laudanum or whiskey, if the pain takes him harder."

"That's it?" Peter said roughly. "You can't cure him? You have no solution, not even something you can *try*—"

Hope-Wallace's mouth drew into a stiff line. "Certainly there are things I could try. All manner of tinctures I could sell to you with my name on them, and half a dozen ingredients that could kill as well as cure him. I could cut open his vein, if you insist."

"Gabe," said Selina. Her voice was reproachful, and the doctor looked chastened.

"My apologies," he said. "It is—frustrating. Not to be able to do more. But I will not hurt this child out of impatience or stubbornness."

"So we wait," Peter said.

"Yes. You wait."

"Will you attend him tomorrow?" Selina asked.

A half smile touched the doctor's lips. "For anyone else, I would say that you've no need of me. But—yes, Selina. I'll come back tomorrow night for your boy."

Hope-Wallace moved briskly to straighten the bedsheets around Freddie, to change the lukewarm water for fresh. He looked out the window, and asked after the housekeeper so that he might make a list of what herbs she ought to acquire from the apothecary. Selina offered to take on the shopping herself.

And all the while, Peter sat, motionless, at the side of the bed.

While Selina was gone, her maid, Emmie, came into the room, bearing fresh bedlinens and clothing for Freddie. Wordlessly, Peter helped her lift his brother's small body. Freddie felt as hot as a brand to the touch, and when Peter peeled off his sweaty shirt, Freddie coughed so hard his body nearly came out of Peter's grip.

"Sorry," Freddie mumbled. "Sorry, Lu—the kitten."

"Hush," said Peter, pushing Freddie's dark damp hair back from his forehead. "Hush. Everything's all right."

When he slipped the fresh shirt over Freddie's head, the boy didn't protest.

"Your Grace," said Emmie hesitantly. "I'm happy to watch the child for a few hours. I've a small sister of my own—I've sat by her many a night, whilst she's been fevered."

"No," Peter said.

"As you wish. Only—that is, Her Grace. She would have you take your rest."

"No," Peter said again. "I can't. I'm sorry."

Emmie nodded and slipped from the room, and Peter was alone again, but for the small boy in the too-big bed.

Perhaps he dozed. It felt like only moments had passed when he felt the cool touch of a hand at the back of his neck, but it was full night. No candles winked in the darkness, and the weather was warm enough that no embers glowed in the fireplace.

"Any change?" Selina said softly at his side. Her fingers petted the nape of his neck, then both hands came to his shoulders, kneading into the muscles there.

"I don't think so." Freddie's face was drawn into sharper lines, and when Peter tried to run a wet linen along his cracked and reddened lips, he whimpered and turned his head away.

"Come to bed," Selina said. "You need to lie down."

"I can't."

"Peter. I will stay with him."

"I *can't.*" His voice snapped out like a whip, but Selina didn't flinch back.

"You aren't helping him if you make yourself ill as well, Peter. You need food and rest. You need—"

"I can't leave him. He might wake. He might need me. When your physician comes back, I want to be able to tell him if Morgan has—"

He choked off the words as he heard them. Too late.

Selina didn't respond for a long time. She stood behind him, her hands on his shoulders, her thumbs tracing circles on his shirt.

When she dropped her hands and stepped away, he clenched his jaw and didn't speak. Shame surged in him. He had failed Morgan, had failed Freddie and Lu. Even now, he could not do what needed to be done. He wanted to curl into his wife and lay his head in her lap, wanted to beg her not to leave him alone. *Selfish. Reckless. Weak.*

And then she pulled a chair from the other side of the bed around to sit beside him.

"How old was Morgan when he died?"

It was so dark in the room. He could barely hear Freddie's raspy breathing, barely see his own hands tangled into the white sheets before him.

"Twelve," he said. "We were of an age. Which should tell you something of our father—he married my mother and fathered Morgan and me within the same trip to New Orleans."

"Who was she—Morgan's mother?"

"Josephine was a French servant in the house. A maid he took a fancy to." He'd asked Josephine once—when he was much older—if his father had forced her. *No*, she'd said. *Peter, child, no.*

But his father had been the new master of the house, Josephine an unmarried girl of eighteen with a little sister to care for. There were many ways a woman could be forced.

"Was he . . . much like Freddie?"

"No." His hands closed into fists on the bed. He couldn't say more. He didn't want to think of Morgan's face, even as he could think of nothing else.

"How did he die?"

Christ, she was relentless in her questions. He opened and closed his fingers on the bedsheets, angry and ashamed of his own anger.

"Consumption," he managed.

"Was he sick for a long time?"

"Selina." He grasped at her name like a lifeline. "Why are you doing this?"

"I don't know!" To his surprise, her voice rose on the words, and he turned toward her, though he could scarcely make out her features in the dark room. "I have no idea what I'm doing, Peter. Only that you are hurting and alone, and I want to be with you, and . . . and take on some of this burden, only you will not let me!"

"Selina—"

"No, I'm sorry," she said over him. "I'm sorry, God, I'm so sorry. I am frightened, and I don't know what to do, and I'm so sorry I can't do more. That's what I should have said, not speared you with recriminations when you do not deserve them."

He didn't know what to do with all the emotions that clogged his throat, burned at the back of his eyes. He seized on the easiest thing to express. "I won't let you take on this burden? Selina, you have done—you have arranged everything. The doctor, the water—even the bed in this room, damn it."

"I—but—" She hesitated. "Peter, those are just *things*."

He remembered when she had said the same about the great empty house, the day they were married. The furnishings were just *things*. "I don't know what you mean."

He felt, more than saw, her helpless shrug. "It's easy for me. To arrange minutiae. To call for someone, to pay someone to fetch furniture or fresh cloths." She drew a breath, let it out shakily. "I do not know how to make someone stop hurting. How to help when . . . when someone is afraid or grieving. I'm not good at things like that, at being gentle or kind or . . ."

He reached out blindly in the dark and found her hands, locked together in her lap. He closed his fingers over hers and squeezed.

"Don't you hear what I'm doing, Peter? Right now—talking about myself, how frightened I am, when all I want to be doing is easing things for you."

"You do ease me."

Her hands unlocked and grasped his, cradling his fingers between her palms. "How can you say that?"

"You make it possible for me to be beside him. You make it so that I don't have to worry that the children don't know where they belong. You have made this goddamned house, which reminded me of nothing so much as my father, into a home. For all of us."

They sat in silence for long moments. He looked at the small outline on the bed that was Freddie, motionless but for the coughs that occasionally rippled through him.

He wanted to talk to her. He wanted to answer her questions and make her understand—who Morgan had been, and their father, and Josephine—and yet it was so hard to do it. He couldn't find the words that usually spilled from him like water from a cup.

"I didn't know he was my brother," he said finally, "for a very long time. Stupid, really—we looked so similar. I was older, by two weeks, but Morgan was bigger. And better than me at"—somehow, a breath of laughter slipped free—"everything, he would have said. Swimming and starting fires and finding the most interesting places to hide. I was better at convincing his mother not to punish us."

He would have expected that seventeen years after his brother had died, Morgan's face would be hazed over by time, but he could still call it up: hazel eyes in a pale face, the deep notch of Morgan's upper lip. Perhaps because Morgan's face had been so like his own.

"Our father married my mother because she was rich, and when they married all of her property became his. She was a woman alone, her parents dead, and he convinced her that he believed in what she did. Abolition. Self-government." Josephine had told him, over a dish of her rice and beans, of how charming Silas Kent had been. How easily Peter's mother had been taken in by his pretty words, wanting to believe that she had found some-one to share her life's work.

"After they wed, he told her he wanted to purchase a planta-tion," Peter continued. "She fought him tooth and nail, and every time he went back to England—which was often—she dismantled what he'd done. She wrote to Wilberforce, to Thomas Clarkson, long letters against slavery that she asked them to read aloud in Parliament. She tried to convert to Quakerism but, because she was married, they wouldn't allow it.

"He was always angry. His name, his reputation—she dragged it through the dirt and spit on it, he'd say."

It was easy, too, to call up these memories—his father, red-faced and screaming. *Stupid selfish bitch! You have no idea what you've done.*

Peter had thought his father might kill her.

"Eventually he gave up. When I was nine or so, he left for the last time. He was sick already, then—yellow fever. He took every penny we had and left us there." *Rot in this godforsaken place*, he'd said.

They would have, probably, if not for Josephine. His mother

had crumpled—she had always been brave, but she had also always been wealthy, had always had servants and caretakers, a cook, people to work for her who loved and respected her. But without money, the house had fallen to decay, vines curling through the walls of the stables, the well filling with brackish water.

Josephine had taken care of Morgan and Peter and his mother too, had single-handedly managed their finances, taught Peter and Morgan to mend their own stockings and pick persimmons when the skins were soft.

"It was a year or two after that that Morgan got sick. He started to cough when we'd swim." *Morgan's face, breaking the surface of the pond, white and a little frightened, gasping for breath.* "He would grow feverish at night and in the morning be fine again. It went on and on—he wasn't hungry. He didn't want to ride any longer. One day I was taller than he was. One day he got in bed and never got out again. That was when Josephine told me that he was my brother."

Selina, who had been silent through this recital, cupping his hand between her own, took a small, gulping breath. "I'm so sorry. I'm so sorry that you lost him."

He let her trace the arch of his knuckles and did not pull away. "I got it into my head that my father didn't know." He couldn't have said why he'd believed it—he'd known his father was a contemptible sod for years.

Hope, probably. Impossible, childish hope.

"I wrote to him. I told him that Morgan was sick. I *begged* him to send us—hell, anything. Doctors. Money. Medicines. And then when he didn't respond, I thought the letter must have been misdirected, so I wrote to him again. And again."

"Oh, Peter. Oh no."

"He finally answered. He said he had no son in New Orleans—not Morgan, and not me." He laughed, and it was a *wrong* sound, here in Freddie's bedroom. Bitter and hateful. "He would have been so goddamned angry to see me here. Living in his house. Spending his money. Ruining everything he thought was so important—the Kent name, the title, our place in this world—all the things that mattered more to him than his own children." His voice broke on the last word, and he hated the weakness in it, hated the pleasure he took in spiting his father, who was *dead*, for God's sake, who *should not matter* any longer, and yet did.

"It wouldn't have changed anything, in the end. Morgan had consumption—it's not as though he could have been cured, even if our father had sent a chest full of gold bars. But he didn't even try—he didn't even see Morgan, didn't acknowledge him." He'd left them—all of them—to rot. Just as he'd said.

Selina tucked her feet up into her chair and shifted her body closer to his, pressing her arm against his arm, tipping her head onto his shoulder. She was warm, and she smelled familiar and real beside him.

"We won't leave Freddie alone," she said. "Not for a moment. I promise."

He swallowed, and could not speak.

"Put your head on mine," she said. "Rest."

Peter drew a breath then laid his head atop hers. Her hair was soft against his cheek.

He had done nothing to deserve her. There was no reason she should be here beside him, all night, holding vigil over his brother.

There was no reason she should care for all of them—no reason except that it was her nature to care, to protect and love and try to set things right.

He didn't know how to make the family he'd always wanted, how to drag the fantasy kicking and screaming into the world. He didn't know how to give Freddie and Lu security, a solid steady hearth fire. He wanted to keep the children safe, and yet part of him was shouting that this was proof—that he could not do so. That he would fail.

He could not think of losing Freddie. He could not bear to imagine losing any of them, and yet it seemed inevitable now: loss and grief and the sickening childish heartbreak over being abandoned.

It took a long time for his anger to dissipate, and Selina said nothing all the while. Merely held fast to his hand. He gripped her fingers in return, holding as if to life itself, and she did not pull away.

She was the heart of their small, fragile family, and he feared what would happen between them if everything fell apart. He trusted her—her calm and confidence and patience—and yet he feared too that she would not want to live in a family as fractured as his own had been. She had been raised in the tight knot of Ravenscroft affection, in the knowledge that she was safe and precious and loved.

Safe, he thought, and tightened his fingers on hers. There was nothing he would not give to keep her that way—Selina and Freddie and Lu.

Precious, he thought, and breathed in the spicy-sweet scent that was bergamot and Selina's skin.

Loved, he thought. *My love*, he thought and had no other words but those.

Chapter 23

. . . And when, dear child, are you bringing your wife to visit me? I am eager to meet her. You've been quite cryptic, but I know you. She must be fine indeed. By the way, I have the estate well in hand—stop sending so much money!

—from Josephine de Marigny, of New Orleans, Louisiana, to Peter Kent, the ninth Duke of Stanhope

On the third morning of his illness, Freddie's fever had not abated. Selina had persuaded Peter to sleep on the mattress Lu had dragged into Freddie's room their first night in the house. One of the children, it seemed, was afraid of the dark. Selina did not know which.

She thought about Lu over at Rowland House and hoped someone would have thought to leave her plenty of candles.

Thomasin would have thought of it. She hoped Thomasin had thought of it.

She'd convinced Peter to leave long enough to wash and

change his clothes. When he came back, he'd brought her tea, too hot and too sweet, as she liked it.

She'd left them only when she had to. Belvoir's—she could not forget about the looming threat of Belvoir's, and the rumors that had begun to swirl about her family. Her banker had revealed that it was a *woman* who had investigated the ownership of the property, and Selina had cross-referenced her membership rolls and her brother's parliamentary opposition until her eyes crossed. Was it the wife of one of Nicholas's political enemies? The daughter?

She did not know.

On the afternoon of the third day, her family came: Nicholas and Daphne, Lu pale and grim between Aunt Judith and Thomasin. Selina made Daphne and Nicholas stay belowstairs—if there was contagion, she would not have them bring it to her nephews.

Lu wanted to see Freddie, and Selina thought that perhaps she wanted to see Peter as well. When they made it to Freddie's room, Lu stood in the threshold, motionless and silent.

"The doctor's seen him," Peter said. Selina's heart broke a little. It had been the only thing he'd wanted for his brother when he was a boy. It was the first thing he said to Lucinda.

Lu's throat worked, but she didn't speak. Her green eyes were wet. Peter moved suddenly toward her, as if to fold her into his arms, but she darted back from him, then fled for the stairs.

Thomasin started to move after the child, but Aunt Judith laid her hand on Thomasin's arm. "Let me."

Selina felt for a moment that what Lu needed was Thomasin's gentleness, her sweeping acceptance—but then, perhaps that wasn't it. Perhaps what Lu needed was Aunt Judith, stern and forbidding, to *make* her believe that everything would be all right.

Instead Thomasin went to the bed, and somehow persuaded

Freddie to take a full cup of yarrow tea, when none of the rest of them had managed more than a sip or two. He slept easier after that, for hours after Lu and the Ravenscrofts had gone.

When Gabe Hope-Wallace returned, he looked at Freddie's drawn face, then briskly performed the same examination he had the day prior.

"Be patient," he said finally, flattening the tube of paper and sliding it into his pocket. "Give him time to heal."

It was hard for her to be patient, with Freddie thin and drawn in the bed, Lu belowstairs, and Peter frozen and terrified at her side. But she bit back her fear and walked Hope-Wallace to the door. He instructed her what to do if Freddie's fever were to break and told her he would come back again the next day.

She brought Peter supper on a tray, coaxed him to sit and eat. When he fell asleep with his head bent onto Freddie's sheets, she kept watch over the boy, and when Peter woke around dawn, she took herself to their bedchamber alone to write to Jean Laventille again and then, eventually, to try to sleep.

When she woke, the sun was high, and she sat bolt upright, alarm flooding her.

Why had no one woken her? She wrapped herself in her dressing gown, raking her fingers through her hair and not stopping to clean her teeth. Freddie's bedroom was a floor below the ducal chamber, and she darted down the stairs barefoot, clutching the smooth dark banister.

At the end of the hall, past the doors that opened onto Freddie's and Lu's chambers, she saw Emmie, wrapped in the embrace of Humphrey, Peter's tall, slender valet. She was crying.

Selina's fingers went nerveless. "Emmie?"

The maid and valet leapt apart. Humphrey looked the very picture of guilty alarm, but Emmie's face broke into a damp grin. "Oh, my lady—that is, Your Grace—" Tears threatened her words. "All's well! All's well with the boy."

Selina turned and pulled open the door to Freddie's chamber with still-numb hands.

Sunlight poured through the open casement window, and caught in the beam of light lay Freddie, burrowed beneath the coverlet that had earlier been tossed aside. Peter lay stretched out beside him in the big bed, fully dressed, one arm thrown across his own face, and the other hand resting on Freddie's head. At the foot of the bed, eyeing her scornfully, was the gray kitten.

Cautiously, she approached the bed. Freddie's face was thin, but no hectic spots of color burned on his cheeks. She laid a hand across his forehead, very gently.

Cool. His skin felt cool. He moved a little, his eyelashes fluttering and a cough breaking free—but less racking than it had been. As she watched, he slipped back into a deeper sleep. The corner of his mouth quirked up.

She gave a little gasping half sob, and sat down hard in the chair beside the bed. Peter stirred, then lifted his hand from Freddie's hair and sat up. His curls tumbled over his forehead.

"He's going to be all right," she whispered.

Peter's warm brown eyes—his beloved grin—

"Yes," he said.

She was lost. She couldn't break her gaze from his, couldn't stop searching his face. Relief, she saw there. Exhaustion, elation. Something else.

"Go back to sleep," she said, afraid of what she might say, afraid of what she wanted so much she could almost imagine it into being. "I'll hurry to Rowland House. I'll get Lu."

He still looked at her. She could pick out the motes of dust in the light spilling through the window.

"Thank you." His voice was thick with sleep and emotion.

She nodded a little and swiped at her eyes before she fled.

* * *

Peter left Freddie's room with one final glance at his brother. Freddie still slept, but it felt different—a deep, comfortable sleep, his breathing a little raspy but unhurried. No longer the desperate gaspiness of lungs unable to take in enough air.

Outside the door, he saw Humphrey's tall form, dressed rather absurdly in worn buckskin breeches and the formal coat that Selina had acquired for him before the nightmare of Freddie's illness had begun. Peter stifled a laugh, but it filled him, buoyant and delighted.

Humphrey jerked around, startled, and Peter had a momentary glimpse of Emmie, Selina's maid, nestled beneath Humphrey's long, bony arm, before she squeaked and darted for the stairs.

When had *that* happened? The bubble of mirth swelled in Peter's chest.

"Your Grace!" said Humphrey, and his voice creaked alarmingly on the words.

"Humphrey," said Peter gravely.

"Emmie—that is, Her Grace's—er—she—" Humphrey sounded strangled. "She says your brother's getting on better."

"He is."

Humphrey's head bobbed in a nervous nod. Then another. He opened his mouth and, when no words emerged, shut it again.

Peter took pity on him. "I'd like to wash and change clothes before my wife returns with my sister."

Humphrey appeared to sag with the relief of having some direction. "Of course, Your Grace. I'll get some hot water—let me go to your bedchamber—" Still speaking, he turned and made his way to the staircase, Peter following in his wake.

Freddie was going to be all right. As Peter bathed, as he let Humphrey lather and scrape away the three days' growth of whiskers on his face, the words bounced merrily through him, an India rubber ball of happiness.

Freddie was going to be all right, and Lu was coming home and he could tell her so.

He met her on his way down the stairs. Lu was coming up, her hair a wild tangle of curls, one pin sticking straight out over her ear. She met his gaze. Little white lines bracketed her mouth, and she didn't speak. She turned down the hall and made for Freddie's bedroom.

Selina was only steps behind Lu, and when Peter met her at the landing, she tilted her head after his sister. "Go," she said. "Be with them."

He hesitated, looking at her. She still looked weary. He moved toward her, cupped his hand behind her head and kissed her hard on the mouth.

"Thank you," he said when they broke away from each other. "For bringing her. Go rest. I'll come for you."

"Call me if you need anything," she said. "With Freddie or Lu or . . . anything."

He squeezed her shoulders once before turning toward the door Lu had disappeared behind. A part of him wanted to tow Selina behind him. She understood Lu better than he ever had. She was like Lu, vivid and ferocious, and she would know how to tell Lu everything he didn't know how to say.

But he couldn't. Somehow it seemed important that he do it himself.

He pulled open the door. Lu stood awkwardly by the side of the bed, her hands tucked into her armpits. Even from behind, he could see that her body was stiff. She wasn't crying.

He came over to her and let his hand rest on her shoulder. "He's going to be fine."

"How do you know?" It was a challenge and a demand.

He looped one of her ringlets around his finger. "We had the doctor out. Selina's friend. She says he's some kind of prodigy, smarter than all the other medical men put together. He says Freddie's lungs are inflamed, but now that the fever's gone, he just needs to rest and get better on his own."

"He's never been sick like this before."

"I'm sorry," Peter said. "I know how hard it is to see him this way."

"What do you know?" Lu asked sharply. "What do you know about anything? You're not from here—you don't know us—not Freddie—or me—"

"Lu. Little one. It's all right."

"No," she said. "No! You made me—you made me *leave* him!" The words came out furious and torn.

"I'm sorry," he said again. "I didn't want you to take ill too. I wanted to protect you. Lu, I never left him alone. Not for one minute. I promise you."

His fingers cupped her thin shoulder, and she reached up and flung off his hand, her body rigid and trembling.

"*I* protect him. *I* take care of him." Her teeth sank into her lower lip.

"You do," he said. "You have done. You've done a good job, Lu."

Her small square hand—so like Morgan's—came up to cover her eyes. She sobbed, once, and then stopped on a gasp. "He's going to be all right?"

"Yes," he said. "Yes."

He folded her into his arms and this time she let him.

"I won't leave you either, Lu."

"How do you know?" she said into his chest. "How do you *know*? Our mother died. Our guardian. Great-great-aunt Rosamund. Everyone left."

"I won't leave you," he said fiercely. "We're a family, Lu. Me and you and Freddie and Selina. The Ravenscrofts. That infernal kitten."

He'd been so afraid. He realized that with sudden clarity. So afraid that he couldn't make Lu trust him, that he couldn't force the Court of Chancery to make the children his. But more than that, he'd been afraid of what would happen if he *did* get them. If Lu trusted him. If Freddie loved him. How could someone like him deserve the keeping of two small, fragile, beloved children?

How could he keep himself from breaking them? How could he protect them from any kind of hurt?

He couldn't. He saw that now, as clearly as he saw Freddie, deeply asleep in the too-big bed. They would be hurt. They would get sick. They would be afraid.

And he would love them through it. He would sit up all night, watching the shadows on their faces change with the slow crawl of the moon. That was what mattered.

That he loved them. That he stayed.

"You can hug me back, you know," he said into Lu's tangled hair.

There was a long pause. And then, very decisively, Lu said: "No."

A laugh unspooled itself from his chest, an unfettered exclamation of delight loud enough that Freddie, in the bed, turned his head toward them and coughed.

Lu ducked under Peter's arm and sat gingerly on the bed beside Freddie. She stroked back his hair and deftly tucked his blankets around him.

He cracked open one hazel eye. "Lu," he sighed. "Finally. Thirsty." The eye closed again.

Lu didn't look up from where she stared down at her brother, but Peter could see the fat splotch a tear made in Freddie's hair. "Didn't you hear him? He needs more tea."

"I heard him. I'll ring for it."

"He'll want Peter too."

Peter blinked at her. "I'll stay. Of course I'll stay."

She angled a glance up at him through dark curly lashes. He had the distinct impression she was biting her cheek to keep her lips from curving into a smile. "Not you, you idiot. His cat."

He reached forward and pulled the stray pin out of her hair, stuffing it into his pocket. "I'm going to tell Selina to fire your fencing master if you don't rename that fuzzy monstrosity."

He was certain she was biting her cheek now. "You shouldn't have given him to us if you weren't prepared for the consequences."

He moved to the windowsill and plucked the kitten up from where it was curled in a square of afternoon sun. "Keep your claws away from my brother," he told it firmly, then deposited it on the pillow beside Freddie's head.

The kitten sniffed delicately at Freddie's face, then picked its way over his chest to curl up beneath his arm.

"He's biding his time," Lu said. "Keeping his claws sharp for you."

He brushed a hand over her mess of curls. "He's in good company then." He moved to the stack of fresh linens one of the new maids had brought earlier that morning and changed the case on the pillow beside Freddie's head for a fresh one. "For you, if you want to nap."

He felt a little foolish as he did it. She was twelve—not a small child who napped. She toyed with the embroidered corner of the pillowcase, and then looked up at him. Her bright-green eyes were suddenly, unaccountably soft.

She nodded, just once. Then she looked down at Freddie and smiled.

Peter felt his heart beating steadily against his ribs. He thought that perhaps he had done all right.

He closed the door to the room gently when he left, whistling a Spanish tune from his childhood. He had tea to fetch for Freddie. A sandwich for Lu, if she managed to stay awake for it.

And after that, he needed his wife.

Chapter 24

. . . the pleasures of love had been to us what the joy of victory is to an army: repose, refreshment, everything . . .

—*from* FANNY HILL

He found her in the bath.

The great square marble tub had been built into the upstairs bathing room by one of his more profligate relations. The benefit, he'd reflected, of his forebear's extravagance was that the tub could not be removed from the premises, and so he'd been able to offer Selina a place to wash rather better than a basin and ewer.

The air in the bath was humid and fragrant. He could see Selina's head tipped back against the wide marble ledge, her hair curled into tiny springs by her ears. Her eyes were closed.

It struck him as mildly alarming. Surely it could not be safe to sleep in the bath.

He approached and then wasn't quite sure what to do with himself. He didn't want to frighten her. She could slip under the water and drown.

That, he supposed, wasn't entirely likely. Still. He cleared his throat decorously from just over her shoulder.

Her eyes flew open, and she squeaked, water sloshing over the ledge of the bath and onto the tile surrounding it.

"Oh," she gasped, sitting up. "Peter!" She glanced down at her naked form, so he, naturally, followed her gaze. "Is everyone well belowstairs? Have you need of me?"

Christ, she was the loveliest thing he'd ever seen. Her pale skin was pink from the warmth, her legs long, her thighs plumply curved.

"I—" he said. "What?"

"Lu and Freddie." He managed to find her face, which had nearly adopted his very favorite glare. "Everyone's fine?"

"Mm-hmm," he said, and then he sat on the square rim of the bath and took off his boots.

"Well, good," she said. "I'll just—finish up here." She gestured vaguely at herself, her lips pursing.

"No need," he said, and he picked up her cake of soap and set to work lathering it into the fine sponge that she'd laid on the tub's wide marble ledge. When it was suitably foamed, he dunked it into the water and swirled it carefully along Selina's shoulders and collarbone. Little streams of bergamot-scented water caressed her breasts, breaking around her rosy nipples.

"Peter," she said, amusement and desire lacing her voice. "Your shirt."

Water had splashed up his forearms, the white linen going transparent and clinging to his skin. He paused to roll up his sleeves, then returned to his task.

Selina licked her lips. He washed her shoulders, her arms, her long tapered fingers. "Sit forward," he said, and when she did, he soaped her back, squeezing the sponge so clear water washed the foam away. He trailed one finger down her ribs, stopping at the flare of her hips.

"I wanted to say something," he said.

"Yes?" She sounded a little breathless, and it pleased him extremely.

"You're stuck with us now. Lu and Freddie. The kitten. Me." He brought the sponge beneath the surface of the water and used it to trace the dip of her waist, the soft curve of her buttocks. "This house. It's yours, all of it. All of us. There's no going back."

"I don't want to go back."

"Good," he said. "We might have to rename the cat."

She laughed, and he slid the sponge over her hip bone, down the crease between her thigh and her sex. "You can—you can be the one to tell Lu," she said. Her voice wobbled.

"I imagined you'd have better ideas about how to bribe her." He trailed the sponge beneath her navel, down one leg and then back up. The sponge slipped from his fingers beneath the water as he caught the slippery curve of her thigh in his palm. Water splashed nearly to his shoulder.

"I—" He looked to her face, saw her throat bob as she swallowed. "I am—sure I could think of something."

"Can you?" he said, coasting his palm up her thigh, laying it flat over her mound. "Perhaps I'm not applying myself."

She made a soft sound and her hips twitched against his hand.

"God," he said. "God, Selina." He'd been trying to tease. To pet and coddle her. But emotion suddenly broke from his chest into his voice at her breathy, wordless sound of need.

Christ, he needed her too. He needed her so goddamned much.

"Stand up." His voice came out low, harsh with demand.

When she stood, water cascaded down her body. He wanted to follow each rivulet with his hands, his mouth, his tongue.

He took her hips between his hands and urged her out of the bath, then pressed her down to sit on the ledge. Water pooled on the floor around their feet. He knelt between her thighs, and the water soaked his trousers, his knees pressing into the slippery marble.

He stroked up and down her thighs, his hands circling closer and closer to her sex. She breathed, a quick shuddering gasp, and he looked up at her.

She was paradise in the afternoon light. Gold, gold all over, her hair, her eyes—soft and heated everywhere he touched. He wanted to wrap himself around her, cover every part of her skin with his. He wanted to claim her, possess her, bury himself inside her wet heat and forget everything that hurt, forget everything except her body.

He kissed his way up her thigh, then let himself bite her, once, not too hard.

She tipped back her head, her hips canting up, her legs falling farther apart on either side of him.

He gripped the softness of her hips as he licked his way up her sex. She was hot and ready for him, pink and wet. He couldn't help the groan that tore from his throat at her taste.

She was leaning back, her hips thrust forward, her hands locked around the marble ledge, and he dug his fingers into her soft smooth flesh. He held her in place as he licked, tasted, sucked on her clitoris. He held her fast, even as she writhed. He would not let her go.

He was all sensation now. Her voice, pleading and urgent. His sodden shirt, rapidly cooling and plastered to his skin. The heat of her beneath his tongue. When she came, hard and trembling, he could feel the vibrations in his cock.

He was mad for her. He couldn't think. He should wait—he should pause to let her breathe—but he couldn't. He stood, unfastening his falls, fisting his cock as he looked at her, flushed and dazed.

"I need you," he said hoarsely, and she smiled, a cat-like curl of her wide, lovely mouth.

"Yes. Please."

He settled himself between her legs, and—Christ!—the asinine tub wasn't quite high enough. He hitched her leg higher up his hip, pressing into her slick entrance, gasping at the tightness of her sheath.

He was saying something—expletives, probably—but he couldn't hear his own words over the blood pounding in his ears. He grasped her thighs in his hands and dragged her toward him. She slid easily across the slippery marble ledge, and he slammed hard into her body.

She cried out, and fisted her fingers into his shirt for purchase. He did it again, and again, working her back and forth over his cock, her body sliding as if oiled over the tub's wide edge.

This was what he'd needed. Selina, wild and breathless and alive, clinging to him as he held her, as he entered her, as he loved her with his body. Pleasure raked across his skin, roaring through him as he thrust into her tight, clenching heat.

He wanted her to come before he did, but the tight clasp of her channel, the sweet pleasure-pain of her fingers dragging against his shirt, the sound of her gasp each time he yanked her hard up onto his length—it was almost too much. He couldn't hold on.

"Touch yourself," he said. "I need you to come."

Her eyes blinked open. Her breath came in shuddering gasps. "I can't."

"You can, damn it."

She looked down to where her fingers held fast to his shirt, and he followed her gaze. Holy God, the sight of his cock in her—her thighs as he worked her over himself—he couldn't breathe.

"I'll fall if I let go."

"You won't."

"I'll fall," she said again, almost desperately.

"I won't let you."

She wrenched one hand away from his chest and shoved it between their bodies, a sob breaking from her. He could feel the urgent unsteady rhythm of her hand, and it drove him half out of his head.

She gasped and stiffened, her head falling back, and he ground her over his erection as she squeezed down hard, a violent wave of sensation that nearly brought him off. He managed, barely, to withdraw, and Selina—beautiful, lovely, *perfect* Selina—wrapped her hand hard around his cock. He thrust himself into the tight circle of her fingers and was lost, finished, blind with pleasure, his release bursting through him like a hurricane, sweeping everything away except sweetness.

When he could see and think and move once again, he let go of her thighs and balanced himself on the ledge beside her. He caught her against his chest, his hand coasting to the plane of her abdomen. He pressed his chin into the curve of her neck. She was soft and smelled of bergamot spice, warm and clean except for the stickiness of his spend on her belly and breasts.

He tightened his hand across her ribs and tipped both of them backward into the water.

Selina shrieked as they splashed into the bath, and he—

"Bleeding Christ," he said. "Hadn't thought the water'd gone so cold."

She was laughing, pushing against him as she scrambled from the tub. Water cascaded over the sides, down onto the slick marble tile. He stood, his trousers and shirt clinging to him, and watched her fetch linen towels from a bureau.

He loved her. He loved her so much he couldn't breathe, couldn't move. Could do nothing but watch and memorize her face as she laughed.

He kept the sight of her in his heart even as she pulled him from the room, as she made him dry himself and lie beside her in their bed. He kept it safe, a perfect pane of glass, crystalline and fragile.

• • •

Peter slept beside her.

"You have heard of beds?" she'd asked him tartly as she'd stripped his sodden garments from his body.

"I've heard of nudity too, and yet keep not quite managing it."

"You're managing well enough."

"Am I?" he'd said, and wrapped his arms around her.

They'd mopped up the water as best they could, then stumbled to their enormous bed and curled up together, despite the fact that it was barely five o'clock and neither of them had eaten supper. He'd fallen asleep almost instantly.

She lay now with her head on his chest. She teased the dark hairs that curled beneath her cheek, slid a finger gently into the hollow at the base of his throat. He was like a great cat, dozing beneath her cautious petting.

She should go downstairs and check on the children. She

should ready herself in case Gabe Hope-Wallace arrived early. She should think about supper. She should plan a menu for tomorrow.

White soup. Roasted pheasant. Some sort of sauce. Carrots. Soup?

Blast—she had thought about soup already, and she was trying to distract her mind, which *was not working*, because Peter had—he had—

I love you, he'd said. Again and again as he'd taken her. *I love you, God, Selina, I love you, I love you.*

Perhaps gentlemen just *said* that during bedsport. Perhaps it was some sort of . . . of animal mating call.

Good God, she was cracked. She racked her brain, trying to recall if she'd read anything about uncontrollable declarations of love in the Venus catalog.

Had he meant it? He had not seemed to notice the words as they spilled from his lips, had not acknowledged them after. Had certainly not said it again, when the haze of passion was gone from his mind.

Had she read anything about unexpected honesty engendered by lovemaking? *In coitus veritas?*

She felt fairly certain she had invented that phrase.

She'd seen an engraving once of a man, drooped pathetically across the lap of his nude and preposterously proportioned sweetheart. *Post coitum omne animal triste est*, it had read. After intercourse, all animals are sad.

She did not feel sad, precisely, here in the bed with Peter, her limbs tangled up with his. She thought of Freddie and Lu downstairs. Peter here with her, his skin warm under her cheek. She touched her thumb to the brass circlet around her ring finger.

No, not sad. Afraid, and cold with it, down in her bones.

How could she leave him now?

He had told her of his father, how they'd been abandoned in New Orleans. His brother—as close to him as Will was to her—who had died and for whom he still grieved. She could not leave him too. She couldn't bear it.

But if her secret came out before the hearing—if her connection to Belvoir's was revealed—what else could she do? She had seen his bleak fear at the prospect of losing Freddie. How would he respond if her scandal caused him to lose both of the children? To lose all the family he had left?

He would hate her. Or, if he did not hate her, she would hate herself.

"Please," she whispered against Peter's chest, barely knowing what she asked for. Things she could never say aloud.

Love me. Hold on to me. No matter what.

His arm tightened around her as if he'd heard. Perhaps he had. He'd told her, had he not? He would not let her fall. But it was not falling she feared. She could face that—the fall from grace, the utter destruction of her reputation and her life.

No. What she feared was that in the moment of crisis, she would not be strong enough or selfless enough to let Peter go.

Chapter 25

. . . I am so glad—so glad—to hear that everything's come right. I know I have not met Freddie yet, but I've been sleepless with worry over the child. You understand why.

—from Will to Selina, upon receiving word of
Freddie's recovery

In the tepid light of predawn, Selina dressed without waking Peter. She peeked in on the children as she passed Freddie's bedchamber. Both of them slept: Freddie in the bed and Lu upon the mattress on the floor, the gray kitten locked in her arms.

Selina's half boots made a rhythmic click as she descended to the lower level. She didn't need a candle, though it was dark in the staircase. She burned with purpose—practically blazed with it.

She was going to Belvoir's. Now, before Regent Street was crowded with shoppers and people-watchers. She was going to call Laventille in, and all his secretaries, and everyone she'd ever worked with, if necessary.

She would find out who was responsible for the rumors about Nicholas and Belvoir's. And she would stop them.

She would not let anything wreck their chances of securing the guardianship. Not now, when they were finally together.

This was how she could solve everything. She would arrange it all—she knew how to fix things. She had to keep the rumors at bay until after the hearing, at the very least. This was the only way to keep hold of what she wanted: the soft beloved contentedness she'd felt in Peter's arms the night before, their new and cautious family.

It was the only way to make sure that she would not hurt Peter. That he would—

That he would still want her.

She directed Emmie (who was emerging from a bedroom that was decidedly *not* her own) to inform Peter where she had gone when he arose, and silently resolved to ensure that Emmie knew where she might acquire a French letter.

The carriage ride to Regent Street was brief, and before long she was hurrying into the alley behind her beloved library. She hadn't disguised herself this time—no servant's garb or even a decorative bonnet. It was reckless, perhaps, but she *felt* a little reckless. It was time to see this done.

To her surprise, there was a figure waiting at the back entrance to Belvoir's. At this hour, she had not anticipated anyone else, and she wondered for a moment if she ought to turn around and run away.

But no. It was a deliveryman, she supposed, or a coal-cutter, and she was tired of being so afraid. She strode forward to take her place alongside the shadowed form.

It wasn't a coal-cutter. It was a woman, cloaked and hooded, and when Selina looked into her shadowed face, two cornflower-blue eyes peeped out from beneath curling lashes the color of moonbeams.

It was, undeniably, Lady Georgiana Cleeve.

Selina opened her mouth, then closed it again. *Fancy meeting you here*, she thought, with a hint of hysteria. *Do you prefer erotic poetry or explicit memoir?*

Georgiana, it seemed, did not find it similarly difficult to summon the spoken word. When she spoke, her voice was devoid of its usual charming bafflement.

"I'm glad you're here," she said. "I had written to Laventille to ask him to meet me here, but I would rather speak to you in any case."

Selina paused briefly to take that in.

To *Laventille*? How did Georgiana even know Laventille? And where were the teeth and the blinking and the non sequiturs?

Something peculiar was going on, and Selina did not enjoy the feeling of being the last to know what.

"I am here to apologize," Georgiana said, "and to warn you. I know about you. I know you run Belvoir's and the Venus catalog."

"You—" Selina couldn't find the words. *Georgiana Cleeve* knew? Lord Alverthorpe's daughter? It made some kind of sense, she supposed—Alverthorpe was one of Nicholas's political enemies, one of the people she'd suspected of starting the rumors in the first place. But she never would have imagined that Georgiana—sweet, lamb-like, ringleted Georgiana—might side with her father in opposition to Belvoir's and what it stood for.

"I discovered your connection to Belvoir's in my financial inquiries," Georgiana continued, "because I wanted to know who was paying for my novels."

Selina could not make sense of the words.

"You—" She could not apprehend it. "You write novels?"

"I've written six in the last two years. The Venus catalog has stocked them all. Three different *noms de plume*." She provided the names, and Selina gaped.

"But those—but those are—"

"Scandalous?" said Georgiana. Her curls bobbed as she tilted her head to the side. "Then I suppose I am in fit company."

"I was going to say excellent!"

For a moment, Georgiana's eyes widened. Her face took on a cast of puzzled bemusement. "I'm sure I do not understand," she said, her voice sweet, her hands clasped together in front of her.

And then the expression fell away. "I'm not sorry," she said, "for lying to the *ton*. But I am sorry for what I'm about to tell you."

It had been a ruse. This whole time. The wide blank blue eyes and the ludicrous comments and—

And Peter had known, or at least suspected. He'd said there was more to Georgiana than met the eye. He'd stopped courting her, suddenly and without explanation.

"Lady Georgiana, I do not mean to offend, but what the devil are you trying to say?"

"For the last several months, I have attempted to uncover who owns Belvoir's because my father has taken it into his head to bring down the library. He found—" Georgiana winced, looking pained. "He found three of my novels in my bedchamber. He did not know they were mine, but once he saw the contents and the Belvoir's bindings, that was more than enough."

"Why—"

"He's searched our rooms since we were children, all three of us. He has a very particular idea of how the Cleeves should behave. My brothers . . . he beat them into the very model of English peers, hunting and riding and fucking."

Selina blinked, taken aback despite herself at the word emerging from behind Georgiana's perfect teeth.

"And I," Georgiana continued, "was to be the ideal wife. Silent. Beautiful. Uncomplaining, no matter what my husband said or did, because he held the purse strings, and I held nothing at all." Her expression was set in tense, furious lines. "To hell with that. I wrote my novels. My mother helped me play the fool so no one—most especially not my father—would ever suspect I was more than an empty-headed doll. And I was going to get out. I was going to run away, and make a home for myself, with *my* money and *my* novels, and I was never going to see him again."

Selina's heart was in her throat. "I'm sorry. I'm so sorry, Georgiana. Tell me how I can help."

Georgiana gave a brisk shake of her head. "I don't need any help. I am doing fine on my own. But after my father found the novels, I set myself upon the path of finding the owner of Belvoir's, so that I could warn her. I thought"—she looked at Selina, her blue eyes piercing—"I thought it must be a woman. You cannot imagine how afraid I was for you. For what my father will do to you now that he knows."

Selina felt cold and sick. "He knows about me?"

"He does. It's—it's my fault. I went to the bank—I pretended I had no idea why the Belvoir's promissory note had come to me and convinced them to send it back to the person who had signed it. That was how I found your man of business and then—well, then I traced him back to you.

"I was a coward." Georgiana's face looked almost pleading. "I wrote you a letter, warning you that you were on the point of discovery and that my father was behind the rumors. I should have come to you in person, I know I should have—but I was too afraid to reveal myself. I wrote you an anonymous note and put it out for the post, and I did not know my father had set a servant to intercept any letters that my mother and I tried to send."

Selina's hand was at her throat. "Are you all right? He has not—"

Georgiana shook her head. "He does not know I am the author of the novels. I did not reveal that much of myself, not even in an anonymous letter. But he knows about *you*, Selina. He knows you are behind Belvoir's and he means to take down the library and you with it. Last night, he boasted to my brothers that he'd learned something new. He told them he had information that was going to destroy Belvoir's and its owner so completely, they'd be the laughingstock of London."

Selina felt dizzy. Belvoir's—her library—Peter and the children—

But she could not think of that, not yet. "Let me help you get away," she said. "Come up with me to the office. I can check the accounts—I'm sure we can arrange for an advance—"

"No. I came here to warn you, and now I have." Georgiana winced. "The guardianship hearing, for Stanhope's siblings— that's soon?"

"Two weeks from now."

Georgiana's face was drawn and pale. "I can try to hold my father off. I can—distract him, perhaps. Cause some other kind of scandal to take his attention off you until after the hearing is over. Perhaps one of my brothers—"

"No," Selina said. The word burst from her, panicked and angry. "No. Keep his attention on me."

Georgiana's lips pinched in. "You don't know him. You don't want him to perceive you any more than he already does."

"No," Selina said again. "Perhaps I don't want that. But it must be that way nonetheless."

It was worse than she'd feared. Just from knowing Selina, Georgiana's fragile independence was threatened. Nicholas's political reputation was marred. Peter might not get the children.

She could not accept that. *Her* choices had brought them to this point, *her* decisions and actions. There was only one way to ensure that the consequences were restricted to her alone. She had to keep the Earl of Alverthorpe's attention directed only at herself.

"You must stop associating with me."

Georgiana looked at her, a familiar glance of confusion.

"You need to leave here. Right away. You must protect yourself first of all. You must give me the cut direct if you see me on the street."

"Selina," Georgiana said gently, "this isn't your fault."

"It is. It *is*."

She had started this whole chain of events, and she'd thought it was because she wanted to help Ivy Price, but part of it had been pride. She was clever enough to pull the wool over the eyes of the whole *ton*. She knew better than everyone else.

No more.

The cottage in Cornwall. The lease her man of business had signed on her behalf.

"I have already done it once," she said.

"Selina, what on earth—"

She grabbed Georgiana's gloved hand. "I will *not* let harm come to you. Or Nicholas. Or Peter, or the children." Her voice was shaking, but she pretended it was not. "I *will not have it*."

"How can I help?"

She felt as though her heart were being torn from her chest. "You can help by leaving. Leave this alley. Do not come back. Send a letter to Lydia Hope-Wallace if you need to contact Belvoir's."

"Selina—"

"No!" Her voice was too high, too loud. She tried again. "No. I have thought of a path out of this tangle, and I am going to take it. I will not discuss it with you further."

"You do not need to be alone in this, Selina," Georgiana said in a low voice.

Selina's throat worked as she tried to swallow. "I am already alone in it."

Will had gone. And Peter—

She had failed. He had come to her weeks ago, so certain that she could handle everything, fix everything—but she could not fix this.

She thought of the exhausted lines of his body, slumped over Freddie's bed. She would not permit the children to be taken from him. She simply would not allow it. Somehow, Peter and the children had come to mean more to her than she could ever have imagined. More than Belvoir's. More than her reputation or her very life.

Georgiana gave a short nod of assent. "I'll stay away from you, if that's what you need."

"Yes," Selina said, "do that."

She watched Georgiana walk away and felt a cold splintering agony go through her. She could not do it. She was not strong enough.

She could pack her things and write a character for Emmie and tell her family—it would crush her, but she could do those things. But she could not leave Peter. She could not abandon him and the children. It would hurt them. *She* would hurt them.

But nor could she stay. It would be worse for them if she stayed. There was no way out—no way to put things right.

She was sobbing, she realized dazedly, breathless heaving sobs in the alley behind Belvoir's. Someone was going to hear her.

She pressed the heels of her hands to her eyes ruthlessly, fighting back her tears, forcing herself to calm down.

And when she was able to breathe again, she made herself stand up straight. She made herself go back to her carriage and when she sat down inside, she imagined herself inside a brittle shell of ice.

She could not think about herself now. She had to do what was right for *them*, for Peter and the children. And the right thing—the only thing—was for her to take herself as far from their lives as she could. They might be angry with her. They might be hurt. But they would survive it because they would be together, as a family.

She took the carriage home and prayed she would not break.

Chapter 26

Dearest brother: You may want to sit down.

—from Selina to Will

It was easy to locate Peter. He was in his study—the room she'd found him in the first time she'd come to the residence, the night she'd arrived to tell him about Belvoir's. She'd had bookcases delivered, so at least now his books were no longer in stacks on the floor.

"Peter," she said softly. He looked up from his quill and the sheet of foolscap, and his face shifted into sweet pleasure as he took her in.

"Thank God you're here. I'm writing in circles, and have run out of synonyms for *bad* and *wrong*. How many times d'you think I can say *evil* before I sound as though I've come stumbling out of a Gothic castle with bats in my belfry?"

She supposed this feeling was heartbreak, as she looked at his beloved grin and felt the words on her lips that would crush everything that had bloomed between them.

"What's wrong?" he asked. He was so perceptive, curse him.

"We should sit down."

He came around his desk and took her hands. She shouldn't let him do that. She should pull back. She should pretend she did not need him.

Damn and blast her stupid eyes, she should *stop crying*. She reached up and dashed away her tears furiously.

"Selina, I am quickly losing any pretense at calm. What is the matter?"

"Belvoir's." She was trembling. She couldn't help it, though she fisted her hands at her sides and tried to steady herself. "I know who's been spreading the rumors. And worse, Peter—he knows now that it wasn't Nicholas at all."

He searched her face. That look—she was so silly over that look.

"You're right," he said. "Let's sit down."

She let him lead her over to the two chairs in front of the fireplace. Where they had kissed and touched. Where she had cried into his shirt.

This time she would not let him convince her that everything would turn out all right.

"Well," he said when they were seated, "it's fucking unfortunate timing."

A hysterical giggle tried to bubble up in her throat, but she choked it back. "It's not ideal."

"Who's found you out? Any chance we can hold them off?"

"No." Quickly she told him about Lord Alverthorpe—he swore again, rather graphically—Georgiana's novels, and her father's intentions.

Peter nodded, brown eyes sharp and focused. "We'll have to act promptly, then. Before the guardianship hearing."

"Yes," she said, and she curled her fingers onto the arms of her chair so that she would not reach for him. "Precisely yes. We must act now. I have considered our options."

"Excellent," he said. "Of course you have. What do you intend for us to do?"

She licked her lips. "You have the difficult task, I'm afraid."

"Anything. Whatever you need, Selina, I'll do."

"You must throw me out of the house."

One eyebrow arched, and he said drily, "Anything but that, I suppose."

"No, Peter, listen." She had to make him understand. "I cannot shield you from scandal entirely. It *will* be revealed that I am responsible for Belvoir's, and the hearing is in two weeks. We do not have time to wait for the scandal to blow over. You must be above reproach."

"You expect me to . . . send you away?"

"Yes. You will openly announce that you were unaware of my actions before our marriage. I have used some of the Belvoir's money to lease a small house in Cornwall. I have—been preparing. Just in case. And we—we should try to have the marriage annulled, if we can. That would be for the best."

It hurt. It hurt *so much*.

She had meant to help him. She had planned and plotted so that he might get the children. All these weeks, and he was worse off than before he'd ever come to her. Even if he did exactly as she said, he might still be denied the guardianship, for having been foolish enough to marry her at all.

A clean break. That was the only solution. Her heart felt split in half, and her fingers were locked to the chair arms so tightly that they ached.

Peter looked stricken, and she did not know how she could stand it. "You—leased a house?"

"Yes," she managed.

"And you expect me to send you away *forever*?" His voice was incredulous.

"It is the only way. If you decry my actions loudly enough, publicly enough, it will give you some breathing room from the scandal. It will be clear to Eldon that you do not approve of what I've done."

"And if I *do* approve of what you've done? If I approve of it so damned much that I'd like to raise a toast in your honor on four continents?"

"It does not matter!" Damn him, why wouldn't he understand? "It does not matter what you believe. This is the only way for you to make yourself respectable enough. This is the only way I can save your family. I have thought through every option, Peter. I have considered every eventuality."

He locked eyes with her. "Then we'll think harder."

"No," she said. Desperation made her voice thin. "No, Peter."

"Tell me you want to go, then." His jaw was wire-taut, his whole body tense and vibrating. "Look at me, damn it, and say that you want to leave. Tell me you want nothing more to do with us."

She looked at his face and opened her mouth. *I want to go. I don't want to be with you. I never wanted to be with you.*

She couldn't do it. She couldn't make herself say the words.

"Selina." He reached across the empty space between them and covered her hand with his own. "I love you."

"You can't—Peter, you *can't*."

His voice was steady, his eyes on hers. "You bring the morning with you. You're the light, sweetheart. When you walk into a room, I can't see the shadows. There is nothing in this world that could persuade me to send you away if I thought you wanted me half as much as I want you."

"You must." She tried to pull her hand away, but he would not let her. "You must, Peter. Or—if not—I shall go on my own. I shall put it about that you've sent me away of your own accord— or—"

"I will follow you. I'll let Lucinda chase you down with her rapier. The three of us will make camp in your stable and greet you with horse manure and tea every time you try to depart."

"Stop it," she said, and now she was crying in earnest, hot terrible tears that burned her nose. "Why are you doing this?"

"You are the heart of us, Selina. There is no family without you."

"There will be no family if you do not follow this course! They will take the children away!"

He stood, and then he dragged her to her feet as well, pulling her up against his chest. "Come here," he said. "Hush now. Hush."

Then he held her, hard and unwavering. "We will figure this out together. I won't let you go."

"You're making a mistake." She heard herself say the words and knew she was lost. She'd already given in. She was going to let him do this—hold on to her. Despite the cost. Despite everything. Despite the fact that surely he must someday come to regret it.

"Sweetheart," he said. "Loving you is not a mistake." He brought his hand to her chin and pulled her face up, a firm, hard pressure with his thumb.

She felt vulnerable and quite thoroughly wrecked as he stared down at her. Her nose was running. He could see—oh, every messy broken part of her. All the depths of want and hope that she tried to keep hidden, the catastrophic desires that drove her.

He saw it all with that clear-eyed relentless gaze, saw it all and wanted her anyway.

He kissed her on the mouth. She felt his hurt and frustration in the hard pressure of his lips, the clasp of his thumb on her chin—and when her lips parted and her hands slipped around his torso, she tasted his soft groan of relief.

She kissed him back, fear and want in equal measure inside her.

And when his hand shifted to her hair, pulling her harder into him, all she could taste was love—his and her own, patient and abundant.

When he finally broke away, she whispered into his shirt-front, "I love you too, you know. I can't bear to hurt you."

"Then for Christ's sake stop talking about leaving." He stroked her hair back off her brow, and then kissed her there too. "Come here. Sit with me. Let's work this out together."

He sat again, shuffling her about in the brocade armchair with him. She ended up half curled atop him, her feet tucked between his thighs, her dress spilling in all directions.

"First," he said, "let's discuss the worst possible outcome. If we lose"—she started to speak, but he shushed her—"*if* we lose, which I very much hope will not be the case, it's not the end. We can appeal the ruling. We can bribe whoever it is they appoint. Hell, we can kidnap Freddie and Lu and sail to New Orleans before the ink has dried on the chancellor's writ of guardianship."

"But it's not what *you* want. Or what I want, either."

"Right." He brushed her cheek with his thumb. "That is why it's the worst possible outcome. But we'll survive even that."

She hated the very idea, hated that he would be forced to accept that result because of her. "If you do not cast me out, surely there is another way you can signal your disapproval of my actions? You could take out an advertisement in the newspaper, perhaps."

He directed a sardonic glance toward her.

"Perhaps not, then."

"I'm more likely to advertise how infernally clever you are, and you know it," he said.

"That would not be advisable."

"Rarely," he said, "do I do anything just because it is advisable. Or else I'd be married to one of your carefully selected candidates and as miserable as a stump."

She let herself lean into him, a luxury of warmth and solidity. "Iris Duggleby would not have brought this down upon your head, at least."

He snorted. "Is that right? Do you mean Iris Duggleby's not a member of your library, then?"

Indeed she was. In fact, they all were, all of the women she'd proposed that Peter marry—Iris and Lydia and even Georgiana, who evidently would have been as outrageous a duchess as Selina herself.

"Simply having a membership is no mark of shame, at this point," Selina said. "It cannot be. Half the *ton* are members by now." She spared a thought for the imminent wreckage of her business and sighed. "We are going to lose so many customers after this scandal breaks."

Peter tapped a finger on the arm of the chair, just once. "Is that right? Half the *ton*?"

"I suppose. I've never done the figuring, but it's not so far off. We are inexpensive, compared with the Royal Colonnade, and our selection is larger. Plus, of course, we have a particular appeal for those who know of the Venus catalog."

"Selina," he said, a rather queer sound to his voice. "Are the *Eldons* members?"

She blinked. "Why—I'm not certain. It's entirely possible."

"The Cleeves are members. The Dugglebys, as you say. The Hope-Wallaces?"

"Yes, of course."

"What about Lady Jersey?"

Lady Jersey was one of the patronesses of Almack's, nearly as terrifying as Aunt Judith. It had always amused Selina to see her name on the membership rolls. "Yes. In fact all of the Almack's patronesses are members. I like to imagine that they talk of vegetable-shaped phalluses over tea."

"About *what*? No—never mind." He toppled her unceremoniously from his lap and leapt to his feet. "Selina—why has the Venus catalog not been more widely talked about before now? Why had I never heard of it?"

She watched him stride toward the window, his mouth curling, half a grin. "No one would admit to it. Not in public. No one wanted to say that they were members, that they'd borrowed books on delicate topics." Belvoir's in general was openly popular—the Venus catalog, on the other hand, was discussed in whispers, beneath hands, in the corners of ballrooms and behind hedges at country estates.

He bounded back across the room to her. "That's right. No one would admit to it. Ha!"

She shook her head against the spark of hope his enthusiasm engendered. "I'm not sure what you are suggesting."

"Perhaps I *will* take out an ad in the newspaper. We'll make it known that Belvoir's is yours and then—by God, Selina, we will brazen it out."

"What on earth do you mean?"

His grin was in full effect now, shatteringly so. "Will it cause a scandal that you run a circulating library? Perhaps. But think— no one will want to accuse you about the Venus catalog because no one will want to admit that they themselves are part of it. Imagine how those patronesses would feel to see their names in the gossip rags alongside your—your vegetable phalluses, or whatever you said."

"You suggest that I threaten to expose my membership rolls?" There was something sacrosanct about her library records: what the patrons had borrowed, the fees they had paid. It seemed rather a wrong thing to make that information public.

But Peter was still smiling at her, a pirate's smile. "You don't need to threaten. You only need to go about town like a cat with cream, nodding at everyone you meet and never once mentioning that you—the Duchess of Stanhope—hold their shocking secrets in your hand."

She had never thought about it that way. She was accustomed to thinking about Belvoir's as something to be ashamed of. A secret guarded so closely that she must never even be seen to enter the doors of the library. Not as something that made her a force to be reckoned with.

She tried to encourage her brain to action, to look for holes in his plan. "But—if even one person reveals the Venus catalog, it will still fall to me. What about Lord Alverthorpe? He might still want his retribution."

"He might. But think of what we know about the man. His damned English pride. Will he want it revealed that his own wife and daughter are members?"

Selina bit her lip, trying to think. "It need not be Lord Alverthorpe. It could be anyone—any of the members who've checked out books from the Venus catalog."

"Oh, indeed. And to whom will they reveal it? All the rest of the members will already know."

"Everyone will know it was I. They'll realize that *I* created the catalog."

He shrugged. "You made it, yes. But they partook of it. And if they try to take you down, well—you hold just as many cards as they do."

"More," she whispered.

He leaned back, eyeing her with delight. "Is that right?"

"I know—who's taken a lover. Which Tory politician has a daughter with a fondness for radical politics. I would not reveal it, of course—"

"But they don't know that you would not." He gave a small, startled laugh. "By God, Selina, if you had a mind to blackmail, you could make a fortune."

She squeezed her eyes shut, then opened them again. "I only wanted to run a library."

Peter pressed a quick, smacking kiss to her mouth. "Don't be modest. You only wanted to revolutionize female education. Makes blackmail look almost decorous."

She felt his kiss linger, imprinted on her lips. "Do you really think this could work?"

"Yes."

It was a perfectly dazzling, perfectly *Peter* sort of plan. No subterfuge or secrets. Everything out in the open, a kind of reckless honesty. She would take responsibility for Belvoir's. Her library would be *hers*, finally, after all this time. Everyone would know it. And everyone would know too about the Venus catalog—

and perhaps, out of fear for their own reputations, they would not condemn her for it.

If this plan failed, it would fail spectacularly. They would be banished from every drawing room in London. Peter's political career would be in shambles; even the most open-minded members of Parliament would hesitate to work with him.

If it failed, they would not get the children.

But they might succeed. This was, perhaps, the only way they might succeed.

"I must go to Belvoir's," she said, rising. "I must see if the Eldons are on the rolls. I do not mean to blackmail them, Peter"— she'd caught the way his eyebrows had risen—"but I must know whether they are aware of the catalog. I think . . . oh, I think Lady Eldon is on our side. But I do not know if this plan will tip her toward us, or away."

Before she could leave the room, he caught her about the waist. "Don't be afraid," he said.

"I am, Peter. I'm terrified." His arms tightened, pulling her into him, and she went willingly. "But it's . . ." She fought for the words. "It's good. Not to be alone."

"Never," he said, his warm breath ruffling her hair. "Not if I have anything to say about it."

Chapter 27

Dear Selina—I think it an excellent plan. I wish I were there to help you see it through. Things grow tense here in Brussels—no more for now. Be brave! (Not that you need any encouragement on that front.)

—from Will to Selina, posted hastily before the regiment's departure

The next morning, she stood in the front drawing room at Rowland House, sick with dread.

Peter had offered to come with her—as he'd come with her to Belvoir's the night before—but she'd declined. "I want to do this myself," she'd told him. She *needed* to do it herself. It was a penance, she supposed, for lying to her family these last two years. For not trusting them. And if they cast her out onto the front step—if Daphne said she could not let Selina be around the boys any longer—well. Selina could understand that. But she did not want Peter to see.

They came into the drawing room in a whirlwind of chatter.

Aunt Judith was speaking sternly to Nicholas, who appeared to be hiding slightly behind his wife. Thomasin dimpled at Aunt Judith, holding out her hand to the other woman as though inviting her to dance. The love and partnership between them glowed as bright as the afternoon.

All of her family. All of them but Will, and Selina felt his absence like a wound.

"Selina, there you are," Daphne said. Her chestnut curls were slightly more tamed than usual, and she smiled broadly at Selina. "We think Teddy has been missing Lu. He's been unusually fussy, and we're pretty sure he keeps saying 'poke stick.'"

"Rapier, I rather think he means," Nicholas put in.

Selina bit down hard on her lower lip. "I'll bring her next time."

"Is something the matter, darling girl?" This was Thomasin—always Thomasin, gentle and serene. "Let me pour you a cup of tea."

Thomasin served them all as Selina gathered her courage. She seated herself on the blue chintz settee and wrapped her fingers around her steaming cup.

"Before the guardianship hearing," she said, "there is something I would like to tell all of you. It has to do with Will—and me—and something we did together two years ago, which I have been carrying on in his absence."

No one spoke. They watched her patiently, her family.

Please, she thought. *Please don't be ashamed of me.*

With a shaky indrawn breath, she told them about Belvoir's. She told them about Ivy Price, and the Venus catalog, and the house she and Will had bought for Ivy and her son. She told them about the Earl of Alverthorpe and Peter's audacious plan.

She didn't tell them about Georgiana's novels. She trusted them implicitly, but that wasn't her information to reveal.

And she didn't cry. It was easier this time, after telling Peter and Lydia. The story of Belvoir's was no longer a private thing, between herself and her twin. It was simply a fact, out in the world now with the Cleeves and Lydia's lady's maid and all those emerald-green books.

And now they knew.

There was a pause when she was done speaking, as though they all waited to see if she had more to say. No one looked at one another, and for some reason Selina took pride in that. They were not the kind of people whose reactions depended upon the judgments of others.

"Well," said Nicholas, "that explains a great deal."

Selina's throat felt dry, and she tried to swallow. "Does it?"

"Mm." He tugged at his cuff, an old familiar gesture that caught her heart. "Why neither of you ever asked for a larger allowance, for one. I'd rather wondered about that."

"Does this explain why your lady's maid is so attached to you, then?" asked Thomasin. "I've been trying to lure her into my service for years. Bribery, was it?" She made a sage little hum. "I should've tried that myself."

"And all those visits you made when we were in Gloucestershire at Broadmayne," Nicholas added. "To Ivy? Yes, of course, that makes sense. I did think it odd that you were suddenly so keen to shop in the village."

"And those gowns!" Daphne nodded. "I thought I'd lost all sense of fashion when you started buying up those eye-poppingly colored gowns." She paused. "Actually, no, I take it back. I still don't understand the gowns. I beg your pardon—perhaps I simply *don't* understand fashion." She looked chagrined.

Selina stared at them all. Daphne, Nicholas, Thomasin, Judith: All four looked at her placidly. Thomasin took a sip of her tea, then winced. Their cups had grown cold in the time it had taken to hear all of Selina's recital.

"Have you all lost your senses?" Selina demanded, almost incensed by their inexplicable calm. "Did you not *hear* me?"

"To be honest," said Daphne, "I think it's wonderful. I wasted a great many years suffering because of my ignorance on such topics. Before I married your brother I was terribly—" She blushed a little, but set her teeth. "Deceived. I was deceived, and if I'd had something like your catalog, I would not have been so naive."

Nicholas caught Daphne's hand in his and drew it into his lap, his expression very gentle.

"I, too," said Thomasin slowly, "could have benefited." She cast a glance to Aunt Judith, who had not, as yet, said anything at all about Selina's revelations. A smile caught at Thomasin's lips, but it was sad, somehow. Selina did not think she'd seen that expression on Thomasin's face before.

"I felt," Thomasin said softly, "so alone, for so long. I felt—oh, peculiar. Abnormal. I thought I would never be quite—quite happy, you know. It would have been good. To know that I was not alone."

Selina turned her face toward her aunt, half blind with tears. "Aunt Judith, you must make them see sense!"

"Child," Aunt Judith said, "you have been very foolish."

"Now, Jude—" Thomasin tried to cut in, but Aunt Judith laid her hand on Thomasin's knee, and Thomasin halted.

"I cannot pretend it's not so. She has been foolish. She will have made her path much harder for herself with this library, with this scandal." Aunt Judith's eyes fell on Nicholas and Daphne, on Thomasin. "I begin to fear that no one in this family knows how to take the easiest road." Her voice was stern but her expression was rather at odds with her tone. The firm press of her lips softened by degrees. "Foolish," she said again, "but brave too."

"Like a Ravenscroft," said Nicholas drily.

"Indeed." Aunt Judith put her hands together in her lap. "Now then, child. Let us put our foolish heads together and work out how to enact your husband's plan."

Selina heard herself make a choked wordless sound. She set the teacup down in its saucer on the table beside her. She turned it carefully so that the handle of the cup was parallel to the edge of the table. And when she had her voice under control again, she looked up at them.

"You are not angry with me?"

"Well, yes, rather," said Thomasin mildly. "You have done a great deal of lying, you know. You might have trusted us."

"I suppose I should have liked to have been warned," offered Nicholas.

Daphne made a delicate snorting sound under her breath. "As though you would have let her do it, had you known."

"Come now," he protested. "No one *lets* Selina do anything."

"For my part, I'd like a free membership to Belvoir's," said Thomasin. "Consider it your recompense."

Selina let out a shaky breath. "Can't," she said. "No nepotism. Wouldn't want to ruin my reputation."

Thomasin—bless her—was the first to laugh. And then they all did, even Aunt Judith, and Selina felt love and relief swamp her. They did not hate her. They were not going to throw her out.

Perhaps she had not expected that they would, not really. Not her family. But she had not expected this either: their solid, steady acceptance of her, in all her turmoil and mistakes.

"My darling," said Thomasin, "don't cry."

•   •   •

They had just begun to work out the details—Nicholas would visit Alverthorpe at his home, Aunt Judith would call upon Faiza's very well-connected mother, Mrs. Khan—when the liveried butler entered the room.

"Your Grace," he said blandly.

Selina looked up. So did Daphne and Nicholas.

She sighed. There were, surely, an implausible number of dukes and duchesses in her social circle.

"You have a number of callers. Shall I tell the Duke of Stanhope and his companions that you are at home?"

Selina stared. Peter . . . and his *companions*? Whom could he have brought with him? Freddie and Lu, perhaps?

Daphne nodded, still holding the quill she'd retrieved from her office between her fingers. She appeared to be keeping minutes of their discussion.

The butler vanished and then reappeared with Peter, who wore the buoyant, slightly hopeful expression of someone delivering a gift. Arrayed behind him were five more people and one white dog. Selina identified his barrister, Mohan Tagore, arm in arm with a lady that Selina did not recognize. Beside Mr. Tagore stood Lydia, looking not at all green, Iris Duggleby, and Lady Georgiana Cleeve.

"Good morning, Ravenscrofts," Peter said. "Looks like you've finished conversing? Good. I've brought reinforcements."

Daphne, who had risen as everyone entered her drawing

room, appeared to be smothering an expression of pure delight. "I believe we'll need more refreshments."

"Peter," said Selina, "where—why—"

Words failed her. She blinked stupidly at the small crowd he'd marshaled.

Peter grinned. "I knew they wouldn't toss you out. I've brought some friends for our morning of strategizing. If we're to perpetrate this scheme upon the *ton*, sweetheart, I thought, well—the more people on our side, the better."

"You—told them? About Belvoir's?"

Peter looked steadily at her. "I told them you needed them. And so they've come."

So, for the second time that morning, Selina told the story of Belvoir's. Lydia and Georgiana, of course, already knew. Mr. Tagore was not a member of Belvoir's, as it turned out, and the lady with him—his soft-spoken wife, Anne—had never heard of the Venus catalog. She looked, Selina observed, quite mightily intrigued.

Iris Duggleby, seated on one of the extra armchairs that Daphne had hastily ordered brought in, gave Selina a lopsided smile. "Oh, well done," she said. "Perhaps later I can make some suggestions for your antiquities selection—it's terribly thin."

Selina strangled her amusement. "I would appreciate that."

She turned to look at Georgiana, who was motionless on the sofa, the little white dog from the Serpentine curled up in her lap. She had not breathed a word of Georgiana's novels, of course, but it had been difficult still to describe Lord Alverthorpe's involvement without turning too much attention in Georgiana's direction. She hoped she'd done all right.

Georgiana took a slow breath and glanced at the door, as though pondering escape. Then she looked back, examining the

Ravenscrofts cautiously. "This is very unwise. This is—" She swallowed. "I had not thought it would come to this. But if there's anyone in the world I can trust, I suppose it is all of you."

And then she told them. About her novels, her false front to avoid discovery, her plan to achieve independence for herself.

There was a little stunned silence.

"All right," said Lydia, whose typical reserve among strangers seemed to have fallen by the wayside in light of the day's epiphanies. "Anyone else have something shocking to reveal?" She turned to Mohan Tagore. "Are you a secret vigilante when you're not arguing the law?"

"Sadly, no."

Lydia turned to Daphne. "How about you?"

"I assure you, when I am not managing our estates or taking care of my children, I spend the eight precious minutes that remain in each day exclusively in bed."

Nicholas choked on a snicker, and Daphne blushed to her hair. "Sleeping! I meant—I—oh, you are all dreadful."

"Perhaps Selina can recommend you some light reading," said Aunt Judith drily.

Amusement tickled Selina's throat, and when she laughed, it felt like champagne bubbles popping, little bursts of mirth she hadn't imagined she could feel so soon.

They worked out a plan together. Daphne took very detailed notes.

Mr. Tagore was going to prepare for any whisper of legal action against Selina—another angry father, perhaps.

Lydia meant to use her ubiquitous network of social gossip belowstairs to spread the word that Selina and Will owned and ran Belvoir's. She briefly related her maid Nora's connections to all the most popular families of the *ton*, and even Selina, who'd known about Lydia's powers for years, felt impressed.

Iris Duggleby offered to have her parents host a soiree. "My mother will be delighted if I express interest in a ball," she said, looking rather grim about the mouth. "We shall use the event as an opportunity for you to stroll around, looking quite knowing and smug and alarming. We can time it so that the gossip will have made its rounds."

"Everyone will be eager to attend," said Thomasin. "They'll want to see how you react. If you try to cower."

"She won't," Peter said. "Not my girl."

"I won't." Her voice rasped a little, but she steadied herself. "I won't cower. We must invite the Eldons."

"To be sure," said Lydia.

"For my part," said Georgiana, "I think it wise if we do not appear to be great friends, Your Grace." She offered Selina an apologetic smile. "For both our sakes. However, I know many people will be eager to speak of you in the coming days. My mother and I have several social events already on our schedule."

She did her teeth-and-eyelashes routine again. "But whyever would the duchess tell us about her library? I certainly would *never* talk about *books* in company. It's not fit for polite society to discuss *literature*. Surely Her Grace has more interesting topics to discuss." Her nose wrinkled adorably. "Hats, I imagine. I hear she's very fond of trimming hats. With fruit, I believe? Little cherries and peaches on her bonnets?"

"Goodness, child," said Aunt Judith. "Stop that at once."

An hour later, Nicholas and Daphne's older son tumbled into the room with a china teacup and a decided lack of trousers, and the conversation quickly ran down.

The Tagores offered to escort Lady Georgiana and her dog back to her residence. Iris summoned the Duggleby carriage.

Lydia, before she walked down the street to the Hope-Wallace house, caught Selina's eye, her face contemplative. "Perhaps," she said, "when this is over, you will put me in touch with your publisher."

Selina blinked. "With Laventille? Why?"

Lydia drummed her fingers on her reticule for a moment before speaking. "I find that I am inspired by you and Georgiana. I have some things I would like to say."

And despite everything, Selina felt a warm rush of pride in her chest at the bravery of her friends.

When they were finally alone in the drawing room, Selina let herself soften against the hand that Peter had placed at the small of her back.

She didn't know if his plan was going to work. It seemed somehow impossible—nothing like it would have ever occurred to her. Nothing like this bold offensive maneuver ever *had* occurred to her, not in the two and a half years since Will had bought Belvoir's. It had taken Peter, with his wide-open heart and his stubborn, headlong determination, to see a new path.

No secrets. No hiding. Not any longer.

And she wasn't alone. That was the part that pulled at her heart, that made her eyes burn as she thought of it.

All these years, she had thought herself alone in this project. Yet Peter had asked for help—had told them that Selina needed them—and they'd come. All of them, unquestioning, had come.

She leaned against Peter, felt his cheek touch the crown of her head. Felt the warm pressure of his hand all the way out the door and to the carriage, until he handed her up and they went home together.

Chapter 28

. . . It came at last, the dear, critical, dangerous hour came;
and now, supported only by the courage love lent me, I
ventured, a tiptoe, down stairs . . .

—*from* FANNY HILL

They decided to begin at Belvoir's.

Peter rather liked the simplicity of it. Selina had told him one of her private rules was that she could never be seen to carry one of the green-bound Belvoir's books, nor could she be caught entering or exiting the library.

So ten days later, after the rumor mill had had time to churn and when the traffic on Regent Street was at its thickest, they marched brazenly up to the front door, pushed it open, and walked into Belvoir's.

It was crowded with patrons. The rumors of Nicholas's involvement had already heightened interest in the library. Though Alverthorpe had not publicly accused Nicholas Ravenscroft of any misdeeds, Nicholas's sudden attention to the earl—who was not one of his friends or political partners—had been noted.

Then Lydia's domestic gossips had gone to work. Peter suspected that Georgiana had had something to do with the project as well, as knowledge of Selina's involvement spread like wildfire in dry grass. He and Selina had paraded through the Park, gone riding in Rotten Row, called on everyone they knew, and brought the children to a number of fashionable destinations—not that Lu had been impressed by anything she'd seen.

They had gotten many long, lingering, interested looks from other members of the *beau monde*, but no one had cut them. They'd been received everywhere they went, and if they noticed people whispering behind their hands as they passed—well, Peter was used to that. He didn't mind in the slightest, not now—because Selina had done something good and important, and he had the chance to stand at her side.

His wife—looking radiant in an amber frock almost the color of her eyes—sauntered through the aisles of books at his side, her fingers resting lightly on his forearm. He'd suspected she would be good at this, ruthlessly competent as always. He had not expected how much she would seem to relish her role.

She tilted her head toward a group of dowagers who stood at the side of the room, whispering as they observed the passersby and looking not at all interested in the emerald books. "Over there next," she said in an undervoice. "Lady Malcolm is the only one of that clique who is a Belvoir's patron. The other two, I suspect, are here for the gossip."

They strolled toward the group. Selina smiled and nodded as they passed others—some friends, some Peter's political opposition—and Peter felt a hot rush of pride as he walked alongside her.

The three older women turned as one when he and Selina reached them. He supposed he and Selina had precedence over all three, but from the cool expressions on their faces, he wasn't certain they felt outranked.

"Lady Yardsley," Selina said, nodding at the tallest of the three. "Mrs. Bucklebury. Lady Malcolm."

"Your Graces." Lady Yardsley eyed them both. "I'm rather surprised to see you here, of all places."

Peter contained a snort.

Mrs. Bucklebury, a petite Afro-Scottish woman in purple, did not greet them. She glanced down and straightened the ribs of her Italian fan.

It was perilously close to a cut, but Selina ignored it and smiled brilliantly at the final dowager. "How do you do this afternoon, Lady Malcolm?"

"Quite well, Your Grace." Her voice was soft, and she didn't look at her companions.

"I was just telling Stanhope about the dinner party you hosted in Gloucestershire," Selina continued. "Do you remember that? A few years back?"

"Yes, certainly, Your Grace." Lady Malcolm had a pale foxlike face and a cap of gray curls peeking out from beneath her bonnet.

Selina looked innocently delighted. "What was it that you served? Venison?" She gazed at Lady Malcolm and said meaningfully, "You prepared the sauce yourself, did you not?"

Peter could not imagine *what* she was talking about.

Lady Malcolm, it appeared, knew very well indeed.

She blanched. "I—perhaps I did. I can't quite recall—"

"And apples!" said Selina. "From your very own orchard!"

Lady Malcolm went faintly green. Peter tried to imagine what apples and *making one's own sauce* could reference.

"I did not know you had an orchard, Mary," said Lady Yardsley.

"Oh—" Lady Malcolm looked at her friend, then back at Selina, eyes round as saucers.

Selina straightened the seam on her calfskin glove, then met Lady Yardsley's eyes. "Oh—perhaps not. My mistake. It was several years ago. I've quite forgotten the details."

Lady Malcolm looked between her friends and Selina. She blinked. And then, cautiously, she smiled at Selina. She seemed to be considering whether or not she could trust Selina's sudden retreat. "Perhaps we could host you again sometime? Your Grace?"

"We would be honored," said Selina.

"Certainly," Peter offered. "I've heard your younger son is a promising new MP."

He had only the vaguest notion who her second son was, but Lady Malcolm looked at him in alarm. He wondered if the younger Malcolm's wife was also a patroness of Belvoir's. He made his smile as bland and unthreatening as he could.

"Lovely," croaked Lady Malcolm. She turned to her friends, who were watching the proceedings with interest. "Alice," she said, "Cecily—I'm sure you'll both be there as well, will you not? I cannot think of a"—she sounded slightly ill—"higher honor than dining with the duke and duchess."

Lady Yardsley assented. Mrs. Bucklebury lifted her fan and fluttered it in front of her face.

"Cecily." Lady Malcolm's voice was strangled. "I am *certain* that you will dine with us. I am *confident* you would not want to miss the pleasure of Her Grace's company."

Silence stretched. Lady Malcolm's face grew increasingly pained. Peter thought she might reach out and snap Mrs. Bucklebury's fan in half.

Finally, Mrs. Bucklebury sighed. "Oh yes, I suppose I would not turn down your invitation, Mary."

And that, it seemed, was that.

Selina chatted briefly with the three dowagers for a few more moments, before placing her hand on Peter's arm. "I fear we must take your leave," she said. "Some business to attend to. Such a *pleasure* to see you all."

They left the group, and Peter set his hand atop Selina's. "Do I want to know—about the venison?"

Selina vibrated with smothered amusement. "There's a book. Lady Malcolm borrowed it so many times and for so long that eventually I simply replaced it in the catalog."

"Is that right?"

"It describes the—er—adventures of a certain female huntress. Modeled on Diana. She engages in a variety of exotic acts with her fellow archers. Arrows, you see. Piercing, er, numerous things. Toward the end, one is informed that Diana prefers a *great deal* of sauce. All over her apples."

Peter tried very hard not to imagine any such thing in the context of the dowager they had just encountered.

"Duchess," he said instead, "don't tell me you are having a good time."

She laughed softly, a little puff of air. "Perhaps—just a little."

The afternoon continued in much the same vein, and Peter felt dizzy with pride in her. In her accomplishments, certainly—but also in the way she threw herself into the role, vibrant and strong. She would have fled society if it would have kept their family safe, the same way she had tried to remake the whole damned world in order to help a friend.

He thought of the way she'd thrown herself into the Serpentine for the little wet ball of canine fluff, and tenderness came in a rush that was almost painful.

There was a brief commotion at the front of the library, and Selina's head snapped up.

It was Lady Georgiana, Peter saw—and then, with a start of alarm, observed the Earl and Countess of Alverthorpe behind her.

Lady Alverthorpe hung briefly on her husband's arm, but he shook her off and made toward the back of the library. Peter felt a brief flash of hazy red rage, but fought it back. Selina was stiff beside him, and he had to be steady right now. For her.

They hadn't expected direct confrontation. They had counted upon Alverthorpe's pride to stop him from announcing his family's association with Belvoir's and the Venus catalog. He might withdraw his membership, to be sure—but they hadn't thought he'd come for Selina.

They'd been wrong.

Alverthorpe was tall and bluff and would have been handsome if his face hadn't been carved with fury. He came straight for them.

"Stanhope," he hissed. "I should have known it when you married into this family. Not something a real Englishman would touch in his life."

Selina stiffened further.

The earl's eyes fixed on Selina. "And you," he said. He seemed to relish the words. "I'm going to run this place out of business. And after that, I'm going to have you brought up on civil charges for the filth you've been spreading."

This was what Selina had been afraid of. Tagore had said she couldn't be prosecuted under criminal obscenity charges, but that didn't mean she was exempt from legal action.

Selina lifted her chin. "I am the Duchess of Stanhope," she said coolly. "My membership rolls include several royals. I'd like to see you try."

Alverthorpe's face grew even more enraged. "Control your wife," he snapped at Peter. "Or I will do it for you."

Peter heard his restraint snap, a quiet pop inside his ears. "That," he said softly, "was too far."

And then, at Alverthorpe's elbow, Georgiana spoke. "Enough," she said. "Father. Enough."

The earl turned on her, and Peter stepped forward, prepared for the earl to unleash violence, but Georgiana raised her voice. "No. I'm tired of being silent."

She'd dropped her muddleheaded public persona. She looked almost a different woman, her mouth a hard slash.

"Georgiana"—Alverthorpe's voice was a threat—"we'll talk about this at home."

"I'll talk about it now. I wrote the books you found in my chamber."

"Don't be a fool—"

"I wrote them," she said, "and three others. I can find them here for you, if you'd like to see them."

Peter felt rocked by Georgiana's sudden revelation of her secret. But Selina didn't miss a beat. "It might be hard to find them," she said. "They're so popular, it's difficult for me to keep them on the shelves."

"You're lying," Alverthorpe said.

"I've lied enough." Georgiana looked her father in the eye. "I've written six hugely popular Gothic novels." He started to reply, but she spoke over him. "Yes—even though I am a Cleeve. Even though I am the daughter of an earl. And if you threaten the Stanhopes again, I will tell everyone in the *ton* what I've done."

Alverthorpe laughed in her face. "You'd destroy yourself? For them?"

"I've been destroying myself for eighteen years," she said, "for you. I've had enough."

Lady Alverthorpe was staring between the two of them, tears painting silvery streaks down the sides of her face. "Georgie," she whispered, "don't."

Georgiana turned to her and, for the first time, looked vulnerable. "Mother," she said, "come with me."

"Try it," said Alverthorpe. "See what happens when you're all alone." His voice was thick with derision. "See how well you'll live with no money—no *ton*, no friends—"

"They won't be alone," Selina said.

"You?" he spat. "A whore masquerading as a duchess?"

Peter felt fury trembling within him but held it back. "They won't be alone," he echoed. "They have us."

And from behind him, he heard a quiet female voice. "And us."

He turned. It was Lydia Hope-Wallace, looking sick with terror, surrounded by her four older brothers like a protective wall.

"How many dukes do you think you can cut and still expect to be received?" Nicholas Ravenscroft emerged from behind another row of books, his wife's arm in his.

And there, coming up another aisle, was Iris—looking mildly affronted at being dragged into a public space—and her parents, the Viscount and Viscountess Duggleby.

Thomasin Dandridge. Lady Judith, her mouth quirked in a sardonic line.

"You bastards think you can get away with anything," hissed Alverthorpe. His eyes darted around the library.

"No," Lady Judith said. "It's men like you who get away with things, Alistair. For years and years and years. And we're saying that it's gone on long enough."

"We're not alone," Selina said to him. "You are."

"I've had enough." The earl yanked his wife toward him. "Let's go."

Lady Alverthorpe stared at his fingers wrapped around her upper arm but didn't move.

"Come on, damn you!" Alverthorpe tried to pull her along with him, and she nearly stumbled, her arm breaking free from his grasp.

"No," she said, her voice nearly inaudible. "I'm staying with Georgie."

"The hell with you, then!" Alverthorpe's face was mottled with rage. "The hell with all of you!"

As one, the Ravenscrofts closed ranks around Georgiana and the countess. Peter wrapped his arms around Selina, heedless of the rest of the patrons in Belvoir's.

And the Earl of Alverthorpe stormed out of the library alone.

• • •

They had the rest of the afternoon to put on a brave face for the gossipmongers who flocked to the library, to act as though the encounter with the earl and his family had never happened.

Selina, of course, managed it like a dream. She bustled Georgiana and her mother off to the Hope-Wallace house, whispering instructions to Lydia that seemed to involve both significant sums of money and all of their favorite scandalous ladies of the *ton*. Possibly a house in Gloucestershire, but Peter wasn't quite sure.

But when Belvoir's closed its doors for the evening, Selina half fell into his arms.

He held on hard.

"They'll be all right," she said. He wasn't sure if she was trying to reassure him or herself.

"They will," he agreed. "The Ravenscrofts are a force to be reckoned with. Alverthorpe doesn't have the stones to try."

She laughed shakily, and then looked up at him. "I'm sorry. Peter, I'm so sorry."

He drew back, holding her shoulders in his hands. "What the devil for? You shattered him like a porcelain teacup, sweetheart. It was spectacular."

"Oh God," she said. "I wish you hadn't seen that. I wish—"

He waited for her to finish, his heart in his throat.

"I wish you didn't have to do any of this." Her voice softened. "You should've let me leave, Peter. I've only made things harder for you."

He wanted to scoff or shake her. But her eyes were downcast, her dark lashes heavy over her eyes, and so he squeezed her shoulders. "Come here."

She came, not quite eagerly, into his embrace.

"I won't leave you," he said. "I won't stop loving you. Even if I have to watch a dozen jackasses call you names and somehow not strangle them. Even if you and your erotic books end up in newspapers across the Empire." He pressed his hands into her hips. "Even if we do not get the children."

"But *why*?" She looked up at him then, fierce and uncomprehending.

"I didn't marry you for that. I didn't want you because you could make me respectable or fix my cursed house or take care of my siblings." He touched the line of her lips with one finger. "I just wanted you."

She said his name. Her lips moved against his skin. "Thank you."

"For wanting you? I promise you, it's no hardship."

She laughed, a little damply. "No. For this brazen, impossible plan." Her eyes flicked to the bookshelves around her and then back to his. "I would not have thought of anything like this, Peter. But if this works—perhaps it's the only way I can have you and the children and Belvoir's as well."

"It will work."

She searched his face. "If it works, it is because of you. Because of the way you turn what could be a crisis into a victory. A flaw into a strength. You see this world and imagine it better, Peter, and I—I think you are remarkable."

His heart battered itself against his rib cage. He wanted—he wanted so much to be what she believed he was.

"I love you," she said, a breathless rush of words. He felt a slow dizzy revolution in his chest.

"Good," he said. "Now can I kiss you?"

She laughed a little, and nodded, and he found her mouth with his.

He felt a little drunk when he finally pulled away from her. Shaky with relief from the afternoon, his body loose-limbed with desire.

"Do you want to go upstairs?" she asked.

He was mad for her, for the flushed pleasure on her face and the eager responsiveness of her mouth, and his desire was shot through with love for her clever brain and her courage and her enormous heart.

"The hell I do," he said. "This time we're finding a bed."

She hummed a little sound and came up on her toes to kiss

his ear. He tried to remember why he shouldn't drag the pins out of her hair and spread the dark-blond waves across her shoulders.

He thought of how she would look, naked in their bed, her hair tangled, her eyes heavy with desire, and groaned into the curve of her neck. He bit her, gently, and she made an approving whimper, tipping her head to the side.

"I am going to make you so happy," he said. It was a promise, a whisper, a kiss. He eased back from her and tugged her toward the back door of Belvoir's. He congratulated himself on resisting the urge to press her up against it.

He pushed open the door, pulling Selina's body full-length against his own. They tumbled into the alley behind Belvoir's, and Selina gave a startled laugh that broke suddenly into an audible squeak of alarm.

They were not the only couple in the alley behind Belvoir's. Peter's eyes fell first on the man, a sturdily built fellow, then the woman, plump and graying. His arm was locked around her back, his face bent over hers, a hairbreadth from a kiss.

At the sound of Selina's squeak, the couple jumped apart.

Peter, still lust-drunk, felt his legs nearly give way.

"Lord Eldon," gasped Selina. "Lady Eldon. Good evening."

Lord Eldon's thick white brows lowered sternly over his eyes. Lady Eldon dimpled at them, looking far less shocked than Peter felt.

"Your Graces," Lady Eldon said, entwining her gloved fingers with her husband's. "We cannot keep meeting this way."

"I *beg* your pardon!" Selina's voice cracked. "We were just—on the point of leaving—"

"Don't rush off on our account," said Lady Eldon graciously.

Selina backed hastily toward their waiting carriage, tugging Peter with her.

"Actually," said Lord Eldon, "please do."

Peter wasn't sure what to do with his face. He handed Selina up into the carriage and tried very hard not to look in any particular direction.

When he climbed into the carriage after her, Selina shut the door with a thunk. And then, quite firmly, she lowered the curtain over the window as well.

Through the thin barrier, Peter was almost certain he heard the muffled sound of Lady Eldon's laugh.

Chapter 29

. . . I will meet you at your house at nine of the clock
tomorrow. Look ducal! Ask your wife for assistance if you
need to.

—from Mohan Tagore, barrister, to Peter Kent, the
Duke of Stanhope

The morning of the hearing, Peter thought rather grimly that they had done all they could do. It had been four days since the confrontation with Lord Alverthorpe at Belvoir's, and the countess and Georgiana were safely ensconced at the Ravenscroft estate in Gloucestershire. He and Selina had made their social rounds. Lydia and her maid had identified any potential sources of opposition and then Lady Judith and Mrs. Khan had moved to quash them. The Dugglebys had thrown quite possibly the *least* exclusive ball of the Season, so that everyone might see the general support for the Duke and Duchess of Stanhope.

Her family, all their friends—everyone had done their best to utilize their positions and associations.

Everyone knew about Selina's connection to Belvoir's, including the Eldons, who were *not*, as it turned out, members of the library. Their daughter, however, was.

Peter hoped it would be enough.

Selina sat in the Court of Chancery beside him, looking calm and formal, a duchess to her satin-slippered toes. While he, the so-called duke, sat with his hands digging into his knees, his heart in his throat.

Tagore had taken the carriage from their house up to Westminster with them, waited beside them all morning before their hearing was to begin. He was robed and bewigged, looking like the Bengali version of one of the portraits in the Stanhope gallery.

Freddie and Lu had stayed at the house, attended by their tutor and several Ravenscrofts. Children weren't allowed at court and—God help him—even if they had been permitted to attend, Peter didn't want them to be there in case it went wrong.

It could not go wrong. Hell, if the force of his determination could will the guardianship into being, it would have happened already.

Selina reached out with her pinkie finger to touch his own, which was locked in a painful grip on his leg. Her gloved finger stroked his, and he felt the steady strength of her there beside him. Perhaps she was only pretending it, that calm, that patience, but it soothed him anyway.

At Lord Eldon's brusque command, Tagore rose to his feet.

He looked every inch the estimable barrister in the great wood-paneled space. He spoke at some length of Peter and Selina's commitment to the children. He managed to highlight Selina's connection to the Duke of Rowland without ever alluding to the Belvoir's scandal, and Peter almost wanted to laugh. Tagore explained in tedious legal detail why juridical precedent for denying guardianship to elder brothers based on inheritance claims did not apply to Freddie and Lu.

"Enough," Lord Eldon cut in. His white brows dove sternly over his eyes as he considered Tagore, Peter, and Selina.

"My lord?" Tagore's tone was cautious.

"I've heard enough of the law. As though I don't know it."

"Yes, of course," said Tagore weakly. "My lord."

Eldon looked penetratingly at Peter. "I want to hear from you."

Tagore coughed and sat down. He looked over at Peter, and Peter felt, more than saw, the thread of anxiety that ran through his barrister. His friend. *Don't cock this up*, Peter supposed Tagore was saying, and goddamn it, he would try not to.

Peter looked up at Eldon, seated and imposingly wigged, and rose to his feet.

"Stanhope," Eldon said, "tell me why these children are better off with you than with another."

Peter felt words rise easily to his mouth, as they always did. "While I did not anticipate inheriting this dukedom, Lord Chancellor, it has come to me anyway. I have the material funds to care for Freddie and Lu, to keep them in comfort. To give them an education and bring them out in society. I have—"

"Fine," said Eldon curtly. "You *have* plenty. What of what you *are*?"

Peter felt Selina stiffen at his side.

What he was. God, there was nothing about what he *was* that made him fit guardian for the children. It was money he had, and a title, and a clever and competent wife he did not deserve.

"Why should I place them with you?" Eldon asked. "Why do you want them?"

Oh, words—he needed words, he needed easy sentences and convincing lies. Eldon's question hung in the air.

"They are my brother and sister," he said hoarsely. "I would want them even if I did not know them. I have a duty to do right by them."

It wasn't enough. It wasn't the right thing to say. Peter didn't know the right thing to say.

He had feared this, somehow feared exactly this. That it would come down to him at the end—to who he was and what he lacked, to the boy in New Orleans who could not make his father happy no matter how hard he tried.

It was his, now, to succeed or fail. There was nowhere else to turn but inward, and all that seemed to live inside him was terror.

But there was Selina at his side, her body vibrating with nervous energy. He thought of her bravery at Belvoir's. He thought of what she'd said—that he could turn a flaw into a strength. That he could imagine the world he wanted and drag it into being.

Selina, he thought. *My family*. And somehow the words were there, steady and true.

"I love them," he said. "I'm proud of them. I may not always know how best to protect them, how to make things go right. But I won't hurt them. I won't break their spirits. I won't leave them. No matter what, I won't leave them."

Selina came to her feet at his side. "My Lord Chancellor," she said. "I wonder if I might say—"

Behind them, people in the gallery—mostly wigged barristers, but some newspapermen and interested visitors—started to stir. A hushed whisper rose. Lord Eldon looked up sharply. His eyes widened, his heavy brows darting upward.

Peter started to get the uneasy feeling that something was going wrong.

It was, unfortunately, a feeling with which he was hideously familiar.

There was a cough. A faint feminine shriek.

And then the door to the courtroom exploded open, and into the room barreled Freddie and Lu. Freddie, looking white-faced and terrified and brave, rode his shaggy bay pony. Lu held hard onto the horse's bridle, half dragging it, brandishing her rapier forward like a small, frock-wearing squire.

Beside him, Selina let out a very soft groan.

Tagore sat frozen. He appeared to have lost the power of speech. He lifted one hand, as though to gesture at the children decisively, and then managed only a half-hearted sort of wave.

"What," said Lord Eldon, "is the meaning of this?"

Peter heard himself talking. "Lord Chancellor. May I present Miss Lucinda Nash and Master Frederick Nash?"

He wasn't certain whether he'd got the order of the presentation right, but at this unfortunate juncture, the finer points of social etiquette seemed a bit beside the point.

Eldon opened his mouth to answer, but Freddie and Lu charged wildly toward him through the center of the room, and Eldon appeared to think the better of trying to make himself heard amid the din of screeching and overturned chairs.

"We can't let you do this!" shouted Lu, her voice pitched high to be heard in the chaos. She, Freddie, and the pony stopped directly in between Peter and Eldon.

Peter realized he had no idea to whom she was speaking. Had they stormed the room to try to stop the proceeding? To try to prevent him from becoming their guardian? He'd thought they were past that—but he knew, he *knew* how hard it was for Lu to trust him.

Alarm crept up the back of his neck. He wondered if he should go to her, try to grab the bridle of Freddie's horse. He must have tensed, poised to spring forward, because Selina caught his arm.

"It's our lives you're deciding," said Lu, her voice carrying. "It was our lives that were at stake when we went to Aunt Edith, and when we went to Great-great-aunt Rosamund. It'll be *our lives*. We want to say our piece."

Peter's heart felt frozen in his chest.

Lord Eldon gazed impassively at the pony, which had lowered its head and appeared to be trying to eat a wig that one of the barristers had lost as he'd darted out of the way. "Do go on."

For the first time, Freddie spoke. His voice was quiet, and Peter had to lean forward to hear him. If the boy hadn't been atop the pony, Peter wasn't sure he'd have heard him at all. He wondered if that had been what got Freddie up onto the pony's saddle—the desire to be heard.

"We want to live with our brother."

"And his wife," Lu put in. "We want to live with the Duke and Duchess of Stanhope."

"And our cat," Freddie added.

"It's our *home*," said Lu, her voice fierce.

Peter had the abrupt sensation that he was going to unman himself utterly and start to cry.

"It's our *family*," Lu went on. "You can't take us away because of some . . . stupid law." She bit down on her lower lip. "If you try it, we shall run away. We'll run back to Stanhope house. You can't keep us prisoner at some stranger's home, you simply can't do it—"

"That's enough," said Lord Eldon, his firm voice cutting off

Lu's impassioned rhetoric. "For heaven's sake, girl. There's no need for such dramatics."

"But—" Lu's rapier had fallen down by her side, and Peter could see that her other hand was in a fist. "But—sir—*please*."

"Master Nash. Miss Nash." Eldon's voice was crisp. "I hereby appoint your brother, Peter Kent, the ninth Duke of Stanhope, along with his wife, Selina Kent, the Duchess of Stanhope, as your legal guardians. As I decree, so shall it be done, now and forevermore." He gestured shortly to a clerk at his side, who was staring, openmouthed, at Freddie and Lu, the pony and the rapier. At Eldon's flick of the fingers, the man started, took up his quill, and began to write very busily on the paper in front of him.

"You—do?" said Lu faintly.

"Yes," said Eldon drily. "I was going to do so anyway."

"You *were*?"

Eldon closed his eyes, then reopened them, his gaze directed heavenward. "Yes. Do not make me regret my decision."

"You won't!" said Freddie eagerly, and somehow his pony took his words as encouragement, and it meandered forward toward where Eldon sat just above them.

"I doubt that," said Eldon. He looked toward Selina. "My wife likes you a great deal, Duchess. I don't like to disappoint her."

"Thank you," said Selina. Her voice, though clear and audible, shook slightly. "Thank you."

Eldon raised one white eyebrow and then looked at Peter. "I am glad you will not break their spirits. However—you might see fit to remove them from this chamber before this animal despoils it."

Happiness was spreading through Peter like a slow tide, seeping into his chest and his limbs and his fingers.

Selina caught his hand in both of hers and squeezed hard.

He looked at her. Her amber eyes were bright and wet, and her fingers were warm.

"They're ours," he said stupidly.

"Yes."

"There's a horse in Westminster."

She laughed damply. "Yes."

"I think we are responsible for removing it, and I hope you have some clever ideas about how to manage that, because I'm not entirely certain that horses can descend stairs—"

Then Freddie slid out of the saddle and took Lu's hand in his. Then they were moving toward him, stumbling, almost running. And then Peter was hugging them, holding them all. Selina's hair tickled his nose; Lu's rapier thumped the back of his leg. Freddie's chest hitched as he cried.

Good God, Peter thought. And then: *God. Ours. Now and forevermore.*

Epilogue

Six months later

Selina let her pelisse fall from her shoulders and puddle on the floor. She spared one single thought for the way it would wrinkle, decided she did not care, and collapsed into the bed at the center of the room.

She flung her arm over her face and groaned.

"Have they killed you?" inquired Peter mildly.

"Yes." She felt the mattress shift as Peter settled himself beside her, his warmth seeping into her body in contrast to the modest bedchamber's December chill.

"Well, at least your death will get this inn into the papers. They'll probably erect a plaque in your honor. The Dancing Dog: The Final Resting Place of the Ninth Duchess of Stanhope."

"She died as she lived," Selina offered from beneath her arm.

"Trying to keep Kent family members from hurling themselves into chaos?"

She laughed despite herself and relocated her arm, tipping her face toward Peter's. "A hairbreadth from catastrophe and loving every minute of it."

They had sent Freddie to Eton that fall. He had been determined to go, his face set and his chin stubbornly lifted, though his trepidation was apparent.

That had lasted all of three months before Lu had dressed in breeches and jacket and taken herself off to Eton after him. She'd bluffed and bullied her way from the headmaster's office into a Latin tutorial before they'd managed to track her down.

"I left you a note," Lu had protested when they'd hauled both children into Freddie's neatly appointed room. "I told you I was perfectly safe."

"Your note," Peter said precisely, "informed us that you had taken a boat to Antigua."

Lu stared at him. "Well, obviously. If I told you the truth, you would've known exactly how to find me."

Several hours later, they had given serious consideration to Lu's arguments for why she should be allowed to stay at Eton, listened to Freddie's pink-cheeked rebuttal as to why Lu should *not*, and removed everyone to an inn with the discussion tabled for after Christmas.

"Do you know," Selina told Peter now, turning on her side to look more fully at him, "I haven't the faintest idea what to do in this situation."

"Mm." He tangled his fingers into her hair. "Neither do I."

"Do you suppose that's just . . . how things will be from now on? Utter pandemonium the majority of the time?"

"Very possibly."

He muffled her laugh with his mouth, and she felt herself relax for the first time since they'd realized Lu was gone. She sank into his kiss, and his fingers tightened in her hair.

After a long, long moment, he pulled back. "I'm so damned glad you're here."

She luxuriated in the warmth of his arm around her, in the curve of his mouth. "There's nowhere else I would rather be."

"You could be tucked into your office at Belvoir's, reading dirty books as we speak."

She shrugged. "Don't think I haven't brought samples in my portmanteau."

His eyebrows climbed. "Have you now, wife?"

She squirmed away and made an abortive dive for her travel bag beside the bed, but Peter was quicker. He swooped upon her and snatched the bag from her grasp, rifling through the stack of uncut pages while she shrieked and laughed beneath him.

She did not know what Laventille had sent her this time, and Peter's staggered face had her mightily curious.

She was fairly certain one of Lydia's more subversive essays had gotten mixed up in the bag, however, so perhaps that explained his expression. In the last six months, Lydia had quickly become one of her most popular anonymous pamphleteers, her reserve nowhere apparent in the radical texts she authored. Lydia had been spending more and more time at Belvoir's—last week Selina had caught her emerging from the upstairs office at a startlingly early hour, ink smudged on her gloves. It was *most* intriguing.

She was just craning her neck to look over Peter's shoulder to see what had caught his attention when he reached back inside her travel bag. "What's this?"

She blinked at small velvet bag he'd produced. "I have no idea. You—"

Oh. He was grinning down at her, looking enormously pleased with himself. She plucked the bag out of his hands and tugged open the drawstring, tipping its contents into her palm.

It was a ring. A brilliant green emerald set in a filigreed gold band.

"Sorry it took so long," he said. "I wanted to get it right."

Her mouth opened, but no words came out.

"You once told me that your private rule was to never have any green Belvoir's books on your person," he said. His eyes were warm and intent on hers. "And now—well. I wanted you to have something to remind you that you've nothing to hide. To make you recollect how proud you should be every time you look at it."

The ring went blurry before her eyes. He had not stopped surprising her—his love and his constancy and that clear-eyed vision for the world he imagined into being.

"I love you," she said. "I love you so much."

He brushed her hair back from her face. "I love you, too."

She slipped the ring onto her finger, opposite from the hand that wore the brass circlet from their wedding.

"Wait," he protested. "That's the wrong hand."

She smiled so hard at him that a tear slipped free. "No, it's not."

"I got this so you could *replace* that makeshift wedding ring—"

"Never."

"It turns your finger green!"

She laughed. "I like it."

"Oh for God's sake," he said, and kissed her.

He was still kissing her—only with her bodice unfastened and her chemise decidedly askew—when a spectacular racket erupted outside their door.

Selina dragged herself away from the temptation of his mouth. She was breathing a trifle unevenly. "Should we—see what that noise is?"

He bent his head to her ear and a shiver ran through her body. "Absolutely not."

She laced her fingers through his curls and kept him there, arching up against him until—

"It's not my fault this time!"

Lu's voice outside their door was muffled but clearly audible.

"I swear it," Lu said, the pitch of her voice rising. "This time it was Freddie—I think he set the Christmas goose free—they seem awfully agitated about it—"

Peter lifted his head, looked from the door back to Selina. And then he lowered his brow to hers and groaned.

She laughed against his mouth.

"I'm going," he mumbled. "I'm going. You stay right here. Do not move."

"I might look through the samples—"

He leaned down and hitched her skirts up to her waist. "Don't you dare move. I will be *right back*." He planted a kiss at the line of her stocking, and she laughed again.

He looked up at her, his curls falling over his brow. "Worth it?"

She felt so much—warmth and amusement and pleasure. Excitement and challenge and sheer delight. And love. So much love. "Always," she said. "Always."

Author's Note

Belvoir's is not real and has no historical basis in fact (as far as I know!). However, all of the erotic books that I reference in this novel are entirely real, including the exceptionally named *Lady Bumtickler's Revels* (1786). The memoirs of Harriette Wilson had not been published yet in 1815, when this book is set, but Harriette Wilson was a real Regency courtesan who was variously attached to a number of peers and significant historical figures, including the Duke of Wellington. Her memoirs are fascinating. "I will be the mere instrument of pleasure to no man," she writes.

Fanny Hill was published in 1748 and remains an intriguing glimpse into the erotics of the mid-eighteenth century. While its author, John Cleland, was in fact briefly imprisoned for obscenity, Selina would likely have been exempt from any legal punishment for her activities, as peers and their wives were excluded from most criminal and civil prosecution in 1815.

John Scott, Lord Eldon, was a real historical figure. He served as lord high chancellor of Great Britain for a number of years in the early nineteenth century, including 1815.

As he is depicted here, he was a conservative politician who resisted calls for change to the Empire—however, he was not overly committed to the ideals of a single party. He was known for his fondness for pranks in his schoolboy days and once survived a stoning. He did, in fact, at the age of twenty-one, remove Elizabeth Surtees from her parents' home via ladder and elope with her to Scotland. They had four children together. After Bessie's death, Eldon never remarried.

I'm very sorry for implying that Lord Eldon was involved in smuggling French brandy. I am sure he was not.

I have presented Peter in this book as a "radical abolitionist." In 1815, the slave trade had been outlawed in the British Empire for several years. However, the end of the slave *trade* did not mean the end of slavery itself—it meant only that to kidnap Africans and sell them in the Caribbean was no longer a legal act. People living under slavery in British colonies were not emancipated, and slavery continued apace.

Abolitionists like Peter had significant power in the British government in 1815. For the text of Peter's maiden speech in the House of Lords, I used William Pitt's 1792 speech in the House of Commons, in which he argues for total and immediate abolition across the British Empire. At the time, William Pitt was prime minister of Great Britain.

However, complete abolition was protracted. In 1833, the Slavery Abolition Act was passed to emancipate enslaved people below the age of six in the colonies. Enslaved people older than six were emancipated in stages over the next ten years.

What makes Peter a particular radical is his opposition to the compensation made to British slavers in the colonies and the metropole. After emancipation, the 1833 act provided for twenty million pounds to be paid in recompense to slavers who would no longer have access to free labor. Compensation was, unsurprisingly, not given to the people whose lives, labor, and culture were stolen from them.

Acknowledgments

How do I even begin to thank all the people who've helped make the greatest dream of my heart come true? (Reader, when I first started typing this, I had caps lock on, and I seriously considered leaving it that way.)

First, thanks to *you*, the reader of this book! It means so much to me that you took the time to read Peter and Selina's story. I wrote it for you!

Oceans of gratitude to my brilliant agent, Jessica Alvarez. Jessica offered representation on *Ne'er Duke Well* six days after I sent it to her and—amazingly—exactly one year ago to the day from when I'm drafting these acknowledgments. What a year it's been! Jessica, you are the best. Pragmatic and soothing, generous and smart, incredibly kind and terrifyingly prompt. You have gone above and beyond every step of the way, and it's a joy to work with you.

Thank you from the bottom of my heart to my wonderful editor, Lisa Bonvissuto. Lisa, I was shaking like a sad little leaf the first time we ever spoke on the phone (in my car in a grocery store parking lot, lol), and you immediately put all my fears to rest. This has since become a trend. You are an editorial wizard, but also so deeply thoughtful and supportive. There is no one I would rather work with on my books. Thank you for your brilliant guidance in shaping *Ne'er Duke Well,* for your excitement about my bonkers ideas, and for laughing at my jokes. I can't wait to make more books with you!

To the art team at St. Martin's, including art director Olga Grlic, as well as illustrator Petra Braun, thank you for the cover of my dreams!! I continue to be amazed and impressed by how you transformed my inchoate ideas into this beautiful piece of art. Thank you, Gwen Hawkes, for loving Peter and Selina first, for helping them land safely at St. Martin's, and for your insightful editorial guidance. Thank you to my sensitivity readers, including Dharani Persaud and Kelsea Reeves, for your thoughtful feedback. To my copy editor, Laura Jorstad; my marketing and publicity team, including Kejana Ayala and Angela Tabor; and everyone else at St. Martin's who's worked on this book—including sales, production, etc., etc.—thank you so much for all the time and care you've committed to the project of my heart. Thank you for helping transform some words I typed at my desk in my pajamas into a REAL BOOK IN REAL STORES!

Thank you to librarians and booksellers, especially to my beloved local indie, Blue Cypress Books, and my kindred spirit Jodi Laidlaw. Y'all are actual human angels, and I adore you.

Thank you to the many wonderful members of the online romance community who have been endlessly supportive of my novella series, the Halifax Hellions, and so enthusiastic about *Ne'er Duke Well.* I have met so many incredible writers and readers through online romance spaces (special shout-out to everyone in SF2.0 and the Kitchen Party!), and I am so grateful to so many people who've been cheering me on every step of the way. Thank you to Bella Barnes, Leigh Donnelly, and Jane Maguire, who read every word of this book, sometimes multiple times, from its earliest instantiations. Special thanks to Jane for telling me that Georgiana needed her own story—we're gonna make that happen for our girl. Thank you to my best beloveds, Felicity Niven, Erin Langston, Maggie North, and Sarah T. Dubb. Thank you to Mazey Eddings and India Holton for being incredibly kind and generous readers, as well as brilliant writers. Thank you, Myah Ariel, Amy Buchanan, Etta Easton, Jamie Harrow, Naina Kumar, Laura Piper Lee, Mallory Marlowe, Danica Nava, Ellie Palmer, and everyone else in the 2024 Romance Debuts group chat. Go read their books, yeah?

To the Heroines of Chaos, with special thanks to Kate Lane and Marianne Marston: thank you for being you, exactly perfect, just the way you are.

Thank you to my raucous and adorable little Vastis, who offered many cover and title opinions, along with interpretive art and lots of snuggles. Thank you to Mama Vasti, who gave me my first-ever romance novel and who has never ever had any doubts that my books would be on shelves some day. None of this would have happened without your constant encouragement, enthusiasm, and unshakable faith. Love you, Mom.

And finally, thank you to Matt. I could not love you more or be more grateful to you. You are my person, my greatest adventure, my rock-solid support, and the love of my life. This one's for you! And the next one too. They're all for you: my first reader and my heart.

About the Author

Scarlet Raven Photography

Alexandra Vasti is a British literature professor who has loved historical romance since age eleven. After finishing her PhD at Columbia University in New York City, she moved to New Orleans, where she lives with her very large and noisy family. *Ne'er Duke Well* is her first novel.

Sign up for Alex's newsletter to receive sneak peeks and bonus content, including Peter and Selina's meet-disaster, two years before the events of *Ne'er Duke Well*. Find out more at:

alexandravasti.com

Instagram @alexandravasti

TikTok @alexandravasti